Rafe caught a glimpse of long, unbound hair and a pale shoulder.

Then woman-soft fingers played along the muscular ridges of Rafe's chest, then up to trace the hard line of his jaw, back down to his neck and shoulder, traversing his arm, stroking his belly and lower to cup, fondle and arouse.

The soft fingers lifted him, cradled him, gently squeezed him, tugged and petted until, his fierce heart pounding in his breast, his blood coursing through limbs suddenly alive, Rafe felt himself grow taut and rise high and higher, harder and harder beneath the sensual strokes.

His flesh radiated a fierce animal heat to her touch and he heard her whisper with a trace of choked fear in her voice, "At last, my black stallion, at last."

RAFE

Peter Gentry

A FAWCETT GOLD MEDAL BOOK

Fawcett Publications, Inc., Greenwich, Connecticut

RAFE

RAFE

1

Steam oozed from the lichenous clay-mud walls where the fierce spring sun struck the side of the pit. A light cloud eddied and swirled upward, barely visible, dissipating rapidly. The pit was thirty feet in diameter, dug deep in a clay deposit that formed a small knoll. It drained to the stream below which in turn drained to the Sabine River. From there most of the water ran south to the Gulf of Mexico. Some found its way to the swamps west of the river. Some was caught by one of the myriad, slow motion eddies and trapped in the murky, stagnant bayous. There the fierce subtropical sun sucked it through tangles of brush and cypress, through quiet air heavy with the mystery of undiscovered eons, back to the sky to fall again and moisten the walls and floor of the pit and turn them into treacherous, slippery footing.

The unusually wet winter and fragrant spring rains had erased the stench of summer's many deaths. Rain would never remove the red taint of the pit's clay flooring, for the clay attracted the blood spilled on it, held it, and would not allow it to be washed away by water alone. Like lust or hate the tint remained and darkened, an accumulative pigment only time might erase, and then only from the earth itself, not from the hearts and minds of men.

The black stood alone near the eastern wall, the sun behind him. His gaze skipped up the opposite wall to the swaying platform hung from the hoisting winch, then slowly travelled down the wall to the spot on which his opponent would be lowered. He didn't contemplate, yet, the size or color of the man he would fight and kill. He spent no time on the weapons he might have to face. Such contemplation would be a waste of time, he knew, for the men and weapons against which he found himself pitted always differed to one degree or the other. It was enough to know there would be a man, and the man would be armed. And the man would try to kill him. A small smile, unseen by the spectators ringing the circle of sky above, played about at one corner of his mouth. It would not be he who died. But now was not the time to think of death. Now was the time to concentrate on the spot soon to be filled by the man he would kill.

Had he glanced to either side of the hoisting block—to any spot on the rim of the pit—he would have seen anxious, excited, hungry white faces staring down at him. He had long since given up examining the spectators, ten feet overhead. They did not interest him. His gaze held the spot even when the watchers called his name.

"Rafe! Hey, Rafe. I got money on you."

"You better be fast, nigger. You gonna have to be fast today."

Rafe, they called him. Short for Rapha, a biblical name meaning giant, given him by his first white master. Two inches over six feet tall, he was aptly named. A long cruel scar ran down his neck and across his shoulder, through the checked, puckered tribal scars on his thick chest, there to curl under the ribs and disappear around his side to end in a slanting gash halfway down his right buttock, hidden by the loincloth, the only article of clothing he wore. He had received the scar in his first fight when, befuddled by the newness of the situation and distracted by the lusting eyes above, he had let the devil with the red beard get too close. Suddenly aware, he had leaped, spinning away from the curving, flashing knife, not in time to

8

escape entirely, but in time to save his life. Stunned, shaken into sobriety, he had gazed for a moment at the blood welling from him, shook his head to clear the pain and waded in, oblivious to the screams from above. The red-bearded man had died quickly, his knife arm broken and dangling useless at his side, his face turning the color of his beard as the blood collected there, unable to get past the deadly vise of massive black hands on his throat. Later the wound festered and almost killed him, but he escaped that death and, emaciated and worn, lived. He had gone to the pit forty times since then and had not been wounded again. He had killed other slaves like himself, Indians, and three more delicious times, other whites. He enjoyed killing the whites.

His fame spread in the three years he fought and he soon drew crowds from the surrounding plantations, once even a party from New Orleans, complete with top hats on the men and wide, round, low-cut dresses on the delicate white-skinned women, slumming up-country far from the fancy streets and cultured homes. They had brought their own champion, a wiry Delta black with a sentence of death on his head and a promise of life should he win. They came to amuse themselves and bet their money against Ezra Clayton's slave. The man was armed with a length of ship's chain. He died with it wrapped around his skull. The fancy crowd sighed collectively and chattered their way gaily back to Freedom Mansion, there to pay off the bets they had lost and drink the rustic cane rum and dance until near dawn.

Rafe was only one of the twenty-five fighters Ezra Clayton owned and trained to fight with machete, saber, knife, axe, pitchfork, whip or chain. They all put on a good show, but Rafe was the favorite. The crowds were bigger and the bets higher when he fought. The towering slave, naked but for the loincloth which barely concealed his manhood from the spectators, could have cared less. He heard neither the shouts of praise nor the taunts.

Little was different on this first day of spring. Nothing but the year had changed. Alone in the coolness of the pit, the one place in the world he could call his own, Rafe waited. The world shrank to encompass no more than the thirty-foot circle, ten feet below the face of the earth. The mossy walls and slippery floor gave him confidence. Here was the only home he could remember with any clarity—the home over which he was the undisputed master. Silently, like some dark and ominous giant, he waited and watched.

"What the hell's holding things up, Ezra? I'm gonna have to get back to the shop before too long."

Ezra Clayton, his eyes hidden under the broad-brimmed Panama which shielded them from the spring sun slanting in from the southeast, looked up lazily to stare at the speaker. He saw a tall man, all bones and skin, balding at an early age. Joe Terson, store- and tavernkeeper of Claytonville, wiped his brow for the umpteenth time and fidgeted before Clayton's relentless scrutiny. "You know how Abigail is, Ezra." Terson forced a ragged laugh, his hands flapping nervously in front of him. "She's always on my back about spending too much time out here."

Ezra's stare held. "You ought to bring her out to Freedom," he said. "Micara would love to visit with her. She sees so few women these days." Ezra removed his hat and ran his almost delicate fingers through the full shock of sculpted hair, snow white already at only forty-five years of age. The lord and master of Freedom never seemed to sweat, as if sweating were too plebian, too far beneath his station. His eyes could be seen, now. A light blue they were, so bright they seemed to burn—or freeze—a hole right through a man. Eyes too hard and cold for the soft, run-to-fat body on the spindly legs. But few men looked at the body. Fewer commented on the legs. All the strength a man might need lay hidden in the eyes, hidden and waiting to be brought to bear on anyone so unfortunate as to cross his path.

"I'll do that, Mr. Clayton. She'd like it. I reckon she'd be happy to visit tomorrow. . . ." The eyes had done their work. Joe Terson had received the message, explicit and implicit. He and his wife would do Ezra Clayton's bidding.

"Go and get a drink from the tray, Joe." Clayton

waved a soft hand, the gesture forgiving, bestowing absolution. "Tell Old Mose I said to let you have a chunk of ice. Rum's mighty tasty with ice."

Terson smacked his lips at the thought. Ice. His eyes widened and he let himself anticipate the sudden, welcome coolness as he turned. The last time he'd had ice was three winters ago on the morning he'd gone outside to find a thin skim of crystal on the bucket. But then it was winter and cold. Now it was spring and already hot. He scurried toward Mose, the old slave with the creased scar on his head, the legacy left behind by a nameless, dead Creek.

Ezra sipped his drink as he cast his eye over the small crowd ringing the pit and loitering in the vicinity. Only ten on the rim itself, and they were a scruffy, sweating lot of gawking fools from nearby small holdings. More frontiersmen than landholders, really, the type who when the time came would be easy to drive across the Sabine and into Mexico. They would hardly bet enough to make it worth the time. Still, their shouts and yells instilled in the crowds an air of excitement. Later in the year their raucous, frenetic bets called across the pit would stimulate real wagers from the more genteel, and it was from these Ezra would profit.

Four small clusters of three or four men stood scattered here and there within close range of the table and cooling drinks. They were all from Claytonville, there because they knew Ezra Clayton expected them. Timid to a man, vicarious bravery would mount as they watched the brutality below. Their excitement, too, would generate some bets as well as add an aura of middle-class respectability to the proceedings.

A dozen small plantation owners from downriver stood near the wagon that had carried them from the landing. They had come upstream from Burr Ferry the night before and camped out at the landing sheds. Owners of fifty to a hundred acres and a few slaves apiece, they were taking a break from spring planting and their wives. They stood packed together, a convivial gathering, their talk spurred and quickened by the homemade cane rum they carried. From time to time a word from the knot of men

11

broke loose and announced the subjects of their debate. The usual, Clayton thought. Always the usual. Crops and weather, slaves, Indians, women and rum, Mexico and the free land they wished they could get their hands on. And wives. Clayton despised the usual subjects, despised the men who could not break from them. They had no flair, no . . . what was it Bernard called it? . . . *panache*. But never mind. Their bets were more substantial. With luck he'd even be able to separate the big Cajun Beaumarchant, from Duggins, one of the twelve. Now there would be a coup. Beaumarchant! His mouth watered at the thought of the war-battered Acadian giant in his pit. He and Rafe together could take on any dozen men. What a battle that would be!

The sound of a shot and a distant yell to his rear drew his attention. He turned to see Bernard and his group coming over Tree Hill. Another ten minutes and they'd be at the pit and the day could get underway. A small frown pulled at the corners of his mouth. He hoped no one had told Rafe. Part of the bet depended on him not knowing who and what he would face. The frown melted away, replaced by the bland expression that revealed and told nothing. He supposed it didn't matter as long as Bernard didn't find out. And Rafe would win in any case. Rafe always won.

His forty-second win. Only eight more and he could claim the promise of freedom Ezra had made. Fifty wins in the pit and a man was emancipated, given a woman, a wagon, two mules, and a boat ride across the Sabine on the stipulation he never again show his face around Freedom Plantation. The thought galled Ezra. He'd never had to make good on the promise, to be sure, and it had seemed a good idea at the time, a cheap inducement to sure death. Ezra decided to be more careful with his promises in the future. Still, he'd gladly pocket the hundred gold eagles and savor the look on François Bernard's face as his one local rival fumed and rode away, once again, in a fine display of Gallic frustration. It would make a very fine profit for the first fight of the year. And as for the promise of freedom for Rafe—he tucked the unpleasantness away in the back of his head. There was time yet to worry. Eight fights, to be exact. He'd decide later.

"Butkis!"

"Yessir, Mr. Clayton."

Ezra examined the man's face as he hurried up. Over fifty, squat and chunky, his red face greasy in the humid air and lined with tiny blue veins, the overseer knew his position was based on his brutality and the utter, dogged loyalty with which he regarded his employer and benefactor.

"Put two more guards on the rim. I'd hate to have any trouble with *Monsieur* Bernard's men. The Creek nature is always unpredictable."

"Yessir, Mr. Clayton. They'll be here in about five minutes."

"And lower a dram to Rafe before they get here."

"Already done, sir. He's lookin' fit."

"All right, Butkis. The guards."

"Yessir!" Butkis saluted and hurried off to the small circle of men squatting around a fire, surreptitiously passing a jug of rum from one to the other. Their muskets lay on the ground beside them. They were a motley, sullen lot with little to be said in their favor save the color of their skin. They were white and could be trusted with firearms.

"Decater . . . Milo . . . get your scrawny asses over to the rim. Them Creeks is apt to cause trouble." The jug disappeared rapidly and he pretended not to notice, passing his attention instead to the muskets. "And get them damned things off'n the ground and primed."

Decater and Milo jumped from the fire, grabbed their muskets and scurried for the rim. The three remaining guards hunkered down, hoping to go unnoticed. One of them turned a young possum skewered on a spit. Fat dripping from the carcass sizzled and crackled as it hit the coals and sent up jagged tongues of flame.

"Where'd you get that?"

"Milo there found it in one of his traps this mornin'."

"It a young 'un?"

"Prettiest little possum you ever seen, Mr. Butkis."

Butkis stepped closer to the fire and drew his cutlass from its scabbard. He grabbed one of the legs and sliced

13

it cleanly from the body. A cascade of drippings hit the fire which flared and sputtered. The overseer thrust the blade through the meat and, blade in both hands, tore off a chunk of the sizzling flesh with his teeth, ignoring how it burned his lips and tongue. He bit into the meat twice more, stripping the useful portion from the bone before swallowing the first bite. Juices dribbled from between his lips and swollen jowls. The three underlings continued to avert their eyes, ignoring the bone Butkis flipped into the fire. The overseer managed to swallow the mouthful without choking before he laughed, belched mightily and wiped the cutlass across his trousers.

"That's good meat, though I'd sooner cut niggers with this blade," he announced. "Carve yourselves a morsel and station yourselves near the winch. And keep them muskets cocked."

The three guards nodded and hurriedly divided the remains of the possum, saving Milo and his sure protestations for later. Each man stuffed his mouth and scrambled off to take up his position and wait nervously for François Bernard. They didn't have to wait long.

Rafe felt the cane liquor warm and loosen his body. Like a huge cat, he relaxed, slack and limp, resting, breathing deeply, evenly, concentrating on the spot, feeling the blood course through him, holding emotion in check as his father had taught him. His muscles tensed of themselves before he consciously recognized the change in sound. A muffled drum of hooves preceded the quickened voices of the whites above him. The horses stopped, and as if on cue the whites followed suit. They had seen his opponent, who was even now being led to the platform. The conditions of the bet were intact. Rafe did not know whom he would fight or what weapons he would face. If truth were told, he preferred to fight that way. A real warrior faced his opponent with a clear mind. His father had taught him that, too, but he did not remember the teaching.

"Well, I'm changin' my bet. My money's on them!" a voice drifted down from the rim.

"Shitfire . . . me too," another chimed in.

"Put up or shut up, boys." The voice was Martinson's,

Clayton's money-man. "Mr. Clayton stands firm behind his nigger. Two-to-one says he kills them both."

Them . . . them both. Rafe shut his ears to the rest and leaned forward slightly in anticipation. So there were two of them this time. What of it? Hadn't he fought two before? And won? He had fought forty-two contests and lived while others—forty-six others—had died. His mind adapted rapidly to the facts while he shifted his weight, readjusting his stance imperceptibly, ready now for the assault.

The A-frame above and in front of him creaked as it took the weight. Only when he heard the spindle squeak and the chain gnash against the sprockets did he look up.

Two bronze-skinned Creek warriors perched astride the ropes attaching the platform to the chain. Entirely naked—there were no women present for the first outing of the year—their flesh was daubed with raucous designs in red, white and ochre. Their eyes bored into him as the platform descended, jerking and complaining at the weight. Rafe relaxed his hold on the machete and breathed deeply. They would be fast.

The Indians were small men with long dark hair that hung straight down their backs. They leaped to the pit floor before the platform hit bottom, landing lightly, their bare feet skidding ever so barely. Each held a tomahawk and hunting knife. Rafe's face was a mask as the warriors shuffled their feet to coat them properly. They were smart, these two, calm and probably well-prepared. He would have to be careful.

Micara put the finishing touches—the Dresden lamp moved a quarter-inch closer to the gilt-edged portrait, and the doily straightened for the fifth time—to Crissa's room. The task completed to her satisfaction, she lit a scented taper, walked thoughtfully around the room to spread the orange aroma evenly, then pinched out the flame and replaced the taper in its holder. The delicate aroma would last.

She stood with her back to the empty fireplace, trying to imagine her daughter in this room again, how she must look after four long years. The northern climate should

15

have done her good. But to come back to Freedom Plantation and spend a life. . . .

Her hand fumbled for and missed the crystal goblet behind her on the mantelpiece. She turned, her eyes darting fearfully back and forth, to find it farther to the right than she remembered. She grabbed for it and raised the glass to her lips, then stopped when she caught her own image in the mirror.

Wrinkles assailed her. The marks of time and pain ran across her forehead and out from the corners of her eyes, which all too often flowed with tears. A brief, mocking fire burned in those eyes as she put the glass to her lips and took a ladylike sip. She mustn't take too much, of course. Crissa shouldn't find her mother, the mistress of Freedom Plantation, unsteady and wobbling in the hall. Unbidden, the eyes welled with hot tears. She twisted violently from the accusing mirror and with both hands shaking, raised the cut crystal and drank deeply, greedily, then stumbled to the hall in search of the decanter.

"May I get you something, Ma'am?"

Micara turned, startled at the voice behind her. The young housemaid, Julie, waited, caught in a curtsy, an open and knowing smile on her delicate ebony features. Micara slapped her across the face.

"Lady Clayton to you," she said, her voice rasping viciously.

Julie ignored the slap as best she could. For a moment her eyes burned darkly, but she nodded, curtsied again and corrected herself as befit her position. "Yes'm, Lady Clayton."

Slapping the young black girl didn't help. The hurt was still there. Bitterness and burning rage and frustration shook Micara as she stared down at the top of the slave girl's suitably bowed head. Hate her as she did, it wasn't the girl's fault. What fault there was lay with her. She alone had played the fool. Micara turned and fled down the hall and into her bedroom, where she slammed the door behind her and sat, panting, on the canopied bed Ezra had so pointedly avoided for the last two years. The decanter was in front of her on the night table. She stared at it. Could she have forgotten placing it there? Without

16

thinking she reached for the warm red liquid and filled her glass to the brim.

Outside in the hall, Julie rubbed her stinging cheek, then smiled at the thought of the secret that wasn't a secret, the knowledge of which brought Micara Clayton more pain than a dozen slaps. The black girl straightened her dress, pressing the bodice tightly over firm young breasts, enjoying the pleasure of her own hands as they travelled down her stomach and to her thighs. She would remember the slap the next time she lay with Ezra Clayton and stole the power of his loins from the puffy-faced woman she served. She moved down the hall humming a little tune, underscored by the echoing distant shouts drifting through the hazy trees, coming from the direction of the pit.

The braves split up immediately, one moving to the left, the other to the right. They stationed themselves across the pit from each other and stopped to stare at Rafe, to take the black man's measure. *Monsieur* Bernard had taught them well—there was no way Rafe could keep all senses riveted to two spots thirty feet apart. He must see to it, then, that the preliminaries were kept to a minimum and dispensed with hastily. The more time he gave them, the greater their advantage. Hardly thinking, he chose the one to his left and moved toward him lazily, the machete still hanging loosely at his side. The Indian sprang away from him and crossed the pit to stand by his companion. The two conferred briefly in soft, barely heard whispers, giving Rafe the few extra seconds he needed for his appraisal. A few was all he wanted. Like sleek hunting animals they moved again, flowing to either side, stalking the black beast at bay.

Rafe backed to the wall and waited, loose, ready for their next move. "Let the lion attack if he wants to," his father had said. "You will learn much from this. Then you must threaten but not attack. From these actions you will know all you need to know, and it will be easy for you to kill him." His father had been right.

The Creeks moved like lightning, pouncing suddenly from both sides. Their tomahawks whistled through the air, one high and one low. But Rafe wasn't there. As their shoulders moved in commitment to the throw, his foot went behind him and pushed him from the wall, sending him rolling over his shoulder to the middle of the pit where he sprang to his feet, knees slightly bent as the braves rushed to retrieve their weapons, a hint of embarrassment clouding their confidence. Their attack had given Rafe the information his father had promised. The one to the right would go high, the one to the left low. *Monsieur*'s trick hadn't worked.

He sprang at them before they could fully recover their poise, his machete whirling in front of him, cutting the humid air in humming chunks. The braves separated, spinning away from him gracefully, their knives flashing behind them as they spun. Rafe stopped before he hit the wall and twisted around to his right, in the direction of the faster of the two. Silence hung over the pit, broken only by the soft pat-pat as the Creek to Rafe's left slapped his tomahawk lightly against his painted leg.

Rafe now knew all he needed. Without hesitation he leaped toward the one on his left. As the warrior broke across to the center of the pit where his companion met him, Rafe hit the wall, spun from it and headed for them. The Indians, taken by surprise by the rapidity of his attack, stood their ground instead of splitting up. Rafe's whirling machete accidentally struck flat-edged against one of the tomahawks, knocking the weapon from the Indian's hand and breaking the machete halfway down the length of the blade.

The charge sent him between the two braves, carried him almost to the wall again. A trickle of warmth ran down his leg. One of the knives had ripped a jagged wound open across the side of his right thigh. His back burned where a tomahawk had struck a glancing blow, ripping from him a chunk of skin and flesh. From above him and as if in a dream, he heard the excited clamor of the crowd as bets changed frantically.

Rafe forced the wounds from his mind and stepped away from the wall. Glistening with sweat, the Indians arced out to the sides and cut back, pressing to the attack, coming in for the kill. Rafe backpedaled, forcing them to come at him at a closer angle. The knives flashed low and high as he had thought they would. His leg went over the low knife, striking the brave in the chest and sending the painted warrior reeling away in a drunkenlike, gasping, slippery fall. Rafe's torso, low, went under the second knife, the broken machete aimed at the brave's exposed belly. The blunt end entered the abdomen with an audible pop as skin stretched in and finally burst, ripping to the sides as the broad blade cut its way through the living organs and struck the backbone.

The mortally wounded Creek staggered back and clawed at the hilt as if to draw it from his body. Instead, he turned it viciously in a suicidal grip. His face contorted in silent pain as the blood gushed freely from the gaping wound and he pitched forward, dead.

Rafe straightened as he heard the scream from behind him. The remaining brave, his shriek of rage echoing hollowly from the walls, launched himself through the air, knife in hand, hate and revenge burning in his eyes. Rafe responded with the only weapon left to him—his hands. His right fist, a massive bony club, struck out like a serpent and met the Indian's face, the left hand simultaneously blocking the swinging knife arm arcing from above. Rafe felt the blow up to his shoulder blade, his right hand and arm instantly numb. The Creek's airborne momentum was abruptly shattered with a loud crack as face bones crumbled and splinters drove into his brain. Dead already, the wrenching snap of neck bones followed, and the Creek collapsed to the packed earth, his head twisted grotesquely back.

Rafe the victor, blood streaming from leg and back, stepped away from the dead men and flexed his fingers as the feeling and searing pain returned to his arm, shooting its length in great spasms. Cheers and curses from the blood-sated watchers above broke into his consciousness, but he forced himself to keep his eyes and face down to the dead sprawled to either side of him. Then slowly he turned and walked to the looped chain being lowered into the pit. Praise rained down on him but he remained as mute as the clay-smeared bronze corpses crumpled behind him. As always, only one man would leave the pit alive.

Ezra smiled graciously to *Monsieur* Bernard, and offered in his most pleasing and infuriating tone to bury the dead braves for the losing landowner. The Frenchman handed Clayton a sack of gold coins and muttering something about letting them rot where they lay, gathered his retinue and stalked off toward his horse. He mounted and rode off furiously, leaving his followers scattered behind.

Ezra waved languidly to his rival's back, then turned to face the pit in time to see Rafe step from the platform. For a moment their eyes met and held. Master and slave. Rafe sucked the blood from his bruised knuckles. Ezra sipped Jamaican rum from a flask of pounded gold.

2

The pitbucks crowded along the western wall of the compound fence, their black faces sweat-shiny and attentive to the sudden shouts of the whites crowded around the pit sunk into the small knoll some two hundred and fifty yards away.

"Wha' happen, Jomo?"

Jomo, battle-scarred veteran of almost as many bouts as Rafe, lifted himself up the final foot or two of the rough pole wall and hooked his elbows over the points. The height of the wall, almost twenty feet, put him at about the same level as the crowd, but he was still unable to see, of course, into the pit.

"Tell us wha's go'n on, Jomo," another black asked, his voice a husky whisper. "Can yo' see anything?"

Jomo spat between the posts. The rough tree bark afforded him little purchase and he was forced to bear the weight of his squat, powerful body with his arms and vise-like grip alone. Muscles knotted along his shoulders and neck. "Don' see nuffin'." He punctuated with another spit. "Don' never see nuffin' from up here 'til they carries 'em out. Dat's de way it is. But Ah climbs and looks anyhow."

The guard left behind for compound duty finished his circuit of the outside wall and began another. His name was Booker, but everyone called him Boo. He hated the name. Approaching the west wall, he could make out Jomo up near the top. Racing from the corner to a position underneath the black, he unslung his musket.

"You escapin', nigger?"

Jomo looked down at the raised musket. Chances were the guard just might be lucky enough to hit him at that range. He put more weight on his left arm, shifting as far as possible behind the stake. No sense in making too good a target. . . .

"I didn't hear you answer, nigger."

"Ah's jes tryin' to watch dat ol' fight, Boo."

"My name's Booker, you som'bitch. Mistah Booker. You hear me?"

"Yassuh, Boo. Ah sho 'nuff does."

"Get your black ass off'n that tree bark. You know you ain't supposed to be up there."

The other slaves stepped back to make room and Jomo loosed his grip and shoved off to the rear, dropping lightly to the ground. Boo thrust his musket part way through the six-inch spacing between two of the thick trunks. "I could blow your head off, if I wanted to, boy. Can get me some nigger brains all over the ground, if you got any. You call me Mistah Booker like you're s'posed to. You got that?"

Jomo grinned broadly, his thick lips parted, revealing bashed and crooked teeth. "Mastuh Clayton wouldn't be appreciatin' no guard killin' off his prized pitbuck niggers, no suh. Ah think he'd take dat unkindly, Boo. Maybe eben put ol' Boo in dat pit wid Rafe hisself. You like dat, Boo?"

The guard flushed, his face an angry red. His finger tightened on the trigger, but he didn't fire. Eventually the barrel wavered, then withdrew from the wall. Boo pressed his face into the opening. "You jus' keep off'n that wall, nigger, or I'll take the cat to you. Mistah Clayton don't mind the cat none. He don't begrudge his niggers their whippins!" With that, Boo stomped off, trying to leave the area before he could hear them snicker at him. He couldn't move fast enough. "I'll show 'em. Goddamn their black asses . . . I'll show 'em," he murmured.

No sooner was Boo out of sight than a muffled roar from the crowd filtered through the wall. The blacks hurried to the sunken tree posts which delineated the compound. The poles were placed a little less than six inches apart and were all at least twenty feet tall. The bottom fifteen feet had been stripped clean, leaving a shiny surface devoid of finger- or toehold. The top five feet were still covered with bark, loose and crumbling now, too dangerous to trust with one's full weight. As if escape wasn't difficult enough, the final foot of the posts had been pared down and fitted with sharp, iron-capped points, rusted now, hot in summer, cold in the winter. The man who would chance blood poisoning on the rusty caps was brave indeed.

Jomo was such a man. Standing on one of the younger Negroes' shoulders, he was barely able to get a grasp on the smooth trunk and hoist himself up. Feet wedged between the rough bark and elbows around the lethal points, he could see the crowd moving away from the pit, clustering in small groups and exchanging money. The fight was over. Two men at the winch turned the handle slowly, hauling up the winner. He could see M. Bernard's party as it galloped away from the small, awkward figure of Clayton. He couldn't tell if the lord of Freedom was smiling or not. Jomo would have felt more confident in Rafe's victory if he had not seen the two Creeks as they had been led to the arena. One Indian was enough, but two. . . .

Jomo scanned the edge of the pit closely, searching for some sign of Rafe. He knew Rafe well, was probably closer to him than anyone else. The two might have considered themselves friends in another time and place, but at Freedom, Jomo knew only too well, a man you called friend one day might be facing you in the pit the next. Better not to have friends. And yet . . . he and Rafe were the two best fighters old man Clayton had. It seemed unlikely he'd pit them against each other.

"What yo' see now, Jomo? Is dat big nigger walkin'?"

"Don't seem fair, sickin' two on him. An' Injuns at dat."

"Injuns is fast an' mean," a third voice explained.

23

"Yo' mark my word. Dey take de measure a' dat Rafe. Yassuh. Dey sho 'nuff cut dat nigger down to size." A touch of the wistful tinged the speaker's voice. A thin, wiry youth with eleven fights behind him, he and Rafe had had trouble between them for some time. Cat hoped to hell Rafe had been wounded. It would slow him up some if they ever had to fight.

A burred head rose slowly out of the pit, followed by Rafe's huge form. Jomo watched, happy in spite of himself, as his almost-friend stepped laconically from the chain onto the boards lining the edge of the pit and stood there facing old Clayton like he owned the little man. "Jes' shut yo' mouf, Cat. Dat nigger jus' step out, mean and big as ebber he was. Looks like dey blooded him, but he standin' and puttin' one foot in front a' 'nother." And with that pronouncement, Jomo bounded back to the compound floor and headed for the gate, followed by his fellow slaves.

Rafe walked alone, the closest guard, Decater, some five paces behind him. The walk back to the compound always affected him deeply. Every time he crossed toward the unlikely tree-barricades, conflicting emotions raged in his breast. Each time he had just killed, and today he had killed twice. Except for the occasional white, he didn't enjoy the deaths he inflicted, saw them as a waste, as crimes against himself. *The sun was high overhead now, filling the air with bright heat.* Each time the scent of blood and sweat and fear mingled redolently, following him out of the pit and hovering around him in a grim miasma that clouded his senses. *Dust puffed from under his feet and caked his ankles and calves.* Each time the remnant of his own fear tucked itself away in his gut, waiting for night and sleepless tossing, waiting for a woman, perhaps, who would take it from him, dilute it with sweat and desire. *The distant swamp echoed a violent chorus of predator and prey.* Each time raw elation surged within him, for it was only during the walk he finally recognized that he was, in truth, still alive. *The guard behind him coughed and spat.* Each time the sight of the looming wall ahead and the gate designed to close

24

after him filled him with a sense of dread, for he then remembered death always waited. *A cloud sliced the sun. The afternoon rain would be on time.*

The walk today was worse. He had been touched, wounded. His right arm hung limp at his side, the pain shooting its length and then into the muscles of his back. He flexed the fingers, his eyes clouding with pain, then clearing as the fist opened and closed, opened and closed until the pain slowly faded to a dull throb. His back was worse. On fire, it seemed, where the skin lay in a huge flap, the tissue below it exposed to the clustering flies attracted by the warm, drying blood. Twice he shrugged his left shoulder, the constricting muscles sending up the flies in a small brief cloud that resettled immediately. Sweat poured down his shoulder and into the cut, stinging sharply with each drop. He quit trying after the second shrug. Only clear water would keep the flies away, cool the skin and stop the salt flow.

The wound on his thigh continued to bleed freely. The Creek knife, razor-sharp, had slit the skin and sliced cleanly through part of the bulging muscle. The wound bothered him unduly, adding to the welter of emotion and confusion. Could it be more serious than it looked? Rafe had heard of redmen who coated their blades with snake poison. He had killed twelve of *Monsieur* Bernard's fighters over the past three years and the Indians brought the total to fourteen. Bernard surely had cause to hate him and would be happy enough to see Rafe dead no matter what the outcome of the fight. It was a cruel, cheating thing to do, but Rafe couldn't discount the possibility. *Monsieur* Bernard was white.

The gate in front of him swung open. Rafe stopped on the threshold. No voice welcomed him; as always, a ritualistic, expectant silence greeted the returning victor. His eyes slowly scanned the familiar compound. Twenty-four black men, black as himself, stared back impassively. They stood arranged in informal order of rank. Jomo, number one pitbuck in Rafe's absence, stood a little to the front, with Trinidad, Dingo and Cat, the thin, angry one, to his rear and the rest arranged randomly around the compound. The sweet smell of dust and sweat min-

25

gled in the air, trapped by the massive walls. In the gum tree over the exercise shed, a mockingbird attempted a complicated melody, breaking off in midstream with an unlikely squawk. The discordant note broke the spell and the men, as if emerging from a trance, shifted positions, relieving tense muscles.

Jomo, all five-feet-eight of him, swaggered toward Rafe and spoke to him in the bush dialect common only to the pair. The words slurred quietly, gutturally, hinting of the dark heat of the old land from which they had been taken.

'You fight good, hey, N'gata?"

N'gata. Not quite brother, more than a friend. It was all one man could mean to another here at Freedom. One cannot kill a brother . . . one must save the life of a friend. But if the bloody-handed spirits bring the face-off, one can kill his N'gata.

Rafe gestured with his head, nodding back in the direction of the pit. "They too fight good, Jomo N'gata. Those two fellas fast like leopards." He smiled. The sound of the old talk eased the tension further, soothed the jangled nerves.

"But you kill them two fast."

"The knife spirit, our blood mother, was good to her son, Rafe."

"Maybe she favor Jomo, too, this summer," Jomo grunted, his face twisting in anticipation of the killing he loved.

"The blood mother favors none but the dead, N'gata."

Decater prodded Rafe in the back with the barrel of his musket. "You two niggers quit that mumbo jumbo and talk like ya' been learnt by Mistah Clayton."

It was a mistake. His nerves still cat-quick from the fight, Rafe spun about and twisted the musket from the startled guard's hands. Decater grabbed for it and then froze, his hands tiny claws that started to shake with fear. His milky face went even paler as he found himself staring down the maw of his own musket. Rafe, half-crouching, held the gun ready to fire. Behind him, Jomo spoke, the easy voice soothing, calming, repeating the words of Rafe's father. "There is no honor in killing a jackal."

The old saying had the desired effect. Rafe relaxed, rose to his full height, broke into a contemptuous leer, then tossed the musket at the startled Decater's feet. The gun went off as the small guard jumped into the air. Rafe turned and crossed the yard to the water trough. Jomo and the others followed, laughing in spite of the hollow fear of what the other guards might do in retaliation.

Behind them Decater staggered to his feet as Butkis and his men headed for the compound at a dead run. Decater grabbed his musket from the ground, drew a lead ball from the pouch at his side and rammed it down the barrel, priming the piece with a cap and aiming it at the retreating slave. For a second time the gun was wrenched from his grasp, this time by Butkis.

"What the hell ya' think y'up to, Decater?" Butkis asked.

"I'm gonna kill me a nigger, goddamit! Gimme back my gun, Butkis. The som'bitch tried to shoot me with it."

"What's the trouble, Butkis?"

The overseer turned toward the quiet voice. Decater froze. Ezra had decided to check on the disturbance himself. He didn't want to lose one of his pitbucks this early in the season.

"Decater here was fixin' to shoot Rafe, Mr. Clayton."

"Shoot who?" Ezra asked, his eyebrows arching in disbelief.

"Rafe, sir."

Ezra turned slowly to Decater. His eyes bored intently into those of the guard, forcing the unfortunate Decater to lower his gaze, shrink back a step and fumble for an explanation.

"Sir . . . he tried ta' shoot me. Woulda' kilt me dead if'n I hadn't . . . uh . . . jumped."

Ezra examined Decater's twitching face, his dancing, nervous gestures. It would be easy, breaking this one. The lord of Freedom relaxed, his eyelids hooding the piercing gaze. He looked as if he'd suddenly lost all interest and fallen asleep. "What's your name?" The voice was almost a whisper.

"Uh . . . Decater, sir."

"Decater . . . Decater . . ." The name rolled silkily, lazily from his mouth, the lips barely moving. "You look like a weasel that's just come up with a rancid hen, Decater."

Decater didn't know what that meant, but it didn't sound very good. "Yessir . . ."

"When's the last time you won me any gold, Decater?"

"Well, I ain't never . . . Mr. Clayton . . ." Decater answered, confused. The man sounded like he was talking in a dream, his voice was so light, so far away.

"I suspect that if Rafe had shot at you, you'd be dead. And if you were dead, then I would have to hang him. And if I had to hang that buck, then he wouldn't be around to win me any more gold." The voice stopped, leaving only silence suspended with the dust motes. "I wouldn't like that, Decater."

"No, sir."

"Now, if that buck can take your gun away from you, I have to consider the possibility I can't trust you with protecting the life and property of Freedom. I might have to find some other way to put you to use." The bright eyes snapped open abruptly, stared mercilessly and with malicious intensity at Decater, who squirmed in total discomfort. "Perhaps in the pit."

Decater's face went entirely bloodless. He struggled to speak but found himself barely able to breathe. Ezra smiled reassuringly, the kind of smile that comes to a man's face as he guts a fish. "Against which one, Decater? Jomo? Cat? Trinidad? Rafe?"

"I . . . I jes' dropped my musket, Mr. Clayton," Decater finally managed to mumble, the words barely audible. "It went off accidental-like."

Too easy. Ezra stared into Decater's eyes, searching for something, anything other than fear. It was a waste of time. The fool was less a man than his niggers. They had a sense of pride, at least. He had never seen fear in any of his pitbucks' eyes. "You should be more careful, Decater."

Ezra snapped his fingers, heard the jingle of harness and the creak of wooden wheels behind him as the coachee pulled up. He turned and climbed into it without looking back, sat stiff-necked as the coachee moved onto the river path and toward the gap in the trees. Beyond that gap, the startlingly white mansion loomed, lazing in the noon sun.

Butkis slapped the chastened guard across the mouth, jolting him back to a semblance of life. "Dumb ass," the overseer muttered. Decater stood with head bowed, the livid handprint standing out on the white skin. Milo, Boo and the others giggled at his expense, enjoying his discomfort. "Boo, you take a meal," Butkis went on. "Decater here'll spell you now that he's got his gun back." Everyone except Decater exploded into laughter. Decater scowled, turned his back on them and began his rounds, disappearing as rapidly as possible around the corner. "The rest of you boys follow me over to the shanties," Butkis went on. "Got to make sure the field hands is fed okay. Maybe even grab us a quick 'un. Get that gate, Milo."

The guards whooped and hollered their approval as Butkis winked and gestured lewdly. This was turning out to be a holiday after all.

Rafe submerged the bucket, filling it to the brim with the cool springwater from the trough. He dumped the contents over his head, dousing himself completely. To his battle-flushed skin the water felt icy. He filled the bucket and repeated the action three more times, shaking the water from his head in great glittering arcs. Jomo alone remained nearby, enjoying the opportunity to relax. Whenever a fight was held at the plantation, training for the slaves not involved was called off for the day. Usually they fought on a Sunday, and as that was a day of rest for them anyway, the respite was nothing special. But *Monsieur* Bernard had brought his Creeks down on a Saturday, giving Clayton's pitbucks an extra day of rest.

Jomo squinted at the afternoon sun. Rafe crossed in front of him and onto the rickety porch where a flimsy overhang offered a meager patch of shade. The blood from the wound on his thigh had begun to coagulate and his back was beginning to stiffen. He sank gratefully onto the single, slatted chair and sagged forward, letting the final shred of tension drain from him.

Moments later the small door in the main gate opened and Old Chulem shuffled in and padded through the dust. Old Chulem was the medicine man of Freedom Plantation. He cured the wounds of the body, and of the heart as well. The slaves went to him for everything. Too enfeebled to work, Chulem had the run of both the fighters' compound and the larger shanty town of the field hands. He went unmolested by the guards. Not a one would strike the withered Negro. Even Ezra Clayton realized the importance of the conjure man to the slave populace: allowing Old Chulem a modicum of liberty about the plantation kept the blacks tractable.

The old man barely managed the single step up to the porch and stood, breathing deeply, gazing at the wound on the thigh. When he finally squatted in front of Rafe, his frail body creaked with the effort. He wasted no time on words, simply drew a pouch from his rope belt, opened it, dabbed his fingers into the fetid depths and withdrew an oily brown glob of herbs, roots and tree sap mixed in bear grease. Ancient fingers spread the wound and worked the mixture in, massaging it into the muscle, loosening the drying blood. A final slather covered the area completely. Old Chulem rose slowly, withered muscles trembling.

"Yo' leave dat po'tice on 'til mornin', hear me, boy?" His voice was dry with age but still rang with authority. "Now turn 'round. Let me care fer dat back, too." Rafe turned, straddled the chair and rested his forehead on the cool wood planking of the shack. "Knife poison ken rot a man sooner'n he can spit. So keep Ol' Chulem's medicine over dem cuts. No woman for you tonight, nigger."

Jomo chuckled. "Ah'll take his women fo' him. Don't yo' worry none, old man."

Rafe nearly dozed as the old, expert fingers worked out the stiffness and eased the stinging pain. Sweet euphoria drifted over him. He was alive and finally calm enough to fully realize and savor the fact. Forty-three fights. That's close to fifty. *Gettin' close to fifty, Rafe,* he thought to himself. Only seven to go. Only seven fights left. Then a rifle and a woman, supplies and a boat ride across the Sabine, and the sweet prospect of never coming back. The swamps stretched before him, then the open land he'd heard of. Open land . . . real freedom . . .

He realized Chulem was finished and turned back to see the old man staring at him. Had the conjure man spoken? Was he waiting for an answer? To what? What was there to say? There were no answers. Only life, and holding on to it any way possible, day by day, fight by fight. Rafe glanced over at Jomo's drowsy face. Jomo liked it, enjoyed the violence, the way it felt to stand over a man just butchered and watch the tortured, dying muscles jerk, the clay drink the red juices. And listen to the cheers and shouts of the men and women above. The ignobility of killing for another's pleasure. Odd thoughts for a slave.

Dammit. Why was Chulem staring at him? Rafe thought of Lord Lucas Clayton, the New Orleans aristocrat who had stared at him the same way before he bought him from the slave market on the docks. Rafe had been only a boy, frightened and determined not to show it. Lucas Clayton had taken an interest in him, and despairing ignorance in any form, saw to his education, made him the pride and joy of the Clayton household. "This is my manservant, Rafe. Speaks better than most white men. Say something for the gentlemen, Rafe."

I think, goddamit! I can speak better than most whites! Rafe screamed in his mind. *I'm not like Jomo and the others, just an ignorant nigger to fight and die for a white man* . . . Old Chulem's eyes bored into him, breaking the thought. "Why you starin' at me, old man, conjure man?"

Chulem rubbed his lips and toothless gums with a dirty finger. He spat into the compound yard. "I'se jus' checkin' yo' eyes fer de poison sign."

"What you see, old man?"

"Poison," he said, starting to turn, then cautiously easing off the porch into the dust. "But not from no knife." The conjure man hobbled off toward the cook shack where a black slave beat a strip of metal and called the pitbucks to their meal. Rafe watched Chulem leave, measuring the old man for the thousandth time, wondering what he knew and didn't know.

Jomo took a length of sugar cane from the basket

hanging from the beam and began to chew on it. "Yo' get yo' po'k today, Rafe N'gata, while the rest of us has ouah rice and beans. You kill yo' man, you gets yo' po'k."

Jomo watched his massive companion step from the porch and, ignoring him, stride across the compound. The shorter man grinned and spit out the torn fibers. He was used to Rafe's silences. They didn't bother him. He stretched his squat, muscular frame, then jumped lightly from the porch and followed the giant. N'gata. Surely he could talk Rafe out of a chunk of that pork. A little fresh meat was good for a man.

3

The boat from Boston arrived with great fanfare, welcomed by an always boisterous, clamoring New Orleans. Crissa, tired and disheveled from the long journey, stood at the rail, glad for the sight of land, happier because this land was familiar, was close to home. The sights at dockside first filled her with warmth and an easy feeling of nostalgia. She remembered how proud and noble her father looked as he stood with arms akimbo and legs planted firmly on the quarterdeck of the warship. But that was almost seven years ago and since then he had, as had so many others, perished on the high seas during the War with England. Since then she had left the land where she was born and raised, left for the far north and Boston and four years of schooling. Now she was back and wanted nothing more than to savor the homecoming. Why then, despite her determination to remain cheerful, did such a disturbing feeling of disquietude insist upon intruding upon her thoughts? Something was very wrong, but she couldn't lay her finger on exactly what bothered her.

The shipboard sounds swelled as officers and crew saw to the unloading of passengers and freight: the noisy, good-natured curses of sweat-lathered dockhands, the rap-rap-rap of feet on the deck, gangplank and dock, the squeal of winches and groan of ropes as cartons of goods were hoisted from the hold and dropped to the deck, there to be placed on the backs of an army of slaves. All was as it should be.

Then above the pleasant cacophony another sound gradually forced its way into her consciousness. The clank of chains. The shuffling of a hundred bare feet scraping on wood. Suddenly a whip cracked and a high-pitched scream rose above the din. Crissa turned toward the sound and saw a coffle of slaves, directly off a boat, making their way down the dock. Men and women chained together, filthy, emaciated, stumbling, evidently in pain. A fat white man strode beside them, yelling from time to time. He carried a bullwhip which he cracked about his head, then about the ankles of the chained blacks. An unfortunate soul tripped and nearly fell. Again the whip lashed out with deadly accuracy and caught a middle-aged black woman across her back, the tip curling around her side and biting cruelly into her right breast, drawing blood. The woman didn't scream, only moaned. Her head fell back and Crissa could see her eyes clenched shut, her mouth wide with pain. A manacled hand tried to reach the bleeding breast, but was pulled short and jerked back viciously.

Crissa was rigid, her muscles taut. Repelled by the sight, she was yet so fascinated she couldn't tear her eyes from the coffle, and watched its passage down the dock and through the huge doors of what appeared to be a warehouse. When the door slammed closed she glanced down at her hands to discover them clenched on the rail, her knuckles white and bloodless. She drew a shuddering breath. Could she have forgotten what slavery was? What it meant? How horribly demeaning it must be for those under its power? Four years in Boston had taught her a new way of life, a way of life which regarded slavery as an abomination in the sight of God and man. Her father had been a slave owner, she remembered. One had to be to get the work done. But he had never transformed men and women into wretches such as these. Or had he? Had she, as so many others, been blind to that which was now so obvious? She had not realized until that moment how deeply the four years had affected her. Shaken to the core, she hailed the first carriage available and disembarked.

The trip through the teeming, crowded streets of New Orleans went by as if Crissa were in a trance. The once familiar streets and buildings shimmered in the hallucinatory heat of the afternoon sun, and dreamlike, she stared as they slipped by. So complete was her withdrawal she barely realized the carriage had come to a halt in front of Le Grande Hotel and the porters had carried her trunks to the lobby.

Le Grande Hotel . . . her mother's last letter had instructed her to proceed there and await transportation to Claytonville. Claytonville. What was it like now? Her mother had never said, beyond the news of the changed name. "Fitzman Corners has a new name," she wrote, "Claytonville. Your stepfather seems inordinately proud of same. I am of the opinion Fitzman Corners had a nobler ring to it, but have had little to say on the matter as, indeed, on all matters these days." From then on the frequency of the letters had declined. Those that did arrive were more and more vague and at times nonsensical and incoherent, leading to dark and ominous thoughts Crissa couldn't dispel.

A dark hand reaching for her broke the spell. A tall, well-dressed Negro spoke in the thick dialect she hadn't heard for four years. Recognizing only the inflection, not the words, she alighted from the carriage and entered the lobby. Le Grande Hotel! The memories rushed pell-mell. A thirteen-year-old girl at her first formal ball. How Le Grande glittered! A fourteen-year-old in bitter mourning for her father. How heavy, how solemn the somber lobby. And now at twenty, a young woman more than a little lost in the confusion of a disquieting homecoming.

A short, squat gentleman tipped his hat in front of her and inquired in thickly accented speech if he might not be of assistance to the mademoiselle. She shook her head and declined in perfectly accented French. The portly gentleman lifted his eyebrows in new esteem of the young woman, bowed and walked off, following the several porters struggling up the stairs with his luggage. He barked at them, urging them to hurry, and when one moved too slowly to suit him, swung his cane viciously to catch the old, white-haired slave a stinging blow across the back of his calves. The porter jerked violently, swivelled his head about and, eyes wide with fright, stumbled and went tumbling down the stairs, the heavy trunk rolling over him on the way down. The Frenchman broke into a string of Gallic expletives and hurried down the stairs to inspect the damage while the desk clerk, all apologies, rushed from behind the counter and nodded obsequiously as the Frenchman pointed out each scuff and scratch on the shining trunk.

Half-forgotten for the moment, the old slave staggered to his feet, his left arm hanging limply at his side. He tried to make his way unseen to the rear of the lobby but the desk clerk grabbed him by the shirt, spoke in a rapid, hissing whisper and dragged the poor soul to the door and booted him in the baggy, worn seat of his pants. The old man squeaked in pain as his broken arm struck the door on his way out. The Frenchman nodded in satisfaction and the clerk, all efficiency, clapped his hands and another black, a younger man this time, scurried from around the corner of the desk, hoisted the trunk onto his back and started up the stairs.

Crissa watched the whole episode with face set in grim distaste. Finally she could take no more, and the amused chatter and laughter of everyone else in the lobby ringing in her ears, she made her way into the street in search of the old man. He was gone. Confused, she turned to her right and made her way along the front of the hotel, glancing down the alley at the end of the building. The alley appeared empty, but as she started down the street again, a soft moan stopped her. She glanced about apprehensively and then entered the dimly lit alley, her slippers barely making a sound on the packed dirt.

The old man, some ten feet beyond the bright line of light, sat on a small, discarded box half-hidden by a barrel, cradling his shattered arm and rocking back and forth in pain. Crissa, nervous now, gasped lightly as the slave turned quickly toward her, his eyes wide with fright at the

36

sight of the young white woman whose strawberry-gold tresses framed an almost perfect face.

The two stared at each other for perhaps thirty seconds, each taking the measure of the other, both nervous and confused by the strangeness of the situation. Finally Crissa reached inside her purse and took out a gold eagle. The coin glittered in the shadow, drawing the old man's eyes to it in spite of the pain.

"Take it," she whispered, hurriedly. The slave hesitated. He licked his thin, cracked lips and stretched out his good right arm. "It's enough to fix your arm and then some. I'm sorry it isn't more."

Suddenly the old man's eyes clouded with fear and his hand jerked back as if burned.

"That's more than he's worth."

Crissa jumped and whirled about. A soldier, his face hidden in shadow, stood no more than a pace behind her, blocking the alley. He was a white man, but she could tell little else.

"They'll say he stole it," the soldier said, a touch of cold amusement in his voice.

Now she was angry. The stranger's amusement bespoke an impudence that fed her frustration born of the injustice she had just witnessed and felt so keenly. Words rushed from her in a torrent. "You have no right! The poor man has a broken arm. Someone has to be kind to him and treat him like a human being. I'll give what I please to whom I please. Why don't you go . . . go fight a war or something!" And without waiting for the soldier's reply, she turned back to the old slave who by this time had gotten up and was attempting to slip away unnoticed. "Wait!" she called. The old man stopped dead in his tracks. "Come back."

The old man turned, shaking with fear. His mouth moved but no words came out. Slowly he took a step toward her, then stopped again, torn between advance and retreat. Crissa walked purposefully to him, took his good right hand and folded his fingers around the ten dollar gold piece. The old man stared first at his hand, then into his benefactress's eyes.

"Go and see to your arm. No one will harm you," she

said gently. The old man scuttled down the alley, disappearing around a corner at the rear of the hotel.

Crissa smiled in satisfaction. At least someone had acted honorably. And as for the soldier. . . . But he was gone. Proud of herself for speaking so forcefully to him and driving him off, she started for the mouth of the alley only to see him step back around the corner and stand waiting for her. There was nothing to do but continue. She had outbluffed him once and could surely do so again.

She had almost reached the street when the soldier stepped back and bowed in deference. All she could see of him was a shock of bright red, unruly hair, previously suppressed by a chapeau bras, the bicorn hat so much in fashion in military circles. The hair was familiar, and now that she thought of it, so the voice had been. It couldn't be. . . .

The soldier straightened up. "Hello, Crissa."

"Steve . . . oh, Steve," Crissa cried in surprise. "Was that you?"

"I thought you'd recognize me."

"In a dark alley? And after four years? Oh, Steve," she broke off, running to embrace her childhood beau. He held her tightly, his arms encircling her, his lips seeking hers. She pulled back abruptly. "How naughty of you. All I could see was the outline of some horrid soldier. Are you a soldier now? How silly you look. Oh, how very, very funny."

Steve drew back, affronted by her comments, only to find himself immediately engulfed again in Crissa's exuberant embrace. He returned her affections rather coolly.

"Steven Bennett, don't be stuffy. I'm only teasing you."

"I'm not hurt, Crissa. Obviously Major Reynolds and the United States Army don't think I look silly. I received my captain's bars and commission only just last week."

"It's also obvious, Captain Steven Bennett," Crissa drawled coquettishly, "that Major so-and-so and the United States Army never ever went skinny dippin' with you in the creek back of the plantation."

"Crissa, please!" Steve looked cautiously about, but the passing pedestrians paid them little heed. "Let's go back to the hotel." He took her arm and guided her back the way she had come. "You came tearing out of there like a woman possessed and walked right past me without so much as a glance. What happened?"

"What happened, Captain Steven Bennett, was a poor old man had his arm broken because some pompous idiot thought to beat some strength into the poor soul's withered frame. I gave him some money to get it fixed and buy himself some food. It looked as if it had been awhile since he'd last eaten."

"That's for his master to worry about, not some stranger. Especially a young girl like yourself. Besides, you'll get him in even more trouble. Who's going to believe that old nigger when he tells them a white woman gave him a whole ten dollar gold piece just because his arm was broken? One or two dollars they might believe, but ten! It was a silly, childish gesture."

"Steve. I've spent the last four years at school. I am now twenty years old and think of myself as a woman. I would appreciate you doing the same."

"Now that *is* silly."

"Captain Bennett, are we going to spoil what should be a pleasant reunion between old and dear friends?"

"Seeing you crouched in an alley with some white-haired nigger after three weeks alone at sea without a chaperone is more than. . . ."

"I think that will be quite enough, Captain. I don't wish to continue this conversation. I assume you have come to escort me to the plantation. Very well. But I will not listen to such language. If you are so proud of your uniform, you could at least behave with the gallantry it represents." She stopped, disengaging her arm from his. "I shall dine at eight in the main dining room. If you wish to join me, I shall be delighted to share your company. I hope to find you suitably courteous at that time." She haughtily turned from the flustered officer and entered the main door of the hotel, leaving her perplexed suitor behind in the street. Steve took off his hat and slapped it against his leg in an age-old gesture of confusion. What man can understand the complex nature of the woman he had dreamed of marrying for all these years?

Crissa Fitzman, clad only in a cotton shift, lay across the broad double bed, listening to the sounds of early evening. The exotic clamor of the French Quarter seeped through the closed shutters and hung heavily in the humid, still air. Sweat streaked her bare neck and rippled across her shoulders until even the shift was too much and she rose abruptly, pulled the garment over her head and stood naked in the light of the pitiful coal oil lamp on the dresser. Steve's words echoed in her mind. A silly girl, indeed. She took a cloth from the rack and dipped it into the basin, wrung it out and wiped the sweat from her neck and shoulders. The cooling towel passed over her breasts, tightening the skin deliciously. She turned to the mirror and gazed at herself. The light from the lamp gave a golden hue to her skin and sculpted her form with deep shadows. Young, firm breasts, swollen slightly from the light touch of the towel, stood in firm relief, each half in shadow, half in light. Her stomach was flat and flowed gracefully to the gentle mounds of mons and hips below, so delicately accentuated by yet more gleaming dark gold hair. Her thighs were full yet firm, her calves shapely and rounded. She placed her hands under her breasts, palpitating them gently with her palms and fingers, then watched, pleased, as the nipples, tingling, swelled with a life of their own. A silly girl, indeed!

The clock behind her struck the familiar melody and she sighed and left the mirror. It was time to bathe and dress, then join Steve in the dining room. *Captain* Steve Bennett . . . well, why not? He was handsome enough, intelligent enough. A soldier, true, and she could wish he were not, but what else was there for a man to aspire to in a town like Claytonville? Or, without money, in the whole of western Louisiana, for that matter. One could be a shopkeeper or join the military. She could hardly blame him for not wanting to be a shopkeeper in Claytonville.

Crissa scowled at the thought of the town once named for her father. When she left for the north and school it had been called Fitzman Corners. Two years later her mother had told her of the change. She wondered what other changes had been made at the plantation during her absence. How radically had the man who had married her mother, a man she had barely gotten to know before leaving, altered the home she remembered? Already she could feel the resentment coming back, building inside her.

"I would have thought four years would have changed things, made them easier to accept. How strange. . . ." Crissa mused aloud. Her words only accentuated the hollow emptiness of the room. She sank into the tub, letting the cooling water envelop her, drifting farther back in a dream of her childhood which spread before her like a feast of genuinely happy memories.

The pecan grove, full of echoes of children playing tag and hide-and-go-seek, was her most cherished spot. Acres of richly laden trees formed a wonderland of cool, shadowed sanctuaries, safe from the fierce southern sun. The sun burned Crissa nearly as dark as the Negro children with whom she played. Her father kidded her about her deep tan and called her "his little darkie."

And there was Ephraim. Dear, kind, "Pa-Paw" Ephraim, the old slave who saved her life and lost an arm in the process. Crissa, barely ten, had wandered from the other children and was sulking over having lost a foot race when the cottonmouth struck. She caught little more than a glimpse of the darting head and curved fangs before her vision was blocked by a black arm. The snake caught Ephraim on the forearm instead of hitting Crissa on the face and the little girl watched, screaming in fear, as the slave tore the dripping fangs from their venomous hold, and whirling the cottonmouth high overhead, dashed it against a nearby pecan tree before he collapsed.

Crissa ran for help and Ephraim was carried back to the main house. Pa-Paw Ephraim lived, but the wound festered, turned gangrenous, and Crissa's father ordered the arm removed. Later, in front of Crissa, John Fitzman gave Ephraim his freedom, secretly of course, and hired him to care for the pecan grove, a duty the black man dearly loved.

Crissa had to smile at the memory of the good-hearted, gentle soul. The way he called the trees his children. He used to tell her, "Chile, ah'm tendin' dese trees fo' de

41

Lawd. When he come on de judgemen' day, he gonna find dis ol' nigger done kep' a place fo' him. Yassuh. Yore Pa-Paw done kep' a place fo' de Lawd to git outa de sun." Pa-Paw Ephraim. He would still be in his grove. Surely there were some things not even four years and Ezra Clayton could change.

Dinner was serene. They dined on shrimp and lobster and curried rice, topping the repast with a thick custard made from eggs, cream and wild honey. They lingered over the final glass of wine, reminiscing over childhood adventures and events. There was much to recall. Later on the terrace overlooking Bourbon Street they found a secluded table and over brandy, their conversation, timidly at first, turned to the past four years. Steve had joined the army only a year after his father, the Right Reverend MacKinney Bennett, died while attempting to cross a flooded stream to reach the deathbed of a friend. And what of the plantation? Steve paused a moment before speaking. "Bigger. Much bigger. Ezra has a knack for running the place. Many more slaves. And more land."

"And mother? How is she?" Crissa asked, disturbed at Steve's reticence to talk about her home.

"Well, no one sees too much of her any more. There's been talk she's been ill. And frankly speaking, I haven't had much call to visit since you've been gone."

Crissa sat back in the shadow cast by the oil lamp bracket. She had sensed as much about her mother and decided the sooner she returned home the better. "When can we be off to the plantation?"

"As early as you like. Crissa, there's one thing I think we ought to discuss." He paused and leaned forward. His eyes showed only too clearly what he felt. "I think we need to talk about us, about what we planned . . . when you returned from school."

Crissa took a deep breath. She had been avoiding this possibility all evening. Steve was more like a brother than lover and she dreaded having to admit it. "Steve, those were childhood dreams. . . ." His eyes tightened imperceptibly as she went on. "I'm sorry. I didn't know you felt

. . . I'm very tired. Do you mind? I'm worried about mother, and. . . ."

"I understand, Crissa," Steve said, his voice filled with disappointment. He rose stiffly, meticulously straightening his uniform, patting the wrinkles out of his blue coat and gray trousers.

"You look very handsome, you know. Very dashing. . . ."

"Please, Crissa, don't try so hard," he interrupted, offering her his hand. "May I? You will need some rest. We have a long trip ahead of us."

They left the terrace and he followed her down the hall, escorting her to her room and unlocking the door for her. She paused before entering. "Dear Steve. I *am* glad to see you. Will you forgive me?"

He smiled wanly. "Of course."

Crissa leaned toward him and gently kissed his cheek. It was meant as a light good-night kiss but Steve was not to be denied. He drew her close and kissed her passionately and deeply. Crissa felt his hands, rough and demanding, on her back. A little frightened, she pushed herself back from him, only to feel one hand grope across her stomach and grasp her firm, swelling breast. She sensed his arousal and broke from his embrace, managed a good-night and quickly stepped inside her bedroom, closing the door behind her.

Steve wandered down the hall. He paused at the door to his room, then continued on to the stairs. A lone gentleman with a Creole prostitute ascended past him with a great deal of stumbling and raucous laughter.

The lobby was empty save for the desk clerk, and the only indication of activity came from beyond a door to his right. He followed the sound into a plush, smoky saloon. A woman detached herself from her lady friends and took his arm even before his eyes adjusted to the dark. He allowed her to lead him to a dark corner, her musky scent rekindling his arousal. He bought her a drink, then another. . . .

Her name was Michelle. She was experienced in the ways of pleasing men. Her tousled hair draped over

43

Steve's naked shoulder and lay in dark waves on the sheet. Twice the young captain had emptied his pent-up desire between the prostitute's legs, each time burying himself furiously inside her as she cat-clawed his back. But with each climax Steve had shut his eyes and fed his mind with images of Crissa, bit his lip to keep from calling out her name.

Even now, the prostitute asleep at his side, he could feel the pressure of Crissa's body against his. And despite his laguorous exhaustion and the late hour, sleep would not come.

4

The women moved like somnambulent shadows across the dirt, bare feet snapping brittle stalks. Neither grass, flower nor shrub grew in the compound, only occasional weeds sucked dry by the thirsty clay. In twos and threes, many quietly timid, others raucous and openly eager, they walked in full knowledge of what awaited them—ravenous sexual appetites they were expected to appease. They passed through the compound gate and headed for the longhouse where Clayton's pitbucks waited like gladiators of old in the heady, sweltering heat of a muggy summer night, waited in one large room lacking anything but the shreds of privacy, a draped slip of burlap or a crate or two, partitioning one excited body from another

One of the women headed for Rafe's hut. For Rafe, more fortunate than the other inhabitants of the compound, slept alone and apart. He was the number one pitbuck and regarded as chief and spokesman until someone should beat him in the pit. The victor would then take his place in the cabin. The sod floor and plank walls would show no sign of Rafe's passing. It would be as if he had never been.

Her musky sweetness disturbed him and he opened his eyes, saw the shape of the figure in the doorway. "Who?"

"Julie."

"I am not to have a woman tonight, much less a child. Go to one of the others."

"Rafe hab a woman any time he wants," Julie said. She stepped into the doorway and approached the dark giant form stretched upon his pallet, barely visible in the faint light, the last edge of the day, from the window behind him. Rafe heard the rustle of her cotton shift as it settled to the floor. She knelt to one side and took his right hand, placing it first on one delicate breast then the other, then pressing it down to her flat, youthful stomach and guiding it still further to the moistness between her legs. "And Ah ain't no girl," she whispered huskily. "Ah stole from the house to bring yo' dis." She moved back and forth, slowly, rhythmically, causing Rafe's scarred hand and wrist to stroke her maiden's pelt.

Rafe drew his hand away, but caught despite himself and in the passion of the moment, cupped her face and drew it close. Beads of sweat dripped from her glistening cheek to his. Her face was a dark sheen against the darker wall beyond. Animal eyes, glistening, hungry, glared down at him. "Julie . . . ? You're the one who works up to the house."

The girl stiffened at the tone of his voice, pulled her face away. "Don' matter. We all gotta work someplace. Ah clean and sometime he'p wid de cookin' an' such."

"You also the one who do her duties in Ezra Clayton's bed. You ain't never gonna whelp him no white pup from yo' black belly. What you tryin' fo'?" The pitbuck cursed as he heard himself begin to allow the slave girl's dialect to influence his own speech. He was proud of the way he could talk. It bespoke culture and position, not servitude. Speech was the only symbol left to him and he had resisted losing its magic for over five years.

Julie's hand swept down toward his face, stopping abruptly as his massive fist rose and clamped about her wrist. She hissed at him like an angry cottonmouth. "Bastard! Ah do what Ah'se to'd, nigger. Same as yo'. Ah'se to'd to spread mah legs fo' de mastuh and Ah do it. Ah do it good. Yo' coulda found dat out fo' yo'se'f. Now you never finds out, nigger."

46

She tore from his grasp and scurried across the floor, grabbing her shift and shrugging the light fabric over her heated flesh. Panting, she turned in the doorway, unable to see Rafe lying in the dark recesses of the hut but knowing he was there all the same. "We do," she spit viciously, "what we's tol' to. What makes yo' any better'n me? Ah screws and Ah likes it. Ah git Mistah Clayton tight 'tween my hot, black thighs an' Ah'm de queen of dis here plantation 'til he go sof' an' roll ober pantin'. Ah screws when Ah'se tol'. Yo' fights when yo' tol'. No diff'rence, 'ceptin' dat yo' killin' yo' own kind. An' yo' know what else? Ah think yo' likes de killin', s'much as Ah like de screwin'. Only when yo' guttin' some po' bastard yo' still ain't nuffin'. Jus' a nuffin' nigger killer. But Ah'se a queen. Yo' hear me? A queen!" She sobbed and ran out the door.

Rafe sighed and rolled over on his side. His leg throbbed, but only a little. His back stung from time to time whenever he scraped it across the coarse burlap of the pallet. Run back to your house, little girl, he thought. White man's waitin' for you.

He raised his hand to his nostrils. She smelled ready enough. Perhaps he'd been a fool to chase her off. Ezra Clayton's mulatto. It would have been a meager way to get back at him. Clayton. . . .

Rafe's memory drifted back to the early days with Ezra. Rafe was Lucas Clayton's trusted manservant in New Orleans. America was at war with England and now the clouds of war had moved south and were gathering over New Orleans. A battle was imminent, waiting only for the arrival of the contestants. The New Year came and went and the air hung heavy with the hush of coming violence. The Lucas Clayton household stored water and provisions in preparation for the worst. And suddenly the storm broke. General Jackson and a wild conglomeration of soldiers, swamp people and pirates against the English. Ezra showed up during the early hours of the battle, shivering from slogging through swamps and bayous, hot and tired from running, trembling with fear of discovery. He and Lucas holed up in the library, but Rafe heard what they said. Ezra had spied for the British and been found out. Jackson's army was after him. Lucas was angry, but what was he to do? The man was his brother.

Somehow the word got out that Ezra was in the house, and before the day was over, even while the final shots of battle were echoing through the muddy streets, a detachment of soldiers surrounded Lucas Clayton's house. Within minutes the house was a raging inferno. No one knew or ever found out how the fire started. Lucas tried to get out but was trapped trying to save his wife and child. The only two to escape were Ezra and Rafe.

The soldiers, a ragtag lot, stopped them to ask questions. In shock and his clothes half burned off him, still coughing from the smoke he'd swallowed, Rafe listened without comprehending as Ezra identified himself as Lucas to the soldiers, none of whom had ever seen either man. When Ezra led him off, Rafe stumbled along, too tired, too broken to understand, much less care, what had happened.

Somehow they made it out of the city. A thin, sallow, toothless man offered them a ride in his *calèche*. They accepted, and on the ragged edge of exhaustion, collapsed into the jolting wooden cart for the ride up the trail along the Mississippi, paying the next to last half-eagle Ezra was able to save from the fire for the privilege. When they got to the junction of the Red River they learned they were being sought, so they managed to wheedle a ride up the Red on a flat boat, working their way for food and passage in order to save the final half-eagle. They got off at Natchitoches, the last stop before the Great Raft halted all navigation to the north, intending to make their way west and into Mexico.

The last half-eagle bought them meager provisions and they struck off on foot along the trail west, ending up at a plantation called Fitzman's Freedom when Ezra was taken so badly with the ague he couldn't walk another step. The people at Fitzman's Freedom took them in, fed them and nursed Ezra Clayton back to health.

Rafe slept for a day and a half once they stopped. Completely exhausted from work to which he wasn't accustomed and half-starved in the bargain, he was in little better shape than Ezra. After he woke up and ate three steaming bowls of jambalaya and a heap of lost bread, the fried bread they'd called *pain perdu* in New Orleans, he fell asleep again. The sound of the calinda, feet beating the age-old dance rhythm on the hardened clay, broke into his dreams and he knew it was Saturday night.

Sunday morning he awoke to see the plantation for the first time. A huge three-storied house of fired brick and native wood sat on the top of a slight knoll. It faced east, with the back open to catch the summer breezes which would later blow off the Sabine River to the west. Two huge magnolias framed it from the front and a stand of giant, ancient loblolly pines stood to its northwest to break the winter wind. The house was in a state of disrepair. Wide steps, some broken, led up to the square-columned gallery which ran the length of the front on two levels. Part of the lower gallery sagged dangerously at one corner, and the whole structure needed paint. As he looked, the front doors opened and a girl accompanied by a huge blue tick hound ran out and stopped to stare at him. He stook stock still when the hound came to him and sniffed inquisitively, then turned and went back to the girl who laughed, and trusting in the dog's good judgement, approached him confidently.

Her name was Crissa Fitzman. She told him all he wanted to know and more. How her father had gone off to war and died aboard his ship. How alone she felt without him. How they'd had to sell many of the slaves. There were only ten left. She took him to meet Pa-Paw Ephraim and the three of them, to escape the cold February winds, sat in Pa-Paw's shack in the pecan grove across the road from the house and talked most of the day.

That had been five years ago. Ezra Clayton recovered, and because he was getting along well with the widowed Micara Fitzman, stayed to court and win her. Another year and Crissa was off to the north to school on the money her father had set aside in a New Orleans bank for the purpose and within another month Ezra and Micara had married and the Fitzman was dropped from the plantation name, leaving it simply Freedom. Within another year the atmosphere at Freedom assumed an ominous note. Ezra, knowing a good thing when he saw it, took over completely. The pit was dug and Rafe, because he knew what and who Ezra really was, lost his position as manservant and was sent to live with the other slaves and fight his first fight.

But he fooled Ezra. He killed the red-bearded one. And the next one, and the next one. He still lived, clung to life with all the tricks and power he could bring to bear. Short of outright execution, Ezra couldn't trick him into death. And of all the years, there was but one good memory—that of the girl, Crissa Fitzman, laughing, willful, beautiful, with long reddish-blond hair down to her waist and a budding, lithesome figure. They spoke rarely after that first day. Rafe, with a black wisdom warning against too much contact with the white girl, kept to himself. But occasionally her eyes rose to find him staring at her. And he would have to lower his or turn aside lest she read in a single glance the dangerous, unfortunate desire lurking there.

Rafe rose from the cot. His flesh felt feverish. Damn wounds. They were the cause of all this. Why else would he be thinking this way? That year, the girl . . . too many years ago, too many deaths ago. Still, the memory rose to plague him. He should have let the girl, Julie, stay. She could have sat astride him to sheath and ride the angry reach of his desire until his bitterness was eased. A woman was good for that. Curse Old Chulem. He had won, hadn't he? He deserved a woman. Footsteps sounded outside. The girl returning?

"Who?"

The moon parted a diaphanous cloud and the compound erupted into shimmering, silvery light. Trinidad stood in the doorway. The giant warrior on the pallet cursed inwardly. Only the young lovesick buck whom Rafe occasionally loaned the privacy of his shack. Trinidad lived for the day when his fiftieth fight would buy his freedom and he could take his woman, Bess, and wagon and team and disappear forever across the Sabine.

"Trinidad. It's me, Rafe."

Rafe rose without a sound, shrugging aside his soul's emotional garments lest they be detected and one day conspire against him. Trinidad jumped back, startled by the giant's sudden appearance in the doorway. Rafe looked at the slim, quick youth and the woman he loved who came to him and him alone faithfully every Saturday and Sunday night and who slept alone the remainder of the week. The girl was dark with thick tribal features split into a grin so warm and inviting one could not help but smile back.

"Thank you, Rafe," Bess called.

The giant pitbuck didn't answer. The deed, the gesture, the action was his way. He did not wait for gratitude nor vengeance. Trinidad and Bess quickly entered the hut and soon were lost in each other's arms, oblivious to the churning thoughts and torturous reminiscences Rafe had left behind.

The gold was arranged in accurately counted stacks. Ten dollar gold eagles in eight stacks of ten with four left over. Half-eagles in eleven stacks of ten with two left over, and five stacks of quarter-eagles with one left over. Martinson, large and blubbery, his face pale and dank with sweat, let the final stack of quarter-eagles clink to the table, counting each as it fell. Ezra sat behind a large oak desk and entered the cash in his books. Martinson rubbed his forearm across his face, wiping away the droplets of salty moisture. "Fifteen hundred and twenty-seven dollars and fifty cents on the nose, Mr. Clayton. I knew I was right. No, sir. I don't miscount very often."

"Once is too often, Martinson," Ezra said without looking up. He blotted the ledger and closed it gently, setting it in the desk drawer.

"Oh, I agree," the bookkeeper said. "I always count it twice, just like you ordered, Mr. Clayton."

Ezra lifted the brandy snifter to his nose and sniffed, enjoying the pungency of the thick peach sweetness. A little sip sent mellow fire down his throat. The fat bookkeeper glanced thirstily in Ezra's direction as the lord of Freedom finished the glass and set it down. Ezra reached over to the crystal decanter and poured another snifter for himself, raising his eyes a fraction of an inch as a faint sigh escaped Martinson. With no indication he would do

51

so, Ezra moved the decanter to another snifter and poured, sliding the second glass in Martinson's direction.

Martinson reached quickly for the snifter, hurrying to secure the proffered drink, eager to be able to gloat to Butkis and the others how he'd shared a drink with Mr. Clayton. Ezra watched distastefully as the fat man realized his greed and sank back stiffly with the snifter held between his palms, rolling it back and forth, sniffing at it delicately in feigned nonchalance. The fool will probably express an opinion now, Ezra thought sourly. Very well. He would pretend to be impressed. Butkis needed a bit of a fall. Getting too big for his britches, and it was always easier to let someone else help. Kept them all on their toes.

Martinson opened his mouth, as predicted, and started to speak when the door to the library swept open and banged against the wall behind it. Martinson jumped, startled by the noise, then sat back, pretending he hadn't been surprised. Behind him, Micara stood swaying in the doorway. Ezra's face flushed with anger as his wife made her way unsteadily into the room and collapsed in a nearby chair, her breath coming in heavy gasps from the exertion. Martinson stole a furtive glance at her then jerked his eyes away uncomfortably, turning to stare uncomprehendingly at the rows of books lining the north wall of Ezra's library.

"Get out," Ezra hissed, his voice barely above a whisper. Martinson looked quickly at him. "Yes, you. Get."

"Yes, sir," he croaked, scrambling to his feet, snifter still in hand. He gulped the brandy quickly and set the glass on the table and scurried from the room, stomach heaving and throat burning viciously, raked by the pale liquid fire.

Micara and Ezra stared at each other across the silent room, Ezra's eyes sharp and predatory, Micara's drugged and bitter but relentless nevertheless. Neither spoke for nearly a quarter of an hour. Ezra patiently sipped his brandy and listened to the great clock, let his rage slow to match the heavy sound, allowed the anger in him to settle before speaking. He was a man who had learned the value of control.

"Micara," he finally said, his voice smooth and satiny, "if you must continue to overindulge, I have repeatedly requested you do so in private. I'm afraid I shall be forced to lock you in your room if you insist on embarrassing me in front of my employees."

Micara's features broke into a surly frown. "Private?"

"Yes."

"Ha! I live my whole life in private. Wha'd you know about private? All you care about is your pit and fighting slaves and gambling and that cheap nigger you take to bed wi' you. Cheap nigger trash instead of your wife. Not . . ."

Ezra was around the desk and across the room in short, quick strides. His right hand shot across in a swift vicious arc, backhanding her, slapping her once, twice. "Shut up."

Tears rolled from her eyes, spilled down her red-streaked, smarting cheeks. "Damn you," she slurred. "Damn you for a . . ."

Ezra cut her off sharply. "You're in no condition to damn anyone. Get upstairs to your room. If you've sobered up for breakfast you may come down and damn me then." He took her by the arm and pulled her from the chair to guide her faltering steps to the door. In the hall, pride helped him decide against calling for assistance and he half dragged, half pushed her upstairs.

"I'm alone in an empty house, Ezra . . . alone in an empty house. . . ." she wept.

"Not for long, Micara, dear. Crissa will be here soon. Only a few days, now. My, won't she be surprised to see how mommy's changed."

"You bastard," she slurred, stumbling against the railing. Ezra toyed with the notion of allowing her to tumble down the stairs but rejected the idea. The timing for such an accident had to be perfect. Perhaps after Crissa left. . . . Now *there* was a thought.

"If it wasn't for me you'd be nothing," Micara continued as Ezra led her down the hall. "All this is mine."

The master of Freedom hurried his drunken wife into her bedroom, spun her around to face him. "Listen to me, woman. If it weren't for *me,* this place would be a hollow whisper by now, just so much empty rotten wood crumbled and fallen down on itself with you sitting atop the whole mess and whining. I've built Freedom. I keep it running and growing. I am the power here and don't you forget it. Freedom became mine when you married me."

"I loved you, Ezra." Micara tried to look coquettish. This was the first time he had even been in her room for many months. "Ezra . . . ?" She reached for him.

Ezra avoided her touch. "Micara, your forty years have aged you. Made you old. You married me out of weakness and fear."

"If Patrick had stayed. . . ."

"But he didn't stay, did he? Didn't stay to help a whining sister-in-law whom he couldn't stand any more. You know why? He was weak like you and couldn't handle responsibility. So now he's probably dead, and serves him right. You're alone and you can't manage Freedom alone. You need me to hold things together and you know it. So you can have pretty clothes, imported sherry and servants. You have all those things, Micara. I've kept my part of the bargain. Now why don't you keep yours and leave me be?"

Micara grabbed for him, pressed her lips against his, crushed her full breasts against his chest. "Stay with me tonight, Ezra. Stay with me? I'll be good, I promise. Better than that little yellow nigger. Stay with me . . . stay?"

Ezra tore her arms from around him and held her wrists pinned to his chest. His hands tightened until his taloned fingers broke the wrinkled skin on her wrists. Micara's eyes widened with terror. "Don't ever," he whispered, the words tiny lashes, "show up sotted downstairs again. Do you understand?" Micara, face knotted in pain, nodded weakly, her head snapping forward as he pushed her from him, sent her stumbling and falling backward onto her canopied bed. He turned and stalked out the door, slamming it behind him. He was gone.

Micara buried her face in a pillow, muffling the sobs that shook her whole body. Finally the wracking spasms subsided and she recovered enough to reach for the crystal decanter of sherry by the bed. Things would be better when Crissa came, she thought. There would be two of them to Ezra's one. Crissa. Her sweet little Crissa. She reached under another pillow and drew out a slim blue bottle of laudanum. A teaspoon? Two teaspoons? It didn't matter. She put the bottle to her lips, drank, then capped and replaced the bottle. More sips of sherry countered the bitterness of the opiate. She shut her eyes and prayed she might succumb to the narcotic sleep before hearing Julie's inevitable footsteps heading down the hall to Ezra's bedroom. She was in luck this time.

Decater waited until his companions began to snore soundly in a deep sleep, courtesy of too much rum and time spent with the field women. His thin bony frame glided soundlessly across wooden planks loose enough to protest the passage of a heavier man. Once outside he traversed the plantation yard swiftly and surely, darting to the cover of the trees in back of the field hands' shacks by the time the moon cleared its cloud cover. He patted the bump in his pocket, suddenly worried he had forgotten it and would have to sneak back. He hadn't forgotten. He sighed with relief.

Silently he crept on to the rear edge of the stand of loblollys, then paused, still in shadow. No sound disturbed him save the soughing of the wind high in the trees and the inevitable chorus from the bullfrog-lined creek. He mimicked a hoot owl. A giggle sounded off to his left and he followed the sound along the edge of the trees until a slight figure stepped into the moonlight and stopped him.

"Yo' brung it, Mistah Decatuh?"

Decater glanced about uneasily. "Sure, honey. Now come here."

"Uh-uh. Yo' gots to lemme hab dat candy fu'st."

"All right. Here. Like I done promised. Peppermint. Bought it maself in Claytonville jus' yestiday."

"Mmmmm, dat sho look good, Mistah Decatuh."

"Now come here and lift up an' lemme see. . . ."

"Yo' promise not ta hurt me? Yo' promise jes ta look?"

"You know I will. I always jus' look. Anyways, Mister

55

Clayton lay down the rules. We cain't touch no black pussy younger'n fourteen, ceptin' we got permission. Now come here."

"Yo' don' tell an' ah don' tell. Mammy'ud skin mah ass. . . . Dis peppamint is sho good, Mistah Decatuh. Ah betta eat it all fo' ah gits back, else deys knowin' sompin's up, I comes in wid peppamint."

"Jus' hesh up, girl. Dammit, hesh up and hold them legs apart and spread it open so's I can see."

"Ah'm gittin' co'd eben if it is springtime. How long you gonna look, Mistah Decatuh?"

"As long as it takes, dammit. Long as it takes. . . ."

5

Crissa and Steve's trip to Freedom Plantation was
considerably easier than Ezra and Rafe's almost five years
earlier. They travelled openly, to begin with, and with
funds enough for staterooms on the Red River Diamond,
a stern-wheeler which, although not large, was comfortable enough even with a three day layover in Alexandria
for repairs to the boiler. Crissa exulted over the trip. The
broad Mississippi, which she hadn't seen for years, was
full of memories. The muddy water swept by them to the
roar of the engines and the constant clacking and creaking
of paddle wheel and gear. The levees, over their heads
most of the time, concealed the land of her youth, offering only tantalizing and occasional glances of chimneys
and roofs.

The two travellers spent hours in quiet conversation,
remembering the youthful days. And if the images their
talk elicited were warm, the changes in Steve were ominously unsettling. Brought up on the edge of the swamp, he
was the son of a self-designated preacher man who poled
the swamps as readily as other men walked the high road.
Bible wrapped in oil-soaked canvas, his pirogue cut
through the murky brown water effortlessly, preceded always by the deep-voiced, off-key booming of gospel

hymns. The word of God as proclaimed by MacKinney Bennett echoed around the boles of a million cypress trees and woke the swamp's primordial inhabitants. The old man had but one dream—that his son should become a real preacher. To this end, from the age of ten on, he sent Steven to spend eight of every twelve months at Fitzman's Freedom, there to learn to read and write.

Crissa remembered a quiet, almost sad boy, one who rarely laughed. A boy who'd never known his mother. A gentle boy. But the boy had changed. Two years older than she, he had grown hard around the edges. Tougher, sterner somehow. More taciturn. Perhaps the army had helped. Knowing the swamp as he did, he made captain easily. He knew the turns and bends of a thousand creeks, knew the men who made a living in the swamp, killing for hide, fur and plumage. This knowledge made him invaluable to the army. When the occasional Creek or far-roaming Atakapan hunting parties raided into the white man's land to steal food and drive off stock, it fell to Captain Steven Bennett, he who had eschewed God and carried gun and machete in place of his father's Bible, to pursue them back into the swamp. Sometimes he found them. They had yet to find him first.

Crissa had looked forward to seeing him again. But now she wasn't sure. He wasn't the same person. She found herself more than a little awed by his new personality and a tiny bit fearful. So she bided her time, making up her mind to suspend final judgement until she'd been back a while longer.

And finally Natchitoches! Saturday afternoon and the Red River Diamond, whistle hooting brashly, eased into the Upper Landing on the shore of Cane River Lake opposite Texas Street. They disembarked to the noise of trade, for Natchitoches was the converging point of important water and land trade routes. A hired chaise, or as Crissa would have it, a shay, with a Negro boy, strangely enough, riding postilion, drove them down Washington Street toward Nicholas Lauve's house where she was to spend the night.

This was the scene Crissa had missed for four long years. Freedom was but forty miles to the west and her father and mother had brought her to Natchitoches often. The noise and bustle, the swirling clouds of dust and humidity were symbols of life and gaiety and extra-special times and treats. She didn't even mind the heat, unused to it though she was after four years in the north. It felt good because it felt like home. She made Steve order the boy to a halt before they reached the Lauves', for a pack train was braying its way up the road toward the landing. Coming from the west, the mules and horses, heads lowered in exhaustion and flanks lathered with foam, were loaded down with hides and dried buffalo tongue, perhaps even silver bars from the mines of Mexico. Crissa remembered the wistful look in her father's eye when such a train passed Fitzman's Freedom, for he too wanted to make the trip one day. Perhaps he would have had he not been so devoted to Micara and Crissa. Only the idea of country had come before them, and for that idea he had died. . . .

Sunday stole quietly into Natchitoches. Crissa awoke in the high-dormered guest room to see the sun steal up over the river. She had stayed at the Lauves' before when her father, John Fitzman, was still alive and a good chess-playing friend of Nicholas Lauve. She shoved the memory from her mind, relaxed to feel the Sunday morning quiet, then suddenly sat up with a jerk. They should be on their way. Freedom was but a day away. She dressed quickly, urged on by the pungent odor of frying ham and dark, roasted coffee rising from below.

Downstairs, Steve Bennett, newly commissioned captain in the U.S. Army guarding the new Mexican border, kicked his booted toe against the hardwood spokes of the brightly painted gig. With its black leather calash folded down so they could catch the cool morning air and the five foot high wheels designed for rough roads, Ezra's gig was one of the best looking in town, one a man could be proud to drive. A strong-limbed brown mare between the shafts shook her head, rattling her harness as if impatient to be underway. Steve moved to her head and stroked the soft nose and shuddering neck. High-spirited, the mare would get them to Freedom before dark if Crissa would hurry and get out and ready to go. Bored with the wait, he sucked at the red weal where he'd scraped his finger while checking the loading of her brass embossed trunk, due to follow the next day on a supply wagon.

A church bell pealed nearby, echoed down the alley-ways, boomed hollowly along the street, strove vainly to carry across the river, only to be drowned out by a swirling cloud of screeching gulls who had followed the boats up from the coast. The morning fog had not yet burned off, and on all sides friendly bearded ghosts, giant oaks festooned with Spanish moss, lurked in the mist. Saturday night revelers had been awake all night, and now that dawn was on its way the town was quiet, only an occasional party-goer straggling by from time to time. The world lay in wait for Crissa Fitzman, and lady though she was, she was also independent enough to make it wait.

Not until nearly eight o'clock did the Lauve House doors swing open and Crissa, accompanied by host and hostess, descend to the waiting gig. Steve doffed his bicorn and offered his hand, his eyes roaming appreciatively over Crissa's bared shoulders. She gathered her voluminous skirts and allowed him to assist her into the carriage. While hosts and guest said their goodbyes he crossed in front of the mare, patting her neck again and speaking softly to the restless beast, then clambered up into the space beside Crissa. Reins in hand, he released the brake and made a clucking sound, lightly touching the long carriage whip across the animal's back. The mare, to the sound of muffled farewells, broke into an immediate trot, its hooves pounding a cadence in the still dewy dust. They were off.

The last forty miles! How short they seemed. Their motion stirred the still air about them and sucked the memory smells to her. Cape-jasmine, magnolia, roses— so early? She had forgotten roses bloomed so early. An acacia, feathery green and gold, floated out of the mist to her right, faded again behind her. Somewhere in the near distance a hound bayed its displeasure at their passage. So little had changed here. So little. And yet Crissa had changed. She saw herself from afar, a timid, frivolous girl, excited and afraid, trembling expectantly. And now a willful, independent, strong-minded young lady looking wistfully to the past.

Before long the gig's steady progress carried them from the town proper and onto the open trail west where they passed the last of the outlying small farms from whose windows drifted the heady aroma of grits, cornbread spiked with molasses and frying fatback—country breakfasts cooked on wood stoves.

For the better part of an hour they rode in utter silence. Steve, country wisdom sensing Crissa's need to gradually assimilate herself into the world from which she had been so long absent, sat hunched over the reins and left her to her own thoughts. Soon they were running along Katichitoo Bayou. Beyond it lay the swamps to the northwest. Grim and foreboding childhood fears reached out from the mossy depths to assail Crissa, plunging her into yet a deeper, gloomier silence. She was thankful for the brace of pistols under the seat, primed and within easy reach should Steve need them. She watched as his right hand strayed from the reins to play along the hilt of his saber. Regardless of its spartan lack of ornamentation and design, it was an utterly lethal weapon when used in close combat. The wire and brass hilt atop the hidden steel bolstered her nerve. Surely she was being childish.

Crissa had forgotten how unsettling this stretch of the trail could be. Because she had grown used to the civilized trappings of the northern cities, the sudden confrontation with the primeval gave rise to a host of unsettling emotions. When she was a child, visions of spooks and savages had burst from behind every lichenous rise where trees, vine-draped and gnarled, exploded in a canopy of moss. The air still and sentient, the old visions crowded in upon her, blotting out the joy of homecoming. The air was thick and moist, barely breathable, a viscous fluid flowing into the lungs and painfully out again. Crissa had always avoided the swamps near the plantation, and when travelling this road with her father had cuddled close to him, peeking out from time to time in spite of what she might see, then ducking back rapidly at the slightest hint of danger.

It took nearly an hour before the road wound away from Katichitoo and the land rose slightly to become rolling low hills covered with pine and, on the higher ridges, hardwood forest occasionally broken by cleared fields planted to cotton and sugar cane and vegetables. Crissa drew a breath of relief. This was the land she knew and loved. "I'd forgotten that horrible swamp," she said with a little shudder.

"It isn't so bad," Steve answered laconically, "once you get used to it. Nothing there to hurt you much."

Conversation wandered in a desultory vein for the next hour until, on a rise in front of them, Fort Jessup appeared alongside the trail. The gig pulled to a stop in front of the low gates, then entered slowly to the salute of the private on guard duty. A half-hour later they were settled on a blanket beneath an elegant magnolia which stood on a grassy knoll out of sight of the fort. Ivory blossoms scented the air about them. Crissa unpacked the lunch they'd brought and set it out. "Four years," she said dreamily. "How could I not remember how beautiful all this is?"

Steve looked out across the rolling land to the west, then back to her. "I never forgot how beautiful you are." His lips sought hers and he forced her back to the ground, his body half covering hers. Crissa could do little but submit as his tongue darted inside her mouth. She tried to squirm free, only to realize her arm was pinned to her side, caught between his legs where she could feel his swelling organ press boldly against her forearm. Gasping, she twisted her head free. "Steve, please . . . no. No!"

He relaxed with an effort, rolled from atop her yet held her down, staring intently into her eyes. "Four years is a long time. I guess I sort of forgot myself." He let her arms go and stood, his ache and longing plainly visible beneath the coarse, snug fabric of his trousers.

Crissa sat up slowly and busied herself with the lunch, keeping her eyes lowered and away from his. He *had* changed. Certainly more blunt, direct and to the point. But life here was hard, and who knew what four years could do to a man? Passion lived in the heat that baked the clay and sucked the moisture from the bayous. Love

62

here didn't wait on niceties. Raised to fever pitch by the shrill cry of cicadas and the pulsing fecundity of the land itself, it sought wild consummation. Crissa would have to handle Steve differently than the more cold-blooded men of the north who were more easily put off, more willing to wait. She looked back up at him. He hadn't moved. "Steve . . . ?"

"Uh?" he grunted tonelessly.

"I'm not ready for . . . that, Steve. Do you understand?"

He turned to her, his eyes raking her body. "No. Not really."

Crissa forced a gay laugh, patted the blanket beside her. "Steven Bennett, you're being surly. Just like some old he-bear come rooting out of the swamp."

"Crissa, you don't . . ."

"Come on. Sit down. Let's eat, okay?" She smiled and handed him a sandwich.

Steve bowed to her will and flopped down on the blanket, tore a huge bite from the bread and fried meat. "Different, isn't it?"

"What?"

"All this." He waved the sandwich in a wide sweep. "The land."

"I don't even know half the names."

"Lot of new ones, especially since the treaty. Lot of easterners coming in. You'll get to know 'em. Claude Duggins has the biggest farm around, except for Freedom and Bernard's place. Plenty of other small free-holders, too. Ol' Claude been rousin' up some of the other farmers. They figure they can bargain with the big plantation owners like your daddy . . . your stepdaddy. Ezra Clayton isn't too happy about the way they're acting up."

"What does mother think about them?"

Steve stared ahead, not speaking for several thoughtful moments. "Micara Clayton doesn't take . . . well, she leaves most of the running of things to her husband."

Crissa sat back, musing on the emptiness and uncharacteristically subdued tone of her mother's letters. Perhaps Ezra Clayton had asserted himself over her father's wife, his home, and holdings more than she had thought. I'm coming home none too soon, she reflected. She roused herself to bright chatter. "Well, whatever, the whole place seems so much more open and civilized—except for you, Mr. Grumpy Bear. The fort . . . even the road seems wider, better, more travelled."

"Ought to be. It's due west to Mexico, besides all the folks going to Freedom for Ezra's shows."

"Shows?"

"Didn't your mother tell you?"

"What?"

"About the pit."

Crissa's face broke into a puzzled frown. "She told me nothing. Since when is there something as brutal as a gaming pit at Freedom?"

"Since Ezra started holding sporting matches. They're right popular. I guess maybe your momma doesn't hold much with them. If she doesn't, she's about the only one. You'll see when we get there."

"Mr. Bennett, you are entirely too mysterious for what is, by this time, a very curious southern lady. What's in the pit? Animals?"

Steve frowned, remembered Crissa's anger in New Orleans, her remarks about slaves. He covered his misgivings with a grin. "Miss High and Mighty won't let her man have a little kiss, she can just wait and find out for herself."

"Well, all right, Mr. Bennett. You needn't be so huffy."

"C'mon," Steve answered, getting lazily to his feet. "You eat any more you're gonna get fat as well as sassy. Besides, we have to get going if we want to get in before dark." He started back to the fort, leaving Crissa to pick up the hamper. The chivalry of love denied. Crissa was back home, surely. She picked up the hamper and blanket and, with one last look over her shoulder, followed him, the question of the mysterious pit relegated to the future.

Cat, restless as usual and jealous about not being matched against the two Creek opponents of the week before, prowled the compound yard looking for trouble, bragging to anyone who would listen how he would have handled the redmen. How he would have left the pit un-

64

scathed. He could afford to play cock-of-the-walk. Rafe was still sore and slowed by his wounds. Rafe watched the young buck with some bemusement, shifted his wounded leg to take better advantage of the sunlight. The poultice had formed a crusty covering beneath which his remarkable healing powers had long begun to assert themselves. The warm rays of the sun filtered into his knotted muscles as back and forth he worked his leg, flexing it, gradually rebuilding its strength and stamina.

Cat had only eleven fights to his credit, but nevertheless had most of the other pitbucks cowed. Deceptively thin and fragile, the slight, trim youth possessed amazing speed and everyone in the compound knew it. Five of their previous number had known it, too. Little good it had done them. Now they knew nothing. Speed or no, he prudently avoided direct confrontation with Jomo or Rafe. Caution with these two was advisable, for though the pitbucks were forbidden under threat of twenty-five lashes to fight among themselves outside the pit, one or two, in the last year, had been discovered dead in the morning. No one knew who had killed them. No one dared assume it wasn't Rafe or Jomo.

"The mamba has no strength, yet he is a hunter of hunters. Such a foe is dangerous and deadly," Rafe's father had said. Cat was like the deadly black snake of the African sun-baked soil. Quick beyond belief, with a razor-sharp, slim, double-edged stiletto in each fist, Cat did not need great strength. "When the mamba strikes first, there is no strength in the world to save you." His father's words brought a twinge of fear to the big man but he forced it from his mind. Fear was not a good feeling to carry inside. It was an enemy and did not help a man stay alive, especially in the pit. A slow smile crept over his face, for Rafe had seen death claim every manner of victim in his brief lifetime. Even a black mamba.

"Yo' leg heals, N'gata?" Jomo sauntered up and squatted down beside Rafe.

"It will be strong enough, never fear, Jomo N'gata. I will be able to give you a good fight when we meet within the circle of clay."

Jomo grinned lopsidedly, a length of sugar cane protruding from his mouth. He spat a wad of chewed fibers into the dirt at Rafe's feet and answered in plantation English, "Ol' Mistah Clayton ain't goana put his two bes' pitbucks agin each oder, N'gata. No suh. He know de value. Yo' and Ah done brung him plenty gold. He ain't goana lose it none by killin' de one ob us."

"I have seven more fights, Jomo," Rafe continued in the more dignified old language. "Ezra Clayton's going to have to give me a gun, wagon and woman. The way I see it, come that last fight and he's going to be sitting in that white house, wondering how to get out of giving me all that. Giving me freedom, most of all. Now who," he paused, breaking brutally into compound talk, the sounds harsh and uninviting, a threat in themselves, "who best got de chance ob takin' me, Jomo? Who got de chance to take de number one man ob Mistah Clayton's pitbucks?"

Jomo's eyes narrowed. His face became incongruously cold and loaded with menace, an expression Rafe had seen on the smaller man only when he was in the pit and lusting for blood. "I reckin' de number two man gots de bes' chance o' takin' de number one man. I reckin' one ob us goana hab to kill de oder."

Rafe nodded impassively, looked straight before him as Jomo rose with simian grace, his face hard and unfriendly. He spoke in a chillingly threatening tone as if shrugging off like a cloak any previous friendship he had felt for Rafe. "Yo' get yo' laig healed, nigger. Ah doan wants to kill me no cripple less'n Ah has to."

"I will bleed on your grave as befits a brave warrior," Rafe returned formally in the age old challenge of warriors. But Jomo had already begun to walk away. Rafe sighed. It was hard to drive away N'gata Jomo, but they must not become too close, must never depend on each other. For he was certain Ezra Clayton would match them. First he would have to contest Cat. Surviving that, Jomo would be next. Rafe rolled so the sun could hit his shoulder. He would kill them both, yet found himself dreading the confrontation with Jomo, for the two men were brothers, like it or not. But Rafe wanted his freedom. He knew that. And he would allow no one to keep him from it. "What a man truly desires he will get," his father had told him. Rafe unconsciously moved his head up and down in silent agreement, then started the flexing regimen once again, gritting his teeth against the throbbing pain which would grow less and less each day until he was once again ready to kill.

Dusk. They were late. An afternoon shower had tired the mare and occasioned a stop to raise the calash. The next three miles seemed more like double their number, for the combined sand and reddish clay stuck to the wheels, weighing them down with sticky muck.

The end of the wet road was a relief for all, especially the panting mare. Steve stopped the gig on the first ten yards of dry earth—it was as if a line had been drawn—here it shall rain, here stay dry—and turned the mare loose to drink in the ditch and crop some needed grass while he scraped the mud from the wheels. Crissa got out and walked back and forth, stretching her cramped legs and back, shooing away battalions of mosquito lions whizzing dizzily about her. Black, blue, green, even red and yellow, they seemed to come in every color of the rainbow. There were mosquito lions in Boston but they were called dragon flies and were rare. She tried to convince herself they wouldn't really bite.

A half-hour passed; little was said. Steve, sweating profusely, lowered the calash again and hooked up the tired mare. They set off again, thankful for the slight breeze caused by their movement. By the time they came to Claytonville, afternoon had given way to an evening marked by piles of red-rimmed gray cumulus clouds rearing to the west. The next day would be nice.

Claytonville had grown. The sign said over a hundred souls and reminded Crissa yet again of the havoc Ezra Clayton had wrought with her father's name. Claytonville. An ugly name, tasting of rusty metal left too long in the rain. Again the question. Why, how, had her mother permitted this? "It's grown," was all she said.

"Two general stores, a smithy, an apothecary, a barber and surgeon, a tavern and a . . ." Steve paused, at a loss for the right word, ". . . gaming house. And the church."

Crissa shot a glance at him. A church? Then why wasn't Steve the preacher? But she had vowed to stay silent.

"It'll be dark when we get there," Steve offered. "I'm glad I sent a rider ahead."

"You should stay the night, then."

"They gave me two weeks to come get you. I have to get back. I'll sleep in Claytonville and be back by noon tomorrow. Besides, it's your homecoming. They'll want to see you. Not me."

"Steve. . . ."

"Don't worry. I'll see you next weekend." He clucked to the mare, urging her into a halfhearted trot.

The lights of Claytonville were soon behind and they were once again in open country, broken now by few trees and no lights, for there were no small farmhouses here. All was part of Freedom Plantation, part of the inheritance she had come back to claim. Steve brought the gig to a halt at the top of a rise. "There it is," he said matter-of-factly.

And so it was. Fitzman's Freedom. But she could tell little, only that lights blazed in windows to welcome her back. Home. *Home again, home again, jiggity jog . . .* "Oh, papa, I wish you were here," she whispered. "I wish, I wish . . . ." But John Fitzman wasn't there. He lay buried with his ship at sea, three points south of east, ten leagues from storm-tossed Cape Hatteras. She reached for the only hand nearby, clasping Steve's fist as it clutched the reins. "It's beautiful, Steve. Don't you think so?"

Steve grunted in reply. Crissa paid no heed, only leaned forward in anticipation as the mare headed for supper and a rubdown.

And suddenly a flare to the right. A knot of pitch ablaze and held high by a dark figure. The mare shied violently to the left, only to be startled back to the right by another flare, followed by an unearthly yell.

"Steve! My God! They've . . ." but she broke off as Steve raised his voice to join the din.

"Hallooo the house . . . !" he called, turning to her with a grin.

As on signal the roadway in front of them blazed as torches were fired to light their way. As they passed, the bearers ran onto the road behind them until, when Crissa looked back, they had formed a twinkling magic procession. Steve, laughing aloud, cracked the whip and the mare broke into one last, frightened stumbling trot, down the last bend and past the edge of the pecan grove—*Pa-Paw, I'm home. I'm home.*—and onto the path leading to the house. No sooner had the gig stopped than a Negro was at the mare's head. Steve leaped from his seat and ran around to Crissa's side and offered her his hand. For a moment she couldn't move, only sit and stare. The house was immaculate. Not a broken step, not an unpainted board. Steve took her hand to break the spell, and before she knew it she was leaping from the gig and running for the broad steps to the gallery. Halfway up the stairs the front door opened. A stranger stood there, arms outstretched to receive her. It was her mother.

The clock was chiming eleven when she finally ran out of stories. All about her the house was silent. Micara nodded sleepily in her chair across the room from her. Ezra sat perfectly still, legs crossed, eyes fastened on her. The chimes ran their course, stopped. "My goodness. I've been talking for two hours solid. I'm afraid I quite forgot myself, mama."

Micara's head jerked back in a losing battle against sleep.

"I'm afraid your mother's exhausted. She been waiting very hard for you. It's a special day for her—for all of us." His tone was light, pleasant, even refined. "If you'll pardon me, I'll see her to her room," he said, rising. "I'll be back down in a moment if you'd like to have a glass of wine with me before you sleep."

Crissa rose and went to Micara's chair. "Mama?" she called, "wake up." Micara opened bleary eyes. "Poor mama. I bored you to sleep."

Micara tried to smile. "No you didn't, dear. I enjoyed listening to you. It's just so late. . . ." she trailed off, looking about and trying to discover where she might be.

"She hasn't been feeling well lately," Ezra said, taking her arm gently. "Will you wait?"

Crissa nodded. "Yes, of course."

Ezra bowed and escorted Micara from the room, leaving Crissa alone. Suddenly tired herself, she moved about the large sitting room. There were so many new things to replace the old, familiar objects she had dreamed of for so long. Papa's chair, gone. His pipe rack, gone. The bust of George Washington, the bellows and poker he'd brought with him from Boston so many years ago, gone. "My God!" she gasped, staring at the wall over the fireplace. His portrait gone too?

"It's safely stored away, should you want it," a soft voice behind her said.

She wheeled to see Ezra standing in the doorway, a glass of sherry in either hand. Did he smile with concealed mockery? Crissa couldn't tell. "I would like," she said as pleasantly as possible, "to see it back where it belongs."

"Ah, but then, one must determine *where* it belongs, don't you think?" He walked to her, handed her a glass, raising his in toast. "To you, my dear Crissa. Welcome home."

Crissa sipped the wine, stared at the man before her. She turned away from him to conceal a slight shudder, looked absentmindedly at the empty space. "I liked my father's portrait where it was."

"My dear Crissa. You must admit a slight . . . awkwardness . . . must you not? After all, there is a new man of the house. I should hardly like to be compared, every day of my life, to the departed John Fitzman."

"I should think not," Crissa said, barely audible.

"I beg your pardon?"

"The house looks better than when I left. You and mother have done wonders with it."

"I . . . we try."

"I remember arriving in Boston. Almost four years ago to the day. I was to stay in a boarding house—a very

70

proper boarding house run by two of father's maiden cousins. It was early summer here and still quite cold there." She sipped the sherry. "I was a lonely girl with few friends, given to excessive daydreaming of home. I pictured it as beautiful. The fields, the pecan grove. The house. Then came my seventeenth birthday. I had been in Boston a little over a month. That night there was a new moon. I sat alone in my room and looked out over the city and cried. I thought of home and suddenly saw it as it really was. The house unpainted, the fields half grown to weeds. Mother was poor and, I thought, alone. As was I. I cried myself to sleep." She looked around the room at the gleaming furniture, dusted and spotless, the sparkling crystal on the sideboard. "It looks very nice now."

"Thank you. I hope you'll be happy here."

Crissa looked at him appraisingly. Such a strange man. Warm on the surface, but cold underneath, betrayed by frigid calculation his eyes couldn't conceal. What was it she saw there? Amusement? Mockery? Determination? Contrivance? Fear? Again the shudder passed through her, a whisper of muted predator's wings casting their shadow over her heart. She hid the premonition with a yawn. "I'm very tired. The last few weeks have been trying. Will you forgive me if I go to bed?"

"Of course."

"You've been very kind," she said, setting the drink down and going to him.

"It's a pleasure to be kind to one so young and beautiful," Ezra answered with a slight bow.

Crissa held her hand out and Ezra took it, started to raise it to his lips, then made a half-fumbling recovery when she shook it instead before turning to the door.

"Crissa."

"Yes?"

"I almost forgot." The twinkling smile again, hider of secrets. "I've arranged for a . . . special event to be held in your honor this coming Saturday and Sunday. A welcome home party."

"It's not necessary, you know. I . . ."

"Nonsense. We shall, as it were, kill the fatted calf. Even if you aren't the prodigal son." He paused specula-

71

tively, then flashed an ingratiating smile. "I hope you sleep well on your first night home, my dear."

Crissa gazed at him a moment, trying to ferret out the secret behind the masklike smile. "Thank you," she finally answered. "So do I." She left the room in a quiet swirl of skirts. A servant waited in the hall to light her way with a taper.

The same moon that lit the pitbuck compound so brilliantly left the lower gallery deep in shadow. Ezra sat in the cane wicker chair and stared straight ahead into the darkness. Somewhere in the distance a bull alligator roared mightily and a big cat screamed. Closer to the house, a myriad of wings and legs scraped jagged edges to produce a chitinous, shrill and never-ending song. Frogs with swollen throats piped and thrummed to their own time. The silence of the country was, in truth, silence in name only.

A soft thump sounded on the porch. Ezra stirred. The Negro boy had fallen asleep, his head thudding back against the post. The white man flicked his cane against the pale soles and the boy jumped alert. "Get out of here. Go on to bed."

"Yassuh," a disembodied voice mumbled from the darkness. A black form moved like a shadow through the door.

Ezra poured himself another drink. Four years. More like five of hard work. And he'd built it from nothing. Ten miserable slaves, a house falling apart, a weak woman with a weaker, useless brother-in-law. Well, he'd done it and Freedom was his. Almost two hundred slaves. The pitbucks. Good cotton and sugar cane. The best rum west of New Orleans. There were damned few plantations in this part of the country in as good shape.

He thought bitterly of the big, fancy plantations farther east on the Mississippi. He would have one someday. Before too many more years passed he would show his face again and damn any man who tried to say him nay. He wasn't the only one who'd carried messages for the British. Some wealthier than he, and they were free to live without encumbrance. He would be too, for money bought all things. Even honor.

Four years. And she had to come back. What had she said? Almost another month and she'd be twenty-one. He searched for the date, found it in the troubled, rum-soaked reaches of his mind. June 22, 1820. Her majority. And under the terms of her father's will, she would legally own half the plantation. Damn her for a minx! That handshake. The look she'd given him when she saw the picture had been removed. She wouldn't be another Micara, to be filled with sherry and forgotten.

But something . . . something. The paper, of course. Signed and sealed. If she'd accept it without a fight. No fights now. He'd have to try to neutralize her some other way. Save the paper for a last resort. Perhaps Steve would help. Steven Bennett. He was foolish enough to be in love with her. Perhaps she would marry him and he'd take her away. A shame, really. Such a nice body. Too bad he wouldn't be able to play with her, and enjoy that ripeness.

Whatever happened would have to be soon. She wasn't a woman to wait and he hadn't worked all these years to lose everything. Wealth and power had always come easily to Lucas Clayton but Ezra had to fight for everything he wanted. Wasn't fair. Damn Lucas, too. Now it was little brother's turn.

Ezra looked around him. Familiar surroundings. Freedom, by God. Freedom to do whatever the goddamned hell he wanted to do and with whomever he wanted. Freedom to show them all. The only time he'd ever known freedom, held it in his hands. He meant to keep it, whatever the cost. The little vixen. Lithesome young woman. Fancy riding her himself. Drive it deep and make her scream like Julie. Like Julie. . . .

He pushed himself from the chair and grabbing the bottle, lurched into the house, sudden desire driving him on in spite of the liquor. The hall was dark and quiet, the stairs a faintly gleaming pathway he followed. In his bedroom a single candle flickered and sent a hundred shadows twisting in a macabre black dance. The figure on his bed stirred, rose and came to him across the candle's yellow glow. Julie halted a moment and let her master appraise her as he always did.

Ezra's lust reached fever-pitch at the sight of her dusky, nubile form. The small, rounded breasts, upturned nipples dark and tightening beneath his stare, the slim curvature of her hips and thighs, the still darker musky shadow of her womanhood. She came to him. Unbuttoning his clothes, she covered each new section of revealed flesh with a flurry of kisses until every restraint burst and he dragged her to her feet and flung her across the edge of the bed. "I'll ride you, bitch," he growled, spreading her legs and planting his feet between them. "I'll ride you to the ground."

He grabbed her hips and raised her buttocks to him, entered violently and rammed himself against her over and over again until the black girl tore the sheet with her teeth to keep from screaming beneath his cruel debauchery. The bloodlust raging, he thrust deeper and deeper, more and more brutally, until at last his sudden shuddering climax stiffened him against her. Seconds later he withdrew and left her moaning, gingerly dragging her bruised flesh the rest of the way onto the bed.

The lord of Freedom walked to the center of the room, eyes glinting with malicious purpose even in repose. He extinguished the candle and crossed to the window. Across the line of trees in the near distance the terrible spikes of the pitbuck compound jabbed holes in the night sky. He could see in his mind's eye the pit beyond. There in the massive hole in the earth lay his true satisfaction: to feel his will manifest. And more. The raw primeval contest. Sweating flesh ripe for puncture, ready to be torn by the vicious teeth of death by machete, axe or knife. To command, to watch men bleed and die, there was release beyond all lust.

"Stop your sobbing, bitch," he said over his shoulder. "It pleasured you more than me. There'll be more this night. You'll earn your keep, earn the easy life I've given you. Keep food in that black belly and the whip off your back."

He left the window and returned to the bed, reached out and pulled her close to him. "Or maybe it's time I

74

found another pretty and gave you to Butkis. Let you bend your back with the other darkies."

Julie's eyes widened fearfully, the pain in her belly not nearly so terrible as the fear of being sent to live with the field hands. "Oh gawd, Massuh Clayton. Please. Yo' . . . yo' de on'y man ken make me happy. Ah's jes' cryin' cause Ah'm so glad to be yo' special woman."

Ezra grinned. He pressed her face against his swollen abdomen, forced her head down farther to the moist hair and damp, sagging organ. He held her there while she cooed and kissed him, licked and teased, her fingers tracing gentle patterns on his flesh. He remained so much limp meat.

The pit . . . think of the pit. The Creek staring at the shattered blade poking from his stomach like some horrid steel growth. Rafe sliced and bleeding from leg and back. *Up, damn you, up, up.* The fist . . . the splintering pop of bone and crushed neck. The spurting lifeless seed, pale white as death itself.

"Use your mouth, damn you, use it. . . ."

Straining to be hard again . . . the brave twisting the broken handle deeper and deeper, ripping, ripping flesh. . . .

The black girl moaned, used every bit of artistry she could summon to finish the job before he exploded in rage. Her hands roved wildly, teasing, probing, exciting until the soft meat swelled and hardened in her mouth. Her lips pursed, slid back and forth. Now larger, almost large enough, now touching the back of her throat. Sensing the moment, she tightened her mouth in time to receive the jetting fluid.

The devil within him appeased, Ezra collapsed on the bed, spent. Sunday there would be more to be remembered. Enough to glut the coming nights. The bottle slipped from his hand and bounced on the floor. Ezra Clayton slept.

6

Morning was cooler than noonday sun, but not by much. The guards' barracks, sweaty air tinged with smell of unwashed bodies and clothes, came to life slowly and with much grumbling and muttering after an alcohol- and sex-filled weekend. Twenty-five of Freedom's thirty-seven guards, and every one of them complaining, bitching about the heat and the day ahead. Ten would relieve the night guards, five of whom were covering the river, the others riding the land boundary of the plantation. Ten would watch the fields and ride herd over the almost two hundred cotton and cane workers. That left five, led by Butkis, to relieve the two night guards on the pitbuck compound. They were responsible for the training of Ezra Clayton's elite.

"You see her?"

"Hell yes, I seen her."

"Shit you did, Milo."

"I did. Me and Decater both seen her, didn't we, Decater?"

"Sho 'nuff did. Prettier'n a twenty-dollar whore. Standin' right out on the gallery staring into the night, over to that nigger Ephraim's grove."

"How come I never seen her then?"

" 'Cause it taken you too long ta' get a hard-on. She already gone back inside and blowed out the light 'fore you could get that teensy little tug-mutton a' yourn up an' off."

"You both full a' bastard shit."

Milo's large ungainly head rose sharply and he brandished his straight razor menacingly. The blade held steady less than six inches from Boo's neck. "You best start watchin' yore mouth, Boo, less'n I be havin' to cut you another'n."

"Both you can shut yer damn traps," Butkis snarled from the doorway. He removed his seaman's cap and wiped the sweat from his forehead onto the sleeve of his shirt. "They's work to be done an' I want all your red asses outside on the double." Milo cleaned his razor and slipped it into the case in his back pocket without paying attention to Boo, who turned and sulked back to get his shoes. Butkis walked out to the grounds, not bothering to wait and assure himself the two feuding guards had obeyed his command. He knew they would.

The remaining guards hurried back to their dressing, disappointed in not having seen a little blood flow. Baggy trousers and shirts on, each man crossed to the barrack's musket and sword racks to gather up and prime muskets and pistols, run whetstones along the edges of sabers, knives and machetes. Each guard was issued a brace of .62 caliber J. Henry pistols, a musket or rifle, and no less than one edged weapon. The personal arsenal of each man was more than sufficient to cow the unarmed field workers. As for the pitbucks, though they might hold their overseers in contempt, they dared not overlook the weaponry arrayed against them. Only a year ago Milo had stopped three of their number from escaping when they rushed the lone guard, expecting an easy kill. Instead, Milo fired his musket and gutshot the leader, then drew his pistols and fired at pointblank range at the other two. The two died immediately, the heavy lead balls nearly taking off their heads. The gutshot pitbuck was left to writhe in the dust as an example for any other who might want to try to escape. He lingered for eight painful hours before his screams faded and died out.

Butkis waited for the men to pile out into the bright morning sun, then assigned them in order as they left their sleeping quarters. The first into the yard got the easier, cooler assignments down by the river. Latecomers were sent to the fields. Milo, third out, surprised Butkis by requesting to be sent to watch the sugar cane gang.

"It's gonna be hotter'n hell out there today, Milo. I kinda figgered on keepin' you in the pitbuck compound with me, workin' them fightin' bucks. How come you wanna watch them cane niggers?"

"Cause Ruby's out there in them cane fields," Boo interjected, snickering, "an' Milo didn't get enuf a' her sugar yestiday."

A foursome of other guards joined in with Boo's laughter. Milo scowled at them, cursing them all for revealing his intentions. A glance from Butkis quieted the jeering guards. "You best come with me, Milo. I catch a man diddlin' with some darkie drippin' pan durin' work time and I'll cut me a slice a' his white ass with this toad sticker." He patted the hilt of his cutlass. "Even if it is meant for niggers. Boo, you and yore good friends there can take the cane fields."

"Aw, shit," moaned Boo. "It's gonna be hotter'n nine hells out there. Give 'em to Milo. He don't care nohow."

"You shoulda kept yore mouth shut, Boo," grumbled one of the other four.

"Git," Butkis ordered.

The five set off at a trot to round up the detachment of cane workers and take them to the fields.

"Let's roust out them pitbucks. Time to get their black asses movin'," Ezra's brutal leader ordered. Milo shrugged, disgusted with the way his plans had fallen apart. He'd just have to get that Boo someday, he figured, falling in line just behind Butkis and following him to the compound.

Crissa awoke to a sound she had not heard in years. The lonely, keening wail of a working spiritual drifted on the still morning air. Mournful, rhythmic, a ballad for the lost and hopeless, a chart for the weary and the tired, undercurrent to swinging scythe, chopping machete and yanking, straining muscles. A song of the oppressed, a tune with which another day's burden might be carried. Hauntingly beautiful and tragic, the melody was the child of incomprehension, birthed in the pain of scarred and battered souls.

The night had passed fitfully. Crissa dreamt of a mother she had known, loved, called her own. A mother who looked a stranger now. Someone she didn't know, yet strangely, still loved. Micara had aged so. True, the plantation flourished and prospered since her marriage to Ezra, yet Micara seemed more a trapped invalid who smiled on command rather than a woman revelling in her own success. She had wept and fussed over the return of her daughter appropriately enough, but her display of emotion seemed exhaustive, dry and shrivelled at the core. And Ezra. . . .

When Crissa left Fitzman's Freedom for Boston, Clayton was a slightly built, dashing man of grace and sophisticated charm. Now he appeared so . . . so degenerate. The hard, mocking eyes full of secrets. Tiny hands clenched in tight little fists. White, protected skin, almost as pale as the shock of ghostly hair. The bloated torso astride those spindly legs. His veneer of cordiality made him seem even more grotesque. She distrusted him.

And the household was totally changed. Old and trusted servants had been sent to the fields—or worse, Micara had hinted during a rare lull in the conversation—and replaced by Negroes of Ezra's choosing. Lithe, attractive, arrogant creatures subservient only to Ezra, they treated Micara with conceited, knowing deference. Crissa flushed angrily as she recalled their attitude, rose from the bed and crossed to her window where she held back the curtain to peer out at her first morning back at home. A score of ragged, tattered Negroes tramped by, two men with rifles urging them on. The blacks passed out of range, their song drifting back to her. The guards bothered her. They had never needed guards at Freedom before. Why now? And armed to the teeth, at that. The only time one needed guards was when slaves were unhappy and rebellious. She couldn't imagine such conditions on what had at one time been a happy plantation.

And what about the grim walls of the prisonlike stockade across the rear garden? What did they contain? And why? Criminal slaves? Could the situation have deteriorated so far?

Her mind was a welter of conflicting thoughts. She was angry at the attitude of the household servants yet felt pity for those unfortunates being herded to Lord knew what tasks. The conflicting emotions of her upbringing and her education raged within her and would not be still. "This will not be an easy homecoming," she sighed aloud.

A tiny wisp of smoke curled up from the pecan grove across the road. Pa-Paw up and about, making his tea. She smiled warmly, fondly. The mystery could wait. There were enough mysteries to last a few days. More important was Pa-Paw. She stepped back into the room and stripped her gown from her body, tossing it lazily onto the bed. How soon, she thought, we slip back into the old ways. In Boston she was expected to care for her own bedclothes, expected to keep her garments and room clean and neat. She frowned at herself, turned and picked up the gown and hung it in the armoire, then quickly made up the bed. No reasonably healthy person needed a slave to make a bed.

The water in the basin was cold, directly from the spring. She sponged herself all over, washing the journey's grit from her body, feeling her skin tingle with each cleansing caress. "Cold water, clean and pure, is the best thing for a man—or a woman," her father had told her. "That spring will run forever."

The armoire was full of her old clothes, carefully kept against the damp. She reached into the stale camphor and cedar-perfumed air to pick an old and favorite sundress and stepped into it, wriggling it up around her hips and over her breasts, then giggling when it wouldn't fasten. She had grown. Crissa moved to the mirror and looked at herself with pleasure. Four years. And now no room for her in the old dress. A wide V ran down her front, barely concealing her nipples, and try as she might, there was no buttoning the garment past the bottom three. She sighed. It didn't matter. Her trunk would arrive soon. She wriggled out of the dress and hung it back in the armoire, shook out the dust and grit from the one she'd worn the day before and put it on. A brush through her hair a few times and a dab of concealing perfume and she was ready.

The house was still quiet. The aroma of frying ham and newly baked bread wafted up the stairs to her and reminded her stomach of the meager fare of the day before. She tiptoed along the upstairs hall, determined to avoid any and all contact with the Freedom household servants. Now wasn't the time, hungry though she was.

The front doors were already open and she flitted through them and into the morning sunlight. Standing there on the gallery, the front grounds and distant acreage displayed in the light of dawn, a momentary panic seized her. For four years she had lived in the browns and grays of a large northern city and now she was assailed by a solid wall of undifferentiated green. She forced herself to take a deep breath, forced herself to separate magnolia green from pecan green from grass green from pine green. So many subtleties and innuendoes of green. Could she decipher the similar undercurrents of mystery and tension in the house behind her? "This is my home," she said aloud to herself. "It was once, and I will make it so again."

Hair glistening golden-red in the morning sun, she ran lightly down the steps and across the drive. The magnolias swirled into focus as she neared them. The dark trunks were heavily scored. Massive limbs meant for climbing and building tree houses—she looked for a sign of the house she and Steve had built so many years ago, but it was gone—angled out to end in heavy, dark green waxen leaves. No one knew who had planted the trees. They were there when John Fitzman built the house. She paused a moment, remembering sitting high in their branches and listening to her mother anxiously calling, "Crissa! Crissa Elizabeth Fitzman, you come here this instant!"

Suddenly filled with a sense of urgency, she ran down

the long lawn toward the road and the pecan grove beyond, stopping short as two ragged men on horseback rode around the bend and stopped. Both were heavily armed, both somewhat taken aback. One of the men doffed his cap, followed by the other. Scruffily bearded countenances split in broad grins; their eyes were dull and red. More like animals, she thought. They frightened her. She nodded briefly and lost no time in crossing in front of the horses and into the pecan grove, for once inside the trees she would be free of their disquieting gaze.

Stepping into the grove was like entering another world, a world of shadows haphazardly split by piercing beams of slanted light. Later in the day the straight rows would become a uniformly dappled magic wonderland where fairies played while leprechauns slept, but mornings and evenings transformed the grove into something even more unearthly. The chilliness of the dew mingled with a splendid, hushed, all-pervading quiet. This was why she had so loved the grove, had been so drawn to it. She wandered amid the pathless, woody sanctuary and her mind cleared and sorted itself. Decisions needed to be made. If her mother had become weak, well, she certainly had not. Ezra must be confronted with the fact that Crissa intended to assert herself. She thought back on her father's will. Fitzman's Freedom had been left jointly to her and her mother. Patrick Fitzman held Crissa's half in trust for her, with provision for her assuming control upon reaching her majority. A reasonable enough will, to be sure, but where was Uncle Patrick? She realized how isolated she had been for the last four years, how little she really knew. But perhaps that was of little import. On the 22nd she would be twenty-one. On that day the mystery would come to an end, for she could legally demand answers.

Crissa turned, catching a glint of movement behind her among the trees. A grouse or pheasant, perhaps. The movement repeated itself, took shape. A diminutive, stoop-shouldered Negro stepped into a patch of sunlight spreading its gleaming light along the grassy earth. The Negro shambled toward her, his eyes squinting to catch a better look, shading them against the bright slant of morning sun. The right sleeve of his ragged linen shirt was tucked into the rope belted about his waist, the fabric pressed flat against his body.

"Who dere? Who comin' to see ol' Eph'em dis early in de mo'nin'?"

Crissa felt tears brim and spill down her cheeks. A little more aged perhaps, but he hadn't changed all that much. She gathered her skirts and ran across the glade, startling the old Negro as she embraced him. "Pa-paw . . . Pa-Paw Ephraim, it's me . . . ," she cried, hugging him, laughing and crying at the same time.

"Who me?" the old man asked, confused by what seemed a wood spirit who had burst into the grove to take him away.

"Crissa. It's Crissa Elizabeth, Pa-Paw. Oh, I couldn't have changed all that much."

"Crissa? Ma' little Crissa? Oh, ma' lawd. Ah done up an' died an' gon' ta' hebbin. Dey to'd me you was comin' an' Ah hear al de ruckus las' night, but Ah toles ma'se'f doan yo' beliebs it lessen yo' see dat chile." He peered inquisitively at her. "Now Ah knows. It's ma' little girl right 'nuff. Lawd, lawd, lawdie . . ." the old man exclaimed, his face beaming.

He stepped back to see her better. "Ma' lawd, Cap'n John's little girl turned into a lady, sho 'nuff. An' she come back to her ol' Pa-Paw, yassuh, come back. Gab'ril soun' dat trumpit, let de ju'gemen' day come. Dis ol' nigger's ready. Ma' little girl done come home."

He led her from the clearing deeper into the grove to the simple shack he had constructed out of dry limbs, broken branches and the few boards he could round up. Crissa felt like a child again. She and Ephraim reminisced, invoking the pleasant memories of the past. The aged Negro freeman continued to live unmolested among his beloved woody children. Ezra had at one time suggested the old man be put to the fields but Micara had stood up for him. Another time he'd tried to make Ephraim skedaddle across the river, but once again Micara had insisted he be allowed to stay. The last incident was several years earlier, and to Ephraim's way of thinking, "Mastuh Clayton done prob'ly fo'got about ol' Eph'em, least ways Ah sho' hopes so."

Ephraim brewed some cherry bark tea in a battered pot, pouring the steaming liquid into two even more decrepit, unmatched cups. Talk eventually centered around new Freedom as it was under Ezra's control. "Honey chile, t'ings ain't de same. Dat Ezra Clayton a mean, mean man. An' de way ob de mastuh is de way dose under gwine be. White mens wid guns an' a' prowlin' all ober, nebber gibin' a nigger no rest. An' mo' workers fo' de extra fields. Dey's sompin' queer in de woodpile. A meanness to de place dat neva' was befo'. Dem darkies workin' in de fields, lawd but dey suffa's. An' whippin'? Land o' goshen yo' nevah done seed de lak. An' worstes' a' all is de pit. T'ain't right. T'ain't right no ways . . ."

A cold, tight wave of fear washed over Crissa. Twice in so many days now she had heard someone speak of the pit. Animal baiting was common but she didn't hold with it at all, thought the sport nauseating, cruel and demeaning. She pressed Ephraim for more information but he doggedly refused to speak further.

"T'ain't fittin' fo' a chile lak yo' is. Jes' keep to yo'se'f lak me. Some things in de worl' ain't fittin' fo' a chile to heah o' see."

And that was that. Ephraim changed the subject, morosely recounting how the grove no longer rang to the laughter of a dozen children playing. There was little time for playing at Freedom these days and the grove was shunned by the little ones, no doubt afraid to laugh even when given the chance.

It was late morning when Crissa took her leave, promising to return whenever she could and assuring the old man she would see to it no one came to harm him or take him away from his beloved grove.

Crissa left the stand of pecans south of the main house. The morning air was still and close, humming with insects. A line of low cedars ran from east to west along the edge of the sculpted and aesthetically pleasing side lawn and led to the partially concealed pointed tops of the walled compound she had seen earlier. Determined to explore farther she traversed the side lawn and approached the compound from the east, skirted another line of protective cedars and found herself at the south wall. She stopped and stared in fascination at the iron-tipped trees, noted the bare trunks, even more formidable from close at hand. This was a nearly impregnable fort and she wondered what it could hold. Moving closer she cautiously peered between the six-inch spacing between the smooth wood surfaces. Her countenance was one of utter perplexity.

Near her two black youths wrestled each other within the diameter of a chalked circle. When one was pushed or shoved over the line a nearby guard flicked the tip of his whip to drive the wrestler back into the circle. She shifted her position and was able to see more of the compound. Several Negroes were lined up before a steaming iron pot, cups and plates in hand. Another black was ladling heaping portions of red beans and rice. Across the yard a cluster of black men squatted or lay prone upon the earth. A heavily bearded, barrel-gutted guard spoke in a gravelly voice similar to the snarling rasp of a cougar. The blacks rose to their feet and scrambled for plates and cups stacked before them. Those who had been wrestling quit and left the circle to join those already in line.

The bearded guard shouted, "Dingo, you bring me that pitchfork over yonder." One of the Negroes who had been wrestling changed direction and headed for a shack, returning with the indicated tool. Crissa tensed, felt a similar uneasiness from the slaves in the compound.

"Here, Mistuh Butkis," the slave called Dingo said, handing the farm implement to the guard.

Butkis turned the prongs to point toward Dingo. "Now you new bucks watch real close. Dingo, which end you gonna have ta' look out fer when a nigger come at you with one a' these?"

"Sheeit, Mistuh Butkis. Gotta watch de pokin' end."

The cluster of young Negroes joined in with Dingo's laughter. Butkis glanced over at them as if to join their laughter, then shifted his weight and spun the implement, sending the wooden shaft slicing through the air to rap with a loud pop against Dingo's head. The Negro dropped like an empty sack. It was Butkis's turn to laugh, his head tilted back, mouth wide open.

"Hey!"

Crissa spun around, her hand raised on reflex to her mouth, stifling a scream.

Milo stared at her wide-eyed, more than a little surprised himself. "Oh," he stammered. "S'cuse me, miss. Uh . . . uh . . . womenfolk ain't . . . uh . . . allowed over ta' here. . . ."

Crissa rapidly recovered her composure and assumed her most haughty air, staring at the lone guard until he lowered his gaze. "I am Crissa Fitzman. This is the Fitzman plantation and I'll thank you to refrain from telling me what I may and may not do."

Milo, thoroughly cowed, nodded his head and muttered, "Yes'm."

Crissa, head erect, primly stalked away, leaving him behind, too stunned to follow her immediately. She rounded the corner and saw the gate in the middle of the west wall, headed for it. Alongside the open gate limbs of a tree had been nailed to the spike-tipped trunks to form a crude ladder to a four foot long platform. There was room enough for a single guard on the platform. He stared inquisitively as the strange woman suddenly came around the corner and headed for him, followed by Milo. His eyes widened as she passed below him. Enjoying the expanse of breast visible from his perch, he shifted the ancient blunderbuss scattergun and leaned over the edge to get a better view. "My Gawd!" he marvelled. "Wait 'til ol' Boo hears about this. He'll shit for sure. Ah got Decater and Milo beat all hollow."

Butkis stopped in the middle of a sentence, realizing the attention of the Negroes was obviously not with him, had strayed to someone or thing behind him. He turned in the direction they were staring. A woman stood centered in the open gateway, her fair blond fragility an incongruous contrast to the rough surroundings. The compound fell silent. Totally still. Dark faces, shiny, glistening and staring. "Shut that goddamn gate," Butkis roared. A nearby guard quickly swung the gate closed. Though not as tall as the stockade walls it was sufficiently high enough to block the view of Crissa's appealing figure as well as obstruct her view of the interior of the compound.

"Mistuh Clayton don't want no one comin' round, missy."

Crissa stared up at the leering guard above her. He too was armed to the teeth.

"No one comin' 'round the pitbuck compound, missy," he repeated.

Suddenly she was running from the compound wall, running with incomprehensible fear at her back, a fear that pushed her forward and away from the mystery of the iron-tipped prison walls, away from the terrible suspicion she had to refuse to face.

Night. The raccoon waited patiently, barely visible in the rapidly fading light. Gray and black pelt blended into the surrounding foliage, became another indistinguishable patchwork of dark and light shadows. Feral eyes probed the depths at the bayou's edge and caught a flutter of movement in the murky water. The glimmer repeated itself, closer this time. The motionless night hunter waited as the remaining light all but disappeared to a chorus of bullfrogs and rasping insects lamenting its passing.

Again a stirring in the water. Closer still. The raccoon imperceptibly adjusted its stance, its wide and unwavering eyes staring past its own starlit reflection to the telltale movement below. Then a flash of paw and claw ripping the glistening, watery surface and flipping onto the bank a dripping mass of roots and a struggling crayfish, pincers held aloft, threatening and snapping at empty air. The carapacial body struggled free of the entangling water plant and scurried for the water's edge. But not quickly enough. The tiny paws seized their prey, cracked the shell in half and dabbled it in the water before tearing the sweet meat from the still writhing tail. Another splash broke the glassy evening stillness of the bayou. The raccoon looked up, eyes glittering greedily, and tossed the morsel in hand behind him. He would eat later. The night hunter once again resumed his vigil.

A movement of shadow in shadow caught the predator's eye and he tensed to leap backward. But not quickly enough. Open jaws, great and terrible with rows of gleaming teeth snapped shut as two bulbous eyes broke through the surface, blinked twice, then sluggishly sank beneath the lily pads, dragging the raccoon down to a watery death. The broken crayfish on the bank twitched and thrashed about, settling deeper into the oozing mud and bleeding itself dry. The first ant found it a few moments later. . . .

The nameless black woman who served as cook for Ezra's household entered the dining room and set a large silver platter of sliced pork near the lord of Freedom. Ezra ignored the servant and ladled cuts of meat on to one plate, then another. A second servant, a young boy of twelve, carried the plates around the table and set one before Micara, another before Crissa. The woman returned carrying dishes of sweet potatoes and fresh greens. All plates served, the woman left and the boy stationed himself behind Ezra, waiting for whatever his master might command.

Micara dawdled at her meal, sipping with feigned restraint at her goblet of sherry. Crissa, though famished, was so preoccupied with unanswered questions she was unable to make any but the feeblest attempt at enjoying the food at hand. Ezra fell to with relish. He ate noisily, each swallow accompanied by a slight muttering from deep within his throat as if he was commenting on the merits of each bite taken. When Crissa could stand no more she shoved her plate away and rose abruptly from the table, her chair sliding back and scraping along the hardwood floor. Ezra stopped chewing and looked up at her questioningly. Micara sipped unconcernedly, lost in the tinted reflection of her face on the surface of the sherry. She finished her second glass and poured a third.

"You've lost your taste for pork and sweet potatoes?" Ezra inquired.

Crissa stood unmoving for a moment, her temper barely under control. "I've lost my taste for many things, Ezra. And I suppose some. . . ."

"I do wish you'd call me 'father'. Ezra sounds so cold."

Crissa glared at him, continued after a slight pause.

". . . something needs be said. Now is as good a time as any."

Micara looked up at her daughter and grinned weakly. "Sit down and eat your supper, dear."

"Don't interrupt, Micara," Ezra instructed lazily. "Your daughter is at odds with herself. The climate, no doubt. She doesn't appreciate pork and sweet potatoes any more."

"Don't make fun of her and don't make fun of me," Crissa said through clenched teeth.

Ezra's hand stopped halfway to his mouth. He placed the fork back down on the plate. No person, man or woman, had spoken to him in that tone of voice for a long, long time. He had become conditioned to immediate and unquestioning obedience and subservience. Now this little trollop dared to order him about. And with a touch of menace in her voice to boot. It surprised him. Caught him off guard. Perhaps amused him a little, but he wasn't sure. Of one thing he was certain. He hadn't underestimated the girl. His assessment of the night before was accurate. She was stronger than she looked. There was only one way to handle such strength: crush it quickly and without hesitation. He would have to break her much as one broke a spirited colt, and the sooner the better. "I am the master of this house, Crissa. Micara is my wife. I will speak to her or any other person as I please. You would do best to mind your manners for such time as you intend to stay under my roof."

Crissa's hands clenched in tight, angry fists. She leaned on the table and glared at him, hate building in her eyes. The clink of glass pulled her attention to her mother. Micara tipped the sherry bottle, sloshing some into her glass, spilling some more on the table. She smiled nervously at Crissa. "Your dinner is getting cold, dear."

Crissa wanted to weep, but the dark anger seething inside her stopped the tears. "Mother, you've had quite enough sherry. In fact, sherry is all you've had the entire evening. Don't you think it's best you went on up and got to bed?" she asked gently.

Her mother shook her head in disagreement. "Nonsense, dear. Why, I'm not in the least bit sleepy, and you were gone when I woke up this morning. We haven't had a chance to talk." She smiled coyly. "Sherry is good for me. It relaxes me. So many pressures, so much to do. Why, I. . . ."

"I trust you remember our talk the other day, Micara. I would hate to have to refresh your memory in front of dear Crissa Elizabeth. Go to your room."

Micara swivelled about in her chair, biting her lip and petulantly shaking her head. She stared at him for a brief moment, eyes pleading silently then suddenly filling with tears as her head dropped forward in acquiescence. Avoiding Ezra's threatening gaze she turned to her daughter. "I'm going to my room now," she said, her voice quivering. "Ezra does so care about me. I hate to worry him. He does so . . . worry. But I'm going to my room. No," she held up her hand, steadying herself against the table with her thighs as she stood, "I don't need any help. You will come kiss me good-night, won't you Crissa dear? Even if I'm asleep? Come and kiss me like you used to . . . like I used to. . . ." She paused, shaking her head in the silence, her mouth rigid with the unpronounceable pain of shattered pride. Suddenly she forced a smile, tossed her head brightly. "There . . . so. I'm fine." She laughed girlishly. "I'm going. I'll take the sherry with me. Perhaps I'll have just another little glass. It helps me sleep."

She stepped sideways from the table and walked stiffly to the door, stopped and braced herself on the frame. With her back to them her voice was strangely detached, the voice of a lost child. "Promise you'll come kiss me, Crissa. John does, don't you, John? Sometimes I'm asleep, but I know he does. Every night he kisses me to sleep and tells me he loves me very, very much." She walked shakily from the room, disappearing down the hall, her muted footsteps fading as she went up the stairs.

Crissa held back the tears she felt welling suddenly in the corners of her eyes. The mention of her father's name, even if only in Micara's muddled confusion, contrasted him sharply with the man at the end of the table and deeply affected her. Suddenly weak, she sat in her chair again and forced her mind clear. The time for crying would be later when she was alone in her room. She forced herself to focus on Ezra who had resumed eating, paying not the slightest attention to his wife's misery or his stepdaughter.

"Now," she said, her voice quiet and subdued, as cold as Ezra's. "Let's start over. What do you mean, 'your roof'?"

"Why, just what I said." Ezra looked up, pushed his plate away and snapped his fingers. The Negro boy brought a cigar and one of the table candles to Ezra and held the candle while his master lit the cigar.

Ezra waited until the candelabra was replaced and the boy left the room with his plate. "This plantation is no longer Fitzman's Freedom, Crissa. It is just Freedom. My freedom. Just as the town at the foot of the hill is my town now. I call it Claytonville. So does everyone else. Your father is dead. Long live your stepfather." He raised the snifter of brandy in salute to himself, emptied it and placed it back on the table.

"Mr. Clayton," Crissa began coldly. "There may be some misunderstanding on your part. I am neither a gull nor a fool. I am not an ignorant townsman nor an indigent farmer to be manipulated at your pleasure. I have spent the past four years at a most reputable school. My father's will specifically stated my Uncle Patrick was to hold my half of his plantation in my stead until my twenty-first birthday. I will be twenty-one shortly and expect to resume control of at least half of this property."

Ezra blew a languid blue-white cloud of smoke into the air. It drifted lazily across the table. He sat back, a self-satisfied smile crossing his face. She was most amusing. More so than he had imagined. Certainly a full cut above unschooled farmers and his imbecilic wife, and perhaps even an opponent of sorts. Crissa was not only beautiful, but intelligent as well.

Ezra rose, bowed curtly and excused himself. Crissa heard his footsteps in the hall. She left the table and followed him, seeing him disappear into the library. She entered behind him. He glanced up from his desk, his smile a frozen mixture of cordiality and menace. Crissa stood mutely before him, waiting. Ezra shook his head, chuckled, then withdrew a document from the desk drawer and held it out to her. She accepted the rolled parchment, untied the ribbon. Inside she recognized her uncle's handwriting. Ezra watched her read, gloating over each frown, each furrow and crease of consternation leading to the final sanguine flush creeping up her face.

She threw the parchment on the desk. "You . . . he can't," she began, eyes flashing. "He had no right, especially without telling me."

"My dear Crissa. He had every right. You were a child and your uncle was responsible for your holdings. Since you weren't here to make your wishes known, he proceeded as he thought best and transferred your portion of the estate to me."

"He had no right to make such a transfer. The land was not his to transfer. I shall fight this. . . ."

"You are a young and headstrong woman with very little say in the matter. You have no rights, and if you think any court of law will disagree, you are free to try. But I warn you. Accept gracefully and you are free to stay here and live. I shall be most generous and you will live well. I shall even see that you marry well. Make the slightest attempt to contest this piece of paper and I will have you thrown out without a penny to your name."

Crissa stared at him in shock. "You are an evil man. I think I have never known a man as despicable as you."

Ezra laughed heartily. "My dear Crissa. Please. No emotional accusations. I am not an evil man. I am a realistic man. A realistic man in a world not of his own making."

"What you have done to my mother is despicable."

"What I have done to your mother is precisely nothing. She chose her own path, freely and of her own volition."

"You lie!"

"Sit down!" The words lashed her like a whip and she obeyed. Ezra's mien, warm and friendly, turned frigid. He breathed slowly until the harsh edge of anger blurred and eased. "Micara," he started, rising and pacing about the room, "placed all claim to this plantation in my name. After all, I was her new husband. And her protector. Her decision was a wise one, for the law out here is tenuous at best. A man had a chance to build Freedom beyond what it had become. In time I did build it to what you see about you now. I *am* the lord of Freedom. I shall continue as the lord of Freedom until such time as I choose to leave."

He picked up the parchment, rolled it neatly. "As for Patrick not keeping you informed, I did not question his motives. I suspect he may have been a bit of a well-meaning scoundrel. He left here the day after he signed . . . this." He walked around the desk and stood behind her. "He left talking of empires—Patrick always talked of empires while others such as I build them—and joined a pack train to Mexico on some crazed expedition. I suspect he has received his just deserts. The trail to deep Mexico is a demanding, dangerous one, full of peril. If the Indians didn't murder him, I imagine the Mexicans hanged him. A well-deserved hanging, I might add, for dreamers are good for little else." He paused, leaning on the back of Crissa's chair, his head over her shoulder. When he continued, the mockery and laughter were barely hidden.

"Still, we shouldn't be too hard on his memory, should we, dear Crissa Elizabeth? He was acting on his niece's behalf. What would a young girl know about running a plantation? Perhaps he decided wisely. You can see for yourself the improvements I've made."

"Whippings and beatings are not improvements," Crissa said in a bare whisper. "My father never stood for them. And those. . . ."

"I am not your father," Ezra interrupted harshly, leaving the chair and crossing back to his seat behind the desk.

". . . those awful men in that prison," Crissa continued doggedly. "So bestial. Slaves and their keepers . . . like animals."

"They are animals. That is why I keep them there. All of my slaves are animals. It takes animals to guard them, to see they do as they're told."

Crissa leaned forward in her seat. "And what," she inquired politely, "of the master? Is he required to be an animal too, or is he one of his own choice?"

Ezra smiled. The girl had spunk. Still he could not let up, could not let her go without making sure the lesson was driven home. "I have given Freedom prosperity," he said, rising and holding out the parchment to her. "Nothing happens without my permission, for I am master. This document—I have another copy, by the way, so you may take it to study at your leisure—says so. As long as I am master, I shall see to it that Freedom continues to grow. And as long as you are my guest. . . ."

"Your guest?" Crissa snapped, rising to face him. "A guest in my own home? We'll just see about that." She snatched the paper from his hand and stalked from the library, quickly ascending the stairs. Julie greeted her in the upper hallway but Crissa pushed her aside and entered her bedroom, slammed the door behind her and leaned against the cool paneling while she caught her breath.

Ezra had showed his true colors early. His position was undoubtedly strong, but she would not be bested, made a common visitor in her own home. Certainly what Uncle Patrick had done was unlawful, but for all her bravado she felt lost and alone, not sure what her next step should be. One thing only was certain. She was determined not to leave, not to give up without a fight. There would come a reckoning.

She stripped the dress from her and let it drop to the floor. Her first day home. What a lovely homecoming! She fell naked on the bed, exhaustion clouding her mind. Tomorrow would be her second day. Time enough then to search for the path. As her eyes closed, she remembered she had forgotten to kiss her mother good-night.

7

An hour deep into the morning sun and the compound was already furiously hot. Rafe had lapped the enclosure ten times and was beginning his eleventh. The humid air, thick and saturated, flowed easily in and out of his lungs. His legs pumped at an unvarying pace as he tirelessly rounded the compound, his muscles moving with the natural grace and coordination of a great hunting cat, his feet thudding a steady tempo on the hard-packed clay. Completing his eleventh lap he trotted toward the shaded spring-fed tank at the north end of the stockade and squatted. The water smelled good. Clean and fresh. He cupped the surprisingly cool liquid and drank sparingly, splashing the water onto his face and over his naked torso.

Rafe stood as Jomo kneeled and thrust his head into the tank, straightened and gulped for air, then repeated the dunking. Water arced out as he shook his head, landed in dust-covered beads on the hard floor of the compound. Rafe watched the pitbucks behind him. Some wrestled, others duelled with sticks and poles in place of more deadly weapons. Dingo and Trinidad strutted among the blacks, arrogant and proud. Clayton had sent them to Nachitoches only the day before. Both had fought and each had won handily. Rafe wondered if Ezra would match Trinidad against him. Poor Bess. Her man Trinidad would not last more than a few minutes in the pit with Rafe.

Jomo rose beside him, his head level with Rafe's chest. "How many?" he asked.

"Eleven."

"Whooo-eee!"

"I'll do twelve this afternoon."

"Yo' 'bout healed up den. Ah ben watchin'. Yo' runs real good."

"I got to. Man who can't run good don't got wind for fightin'."

"Weapon what count," Jomo disagreed. "Dat an' de man."

"Maybe. You say so."

"Axe an' knife. No knife neber done beat no axe," Jomo growled.

"It's called a machete."

"Don' care what'cha' calls it. Yo' always tryin' ta talk fancy. Hell, purty words ain't goana sabe yo' hide. Blade don' neber beat no axe. Axe don' bus' on any blade 'ceptin' 'nother axe. Yo' ain' neber goan see dat lan' cross de riber, Rafe."

Rafe strode away silently. He regretted the change that had come over Jomo. Perhaps he never should have said anything about what he suspected to be Ezra's intentions. Their inevitable contest would not be for a while yet. There would have been time for camaraderie. But too late. Now there was only time for both of them to think about and plan the coming fight. Time to watch each other, ferret out weaknesses, assess strengths and seek advantages. The prize was Mexico, where a man could find his own freedom. Rafe knew nothing could make him hesitate nor hold back the killing slash or thrust. He would not jeopardize his only chance for freedom.

Near the center of the compound two A-frames jutted from the ground. They stood twenty feet apart and were joined at the top by a pole some fifteen feet off the ground. Fifteen twenty-four pound cannonballs were suspended at various heights from the cross bar. Each of the balls was set in motion swinging back and forth at varying rhythms. A man running the balls had to go from one A-frame to the other through the maze of iron pendulums. The task required agility, concentration and coordination. Those who learned to run the maze without being touched by any of the balls, those who survived without broken bones, were an important step closer to being champion fighters indeed.

Milo had several of the newer pitbucks lined up between the legs of the north frame. Two of the guards had set the cannonballs swinging. Milo clapped the young Negro first in line on the shoulder. The youth confidently leaped forward past the first weight and directly into the path of the second. He twisted in time, barely missing it, only to catch the third on his hip. He was knocked sprawling into the dust, his scream of pain muffled by the dirt. Milo shook his head in disgust and signalled the second pitbuck to start. Brutus was an older man recently transferred from the fields. An incessant brawler, he was sent to the pitbuck compound when Ezra decided his quick temper and hardened physique would best serve Freedom's interests fighting in the pit. He covered half the distance, snaking his way through eight of the whistling balls before the ninth clipped him on the shoulder, spun him around and into the path of another weight which slammed into his stomach. He landed ten feet away, doubled up on the hot earth, retching and gasping for breath.

The remaining three pitbucks in line looked at each other nervously, each indicating the others should go first. The sour smell of their fear was evident. Rafe crossed in front of the youth next in line, a congenial-looking boy named Tater. Milo looked questioningly at the black man towering over him and his hand sought the reassuring comfort of the pistol in his belt. Rafe grinned at Milo. "Gonna he'p these young bucks keep their heads where they belongs. Up on top o' their shoulders," he said.

Milo shrugged. The cannonballs were set in motion again. The black giant flexed his shoulders and breathed deeply, sending a cascade of muscles rippling across and down his back. He stepped out smoothly, cleared three of the pendulums, dropped back, ducked, stepped forward, twisted his body, bobbing and weaving, ever calm, ever alert. He bounded the remaining two yards and landed lightly on his feet near the opposite poles, untouched and breathing no more heavily than if he had been out for a short walk in the cool of evening. Tater and the others were awestruck. Even Milo, who had seen Rafe run the balls before, stood quietly and respectfully for a moment before he drew himself up to his full height and bellowed at Tater. "What the hell you gawkin' at? You seen how it's done. Now git yore black ass movin' an' do it yourself. The rest of you niggers is gonna keep at it 'til you do it right. Mistah Clayton done taken you outa' the fields, give you women every week and two meals a day. You better off than any of them pickaninnies that gotta work the crops an' you ain't about to waste his kindness by gittin' yo'self kilt the fuhst time out. Not whiles I got anything to say about it. No siree."

"Any trouble, Milo?" Butkis, his face red and sweating from the fierce southern sun, approached from the gate.

"No trouble, Mistah Butkis. Just puttin' the fear into these niggers. They becomin' almighty slow."

Butkis drew a strip of jerky from his pocket and wadded it into his mouth. He shook his head from side to side, showing his utter disenchantment and displeasure at the newly conscripted fighters. Rafe walked up to stand beside Tater and the others. "You doan train a man by bustin' his laig. You doan keep him alive by smashin' in his head. They ain't ready to run the balls yet, Mistah Butkis. Only been here a week."

Butkis' eyes narrowed, glittered like a rodent's caught in the glare of a lamp at night. "Jomo!" the overseer barked, stopping all action in the compound. Everyone looked at Butkis, wondering what was going to happen. "Nigger, git yer black ass over here."

Jomo trotted across the compound. "Yassuh, Mistah Butkis."

"Special doin's, Jomo. You gonna fight Sunday. You an . . . Tater here . . . an' one other. . . ." He cast about, pretending he hadn't already decided, letting his gaze hold

100

on each in turn and holding all in suspense. "Yeah. Brutus. The nigger who likes to be fightin' all the time. He'll be a good'n."

The evil-tempered slave who had the wind knocked out of him looked up, got painfully to his feet and moved closer so he could hear.

"Ah fights alone," Jomo muttered.

Butkis's hand lashed out before anyone saw it and slapped Jomo across the face, the slap ringing out in the sudden silence that gripped the compound. Bodies tensed unconsciously. Still the silence held, broken now by the dual clicks of two muskets being cocked. "You do like I tell you, nigger," Butkis said calmly.

Jomo lowered his head so the overseer would not read the murderous intent in his eyes. "Yassuh," he mumbled.

"What you say?" Butkis inquired innocently.

Jomo took a deep breath. "Yassuh, Mistah Butkis, suh. Ah hears yo'."

Butkis smiled expansively. The tension eased. "That's better. Believe me, nigger, you gonna be glad for the company."

"Mistah Butkis," Rafe broke in quietly, "Tater an' Brutus ain't ready fo' the pit yet."

"Yo' worry 'bout yo' own skin, Rafe. Ah kin fight," Brutus retorted angrily. "Ah cain't fight no goddamn iron ball but Ah ain't seed de man Ah cain't gut."

Butkis nodded. "See, Rafe. He's ready. Ready as sin. An' Tater here'll learn quicker in the pit than he will walkin' the balls. You bucks get plenty to eat an' sleep lots for the next three days, 'cause Sunday gonna be special. Brutus, you an' Tater go to the front shack before this day is out an' pick what you gonna fight with. Git used to 'em for the next few days 'cause they'll be keepin' you alive once you get down inside that pit."

"It ain't right, Mistuh Butkis," Rafe persisted.

The overseer swallowed the lump of chewed jerky before continuing. "Rafe, you may be the number one nigger amongst these here boys, but you ain't shit to me. Now, you want a taste a' the cat, you jes' sass me one more time. They's fightin' an' that's that. You hear me?"

He didn't wait for an answer but stalked off the way he came, taking Milo and the other guards with him. The big gates slammed shut, leaving the silent blacks alone.

The closed gates meant freedom of a sort, and muffled conversations started as the blacks discussed the fight and who the opponents might be. Rafe stood alone and unmoving, seething with anger. Perhaps the price of freedom was too high. It would have given him almost as much satisfaction to break the overseer's neck.

Cat swaggered up to the powerful black man. "He put yo' in yo' place, boss. Down heah wid us plain-ass niggers," he taunted.

Rafe stared impassively at Cat, made himself relax and keep an eye on the pitchfork the young man held. "I doan feel like playin' no games, Cat. Doan you vex me now," he said in a low, dangerous voice.

Cat didn't know any better. "Which end de one to watch fo', nigger Rafe?" He gestured first with the iron tines, then the blunt shaft. "Come on, nigger. Yo' de number one pitbuck. Show us which end de one ta duck."

Tater and the rest stepped back, giving the two pitbucks plenty of room. The entire compound held its breath.

"C'mon, boss. Pitchfork a' comin'. Which end de one to watch?" Cat feinted rapidly with first one end then the other, each becoming a blur of motion as the pitchfork sliced the air with an eerie hum. Rafe's powerful right arm shot up and down. A loud crack, and Cat leaped back, the iron prongs of the fork singing past his face and clanging against one of the cannonballs. Most of the wooden shaft sliced across the dusty compound floor. A lethal sliver of wood stuck quivering in the ground between Cat's feet.

"What pitchfork?" Rafe asked quietly. Without another word he turned and left the smaller man to the humiliating jibes of the other pitbucks.

Butkis hated horses. He sat astride the big gelding, distastefully guiding the animal down the sloping farmland, leading the way toward Claytonville. The brutal old seadog scowled back at his two companions riding close behind. He was determined they should not see his discomfort. The gelding stumbled, lurched and almost lost his rider. Butkis drove his booted heels into the animal's flanks and jerked cruelly on the reins. "By my mother's salty dugs, I swear I'd sooner ride the tumblin' deck of a broached whaler than straddle this goddamned critter a moment longer," he swore aloud.

"You say sumpin', Mistuh Butkis?" one of the guards behind him inquired.

"Jes' shut up and ride," Butkis growled in return.

The guard who had spoken turned to his companion with a what-did-*I*-say? look. His partner shrugged. They rode on.

Claytonville, although growing and prospering due to the trade with Mexico and the numerous visitors to Freedom Plantation, was still a mere crossroads around which clustered an assortment of shops and businesses. To the northeast wound the road to Nachitoc⁝ :s. To the southwest the deeply rutted high road to Burr Ferry passed through rich farmland. North of the crossroads the townsfolk had built their homes. There the ground was higher and the proximity of the houses to the businesses gave an illusion of greater size to the town and enabled the citizens to assume an aura of importance they otherwise would not have.

Joe Terson finished sweeping the porch of his general store. He propped the broom against a post, removed his glasses and wiped each lens with a rag from his hip pocket. Replacing the spectacles on his beakish nose, he inspected his precious display window which had cost more than he cared to remember. The bevelled glass boasted a huge and fancy engraved "T" and had been shipped all the way from New Orleans. He polished the pane with delicate and meticulous care.

"Mornin', Terson."

The shopkeeper stared at Butkis's reflection in the glass. Butkis frightened him almost as much as Ezra Clayton. The townspeople of Claytonville he had known most of his life. The small farmers down the Burr Ferry road and back toward Nachitoches he knew by first and last names. They'd been trusted customers ever since they had moved in. But Clayton and his guards were something else. Even though good customers, they were indifferent, hostile vagabonds who carried their bravado in a brace of pistols. They flaunted cruel mean streaks and short tempers prone to sudden and violent eruption. At those times small farmers or townfolk had to watch out, for they knew one of them might be hurt. Terson coughed and stammered a greeting to the overseer. Butkis dismounted, instructed his two lackeys to busy themselves nailing up the hand-drawn bills Ezra had instructed them to take to town.

"What's this, Mister Butkis?" Terson managed without stuttering, accepting the proferred piece of paper from the guard.

"Mistuh Clayton's stepdaughter come back home. Mistuh Clayton's gonna hold a celebration come Saturday an' Sunday. Big doin's."

"Why yes. Abigail thought she saw the Fitzman girl yesterday, and folks have been talking. Haven't seen her yet, myself. Expected her to visit . . . ."

"Mistuh Clayton," Butkis interrupted, "wants Miz Terson to help with decoratin' an' such fer the party. She's ta' be there Friday evenin' an' stay over."

"Why, certainly," Joe answered nervously, glancing about. "Yes. Abigail will be more than happy to help out."

A thin-lipped, hawkish woman stepped onto the porch, started to say something to Joe but stopped short when she saw Butkis standing in front of her. The overseer leered at her, tipped his cap. "Mornin', Miz Terson."

Abigail nodded icily in the overseer's direction before speaking to her husband. "Joe, Elmer needs help with that crate of apples that came in this mornin'."

The shopkeeper's face rose in astonishment, but catching his wife's signal, he broke into a happy smile. He spouted a dozen rapid apologies to Butkis and followed Abigail back into the store. "Abigail, what on earth . . . we don't have any apples. It's too early for apples."

"He don't know that."

"But what happens if he comes in and asks for apples?"

"We'll just tell him we don't have any."

Joe threw his arms in the air. "But Abigail, he . . ."

"You listen to me, Joe Terson. I hate these men. Worse than niggers. They're not only dumb but also . . . bestial. Yes, that's it. They make me think of beasts. I was afraid you might be in trouble."

"Don't be silly," her husband retorted. "Why, Ezra Clayton and I are quite friendly. He wouldn't let anything happen to me. Didn't he just last week . . . . ?"

"Ezra Clayton considers us just so much property. Thinks he owns us just like his niggers."

"Now don't you say that, Abigail. Don't you ever say that."

"It's true!" Abigail punctuated the remark by slapping her hand down on the countertop.

"Abigail, please. . . ." Joe looked around, fearful anyone should have heard or seen her outrageous display. "Elmer . . . ."

"Elmer's still gone from when you sent him down to the Grovers'. You know that."

"He could come back. Anyway, that ain't got nothin' to do with what we're talkin' about. Now, Mister Butkis come by to tell me Ezra has requested you show up at Freedom Friday afternoon and help Micara pretty the place up for a party honorin' Crissa." His wife's face twisted in distaste and Joe hurried on before she could interrupt. "Now does that sound like he thinks we're niggers? Gonna be a big to-do, and that's good for us, 'cause they'll be needin' supplies." He waited apprehensively.

"Did he say 'request'?"

"Sure he did," Joe answered quickly. "Butkis said that very word," he lied, hoping she wouldn't read it in his eyes.

Abigail, her dignity soothed, patted her hair in place and stalked off to the back of the store. Joe shuddered, sighed in relief. It made him sick just thinking what might have happened if his wife had decided not to acquiesce to Clayton's demand.

Black Bedetta sent one of her girls scurrying up the brothel stairway and down the hall to knock three times on Lutibelle's door. The door opened slightly in response to the signal and a raffishly handsome man whispered, "Yes?"

The prostitute repeated Black Bedetta's message in a low tone. The room's occupant nodded, closed the door, pulled on his trousers and stuck his McKim Brothers pistol in the rear waistband. A moment later he opened the door and stepped into the hall. Barefoot and wearing faded trousers with worn suspenders pinching the naked flesh of his shoulders, he followed the prostitute down the stairs.

The smell of hot, spiced tea and biscuits assailed his nostrils and set his stomach growling. He rubbed the flat, hungry ache away and moved toward the back sitting room. Bedetta sat by the window at a small round table.

"Yes? What is it you wanted?" the man asked, his voice tinged with aristocratic impatience.

Black Bedetta's face split into a wide grin nearly lost in a sea of fatty creases and wrinkles lining her face and neck. "Tea?" she asked. Her corpulent arm reached over to tilt an ivory china teapot and pour a clear reddish brown liquid into a matching cup, empty but for a leaf of mint. The tea smelled strong and heady. Bedetta's breasts, massive and unbound beneath her tentlike dressing gown, swelled to even more frightening proportions as she pressed against the table. The grin never left her face. "It's got brandy in it. An' clove . . . an' mint."

"I don't want any tea," the man said petulantly. "Besides, I couldn't afford what you'd probably charge me. The room itself is an audacious robbery."

"Tea I give to you. For free," the fat black woman responded. She squinted at him for a long, silent moment. Without taking her eyes off him she sliced a hot biscuit, spread it with butter, ladled a hillock of peach preserves on one half, covered it with the other and popped the whole concoction, seeping now, into her cavernous mouth. Not a crumb touched her lips as she poked it back toward her throat with a thick finger. Her cheeks bulged only slightly, the motion of chewing even less noticeable save for the jiggling rolls of fat where her chin should have been. She beamed at him anew.

"Dammit, nigger, what is it you want?" The man was uneasy now. The madam was up to something, though he couldn't be certain exactly what. To emphasize his seriousness he reached behind him and drew the pistol from his waistband, cocked it and lay the weapon on the tabletop in front of him.

Black Bedetta appeared not to notice the gun. Her hand dwarfed the dainty tea cup as she lifted it to her lips and drained the tea in one swallow. She pulled the cup from in front of the man over to her and drank its contents as well. A girlishly youthful prostitute, newly arrived, brought a thin black cigar to the table and lit it for the madam. Black Bedetta inhaled deeply, threatening to send her mammoth breasts bursting through the light material covering them. "A quarter-eagle a day," she said. "From now on."

The man stood abruptly, knocking the chair over backward. "What?"

"A quarter-eagle. Two and a half dollars." Bedetta's voice remained calm and unconcerned even as the man grabbed the pistol from the table and levelled it at her.

"We agreed on a dollar. And I don't use the girls. A dollar is too damn much, you nigger slut, but a quarter-eagle . . . Hell, you haven't a tart here worth that, much less an empty room."

"I'll have your gear fetched an' you can find some'eres else to light."

"You know there is no other place."

"A quarter-eagle or outside. Mebbe that ruffler Butkis might find you lodgings."

The man lowered his gun, his face blanching. "What's this? What about Butkis?"

"Why, he come to town, Lutibelle tells me. Come this mornin'. An' when Butkis come down from Clayton's hill, he always stop in fer a bit of gamin' with one a' my white girlies. He not alone, neither. Two a' his roisters is with him. They'll follow him here, mark my word."

"Dammit to hell, woman, I need that room. Butkis would probably recognize me. The others are no problem, I imagine, but Butkis . . . Damn!"

Black Bedetta watched him closely, her eyes dropping

down to his waist. She tossed her head girlishly. "Well, there is one room I might jes' let you have fo' free."

Lutibelle entered from the front porch. "Mistuh Butkis headen' dis way, ma'am."

"Take me there. Be quick about it," the man said, his voice tight and hushed with urgency.

Bedetta, the infernal grin still slashing her dark face, rose ponderously from the table and moved with surprising adroitness through the sitting room toward the back of the house. Coming to a heavy oak door decorated with an assortment of crudely explicit carvings, she stopped to fumble with the lock. Her breath came in short, heaving rasps, the only sound discernible this far back in the brothel.

The door opened. Bedetta waddled through the door, the man following her, his face wide with surprise. The room, draped in white silk finery, was half filled with a magnificent canopied bed also covered with white and lumped with huge, brightly colored pillows of different shapes. "Whose room is this?" the man asked, moving past her in awe, already knowing the answer.

"Mine," Bedetta answered, her voice husky with desire. He turned to ask a question in time to see the dressing gown slide from her fleshy shoulders and land in a heap at her feet, revealing a mountain of flesh, black and shining. She cupped each ponderous breast, the nipples bulging as her fingers prodded each palm-sized dark aureole. Like some great black storm cloud she moved close to him, shutting the door with her foot as she stepped out of the crumpled gown. The man stood silent and awestruck in front of her, unable to move as the pistol slid from his hand and dropped to the floor.

"I'se got mah mo'nin' hongrys, honey," Bedetta chuckled, sliding his suspenders down and unbuttoning the top of his trousers. "But doan you worry none. There's been mo' white in me than most folks 'spect." Her hands ran the length of his inner thighs as he joined her in nakedness. She led him to the shipsized bed. "We gonna make this first 'un quick 'cause I'm gonna have to be up front to handle our friend Mistuh Butkis." Appalled, he eased down onto the bed, feeling himself harden in spite of himself as her fingers deftly teased him. "First I aims to sample what I'm hidin'. An' you can stay fo' free, honey." She patted his manhood, her hand folding around him, guiding him between her massive thighs. "Yassuh, you can stay fo' free as long as it's good fo' ol' Bedetta. . . ."

Butkis watched from the thin mattress as the prostitute pulled her cotton shift back over her head and patted it down along her thin frame. The soiled fabric clung tightly to her smallish breasts, adding misleading dimensions to her form. "I deserve another," Butkis growled. "The first one was good. I ken work up to 'nother, by heavens."

"Don't matter what you ken work up to unless'n you ken work up to more money fuhst."

"Aw, honey, I already done paid."

"You paid fo' one an' I give yo' one. Kep' it goin' extra long, too. Now don't you gimme no hosshit 'bout another. Not unless'n I see the color of silver."

Butkis threw back the covers and half rose in bed, revealing his hardened desire, a pole of lumpy flesh beneath a belly that had been the willing recipient of too many jacks of ale. "Well now . . . supposin' I was of a mind to take me some more of yore sweet ass as an extra sumpthin' to remember on my way back to Freedom. Maybe you forgettin' who you got in this room. Maybe I'll be takin' what I want an' if you don't give it free and good I'll be carvin' on that pretty white face o' yores. Give you another scar to match the one you already got."

The whore did not even turn to look at him. Facing a wash bowl she lifted her shift and began to sponge her privates. She shrugged. "Mistuh Butkis, you don't half skeer me as much as what Black Bedetta gonna do to me if'n she catch me givin' belly-warmin's for free. Now you ken make me do what you will, but you better enjoy it 'cause Bedetta will be comin' round to claim that stick o' yores for her very own. She'll razor it off you and hang it over her door."

Butkis looked as if he might spring for her after all and the prostitute feared the Clayton overseer would risk another chance between her legs. Instead he scowled and sat back against the iron latticework at the head of the bed, reached down to the floor and after a moment's search found his bottle of rum. "Well, then," he patted the bed next to him, "come and drive another nail with me." He held the bottle to her. She wetted her lips and looked at the door, almost expecting Bedetta to be there. Then she looked suspiciously at Butkis. He protested innocently. "A bit o' grog is all. You gave it to me good. Now I've a little extra for you," he said.

The prostitute brushed back her straggly brown hair and climbed onto the bed, sat beside the overseer and took the proffered bottle, tilting it to her mouth and swallowing long and deep. Butkis, hiding his erection under the soiled sheet, reached inside her shift to provoke one small breast, rubbing his calloused seaman's thumb over her nipple. He sang softly in a guttural voice an old sea ditty he'd sung as a whaler while scouring the ocean for its mountainous quarry:

> "O, I harpooned whales and drunk me grog
> on a thousand ships or more,
> but the only berth I dearly love
> is 'tween the legs o' a Yankee whore."

The girl shoved his hand away from her breast. "No more a' that."

Butkis grabbed the bottle from her and took several swallows before handing it back. As she drank he sat up, grabbed her ankles, pulled her down flat on the bed and forced her legs apart. The prostitute, too startled to cry out, gagged on the rum still in her throat as Butkis mounted and drove himself into her with increasingly rapid strokes until he peaked, his head thrown back and a growling moan issuing from his throat. The girl kicked feebly, then gave up.

His goal achieved, Butkis pushed himself away and reached for the bottle before the final dram of run emptied onto the sheets. He crossed the room and stepped into his trousers, sliding them up over his bare rump, then pulled on his shirt and buckled his pistol belt around his waist.

"Bastard," the girl gasped, still coughing and spitting,

trying to clear her lungs of the fiery fluid. "Bedetta will geld you for this."

"No she won't, 'cause you ain't gonna say a thing, doxy. Yore gonna keep that stick-suckin' mouth o' yores quiet 'cause you know that you gonna have to tell that big bag o' blubber how you drunk my rum when you should a' been headin' downstairs. An' she'll not be likin' that a'tall." He pointed the bottle at her menacingly. "You ain't," he continued quietly and slowly, "tellin' no stories. Anyway, figger that quick 'un was payment for the rum you spilled. Course, I'd wash me mouth out if'n I was you. I 'spect ol' Bedetta ken smell likker on a girlie's breath quicker'n a sailor gets the stick."

The prostitute thoughtfully fingered the white scar that spoiled her jaw, running its length from ear to chin. Black Bedetta had left a mark on her once before. She didn't relish the idea of a second kiss from the madam's straight razor. "Go yore way, Mistuh Butkis. But when you come back 'round, don't you be buyin' my services 'cause it'll get you nothin' but grief over havin' throwed good money away."

The overseer drew his cutlass and stepped near the bed. The girl's breath caught in fear. He rested the point of the heavy blade on her inner thigh and forced her legs open. Her eyes widened and she stiffened as he lifted her shift to stare at her musky femininity. It was seconds before she realized he was chuckling, the laugh coming low and mean from his throat. He let the fabric drop and deftly slipped the blade back in its scabbard. "There's plenty better here to ask for," he said quietly. "An' tighter, too," then turned and strode from the room.

The lower hall was dark, even in daytime. Butkis started for the front parlor where his companions waited, then sensing danger, spun around and stared into the darkness at the back of the house. A door closed. Drawing the pistol from his belt he stealthily made his way along the wall. The light from an outer room faintly illuminated the dark recesses and he could make out a single door at the end of the hall. He approached silently.

The man in Bedetta's room cocked his pistol and aimed its .54 caliber load directly at the door. He had

111

seen Butkis and in his haste shut the door too noisily. He knew it and cursed himself, but it was too late now for recriminations. He would have to run for it, and assuming he could kill Butkis, hope he could win his way past the two guards before they could contest his passage. The latch began to move. Why hadn't he bolted the door? Damn it. Damn, damn, damn, he repeated angrily to himself.

A door behind Butkis opened and the hall flooded with light. "What you doin' messin' wit my room, Mistuh Butkis?" Bedetta shouted from the doorway. Butkis whirled about, startled at the sudden noise and light. The man in the room slumped in relief. "Lawd have mercy but he gots a gun," Bedetta continued, advancing on him. "You don't need to deflowa' me at gun point, honey. Why, you ken hav this any ol' time." The fleshy madam lifted her silk skirt and revealed the black vastness of her thighs.

Butkis saw his two companions grinning at him from the parlor door. He scowled at having been taken unawares. "I was lookin' for those two rumskins and thought I seen one head this way. You get that big black fleece o' yores out o' my face an' we'll be goin'." He hurried past the madam and gestured violently for the two guards to follow him.

Once outside he turned on them. "Wipe them grins off'n yore faces," he said venomously, "else it's the cane fields from now till doomsday for the both o' you." The two expressions changed from mirth to one of supreme sobriety. "An' not a word o' this to a soul," he continued, "or I'll split yore tongues on my blade an' feed em' to you with yore beans." He swung awkwardly into the saddle and rode out at a gallop, followed by the two thoroughly cowed guards, totally unaware of the pale, handsome face that watched them from the window of Bedetta's bedroom until they were lost from sight.

Rafe finished his twelve laps for the afternoon. The sweat pouring off him, he squatted at the tank a long time, outwardly calm, inwardly a seething ball of doubt and tension. When he could no longer take the nagging fear, he made his way to Old Chulem's hovel, a tent made of hides and wood. The entrance was low and he had to crawl in on all fours. Old Chulem sat in the gloom, a brass cup set before him. The cup held a few small brownish green leaves which were burning and sending up a slim, tenuous gray coil of scented smoke. The old man was staring at the leaves, mumbling an unintelligible chant. Rafe waited, slumped forward, legs crossed. Little used to the fetid odors of Old Chulem's abode, he looked about apprehensively. Fetishes hung on the walls. Some were man-shaped, carved of wood or fashioned from mud-covered reeds and twigs. Several were carved from bone. There were other shapes, too. Recognizable animals, the hunters and the hunted. Reptiles. And more. Nightmare shapes, fragments of despairing dreams, of demons, and eaters of spirits. The latter were evil totems and occupied a niche all to themselves. There were quills from an assortment of fowl, small clay bowls of unguents and poultices, all exuding singular pungent odors. Skulls hung from the hide roof, suspended by vines or lengths of twisted cord. Old Chulem's hut was a place of mystery, of dark ritual and age-old superstition.

Old Chulem himself was a dabbler in secrets sometimes best left untouched and unremembered. His had been a tribe living in the cloistered confines of a narrow valley on the fringes of the African delta. His remote ancestors were among the first of men. They had been some of the first to witness the unfathomable terrors of a dangerously capricious world, the first to try to understand and cope with nature, the first to try to predict and control their environment with primitive magic. Old Chulem was a proud product of the dark wisdom his ancestors had garnered over the centuries. And now, far from his native land, he practiced the ancient workings of his cult.

He looked up and stared at Rafe. One long bony finger rose to point at a man-shape carved of a chunk of meat that had hung on the wall so long it had begun to mummify. Chulem's toothless grin was all the more dreadful because of his tattooed gums. "Ezra Clayton," was all he said. His laugh was more a wheeze. Old Chulem squinted in the gloom, his finger lowered to probe at Rafe's thigh. "Yo' leg?"

"Better."

"I seed yo' walk de balls."

Rafe uncrossed his legs, crossed them again.

Old Chulem shook his head. "Shouldn't worry 'bout dem young bucks. Food fo' de rats an' snakes. If not now, yo' prob'ly be killin' 'em fo' too long." The old man could feel Rafe wasn't listening, wasn't paying attention, only waiting for him to cease his gabble. He sighed. "What yo' come to Ol' Chulem fo', Rafe?"

"Throw the bones, Chulem. Throw the bones an' tell me what you see. There's fightin' come Sunday."

"Ah don't need no conjurin' to see what's ahead. Blood. Yo' knows dat well as Ah do. Blood flowin' in de pit. An' bloody death . . . yassuh."

"Throw the bones, old man. There's a fear in me. Somethin' happenin'. Not wrong. Not right. A change maybe. I'm not fightin', yet I feel in my gut . . . throw the bones, Old Chulem, dammit, read 'em fo' me. See what comin'. I gots to know." The more urgent he became, the more Rafe lapsed into the compound dialect. I'm losing it, he thought. It I don't get out soon, I'll be nothin' more than a compound nigger jus' like the others.

Old Chulem sighed despondently and took his box of white bone fragments from behind him. He shook them twice and emptied them onto the ground, scooped them up into the box, muttered, threw them again. He repeated the action a third time. The fourth time he let the ghostly white shards lay. He bent his withered frame, his eyes studying the fragments cautiously and with great deliberation. He remained unmoving for a long time. Twice Rafe suppressed the urge to flee the old man's presence, to flee into the clean air. There was too much of the dark here, too much of the spirit world into which a man ventured only at great risk.

"Much death," the old man began. "Much death. Red gold. Ah sees dead men an' de cat. Ah sees fang an' jaw. An' mo' . . . but Ah cain't say." He hurriedly scooped up the bones and deposited them back in the box and shoved it behind him.

Rafe grabbed the withered arms, held them tight. "What else, old man?"

"Leabe me alone, boss. Bes' leabe Ol' Chulem be."

"What did you see?"

"Ah tol's yo' what Ah seed. I doan tells yo' no mo'. Now go 'way."

Rafe dropped the conjure man's arms and backed away from him, scrambling out from the stifling lair. The bright light confused him and for a moment he did not know which way to turn.

Old Chulem clutched a fetish and chanted an incantation in the dark. He had seen beyond Sunday.

8

Torches flared, lining the carriage path to the house in a manner reminiscent of the night almost a week earlier when Crissa first arrived. Thrust into the ground at six-foot intervals, they illuminated the gathering throng of townspeople, farmers and trappers on the way to pay their respects, garner the much-desired favors of Ezra Clayton, and partake of the abundant refreshments and entertainment for which Freedom was rapidly becoming famous. Claytonville was virtually emptied as were many of the surrounding farms. The tone of the evening was one of eager anticipation. There was gold to be wagered on the next day's event. No one could guess what Ezra planned for the pit, but it was certain to be novel and exciting.

Tables were set up on the front and side lawns. On them were heaped the rewards of nature's bounty and man's ingenuity. Slabs of venison, roasted and dripping with its own juice; wild turkey, cooked whole and stuffed with rice and herbs; vegetable pears stuffed with crabmeat; jellied pigs' feet; and bowls of steaming jambalaya done up with ham and sausage with more bowls of gravy almost thick enough to hold upright the huge wooden spoons. A huge kettle of hot, spiced chicken gumbo simmered over an open fire. Another table held desserts—

loaves of fresh bread and bowls of fig, jujube, dewberry, muscadine and scuppernong preserves. Behind each table were two fan-wielding slaves to keep the flies and mosquitoes away. Other slaves from the fields had been specially bathed and clothed and trained to wander through the crowd with trays full of cups of coffee or bottles of rum.

A platform was set under the magnolias and on it sat the *fais-dodos,* the Acadian troubadors with their violins and accordions, hired for the occasion. In front of them on the lawn, town and country folk danced between food and drink. Off to one side eight or ten tables were set up. There some of the older ladies were playing a furious hand of *vingt et un.* Two tables were surrounded by men watching fierce poker games which would last the night. Farther off and beyond the glow of the lanterns a person had to walk carefully, for Saturday night in western Louisiana was an occasion for more than dancing, eating, drinking and card-playing. Young and not so young lovers sought the shadows of the cedars, from which came an occasional giggle or cry of delight as flesh met flesh under hastily raised skirts and lowered trousers.

Dressed in an immaculate white frock coat, Ezra was the perfect host, the soul of gentility and congeniality. He roamed about, laughed, smiled and greeted all with quiet dignity as befitted his position. Few knew he had made it a point to post several of his guards at various key points on the perimeter of the party.

Micara was nowhere to be seen. Hidden in her room, she drained another glass of sherry and lay back on her bed, barely able to distinguish the voices outside her door, but hardly caring. She just wished they would leave. "I just don't know what else to say to her, Crissa." It was nosy Abigail Terson. "She won't listen to me and I'm her best friend. Or was. I haven't been invited up for . . . I don't know how long. And now she'll barely talk to me."

Crissa murmured something unintelligible in return. The door opened and closed before the Terson woman could repeat herself again, as she had been doing for the last twenty-four hours, and Micara's daughter approached her mother and sat down beside her on the bed.

"Mother?"

Micara pretended to sleep.

"I know you're awake, Mother." Micara sighed, opened her eyes and tried to focus. "Please join the party with me. I shall have to talk to all those people and would hate to have to do it alone. I'll never remember their names without you there to help me."

Micara stared at her daughter from beneath heavy lids. The girl swam into focus and she reached up to stroke Crissa's cheek. "I'll be down shortly, dear. Run along and find Steven. I . . . I need to be alone a moment more. It's been too long, I'm afraid, since the last party I was . . . invited to."

"Mother, you. . . ."

"Shhh. I promise." She laughed woodenly, rose and ushered Crissa from the room, shushing her again when her daughter attempted to protest.

Outside in the hall, Crissa once more was confronted by Abigail Terson. "Won't listen to you, either, will she? And you her daughter. Them decorations downstairs? All my doin'. Tweren't no one but the niggers to help, and them surly. And Ezra Clayton? Humph. Not one word of thanks from the likes of him!"

Crissa took the older woman's arm and steered her toward the stairs. "Mr. Clayton has been terribly preoccupied with personal problems," she confided. "I have, too. I'm afraid it was terribly gauche of us not to thank you, for I do."

"What?" The older woman stopped, a little perplexed.

Crissa smiled. "Thank you, of course. There wouldn't even be a party had it not been for your help."

"Oh . . . well. . . ."

"No, I mean it. And you know it. You've been simply marvelous and certainly more than generous. I wanted to invite you over next week so we could spend some time and thank you properly, but hadn't had the opportunity. I hope you'll forgive me?"

Abigail patted her dress, swelled with pride. "Well, of course. . . ." She stopped, at a loss. "I'd best be joinin' Joseph downstairs. No tellin' how much trouble that man'll get himself into before the night's done." Abigail

Terson shook her head in despair and, her ego boosted by Crissa's flattery, marched regally down the stairs.

Crissa fled to her room and closed the door behind her, choking the tears back. The room was dark and she stood unmoving until her eyes adjusted to the gloom, then moved to the bed and flung herself full length on the sheets. The week had passed in a welter of confusion for her. First the change in Steve, the glimpse of the mysterious compound with the dangerous-looking slaves, then the confrontation with Ezra which had left her shaken to the core. Next the wagon with her trunks arrived and she busied herself with settling in for her stay. Hours had been spent alone in her room considering her position *vis à vis* Ezra and the plantation and writing letters to friends in Boston and the bank in New Orleans.

And Micara? Her mother? Or more accurately put, what was left of her. A shell of a woman. Micara became her prime concern; to help her repair the ravages of too much sherry, recover her spirit and strength, and then together, force a reckoning with Ezra Clayton, together assert themselves and regain control of the affairs of Freedom. Of Fitzman's Freedom. She still wasn't at all sure of how she should go about such a task. Ezra had spent part of the week away, the rest at home but sequestered. The few times they met he was as charming as possible, obviously taking pains to assure her he could be pleasant so long as she accepted his role as master of the plantation. The party was an even stronger promise of his assurance. Crissa wasn't about to let herself be bought for such a small price.

A knock sounded on the door, followed by Steve's voice calling her name, breaking her reverie and bringing her back to the present. She sighed, rose from the bed, gathered the voluminous skirts of her gown and joined Steve in the hall. The young captain was resplendent in his uniform. He bowed as Crissa appeared. "I had to get special permission to attend this party," he said in a low and supposedly seductive tone, "and I'd hate to waste what little time I have wandering around without you."

Before Crissa could reply another voice interrupted. "Captain Bennett, sir. A gentleman does not come calling for his lady by knocking on her bedroom door. Such conduct is hardly proper," Micara said from the hall outside her room.

Crissa brightened. "Oh, Mother, Steve used to follow me to my room all the time when we were children."

"My dear," Micara laughed a little giddily, joining them at the head of the stairs, "the world has come to a pretty pass indeed if I have to point out you are no longer children." She held out her hand to take Steve's arm. The officer blushed and bowed, took her arm in his. "Will you dance with an old lady, Captain?" she asked coyly.

"I dance with none but young ladies, madam. I'll be glad to dance with you," Steve answered gallantly, starting down the stars.

Crissa followed, trying to smooth the worry from her eyes, as they descended into the din of the party below.

The compound was empty and still. Somewhere a whippoorwill cried a last mournful note before hiding for the day. A mockingbird woke and sang a greeting to the morning that was young enough yet not to have seen the sun. Rafe had listened to the clamor from the plantation house and grounds for a good part of the night. Foremost in his mind was an attempt to revive the image of Crissa Fitzman. He hadn't seen her when she had captured the attention of the compound earlier in the week, but word had reached him, for the pitbucks had talked of nothing but the blond girl all the next day. He had finally fallen asleep to the thin wail of the violins and accordion, then dreamed of the slim-hipped, youthful girl of so long ago. In his dream he could picture her well enough—the reddish-gold hair, the pug nose and bright green eyes she said were inherited from her father, small pert breasts under the light cotton dress and strong little-girl legs. And in his dream he stood in front of himself and said, "Ain't right you think on the likes of her, nigger. White man see that pole stickin' up, he cut yo' balls off at yo' neck." Rafe stirred, rose from the shuck mattress and made his way to the door, dream and admonition vivid in his mind. In spite of the warning he couldn't drive her out.

The mockingbird cried again, answered this time by the myriad sounds of distant waking swamp and forest. Across the compound a figure stirred near the spring and a squat, simian shape that could only be Jomo rose and stretched. Curse Old Chulem, Rafe thought. He was an old bone-rattler better off buried. No sooner said, Rafe quickly denied the silent words lest the conjure man read the curse and hold it against him.

Jomo left the spring and crossed the compound toward the longhouse. Suddenly he changed course and headed for Rafe. The giant black noticed a gleam of metal in Jomo's left hand. The smaller man stopped and stood before Rafe, stared at him a moment then held his hand up to hold the double-edged axe blade even with Rafe's face. "No sleepin', Boss?"

"You can see that."

"How come? Yo' ain't gonna be fightin' today. Maybe yo' worry Jomo might be dyin'."

"Not worried o' that, Jomo. What Mistah Clayton got planned fo' you make less work fo' me when my freedom fight come."

Jomo's eyes narrowed to slits and he said very quietly, "Number one pit nigger gets to come watch when he not fightin', if'n he want to. Yo' come an' watch Jomo. Yo' see dere not a man ken beat me. Not one man, not two, prob'ly not tree o' fo' dat Ah cain't go up 'gains' wid dis axe an' whup 'em. Yo' watch dis day, nigger. Ah be eatin' pohk tonight."

Rafe stood unmoving as Jomo left. Old Chulem's words echoed in the corner of his mind. "Ah sees fang an' jaw," he had said. "Fang an' jaw. An' mo'. . . ." Rafe shook the worry from his mind and walked slowly to the tank. It would be a hot day for killing.

Those who went to their homes for what was left of the night returned to Freedom right after Reverend Leahy's service, held early to accommodate the goings-on. Claude Duggins and the other small landowners from downriver and the dozen or so trappers from across the Sabine slept under and in wagons and on the lower gallery. Soldiers with a free weekend from Fort Jessup spent the night in

Claytonville in the Coonskin Tavern and Black Bedetta's, then set out early for Freedom and a day of entertainment and gambling. *Monsieur* Bernard and his family were put up in the big house overnight, for rivals though he and Ezra Clayton were, gentry was gentry and had to be treated as such.

Revelers from the night before who had stayed on the grounds wearily shoved themselves away from food-laden breakfast tables and began to wind their way across the lawn toward the compound and the pit beyond where they planned to stake out prime space for viewing whatever Ezra Clayton had prepared for them. There was much speculation, and betting on the nature of the contest got under way early. Ezra Clayton liked a well-kept secret.

The atmosphere inside the house was cold and tense. "I'm not going," Crissa averred. "I think that sort of thing is horrid. I'll have nothing to do with your animal fights. I'll have nothing to do with them," she said, turning to leave.

Ezra stepped in front of her, blocking her attempt to reach the library door. "The contest is the high point of the festivities, Crissa. The climax of a party in your honor. You are expected; your absence would be noted. Surely you wouldn't spite my welcome?"

"A bitter welcome marked by the baiting of dumb animals? Yes. I would spite it."

The door opened and Micara entered. "Oh there you are, darling. Come. We mustn't be late. I'm sure Ezra has arranged a magnificent excitement in your honor."

"Mother, you've been up nearly all night. Don't you think you'd better rest some?"

"Nonsense. I'm having a lovely time. We haven't seen a ball like this in years. I shan't be put away to bed and miss all the excitement." She stumbled, spilling some of the sherry. "Oh dear," she laughed, wiping her hand on her skirt, "I'm afraid I'm a trifle light-headed from the gaiety of it all." A tiny panic-stricken look clouded her face. "Please escort me, dear? I don't want to go alone. . . ."

Ezra leaned in close to his stepdaughter, stirred by the

123

light lilac fragrance and the smooth flow of flesh from neck to shoulder to breast, barely restrained by the daringly cut bodice. "Micara dearly loves my little excitements. If she wants to go and wants you to accompany her, I think it would be less than daughterly of you to refuse. After all, she is your mother." He smiled wolfishly at her, allowed his eyes to rake her from leg to head then looked directly into her eyes. "Besides, how do you know what will happen? You might be surprised." His eyes dropped obviously to her breasts. "Many times those experiences we most seek to escape turn out to be the most pleasant."

Micara seemed not to observe her husband's brash suggestion and took her daughter's hand. "Do come along, Crissa. Everyone expects you, and I'm sure Steve is frantic over your absence. It's a pity he isn't around more often."

Crissa allowed herself to be led out to the empty lawn where the shay waited. Disgusted with herself for allowing them to coerce her into accompanying them, Crissa Elizabeth Fitzman climbed reluctantly into the shay and held her mother's hand.

Rafe stood inside the main gate where he could hear the crowd gathering around the pit. The hum of voices rose and fell, punctuated by an occasional shout or cry of greeting. The crowd was obviously large. Ezra Clayton was throwing one of his special matches and Rafe feared for his companions. Rumors and speculation had flown about the pitbuck compound since Butkis had announced the coming match. And while none could tell what the three would face, Rafe knew in his bones they would be pitted against a particularly dangerous foe. He tensed slightly as he heard footsteps behind him, then forced himself to ease the worry from his face when he saw Tater at his side.

"B . . . B . . . Boss?"

Rafe turned to look at the youth, casting a practiced glance at the machete Tater held with a death grip. "You practice with that machete, boy?"

"Yassuh. Me an' Brutus both. But Brutus gots a mean

124

streak. Won't hab nuffin' ta' do wid me. Who yo' figger we goana fight?"

"No tellin', boy. Who or what. Jes' keep near Jomo. Listen close to what he say an' watch close to what he do. Take care don't nuthin' o' nobody get to his back an' he do what he can best he can. Maybe you live to get your woman an' wagon."

"Yassuh. Ah'll sho' keep mah eyes open. Ah always be quick. Used ta' steal 'taters from de field when Ah was jes' a pickaninny. Don't nobody catch me. Dat's how Ah come ta' be called Tater. Ain't nobody goana mark dis boy, no suh."

"Don't you be too proud, boy. I gots marks on me. Jes' you do like I say. You watch Jomo. He ben 'round a long time." He sensed the youth stiffen as the small door in the gate opened and Butkis, accompanied by Milo and Decater, walked a few paces into the compound and halted.

Butkis stared at Rafe. "What you doin' up here, nigger?"

Rafe stared back, kept an eye on the overseer's cutlass arm. "Mistah Clayton say the number one pitbuck get to watch when he got a mind to. Today I wants to watch."

"Can't git enough, ken you?" Butkis snarled. "Can't git yore fill o' blood an' cuttin'. You come along then, but mind you, I'll be keepin' my eye out. You try anything an' I'll spit you with this." He patted the cutlass meaningfully. "Where the rest of them niggers?"

Rafe looked back toward the longhouse just as Brutus sauntered from the door and swaggered across the compound, slapping the flat of the razor-sharp machete blade against his thigh. Jomo followed hard on his heels, his squat, powerful torso moving with fluid but heavy, sure steps. The two stopped a half-dozen paces in front of the guards and waited. Rafe nudged Tater and sent him scooting to take his place at Jomo's side. Behind them the longhouse emptied of pitbucks. Twenty-one black and shining bodies arranged themselves on the hard-baked clay, expressionless faces masking whatever emotion each might feel as he watched his comrades prepare to leave, perhaps never to return.

Rafe's eyes locked with Jomo's. Though neither could

read the other's thoughts with any precision, each recognized the lean and savage anger, the all-consuming hate of world and time and place. Rafe wondered if perhaps Jomo, too, had sat with Old Chulem, had listened to the conjure man's warning and acknowledged the aura of atavistic fear in the old man's words. Perhaps Jomo, too, tasted the premonition of death beyond the usual. Rafe wanted to apologize, somehow, tell Jomo they were fools to no longer be N'gata, fools not to be brothers and stand together to fight the hate as one, at least until that final terrible fight brought them together as foes. But the light in Jomo's eyes forbade such words, and Rafe was always one of silence.

"Weapons," Butkis growled.

Jomo stepped forward and passed his axe handle first to the overseer. Brutus and Tater cast a questioning glance at Rafe. "You get 'em back," he reassured them. "Pitbucks not allowed to carry no weapon through a crowd." The two followed Jomo's lead and gave up their machetes.

"All right. Let's go." Butkis took a last look at the pitbucks near the longhouse. "Don't want no shit from y'all," he said, then turned and led the way through the gate. Once out the door, the procession took on the aspects of a somber parade. Butkis, cutlass shining in the noonday sun, swaggered in the lead. Rafe, head high and steady, strode with an easy animal gait. Jomo walked alone, swinging his arms, savoring the welcome tension as it built to where he knew it would sustain him. Brutus and Tater, side by side, walked behind Jomo, Brutus cockily, Tater stiffly, wiping his hands from time to time on his loincloth and wanting desperately to take a pee. Behind them all strode Milo and Decater, muskets cocked.

The path was worn deep by many such processions, worn like a wagon rut where it rounded a brief hillock covered with peach trees. Rafe walked toward the trees as for the first time. Never before had he chosen to watch another man fight, for he feared seeing too much. He cared not for long-range analysis and planning. Such knowledge led to complacency and one's own death. Better was the instant appraisal, the decision based on in-

126

stinct and training, the action growing out of the moment at hand. Over forty times he had passed this way, and for the first time he felt fear and a nameless dread stalking him from behind. The fear surprised him and he questioned its presence, for he was in no danger. And then he understood. When he walked to fight, the sure awareness of his own ability accompanied and comforted him. Death was always ahead, true, but he would have a word in its manner and so did not fear. Rather, his senses were heightened, sharpened in appreciation. The air. The trees. The song of birds. And especially the sweet summer smell of peaches.

Odd, fear washing over him now. Always before fear walked with him back from the pit. At those times he never noticed his surroundings, only the heat, the dust and his own conflicting turmoil. With death behind him, the miracle of his own life filled him with awe and left him quaking.

The peaches reminded him, jarred him back to reality. They would see the crowd when they rounded the hillock. He glanced back. Jomo was Jomo, tension-sprung for the fight ahead. Like a good fighter, Rafe thought, his mind was empty of anticipation and apprehension. Brutus was too cocksure, too eager. He could be dangerous if Jomo mistakenly decided to depend on him too fully. Tater was in bad shape. His eyes already wide, he stumbled, caught himself, wiped the sweat from his face. If only he stayed close to Jomo, caught his strength. . . .

They could see the crowd now, clustered around the top of the small hill, an empty ring of people around an empty hole in the ground. A hole in the ground. . . . Where every man ended up sooner or later.

Crissa clenched and unclenched her fists, uncomfortably aware of the buzz of humanity around her, the smell of too many bodies too long in the sun. A feeling of nausea crept into the pit of her stomach and refused to be dislodged. To her right, Micara half dozed in the heat, woke from time to time to look about and smile vacantly at some half-seen, half-remembered face. Ezra sat in a large wicker chair to her left. She could feel his presence

127

boxing her in. Her spine ached with tension and she wished Steve were there to act as a buffer between her and Ezra, but he was inexplicably missing.

Suddenly a hush fell over the crowd. She couldn't see over their heads, only knew something must be happening. Across from her a cleared space of some two or three yards was roped off. She looked there, not knowing what to expect.

Butkis, heavily armed, appeared first, followed by a giant Negro walking arrogantly, a slave aloof from his masters. He was familiar, she thought, but couldn't place him. And then three more, followed by two guards with guns. Her chest tightened. Why slaves? Perhaps she had been wrong about the animal baiting. A friend had taken her to see a fisticuff exhibition back in Boston. She had thought it senseless but at least no one was seriously hurt. Was this to be more of the same? She had suspected, expected, something more cruel from Ezra. She looked sideways at him, caught a glimpse of his smug, knowing smile and quickly turned forward again. Micara squeezed her arm and Crissa responded to the pressure, patting her mother's hand. Micara was staring across the pit. Crissa followed her gaze to the giant Negro and she studied him again. He faced her now, stood at the edge of the open hole and looked across, first at Ezra, then at her. Suddenly her breath caught in her throat. She recognized him! Rafe, the boy who'd come to Freedom with Ezra. A gentle, quiet boy, well-spoken, well-educated, for a slave. Why, he was even able to read. She had talked with him a time or two until he became withdrawn and took pains to avoid her. She looked away, ashamed of her presence. Micara did not look away. She studied every bold line of his naked torso and thick, strong legs.

Butkis nudged him and Rafe absentmindedly stepped aside, entranced by the beauty of the girl who had changed and become a woman. He had not changed, he thought bitterly. A slave when first he saw her, he was yet a slave. Just another one of Ezra Clayton's niggers. Worse. A pitbuck. A killer of men. He had no right to feel the ache stirring his soul and coursing through his body.

128

The end of a rope flicked his arm and he jerked his head as Butkis shoved a coil in his direction. "Hold one end a' this an' lower them niggers into the pit," he said brusquely. "Seein' as you're here, you might as well be of use."

Rafe grabbed the rope, held one end and threw the coil into the pit. The crowd around him started buzzing again, trying to figure out what the contest would be. Butkis slapped Brutus on the shoulder and the older man confidently grabbed the rope and, while Rafe braced himself, slid down hand over hand to the clay floor. Tater was next. He moved in front of Rafe and wiped his palms on the loincloth once again. His eyes were bugged and his breath shallow. "Easy, boy," Rafe murmured. "Keep close to Jomo." There was time for no more. Tater nodded stiffly to Rafe and dropped over the lip, lost his grip and slid to the clay floor, much to the amusement of the crowd. Tater scrambled to his feet and grimaced as the pain from the rope burned into his consciousness.

"Dumb ass," Butkis shouted down. The crowd laughed uproariously.

Jomo scorned the rope. He held out his hand to Butkis, who handed him the axe. The pitbuck stood at the edge of the pit, tossed the axe in and leaped in after it. He hit the clay lightly, and to a roar of appreciation from the crowd, rolled lightly and came up in dead center of the pit, weapon in hand and held high overhead. Brutus and Tater grinned weakly and looked inquisitively at each other, then up to Butkis when he yelled at them and tossed down the two machetes. Both men retrieved their weapons and went to stand by Jomo. The crowd roared its approval, signalling its readiness for action. Three against something. It was going to be a hell of a fight.

Crissa went pale at the sight of the weapons. The men were meant to kill, perhaps each other. She searched the crowd for Steve, who was still nowhere to be seen, then for anyone who might stop what she suddenly feared would follow. Half rising, she felt a hand on her left wrist, the fingers clamping viselike. Speechless with horror, she sank back weakly in her seat, staring at the little beads of sweat popping up around each hair on the clawed hand restraining her. Ezra's hand.

"Who we fightin'?" Brutus muttered, watching Jomo and then Tater for any threatening move.

One of the onlookers, a trapper, shouted, "What in hell we bettin' on, Ezra? Three niggers ain't nuffin' special. Hell, I ken see niggers fight one t'other in Nachitoches any ol' time. Don't need to travel no forty mile, even if'n yore rum is a sight betta' than most." The trapper sent a dark brown stream of tobacco juice down into the pit while his rum-drunk cohorts echoed his remarks.

Other members of the crowd took up the question, threw it back and forth.

'What the hell, Ezra?"

"C'mon, Mistah Clayton, what they gonna *do?*"

"Five dollahs says it's Injuns, right Mistah Clayton?"

Ezra merely smiled enigmatically, then raised a hand to quiet the commotion. All eyes watched as he waved a languid finger to Martinson who leaned over and listened as the master of Freedom spoke in his ear, then turned and made his way through the crowd.

The grumbling grew as men full of rum and standing in the noonday heat grew restless. Suddenly a new sound was heard and quickly overrode the murmuring crowd. Because he was waiting, expecting something, Rafe heard it first. The snarling of a beast—of several beasts. Jomo, Tater and Brutus could hear nothing yet, nor would they until nearly too late, for by now the hushed word had run around the packed spectators and set them to buzzing again, started them excitedly exchanging bets made up on the moment.

Rafe shielded his eyes, squinting them to see. A line of field hands wound their way through the roped-off section and made their way to the edge of the pit. The slaves bore five wooden cages, carrying them on poles run through the bars. Rafe caught only a flashing glimpse of reddish-brown fur. It was enough. Wolves. His blood ran to ice.

The cages were brought to the lip of the pit, set side by side, the front doors hanging a few inches out into space.

Ropes were hooked to the latch pins and passed back to Milo who would, unseen, yank them simultaneously and loose the animals inside.

Below, Jomo backed away from the center, shouting for Tater and Brutus to join him at the wall. Brutus, closer to the cages than Tater, scampered to obey, cuffing Tater as he passed him. Tater, frozen, didn't bat an eye when struck. Terrorized, he stared up at the cages as the machete fell from his hand and a thin line of drool started to run down his chin.

"Pick up yo' knife!" Jomo called to him. "Pick it up an' git ober here wid us, Tater. Them's wolves. We gotta fight 'em togedder o' we ain't never leavin' dis place alive." Tater's back was to him and he couldn't see the blank look on the youth's face. Nor did he try. Jomo kept his eyes glued to the cages, watching the pins for the slightest hint of motion.

"Ah ken fight men. Ah ain't afeared o' no man," Brutus repeated over and over again.

"Them ain't men. We goana hab ta' watch out fo' each oder. Careful o' yo' blade. Slash 'em, 'cause it liable ta' git caught if'n yo' stabs," Jomo instructed quickly. "Kill one an' git free afore de nex' one come asnappin' at yo'. Tater!"

Tater didn't move. "Tater!" Jomo didn't dare go to him lest he be trapped in the middle of the ring with five wolves falling around him.

"What de hell matta' wid dat no good Tater?" Brutus asked.

"Froze up. Wild beast do it ta' some folk. Git so's dey cain't move." He worked his shoulders, loosening the tense muscles, readying them for the work that would follow.

Fang! Old Chulem had said fang. Rafe searched the faces of those around the ring. Only in Crissa's did he find pity, and that rapidly becoming masked by shock.

"Gonna see sumpin' now," Butkis said from his side. "Ya' can thank yo' heathen gods yo' ain't down there, nigger." Butkis laughed deeply.

"Ain't right," Rafe answered, barely able to keep his

131

voice under control. "Tain't right a'tall. Brutus and Tater, shit, that's like sendin' Jomo down there alone. Against wolves."

"Mistah Clayton jes' wanna see what his stock is done made up of. There they go. This is gonna be sumpin'!"

Ezra raised his hand, held it a moment, then waved. Behind the cages and out of sight of those below, Milo jerked the ropes and pulled the pegs from the latches. The spring-loaded doors popped open, traps slid back and the wolves leaped and tumbled to the pit floor, sending the crowd into a screaming frenzy. Lean, hungry and thoroughly vicious after two weeks of mistreatment and near starvation, the five wolves, four bitches and a hoary old male, landed in a tangled, snarling heap.

The animals, each over eighty pounds of lithe, primitive canine fury, snapped and growled at each other a moment until their pack instinct took over. They began to circle their prey and an expectant hush fell over the crowd. It was a moment before anyone recognized the keening wail.

Tater was crying. And then he urinated, the warm fluid soiling his loincloth and running down his leg to puddle on the hard clay floor. Someone above called attention to the frightened boy and soon everyone was laughing.

"Hey, pickaninny, that yore weapon? Gonna pee on them wolves?"

"Might work at that. Stinks from here!"

Three of the wolves skulked toward Jomo and Brutus. The other two focused on Tater. "Pick up yo' blade, dammit, boy!" Rafe shouted. "Pick up yo' knife." He shut up as he felt the muzzle of the musket prod him from the rear.

"Keep yo' mouth shut, nigger," Milo said.

The scream started deep in Tater's chest. It welled up in his throat and spilled forth in a long, drawn-out wail of abject terror, set to the laughter of the spectators. Jomo stepped toward the boy but was forced back as one of the three wolves darted toward him and Brutus. Tater had separated himself and he was on his own. Jomo concentrated on his own problems.

The boy, against all logic, suddenly became aware of

the wetness. He tore away the waste-soaked loincloth and stared down at the erection fear had given him.

"Look at the pecker on that young 'un, will ya'?" someone shouted.

"That's the spirit. They she-wolves anyway. You got 'em on the run!"

One of the prostitutes from town leaned over the edge and catcalled, "How come yo' never showed me that youngster 'til now? Woooo-eeee!"

"You done it now. Broke mah mule's heart!"

And another voice, lost in the din of bets made and changed, raucous laughter and jibes. "Somebody stop this. Oh, God . . . somebody . . . somebody stop this. . . ."

Crissa tearfully continued pounding at the hand clenching her wrist, holding her immobile.

The first wolf struck high. Tater feebly attempted to protect himself. The animal's snout slammed against his cheek, one fang catching the flesh and tearing it open, ripping away a bloody flap of skin. The impact knocked him off his feet and spun him out of the center of the pit where the second animal waited. Jomo once again attempted to reach the youngster, but because Brutus wouldn't follow, was forced to keep the remaining three at bay, swiping with his axe at one and then the other.

Tater kicked high as the second wolf leaped. His foot slipped along the sleek bristling fur as the animal lunged inside the youth's attempt to ward him off. The wolf was a hunter and knew where to strike. The yellow fangs aimed for the stomach, missed as Tater arched to get out of the way and tore deep into the boy's groin. Tater's mouth opened, but there was no scream left. Pain blotted out all ability. His legs kicked at the ravaging beast that continued to tear at his genitals. His right hand groped for the machete and found it, but the first wolf found his arm at the same time. Fangs closed on his wrist and the machete skittered away uselessly. No one heard the bone snap.

The scent of the fresh kill aroused the other wolves to a blood fury and they closed in. Tater, barely alive, was dragged across the clay floor by the crazed beasts. Jomo, free now, screamed for Brutus to follow and ran to Tater.

He knocked aside one animal, kicked a second squarely in the side. The wolves jumped away as Jomo attacked. Four made it out of range of the deadly axe. The fifth jumped a trifle more slowly, reluctant to leave the soft, easy meat. The axe clove its skull, spilling the living matter on the floor of the pit to mingle with Tater's blood. Jomo freed the blade with a quick twist and turned briefly to check on Brutus. He was alone!

A slinking form behind him caught his eye and he tried to turn toward it, tripped instead on Tater's outstretched arm as the leader, the male, returned to the attack. Desperately trying to regain his balance, Jomo slipped on the blood-soaked clay and the wolf's fangs snapped, tearing his shoulder. He rolled backward, throwing the animal off before it could sink the fangs for a hanging grip, sprang to his feet and slapped aside a second beast with the flat of the axe. For a brief second he was free and managed to stoop and grab the machete. Tater twitched from time to time, a great bloody cavity where his lower vitals had been.

Brutus, berserk with fear, flailed wildly about with his machete. A streaking red-brown form flashed upward past his guard, slamming him against the wall. As fangs sank into Brutus' chest, animal and man fell to the ground. Brutus dropped the machete and began to pummel the wolf with his fists, rolling over and over until the two became a black and tawny blur on the clay floor. With a final supreme effort, Brutus loosed the wolf's vicious grasp by tearing off one of the animal's ears. The beast howled and snapped at his arm, but the black man kicked free and staggered to his feet, blood spurting from his lower neck and covering his chest in a gory, crimson bib.

The other wolves, excited by the prospects of a second kill, joined the attack on the now helpless black. Only the giant old male stayed to snap at and worry the threatened Jomo. Brutus lurched crazily toward his machete, the screams of the crowd a ringing, blurred roar in his ears. A flashing form knocked him sprawling. Bone-crushing jaws closed on his ankle, snapping the bone and nearly tearing the foot from his leg. He saw the next wolf too late, was unaware before fangs raked his face. He punched them away, his fists flailing blindly as the beast at his ankle started to drag him through his own blood across the pit.

Then cruel, gleaming jaws darted inside the wildly thrashing fists. The one-eared she-wolf closed on his throat, striking like a shark, her muzzle sinking deeply in the hard muscles, turning red and matted with his fluids. And still he continued to brawl, arms moving slower now as some machine winding down, even as the yellow-fanged canines tore through muscle and veins. Finally there was not enough blood left to sustain his life and Brutus' arms sagged lifeless to the clay. His fists, gnarled and misshapen from a life of brawling and harsh labor, slowly unclenched, finally empty of anger. When the she-wolf finally let go, his head hung back crazily on a thread of flesh.

Bets were won. The second to go down. Three-to-one said the nigger with the axe stayed the longest. Three-to-one won. And then the bets on how long he would last. One man, one nigger, against the four crazed wolves. Rum was forgotten. Two eagles said he'd kill two before the others got him. One gold eagle against ten said he'd kill them all. Five planters took twenty dollars each of the confident hundred wagered by another that the old male would be the one to take him. . . .

Jomo stood alone, besieged. The wolves were more careful, now, closing in steadily from all sides, hunting slowly and purposefully. One got too close, grabbed the axe blade and almost succeeded in dragging the weapon from Jomo's sweaty grasp. Jomo drove the point of the machete into the knotted muscle of the bitch's shoulder and with a yelp she let go and darted away, snapping angrily at the wound. The others ignored her, walked stiff-legged toward their prey. Jomo shrugged the wounded shoulder and, his back to the wall, moved to his right, slowly circling the pit, never allowing them to center on him, coldly waiting for the moment to take them one by one.

Rafe watched on helplessly as Jomo circled, passing directly beneath him. Even as he watched and analyzed, the cold thought echoed through his mind over and over.

Ezra sent them to die. They weren't ready. The thought built its own rhythm, pounded in time with his blood. Around him the spectators were near frantic with the spectacle. Even Crissa? He dared a glance. No. He searched the onlookers. The girl was gone. At his side, Butkis began to mimic a wolf howl. Some of the others took up the crazy sound, howling in glee. The pack was closing in. The leader broke off from the others and came around to intercept Jomo's path, cutting him off. The bitches came in from three sides. Big, husky brutes, darting forward and back, forward and out again, barely outside the range of the blood-stained blades.

Butkis was beside himself with amusement. He sent a stream of spittle off to the side, twisting his body to accept a clay jug of home brew from a nearby trapper. The brass hilt of his cutlass gleamed in the sun. A hand, burnt dark from the sun of two continents, swept down to cover it. . . .

The she-wolf snapped at his left and Jomo clubbed her with the flat of his axe, spun and hacked a chunk of meat from her companion in front of him. The machete blade glanced off bone and bit into the clay floor. There wasn't time to bring it up. Jomo tugged, the sweat streaming from his face. He could see the third bitch coming for him, could do little more than hold out the axe and hopefully fend her off. But if the leader attacked with her. . . . He turned, eyes gleaming.

Then a scream, a terrible warrior's howl, and a black form hurtled from the air above. The male leaped back. The bitch was not so swift. Rafe landed on her, knocking her to one side, the full force of his weight behind the cutlass skewering the animal and driving the blade deep into the clay, pinning the writhing beast to the pit floor.

Ezra came to his feet, his drink spilling to the side, his face registering total surprise. Butkis groped at his belt, unable to accept the fact Rafe had taken his cutlass.

The male rushed Rafe even as the giant rose to his feet. He caught the animal in midair by one paw and fell back, snapping his powerful wrists as he dropped. Howling with surprise and pain, broken leg hanging limp, the startled

136

wolf slammed into the far wall and fell to the ground. Jomo reacted quickly, a huge grin on his face and a jubilant battle cry in his throat. He shouted Rafe's name, jerked the machete free of the sticky clay and tossed it to him. Whirling to knock aside the she-wolf, he leaped close to the giant pitbuck. The two, tall and short, stood back to back in the center of the pit.

"What yo' doin' down here, nigger?" Jomo managed between gasps.

"Don't know, N'gata," was all Rafe could say. "Don't know. Just here is all." There was time for no more, only the exhilaration of battle.

The wolves attacked. They regrouped and came in low and snarling, darting past the blades only to be driven back by a well placed kick or two. They fell back and began circling. Rafe and Jomo waited patiently, breathing deeply and biding their time, two old hands resting and gathering their strength.

Above them Butkis grabbed a pistol and aimed at Rafe. He glanced across the yawning mouth of the pit. Ezra's eyes bore into him and the lord of Freedom shook his head, "No." Butkis swore to himself, swore to repay the nigger below for taking his cutlass. No nigger ever. . . .

And finally the wolves closed in, sprung to the attack. Jomo and Rafe lunged as one at the old she-wolf. The beast, unable to halt her momentum, dove into the whirling steel trap set by her intended prey. The machete sheared away one front leg as she passed Rafe, and Jomo's axe broke her back a second later. Red fur and black skin, yellow fangs and biting blades. Rafe ducked beneath the old male as he sprang awkwardly to help his dying mate. The machete sliced the red, furry belly and the wolf crumpled to the ground, walking on his own entrails. At the same instant Jomo's axe caught the last wolf in the neck. Their dying howls rose to fill the pit, then stopped simultaneously as the two black warriors ended their pain with fiercely driven killing blows.

The only sound left was the thin whine of the skewered female, still alive and pinned to the clay floor. Rafe went to her side. The wild eyes glared up at him, full of animal

137

hatred. The giant black raised the machete slowly, brought it down swiftly.

Suddenly, it was very, very quiet.

9

The final strains of the fiddle played out. The last dancers stood about wearily, recalled high points of the weekend, climbed into carriages and calèches and made their way into the dusk. Crissa sat in her room, well away from the window, half listening to the retreating, slim threads of sound. Little remained of the candle she so ardently watched. Soon the flame would sputter and fail and the room would return once again to darkness. She had forgotten to bolt the door and regretted the omission when it opened to admit Captain Bennett.

"Crissa?" Steve called softly.

"I'm here." He closed the door, walked to her. "Where were you?" she asked dully.

"Tapper Solomon came across fresh sign. Atakapan. Early this morning. Maybe a hunting party, maybe a raiding party, maybe just snooping around. I went out to look and see if I could figure out what they were up to."

"Why didn't you tell me?"

"There wasn't time. Besides, you were asleep."

"No. I mean the pit. Why didn't you tell me about the pit?"

Steve sighed, crossed and sat with his back against the

139

window. "I didn't think you'd understand. And after seeing you with that ol' nigger in New Orleans. . . ."

"You are so right. I do not understand. Men butchered for sport? You call that entertainment? The very idea is disgusting, nauseating. Even my own mother was there to watch."

"This isn't Boston, Crissa. Oh, I'm not in favor of it myself, but they *are* only darkies. Some even manage to win their freedom. Even the niggers figure it's worth the chance. And if they weren't fighting in the pit they'd be cutting up each other and causing Lord knows how much trouble among the peaceful darkies. Those pitbucks are criminals and troublemakers."

"Rafe was no criminal."

"Who?"

"I recognized him. He came here with Ezra five years ago. An intelligent, sensitive young man."

Steve rose abruptly, stepped close to her. "Rafe," he said disgustedly, "is the worst of the lot. Worse than any of those they killed in the insurrection in Saint Charles Parish. He's killed over forty niggers, two or three white men and some Indians to boot. He hacked them to death with a machete. And you talk of him as if you were childhood. . . ."

"Stop it. Please leave. Go on back to . . . wherever you're going."

"This is Louisiana, Crissa. It's frontier. Your Boston-learned code of ethics and morals is meaningless out here. You should know that."

Crissa did not answer. Steve stared at her a moment more, then shrugged in a helpless gesture of resignation. He turned at the door, sudden anger rising to spite her childishness. "By the way. They'll be whipping your old friend. The sensitive, intelligent one."

Crissa spun in her chair. "Why?"

"He broke up the match. Jumped in and helped one of the other niggers fight off the dogs. Bets had to be called off. A lot of upset people."

Crissa was out of her chair and pushing past him through the door before he finished. The house held only a few revelers. Most had left for home and the few left inside were women waiting for their men who had gone outside for the whipping. Crissa rushed through the hall and stormed onto the front gallery to find the front yard empty. She ran to the end of the gallery where she could see a crowd gathered behind the line of trees separating house from compound. Several torches illuminated the rapidly gathering darkness. She caught her breath and ran off the porch, hurried toward the circle of burning brands.

The crowd of men gave way before Crissa's frantic importunings. Inside the circle she saw Ezra standing with hands behind his back, his toadlike body held primly erect. In front of him stood Butkis, a cruel cat o' nine tails gripped in his swarthy fist. Towering over the guard's none too slight bulk stood Rafe, his back naked and glistening in the flickering light.

"This is gonna pleasure me, nigger," Butkis snarled. "Oughta have a bullet through ya' for touchin' my cutlass. Yore lucky Mistah Clayton don't see it that way. Now I'm gonna make ya' feel not so lucky."

"Stop it!"

Butkis halted his swing, turning to stare in the direction of the voice. Rafe looked over his shoulder, as surprised as anyone.

"There is no call for this," Crissa said. "He risked his life to save a friend. He shouldn't be punished." She realized with a sinking heart how weak, how ineffectual her entreaty must sound when she heard a muffled laugh behind her, followed by a barely concealed snicker.

Ezra's eyes probed the small circle of men, silenced them. He turned his back on Crissa and spoke without looking at her. "We are all impressed with your gracious plea, Miss Fitzman. Mercy even when misplaced is ever befitting a young lady. Rafe knew the law when he interfered. He knew the punishment. Thus he is not tied, but stands here of his own volition. He expects ten lashes—a moderate price and one he knew only too well.

"Many of our friends here have been put out. They placed bets which had to be cancelled. Money was surely lost. It is only befitting the nigger responsible be punished. I could have him shot for what he did to Butkis. However, I can afford to be lenient. If you wish to stay, you are free to do so. If not, I suggest you leave immediately. Proceed, Mr. Butkis."

Before Crissa could protest further, the whip rose and cracked down across the giant slave's back. The massive muscles bunched involuntarily in response but the man did not flinch. Crissa stared mesmerized as the cat fell away, revealing already red and swelling welts. The overseer's arm went back slowly, the forearm bulging. A moment of time stood still and Crissa could see only the fist clenched around the handle of the whip, the white knuckles standing out in the firelight.

Butkis swung again, putting his whole body into the cat. When it struck the Negro groaned in spite of himself, swayed forward slightly then straightened again. Crissa felt her back turn to fire and her stomach churn. She heard herself starting to cry, tasted the sweet, acid slipperiness in her throat. No one watched her, paid her the slightest attention. Nearly gagging, she fled through the ring of entranced, tight-lipped farmers, trappers, and townsmen and ran through the trees and up the path to the house. The steady, inexorable sound of the cat followed her, pushing her forward until she was safely inside, leaning against the kitchen door, panting for breath and holding her stomach lest she retch.

The slave girl Julie came out of the pantry. There were crumbs around the girl's mouth and she carried a partially eaten piece of cake. She stopped, stared at Crissa a moment, then curtsied briefly. "Miz Clayton gone ta bed, ma'am. She to'd me ta tell ya'."

Crissa steadied herself, took a deep breath. "Thank you, Julie." The black girl seemed anxious for her to leave. Crissa obliged, casting a quick glance over her shoulder at the door. The slave girl had set the cake down on the table and was proceeding to stuff bits and pieces of it in her mouth.

Much of the house was dark but the hall was dimly illuminated by a light from Ezra's library. She halted momentarily, feeling utterly weary. If Steve was in the library she didn't want to see him, didn't feel up to another scene with him. Ezra's corruption had touched even the young man she once . . . loved? It was hard to tell. What did a sixteen-year-old girl know of love? She went quietly up the stairway into the dark.

A few minutes later and she lay in bed trying to relax, trying to loosen the bunched muscles so she could sleep. By now they had surely finished with Rafe. She tried to remember the sensitive, intelligent young man she had known, comparing him to the muscled, grim-visaged giant in the circle of burning torches. The contrast bordered on the unbelievable—a killer, Steve had said, a man trained to one purpose—death. She had heard those killing screams, seen the flashing blades at work. More than forty men, Steve had said. Incomprehensible. . . . But the pit was there, blood-soaked, gaping. The pit. . . . Rafe. . . . She huddled alone in the dark room, surrounded by the memories of the dreadful day. Poor Rafe. . . . Poor Freedom. . . . She dreamed of blood.

Ezra watched Rafe disappear into the shadowy darkness of the compound, walking under his own power. And after standing up to the cat. But then somehow Ezra knew he would. Rafe would unflinchingly withstand his punishment and walk away from the whipping just to spite them all. No. Not them all. Just Ezra, the man who had never owned him, never would own him. When the gate slammed to, he waved Butkis away, sent the shay on empty. He would walk.

The night was clear. A slight breeze from the east cooled the air and kept the mosquitoes back at the river where they belonged. The ghostlike figure pondered the future. There weren't too many fights left for Rafe. Only seven? No more. Ezra knew in his soul the black man would come back across the river if he ever got free. Come back and kill the white man he must hate. There would be little to stop him, for freedom was the only weapon he lacked. With freedom, he would be more powerful than ever. The sound of an alligator booming in the distant swamp gave him pause. They too had been hunted and killed, forced to live in the deeps of the swamps. He saw he was wrong. Rafe would not come back for revenge any more than would alligators seek revenge. He would simply ignore Ezra, for when all was said and done, Rafe did not fear the white man. Did not fear him at all.

A cold anger seeped over Ezra, an anger swollen with hate for the black man. Rafe was too big, too strong, too confident of his own physical ability. The display that afternoon was indicative of how Rafe thought. He entered the pit not through fear but in exhilaration. Very well, then. He must be taught fear, the white man thought coldly. Every fight from now on would be calculated to break him down bit by bit. He would win three or four more times, but each would take something more out of him, each take him one step closer to destruction. Stripped of impunity, forced to stand in naked isolation in the face of ever more fearful odds, the reality of his own vulnerability would begin to erode his prowess. Then it would be time to arrange a situation, a fight Rafe could not possibly win. And he would know fear, and die.

"You got a moment, Mistah Clayton?" Ezra scrutinized the man who materialized out of the shadows. Duggins, the dirt farmer who aspired to greater things. A troublemaker bent on posing difficulties for the lord of Freedom.

"Walk with me back to the house, Claude. We can talk."

Duggins glanced back into the shadows and was instantly joined by three others, one of whom held a torch, who fell in stride behind him. "Well," Duggins started, "ol' Charley Statton here has been . . . uh . . . complainin' to our little association. It seems you've laid claim to his bottom land jus' south of where your boundary used ta be."

"That's because it's my land, Claude."

"He don't think so. Charley's been workin' that land for nigh on six years. The Fitzman line is back a quarter-mile from where you moved it."

Ezra's face clouded menacingly at the mention of Fitzman's name. It had been coming up far too frequently recently. He stopped. Duggins took a step past him before stopping, then turned back. The three farmers who had been following collided with each other, caught off guard by Ezra's abrupt halt. "The land in question is Freedom property," Ezra said coldly. "Fitzman was a fool. The original survey established the acreage as his but he allowed some ninny of a dirt farmer tillage. So Statton moved in and decided the land was his. Well, not according to the documents in Nachitoches and in the state land office. Statton is squatting on Freedom land and he'd best remove himself. I'll not discuss it farther."

"T'ain't right, Mistah Clayton," Statton said from behind him.

Ezra ignored him. "You tell him again for me, Duggins. Off he goes. The only thing I'll talk to you about is Beaumarchant. I made you an offer awhile back. You interested or not?"

"I cain't sell no white man, Mistah Clayton. Not even a fella the way Beau is, all mussed up. Beau saved my hide durin' the battle down at New Orleans. I ain't puttin' him in with niggers."

"If he's so mussed up, as you put it, he won't know the difference."

"I would. Wouldn't be right."

"Well then, how about you keeping him and me fightin' him for you?"

"No."

"I'd start him out on one of my young ones if you're afraid he couldn't fight one of the good ones."

"I ain't doin' it, Mistah Clayton. I owe him. He's my friend."

"And too good for killin' niggers," Ezra said scornfully. "Well, if he isn't strong enough to kill a nigger, I guess I don't want him anyways."

"I didn't say that."

Ezra stopped. "What did you say then, Duggins?"

"I said I wouldn't sell him," he answered, his voice tinged with ugliness.

Ezra turned back, a little smile on his face. He looked from one man to the other, focused on Duggins. The smile disappeared. "Tell Statton I want him off. Now. I'll have my men down there to see he's gone, come next Monday. Now get out of here."

Duggins stood stock still, stopped his companions with

a gesture. His shoulders hunched dangerously, eyes glittered with a meanness Ezra hadn't seen before. "You may be a pretty big man in these parts, Clayton, but you got no call to talk that way. This is your place, so we'll go, but I want you to know somethin' first. You ain't that big. You send your men down there Monday next an' the rest of us'll be there waitin'.'."

No man spoke to him so menacingly. Ezra bristled. "There aren't enough of you, Duggins. Don't be a fool."

"I ain't. Charley's my friend. So are the others."

"I won't give up on this, Duggins. You know that."

They stared at each other in the flickering light. Duggins turned first. "We'll see your men Monday, Clayton. You tell 'em to be ready for bear."

The man with the torch stopped Duggins, whispered rapidly in his ear. Ezra strained to listen, could hear no more than isolated, meaningless syllables. Duggins took the torch, walked back to Ezra. "Charley's got an idea, Clayton. You wanna hear it?"

Ezra didn't move, didn't speak.

"He says, why don't we save a lot of trouble? If it comes to shootin' we're gonna have the troops from Jessup down here before you can say jack spit. That ain't gonna do nobody no good. We got a man, you got a man. 'Stead of all of us fightin'—an' even if you don't come along we'll find you—why not jus' them two. Beaumarchant 'gainst Rafe."

"No."

"Rafe wins, you got Charley's land an' mine, too. Beau wins, Charley gets his land back free an' clear an' you pass title to ever' thing south of Littlejohn Creek to me."

"No bet. I have the land Charley's on already, and I'll have yours soon enough."

"That's somethin' you ain't sure of. This way's quick an' easy. Your place'll be a quarter bigger, jus' from one fight."

"I'm not interested," Ezra barked, turning.

"You afraid, Mistah Clayton?" The words were spoken softly but cut into Ezra's back the way the cat had into Rafe's. He stopped, anger rising in him.

"Ezra Clayton don't have a nigger what can whup a man with half his head shot away? A man what can't even talk?"

Ezra's fists clenched, unclenched. "Won't work, Duggins. . . ."

"You're man enough to steal from a woman an' a girl, but not bet with a man? 'Pears to me you ain't much, Clayton, lessen you're a thief."

He turned, face white, anger half choking him. "You're on," he said hoarsely. "Four weeks from today, when Rafe's back is healed. When he wins, you get ready to get the hell out of Louisiana fast, or you won't have more than three hours to live."

Duggins grinned. "Ain't no way your nigger can win. I jus' got me a plantation as big as yours, Clayton." The farmer nodded a brief farewell and left, leaving Ezra standing alone in the dark. And only when they were far enough away did the three farmers gather around Duggins and discuss the terms of the wager.

The anger subsided and Ezra was left more than a little worried. Duggins had suckered him into a bet and now he had to calm down and think it out. Rafe against the Cajun. If Rafe won, the land would become part of Freedom. He'd be rid of Duggins for good and Rafe would be torn up bad enough to start putting the fear in him. He'd still be good for three or four more fights, still be good enough to win enough to remain worthwhile, yet softened up considerably and easier prey for the last two fights. There was much to gain.

But there was much to lose, too. If Beaumarchant should win, and he well could, for he was a monster, Ezra's problem with Rafe would be dealt with, to be sure, but not the way he wanted. The fight could be very, very expensive, for Duggins would win far more than Ezra was prepared to pay. There had to be some way out, some way to ensure Duggins would never take even one square foot of Freedom land, bet or no. Ezra regretted his loss of temper. That Duggins should force him to make a mistake was unforgivable. He would pay dearly, one way or other. There were ways, and there were four weeks in which to find the ways. Ezra Clayton smiled faintly to himself, started back to the house. A confident man always won. He would win.

The mansion was dark. The guests were all gone and Freedom was quiet, sunk in sleep and exhaustion. Ezra wearily climbed the steps to the gallery and stood watching the night. A good weekend, all told. Exciting. And Julie would be waiting. She would be good to ride tonight, especially after the day's events. A pity about Crissa. Now there was a pleasant bit worth the effort. Though time was out of joint for the nonce, there would come the day when Crissa Elizabeth Fitzman would bare her body willingly. She'd give in, all right. The episode at the pit would have gone a long way toward breaking her down. A few more and she'd be ripe. He'd seen them before. Virtuous, untouchable, until the blood lust hit them and they pleaded for it, pleaded to be mounted and ridden like the animals they were. The little fool . . . to plead in that bush nigger's behalf. Now there was a tale to be tattled about. He owed her for that, too. . . .

A dull glow issued from the library. He entered the book-lined room. The lamp was on his desk and he'd not left it there. Someone had moved it. Suddenly very tense, Ezra crossed to a shelf, removed a large book and took a loaded and primed pistol from a niche in the wall. Warily, he crossed to his desk. A folded and wax sealed note had been addressed to him and placed on top of the desk. "Ezra" was written in elegant penmanship across the front and his face drained as he recognized the handwriting. He tore the seal away, ripped open the envelope and pulled the paper out to read . . . nothing. A blank page.

"A lovely party, Ezra."

Ezra spun about, taken completely unaware. A raffishly handsome man stood in the door, a brace of pistols in his hands. Ezra's own gun rested on the desktop, for the moment out of reach. "Why Patrick, what a surprise."

"And a far from pleasant one, I'll warrant."

"Come in, come in," Ezra answered heartily, his mind whirling. "Close the door."

Patrick Fitzman stepped into the room. "Wouldn't want any sudden visitors like Micara or Crissa? I should imagine not." Patrick crossed to the desk and confiscated Ezra's pistol before putting his own in his belt.

"I thought you were in Mexico."

"I was. With James Long. But I came back, as you see. I've located the place I want. The land is there for the taking and holding, but I'll need funds to hire and supply the men who are going with me."

Ezra poured two snifters of brandy, slid one across the desk to Patrick. He scowled at the mention of money.

"That's right, Ezra. That's why I'm here. The money you paid to fix those property claims and to transfer Crissa's inheritance is long gone. Carving an empire out of the wilderness requires capital from time to time."

"I have paid you all I intend to."

Patrick sipped the brandy. "This is very good brandy, Ezra." He looked around the room appreciatively. "You've done wonders with the place. I used to caution John about staying away so long. I was right. The place fell to ruin. But you, Ezra, have done a splendid job. I congratulate you." He raised his glass in a silent toast. "Of course, you had so much with which to start. Even so, I trust you will be so kind as to remember it was I who arranged for the transfer of the title, I who bent the law and saw to it you were able to acquire total and complete control."

"And it was you," Ezra interrupted, "whom I paid to disappear forever. Paid handsomely, too."

"Not so handsomely, and not enough."

"All you will get."

"No!" Patrick's hand slapped with a resounding bang on the desk. Both men stopped, listening for any telltale sounds indicating they had wakened the household. When none was forthcoming Patrick continued. "I have not come to beg, Ezra. You will give me that which I wish. I can make trouble for you and you know it. I'm certain Major Reynolds, among others, would be most interested in anything I might have to tell him."

"Don't be absurd. They'd put you away as well."

"You forget," Patrick laughed, "I know the law. Justice will be lenient should I choose to play the repentant. The courts would treat you more harshly. Robbing a poor innocent of her inheritance, scheming to confiscate the small farms in the area. . . ." He paused meaningfully, looked directly into Ezra's eyes. ". . . And of course, we shouldn't forget, spying for the British."

Ezra bolted upright in his chair.

"That's right," Patrick continued. "I spent a great deal of time in New Orleans. Met an interesting chap, a Major William Paxton, who . . . but that's another story. I doubt you're interested in the details, though Major Reynolds would find them, shall we say, fascinating? I will need three thousand dollars. In gold. A thousand each in quarter, half and full eagles."

"Impossible."

"They shoot spies, Ezra."

The lord of Freedom sagged back in his chair, his face sullenly registering defeat for the second time in as many hours. "I shall have to travel to Nachitoches."

"I thought perhaps. If you leave tomorrow morning you should be able to conclude your business Tuesday and be back Wednesday. Long and I have friends there. They will know if you get the gold, so please don't try to pull some stupid bluff. When you return, we shall meet again. I'm not anxious to tarry overly long."

"Where are you staying?"

"Really, Ezra. . . ."

"Then how shall I find you?"

"Midnight, Wednesday. In the pecan grove, near the rear atop the old Indian burial mound. Wear your white frock coat, bring the gold and come alone." He rose, thrust Ezra's pistol in his pocket. "And Ezra, please remember. Your white coat will make an excellent target. I have become an expert pistol shot." He stepped to the door, opened it to check the hall. "Kiss my dear sister-in-law for me," he muttered sarcastically, and was gone.

10

Milo spewed a stream of tobacco and saliva, wiped his mouth with the back of a broad hand and grimaced at the raw, bruised flesh on his knuckles. Boo stepped out of the barracks. His babyish good looks were spoiled by a puffy lip and a dark welt under his left eye. He avoided Milo and stepped off the porch, looking up at the main house. The tall gangling guard with the bruised fist stared at him. "How's yore eye, Boo?"

"Mah name's Booker. You'd best be callin' me that."

"I thought we settled that last night. Now the way I figger, I call you anything I want. Of course, if'n you want to go 'round again, I got me another hand I don't mind bruisin'."

"You boys troublin'?" Butkis gruffly inquired.

Milo stood as the overseer approached. "We just havin' ourselves a chat, me an' Boo."

Decater stepped onto the porch, followed by Martinson and several of the others. Martinson yawned expansively, raking his pudgy fingers through his hair. "Some party. Yesterday wasn't hardly enough to rest up. Real doin's, I call it."

"What would you know about real doin's, fatguts?"

Milo scoffed. "You ain't never gotten further than the food tables."

Martinson looked wounded. "I'll have you know . . . ."

"Sheeit," Milo continued. "The real partyin' takes place off in the bushes, don't it, Butkis?"

Several of the other guards guffawed knowingly. Butkis sneered and aimed a cuff at Milo who ducked away. Decater perked up. "You better be watchin' what you say about Mistah Butkis, Milo."

"Hell, you stubby scrawny-necked fart catcher, what d'you know? While you was drinkin' yo'self asleep, Mistah Butkis was gettin' it an' gettin' it good," Milo told him. "An' I was too. So was Pete, Rooster, Caje and Arvid. Even Boo dipped his wick."

Butkis sighed aloud, his right hand scratching vigorously at his privates. "That Miz Leahy, she jus' couldn't get enough. Guess the good Reverend ain't up to givin' her all she wants. She worked us 'til we was limp as bank notes. Never seen a woman take to it quite like she did, A'course, the rum helped. Still, she knew her tricks. That was prime stuff. But I give her a good reamin'. An' then some."

Martinson shook his head in disbelief. "The Reverend's new bride. What's the world comin' to?"

"She got a dark hole like all the rest of 'em, preacher's wife or no. Yessuh, she took to Mistah Butkis' cutlass quicker'n that nigger Rafe." Boo laughed, thrusting out his hips and grabbing his privates in an age-old gesture.

The ribald laughter ended abruptly. Butkis' face flushed crimson. Boo went pale realizing what he had inadvertently blurted out. The overseer whipped his sword from his belt. The point wavered to and fro, inches from Boo's throat. "Ain't nobody gonna touch mah cutlass again. Nobody. I got careless with that nigger an' you seen what he got. An' that ain't all. If'n that nigger win his freedom, I'm gonna be there waitin' fo' him across the Sabine. An' I'm gonna hack off his right hand 'cause it did the grabbin'. Then I'll take one o' his eyes an poke it out with the point o' this blade."

Boo shrank back as the blade skimmed barely inches away from his widened eyes. The point slowly dropped to his chest, lowered farther to touch his groin. "An' when that big nigger is howlin' like a pickaninny, I'll be slicin' his balls so's he won't never have him no little ones of his own to grow up an' lay a hand on one a' his betters. You understand me, Boo?"

Boo nodded. Beads of sweat coursed down his face to cover his puffed lips with a film of glistening sweat. Butkis replaced his sword and faced the guards. "We're short-handed again today, what with them Mistah Clayton done taken to Nachitoches. We only workin' the cotton today, jus' like yestiday, only maybe we split some off this afternoon to hoe some a' the corn. We'll keep 'em all in them two north fields where you roisters can keep a close watch on 'em. Now, jus' 'cause Mistah Clayton been gone a day, no need to ease off. He'll be back tomorrow an' sure enough want to know what ever'body been up to. Let's go." Butkis gestured toward the field workers' shanties and the guards fell into stride behind him.

"You sure are a stupid one, Boo," a guard muttered. Another dug scratching fingers into his crotch and angrily exclaimed, "I think Miz Leahy done give me the stick."

"You pissin' green?" his friend queried.

"Ain't pissin' at all."

"Who'd you dip after?"

"Boo. He went jus' afore me. Why?"

"Boo . . . ? Sheeit. You got the stick all right."

"Hey," a third guard called. "Lookie there. . . ."

"What?"

"Comin' from the house. Ooo-weee!" His companions followed his gaze.

"Nicest bit a' showblubber this side a' New Orleans," Milo offered. "I'd take her ahead of the Reverend's wife any day."

Crissa was walking toward the guards, hurrying to intercept them. Butkis failed to notice her until she was almost beside him. "Mr. Butkis," she called.

Butkis halted as did the men behind him. The burly overseer was obviously surprised at seeing the young woman so early in the morning. Crissa glanced at the faces staring at her, sensitive to the lascivious intent behind each moistened lip or scrutinizing appraisal. "Mr.

153

Butkis, many of the slaves worked all weekend for the party. They did not have their day off. They will not be going to the field today or tomorrow as a reward for working so long and well."

Butkis stood back, his hungry eyes exploring the lush figure pressing, straining at the cotton bodice, the tiny feminine waist above the sea of skirt and petticoats. "Is that so, missy?" he asked with a leer.

Crissa boldly returned his stare, countered with an air of haughty, authoritative arrogance. "I am Crissa Elizabeth Fitzman. The land upon which you are standing was my father's and is mine in partnership with my stepfather. For as long as you remain at Freedom you will not forget this. I am Miss Fitzman to you—" she glanced at the others "—to all of you. The slaves will not go to the fields today."

"Mistah Clayton won't be likin' this, missy . . . uh, Miss Fitzman. Them niggers, now, the way I see it, they're here to be workin' and workin' they'll be. We'll be on our way now to roust 'em out," he said, starting away from her.

Crissa planted herself firmly in his path. "You will do nothing of the kind. I have given you an order."

"I already got my orders, *Miss* Fitzman, an' I don't know nothin' about no partnership. The field hands got to chop that cotton."

"You have new orders. The slaves had no time off this weekend so will have this day off. And tomorrow as well. Had I thought of it, I would have given them Monday too. Should you choose to disobey me, I shall terminate your position and you may go and look elsewhere for employment."

"Can't nobody do whatever you said. Can't nobody drive me offa here without Mistah Clayton's say so. He took me on an' only he can let me go."

"Very well, Mr. Butkis. I shall send a rider to Fort Jessup and we shall see. Major Reynolds is an old family friend. He and my father were very close. I'm sure he'll be dismayed to hear of insurrectionist conduct on your part and be more than happy to supply a small detachment of troops to see to your removal."

154

Butkis started at the mention of Major Reynolds, for he knew there was bad blood between him and Ezra Clayton, knew the major might just respond to her call. There was not a man alive he feared, yet troops . . . he wouldn't want to have to face a detachment of armed soldiers. Of course, the little Fitzman trollop could be bluffing. If so, she played a good hand, one he'd be happy to leave for Clayton to call. Even so, it galled him badly, for he was a man not given lightly to backing down.

He had to admit the little bitch had spunk and more. The way she looked at a man gave him pause. The same look Clayton had, in a way, only more natural, like the coldness and determination was bred into her and lay waiting for the right time to come out so she could ride roughshod over whoever might get in her way. He shrugged and instructed the guards to leave the field hands be, sending only enough men to relieve the night guards and patrol the squalid shanty town and compound. When he was finished and his surprised underlings hurried off to their appointed tasks, he returned his attention to Crissa. "You satisfied?"

"Very much so, Mr. Butkis. Thank you." She turned to go, then stopped and faced him, a little smile on her face. "Oh, yes. There is one more thing. There was an abundance of food left over from the party. I have instructed the house servants to carry it to the field hands and pit-bucks. You will, of course, do nothing to impede them."

"But . . . ."

"That will be all, Mr. Butkis," she said curtly, dismissing him before he could protest, then swirling away in a billow of skirts. Open-mouthed and utterly at a loss, Butkis continued to gape long after she disappeared around the corner of the house. When the first of the inside slaves appeared with the large trays and headed for the field hands' quarters, Butkis spat and turned disgustedly back toward the barracks. No good would come of any of this, he was sure.

"G'wan, get outa' here," he snarled angrily to those guards left. "I guess you got the rest of the day off. Might jus' as well the white folks rest too, seein' as the damn niggers are." He stalked into the barracks, face livid.

A Tuesday off! None had seen the likes. For the first hour the slaves hid in their quarters and talked it over. When they decided nothing terrible had happened they came out of their shacks to find the food waiting. Before another hour passed they were full and lazing in the shade, soaking up their good fortune despite their disbelief. The noon bell rang and they listened contentedly. When no one came to take them to the fields they finally believed and settled down to enjoy the unaccustomed idleness. Some slept. Others, mostly younger, filtered away to the creek to swim or to the trees to spend the afternoon making long, slow, lazy love.

"Ah'm skeered, Mistuh Decatuh. It daytime. Somebody gonna come see us fo' sho'."

"Ain't no one comin' in this neck a' the woods. They all got their own quiet place, or back eatin' white folk food or sleepin'. Yo' mammy same as all the rest."

"But yo' ain't never ast me ta do nuffin' like dis. Ah's jes' supposin' ta watch yo'. Dat's wha' yo' say."

"Well, it don't pleasure me to have ya jus' watch no more. An didn't Ah bring ya' the extra peppermint?"

"Sho, Mistuh Decatuh. But Ah's still skeered."

"Got no call ta be skeered. All yo' sisters already done it. It don't hurt them none when their men done taken 'em. An' it ain't gonna hurt you."

"Yo' promises ta bring me a purty dress? Yo' swear it?"

"Hell, yes. Now lie down. That's it. Open 'em up."

"Ma will gimme a lickin' if'n she fin' out."

"Ah give you one, you don't quit yore jabberin'."

"Ah ain't ready."

"Shut up."

"Eben sissie had two year on me afore it happen ta her."

"Sissie ain't smart like you are. She don't get no peppermint, neither. Now am Ah gonna have ta slap ya' quiet?"

"Oh, Lawd, Mistuh Decatuh, I'm skeered. I doan wanna, even fo' peppa '. . . Oh, Lawd . . . !"

"Dammit. . . ."

"You tearin' me up. It hurt . . . stop it . . . Oh, Lawd. . . ."

"Shut up!"

"Mammy . . . !"

"Keep yo' voice down."

"Mammy . . . it hurt so. . . ."

"Goddamn pickaninny slut. Hold still. . . ."

"He'p me, mammy. . . ."

"Shut up!"

"Aaghhh . . . Lawd, lawd . . . mammy, ma . . . !"

The scream was cut short as the bones snapped. Decater finished in silence. The sun drifted into the afternoon sky, the lengthening shadows unaware of what they hid. When dusk came the pile of leaves and dirt looked no different than any other natural mound among the trees.

The stifling interior of the shack offered scant relief from the blistering heat still rising from the baked clay floor of the compound. Rafe awoke from a deep sleep. It was almost dark. He'd slept a second day, Tuesday, away. He moved his shoulders gingerly, testing his back. Old Chulem's medicine was good. Only two days of absolute rest and already the pain was nearly gone. He eased himself to a kneeling position, careful not to rub off the poultice slathered over his back. The stillness was broken by scuffled footsteps. Rafe turned to see a squat shadow in the dim outline of the open door as Jomo stepped into the room and squatted down beside the pallet. Rafe tensed, momentarily distrusting the smaller man who had avoided him since the fight. Jomo thrust something toward him and Rafe sniffed eagerly, the odor wakening a nearly forgotten memory. "What's that?"

"Cake."

Rafe's brow creased, his mouth dropped open. "What?"

"Cake. I saved some fo' yo'." Jomo held a glob of something white in his hand. He broke the piece and handed half to Rafe. The massive black held the cake reverently, staring at it unbelievingly in the dim light before tentatively dipping a finger in the icing and tasting the almost gagging sweetness of the confection. His eyes closed in ecstasy and he swallowed over and over again as the saliva poured into his mouth. Finally he could speak. "Where in hell you get cake? Hell, the whippin' I got ain't the half of what you can expect if they catch you stealin' white folk's cake."

The two men ate in silence. Jomo squatted on the floor, savoring his share slowly and deliberately, careful not to miss a crumb. Years had passed since Rafe had tasted cake. Five years and more since he worked in Lucas Clayton's house and had access to all he could eat of whatever he wanted. He rolled more of the icing around in his mouth, let it melt of its own accord, finally swallowed reluctantly. Jomo saved one large bite for last, stuffed it in his mouth and grinned hugely. "House niggers brung it over," he said. "Ol' Ezra Clayton gone to Nachitoches yesterday an' dat little girl done taken ober. She say ain't no one goan to de fields 'til de mastuh come back. Jes' lahk grabbin' two extra Sundays. Down amongst de field niggers Ah ken hear de singin' an' dancin'. Dey's whoopin' an' carryin' on lahk yo' nebber seed. An' dem house niggers done brung all de food t'weren't eaten at de party to dem."

"She done that?"

Jomo nodded. "Trinidad done hear de guards talkin' as how she eben made ol' Butkis back down. Ah lahks to see dat. 'Deed I do."

"Ezra Clayton ain't gonna stand for that."

"T'ain't mah worry. Ah jes' eats mah cake lahk a house nigger an' keeps mah mouf shut."

Rafe swallowed the last sugary morsels and licked the crumbs from his fingers. His mind roved back to the pit and later the whipping post. Crissa Fitzman had been there. Did she remember him? Recognize him? And did it matter if she had? Wasn't he just another of her niggers, no matter how kind she tried to be? Was he any more free for having been fed cake instead of beans and greasy rice? And what would be changed if she had seen him? He was still going to have to fight seven more fights, still have to win his freedom the hard way. Damn her cake anyway. He almost wished he could spit it up, throw the churned mess at her daintily slippered feet.

"N'gata?" Jomo asked awkwardly in their native dialect, "why you leap into the pit to face death with he who will try to kill you? Why risk your freedom dream to save the one who may end it?"

Rafe thought of the wolves leaping to the attack and the exhilaration of the fight as he and Jomo matched them steel for fang, blood for blood. He hadn't wondered why. Now the reasons seemed clear enough. "Because it was a good hunt, N'gata Jomo," he answered quietly, contemplatively. "Anyway, a long time to go before we fight. Six more fights."

Jomo hesitated, finally found the words. "Ol' Chulem say 'no.' He saw fang and fang came. And he saw more. . . ."

Rafe looked sharply at the dark shadow only inches away. "That old man isn't the only one can see. He read bones, I feel things in mine. Come the end of summer, I'm leaving here a free man. A wagon, a woman, a team and a gun. A free man."

"Conjure man say he see different."

Rafe struggled to his feet, held his back straight against the pain and walked the few steps to the door. Outside a torch weakly illuminated the compound. Pitbucks lazed in the darkness around the longhouse and near the spring. A huge platter of food, white man's food, nearly empty now, rested near the water tank. The question gnawed at him and he didn't want to ask, but did. "What he see?"

"You bein' free. The next time you go to the pit will be the last time. You won't walk away. And you'll be free."

Silence hung between them, hung like the stars that reeled dizzily across the night sky and reached for the new day. When morning came, Rafe would be outside waiting for the sun. He moved his shoulders and flexed the stiff muscles in his back. The sooner he started, pain or no, the sooner he would heal and the more ready he would be for whatever came next.

Claude Duggins scratched his coondog's ears and

watched the sunrise, staring across the green stalks of young sugar cane stretching out to a far line of cottonwoods in the distance. This was his land. More acreage than any two of the other small farmers.

Small farmers. The thought galled him. Freedom made his holdings appear paltry. Duggins was a simple man. He'd worked hard every moment of his life. Fought in the war and been wounded twice. Mustered out in New Orleans and headed into the wilds of western Louisiana. He'd never see forty again and felt the desperation of wanting to have something, be something more than a one-crop farmer. Lord of a plantation. That was what he wanted. Title. To be one of the gentry despite his calloused workman's hands and grimy nails. He deserved success, but there were always men like Ezra Clayton beating down the heads of those who attempted to rise above their station. Clayton's control of the village businesses assured high prices for everything needed on a farm unless one packed in from Natchitoches. But this was also an expensive proposition, for pack trains supplying the small farmers were always attacked, or met with mysterious accidents. One did well to push profits above a bare subsistence level. And there had been an unfortunate fire the year before. The raging flames destroyed part of Duggins crop, forcing him deeper in debt to the bank in Natchitoches. Duggins cursed the money lost on the pit fight only two weeks earlier. Damn Bernard's Indians anyway. He'd counted on winning, couldn't afford what he'd lost. He looked out across the cane fields where his twenty-five field hands were starting the day's work. Twenty-five niggers, he scowled. Ezra Clayton had two hundred.

The struggle wasn't all one-sided. He'd gotten Clayton's goat right enough by organizing the other small farmers to protect and assist each other through hard times, natural or man-caused. The association helped, but not enough. Despite his efforts, Duggins was still behind. He needed money and no bank or man would lend him any more on his land or crop. Of course if he managed to acquire more land . . . to double what he had. . . . Clayton's land with its crop of cotton nearly on the bud would be more than enough to pay off his debts and then some. He'd even be able to afford a woman. Yessir, travel to New Orleans and find himself some pretty little minx eager for plantation life. Claude Duggins would be somebody. To hell with his neighbors then. He'd show Clayton —and Bernard too—a thing or two about gentry, by God.

A slight breeze sprang up from the north and Duggins turned gratefully into the vaguely cooler air. A work song, sung by one old woman and taken up by the other slaves, drifted from the fields. Behind him the clank-clank of hammer pounding iron rang clearly in the morning air. The farmer smiled, remembering the bet he had forced on Ezra. Gotten his goat then, too, makin' him bet his land on a sure loser. Beau would tear Clayton's nigger apart piece by piece and then look for another one.

Beaumarchant. A good man, once. Duggins felt a pang of guilt at the thought of his giant Cajun friend. They had fought together under Andy Jackson in New Orleans. Duggins was wounded in the leg and Beau carried him to safety as the British neared the breastworks. Carried him like a baby, by God, not even working hard. Mortars and cannon turned the air into a corner of hell, raking the ground and tearing up trees and men. A shower of screeching rockets rained down on them and a burning fragment spun into Beau's face, searing the left side and cracking his skull. Somehow he lived, crawled on with the unconscious Duggins in his arms, an animal whose muscles had told him where to go.

The fire that burned the Cajun saved him, for the wound was sterile. And Duggins, game leg and all, nursed the friend who had been transformed into a grotesque mockery of a man, a silent, childlike brute. When the time came, Duggins took out in a wagon full of goods needed for farming. Beau rode quietly at his side, a massive dull-witted mountain, stronger than any man Duggins had ever known. He brought Beau along not out of gratitude nor a sense of duty alone. Western Louisiana was rough, dangerous country and more than once as the farm took shape and the first crop went in the ground, his friend's terrifying strength made the difference between success and failure.

Duggins had not told Beaumarchant of the bet with Ezra. Nor had he ever taken him to see a pit fight at Freedom, for being near a fight drove Beau into a wild, uncontained fury. Ezra's guards would have shot him down, as well they should have, for there was nothing else could stop him. So Duggins went alone or with friends, leaving Beaumarchant behind with instructions to watch the slaves lest any be of a mind to escape. Beau was good for that. His presence alone cowed even the most recalcitrant black.

Hesitation was more dangerous than haste. Duggins wiped the sweat from his face and neck. Tiny droplets still glistening in his beard, he walked toward the open barn. At the end of a line of stalls Beaumarchant labored over a glowing forge. The heat outside was nothing compared to the area around the forge, but the Cajun little seemed to mind. Naked but for a pair of faded cloth army trousers, he lifted a glowing red bar of iron from the fire and lay it across the anvil, took up a short-hafted hammer and began to shape the vibrant crimson metal. Bits of incandescent iron like tiny meteorites scattered upward and out with each ringing blow. Fire danced in Beaumarchant's dull eyes and lit his scarred face, giving his disfigured features the altogether incarnate appearance of a massive mountain troll at labor over the fires of hell. Having once been scalded by brimstone, he had returned to the flames that had broken his mind and puddled half his face.

He thrust the iron into a tub of water. A voluminous cloud of steam erupted from the bath and enveloped the giant form in an eerie drapery of ghostly gray.

"Beaumarchant," Duggins said softly as if uneager to disturb the brute. The Cajun glanced up, smiling and happy to see his friend. The smile was only half a smile for the left half of his face was frozen in a shiny red and white scar that didn't move. "Beaumarchant. I must talk with you."

Beaumarchant nodded, dropped the tongs and sat on a

162

log. He always sat when his friend talked to him, for then he could concentrate better, remember the words his friend said.

"There is to be a fight. And he who wins will get much money, much land. Do you understand?"

Beaumarchant thought a moment, nodded.

"Good. It is Ezra Clayton's land that is wagered. He is one who looks down on us and thinks we are dirt. He has a nigger who fights. Who kills white men. This nigger has said he will kill you, Beau." The giant started to rise, sat abruptly when his friend motioned he had more to tell him. "He has called Beaumarchant and Duggins fools. You he has called a coward and says you dare not fight him." He paused to let the information sink in, watched as realization came and the massive head swayed back and forth with the slow beginnings of anger. "I have told him you are a brave man and not afraid to meet him. That you will tear him into pieces in front of everyone. Clayton does not believe me, but he will find out. Will you fight this nigger?"

Beaumarchant thought for a moment then reached in the tub and picked out the cooled iron. His terrible visage set, he grasped the ends of a new horseshoe and, barely straining, bent it straight, then tossed it back into the fire. Duggins understood. It had been easier than he thought, and now the asking was over, he didn't feel nearly as bad as he thought he would. He watched as Beau turned back to the forge, picked up the tongs and turned the iron. Thank goodness the Cajun hadn't gone berserk with the mention of a fight, as he might well have. Duggins watched the rippling muscles as Beau pumped the bellows. He went to the giant's side, touched him lightly on the shoulder. "Beau," Duggins said over the roar of the flames, "you can kill that nigger as slow as you like. Hear?"

The light of the fire reflected on the shiny scar. A semblance of a death's-head grin split Beaumarchant's gnarled features.

Duggins left the shed, stood in the growing heat of the sun, cool in contrast to that of the forge. He smiled. A little less than four weeks. He'd have to buy more slaves, of course. Perhaps from Ezra himself, who wouldn't need quite so many with a quarter of his plantation gone. The thought was amusing. He tried to picture his adversary's face. . . .

Ezra gazed steadily ahead, lost in thought. Midmorning and the shay tore along the highroad at a run, the horse still fresh enough after an early start from Fort Jessup. Dust drifted back from the two guards riding point. Behind him rode a foursome of well-armed men. Clayton kept his left hand inside his coat where, beneath the cloth, a pistol was aimed at his driver. Between them rested a blunderbuss. Ezra took no chances. Not with three thousand dollars in gold. They rounded a pair of Indian mounds similar to the one at the rear of the pecan grove where he would rendezvous with Patrick Fitzman. He had until midnight to formulate a plan.

The trail split and ran through a small stand of oaks, then wound down into Claytonville. They slowed not at all. The six riders and shay made such a clatter that people came out of their shops and houses to watch. A thin, bony white girl waved from the top window of Black Bedetta's and two of the guards waved back. Patrick Fitzman heard the commotion but didn't go to see. He was busy with Bedetta in the huge white bed.

Dogs yelped and ran for cover. Children squealed at the noise and activity, raced alongside the shay as far as they could. Joe Terson, sweeping the board walkway fronting his store, laid the broom aside and raised his hand in greeting. The shay passed and Ezra ignored him. Inside, Reverend Leahy's new bride lowered a bolt of calico and gazed wistfully at the carriage. Abigail Terson ran to close the door and shut out the rolling cloud of choking dust, cursing Ezra Clayton and his bullies and his money, the likes of which she knew her husband would never come close to having. Money was there for those who already had it.

Ezra frowned when they passed the road cutting south to Burr's Ferry and Duggins' place. Patrick Fitzman was problem enough without Duggins and Beaumarchant. But to everything its own time. Patrick Fitzman first, then Duggins and his half-wit monster.

They passed the last business and headed up the higher ground, at the crest of which Freedom began, leaving behind them a meager stillness to settle with the dust. . . .

"Empty!!" Ezra shouted furiously. The word echoed back to him, carrying back down the hill to Claytonville, shimmering in the distant heat. He shaded his eyes and peered across his other fields of cotton, cane and food crops all the way to the stark white plantation house gleaming beyond the matched magnolias. All were devoid of life.

"Empty!" he screamed again, his hands outstretched, his back arched. . . .

The shay came to a careening halt in front of the house, almost running down a guard who stumbled and fell, rising shakily to his feet only to find himself staring down the awesome maw of his employer's J. Henry pistol. "Where's my niggers?" Ezra asked, his breath coming in furious rasps. The pistol in his hand did not waver an inch.

The guard, usually a surly youngster, doffed his cap. "Suh, they back at the shanties."

"What the goddam hell they doing *there?*"

"Miss Fitzman . . . ." the youngster's voice cracked into a higher pitch and he tried again. "Miss Fitzman done declared a holiday and given ever'body yesterday an' today off."

Ezra went livid with rage. The guard, quaking now, backed from him. "Get Butkis. I want to see him. I'll be inside. You tell him I want him right now."

"Yessuh!"

"Git!"

The guard leaped away, tripped, regained his footing and scrambled off around the corner of the house. Ezra dismissed his escort, and pistol and satchel in hand, entered the house. The Negro manservant stepped aside as the door swung open then slammed back on its hinges. He recovered enough to bow as Ezra entered.

"Where's the girl?"

"Miss Fitzman an' her mother gone on a picnic, suh. They won't be back 'til later this aftahnoon. They say they be spending the day with Madame Bernard."

Ezra cursed and started for the library, stopping suddenly to scrutinize the gray-haired servant. The slave coughed nervously, tried, too late, to leave. "Come here," Ezra commanded shortly. The slave advanced, stood trembling in front of the threatening figure. "I know you."

"Yassuh."

"I sent you to the fields, sent you to live with the field niggers. What're you doing in my house?"

The old man lowered his head and answered in a cultured voice. "Miss Fitzman. She found me. Told me to come back here to the house to work like I used to."

Ezra raised the pistol, pointing it at the manservant. "Take off those clothes," he ordered, his voice bristling with quiet menace.

"Suh?"

Ezra cocked the pistol. Sweat beaded the servant's brow and upper lip. His white burred head bobbed up and down quickly in acquiescence as he hurried to slip out of his butler's coat and lay it across a chair.

"All of them," Ezra commanded, jerking the gun under the older man's face. The slave proceeded to remove his other garments; vest, cravat, shirt, trousers and polished shoes. His thin, naked frame shivered despite the humid stuffiness of the hall. Fear was the deepest chill of all. "Now you git back to the field shanties. And if I ever catch you near this house again I'll hang you up by your pecker."

Tears of shame mingled with the sweat. "Yassuh," the old man replied weakly. He opened the door and stepped out onto the gallery, his bare feet hardly making a sound on the wooden floor. He went down the front steps and headed for the field shanties, his head bowed to avoid the eyes of anyone he might meet. Naked, he returned to the shanties. No one laughed, not even the guards.

Back in the house Ezra poured himself a glass of whiskey. He removed his coat, stripped away his sweat-soaked shirt and ordered Julie to bring him a wet towel and fresh linen. The lithe mulatto lost no time, hurried up the stairs to Ezra's room, wet and wrung out a towel, found a white shirt and scampered back to the library, nearly colliding with Butkis in her haste.

Butkis started to snarl and cuff her away but Ezra was there watching, his eyes beady with anger. The overseer stepped aside and let the girl go first, silently entering the room after her. Ezra grunted and grabbed for the towel, and ran the wet cloth through the damp hair on his chest, threw it aside. Julie held the shirt for him, then buttoned it. "Get out," he commanded hoarsely. "Wait upstairs. Pretty yourself. You smell of scullery sweat. I'll be along as soon as I'm finished with Butkis."

Standing in some semblance of attention, the overseer shuddered inwardly at the way Ezra said "finished." The girl fled the room, in haste to be as far as possible from what was about to follow. The door slammed behind her, locking the room in silence.

Ezra sat, poured himself some more whiskey and turned his cold, piercing eyes toward Butkis. "Who am I?" he asked, his voice ominously pleasant.

Butkis fidgeted. "Sir?"

Ezra's hand slammed down on the desk. The guard jumped despite himself. "Who am I?"

"Mistah Clayton."

"You're goddamned right." Ezra sipped his whiskey, his eyes, calculating, showing no trace of the seething rage just below the surface. "Who pays you, Mr. Butkis?"

"You, sir."

"Who feeds you?"

"You."

"Who?" Ezra barked.

"Sir," the overseer amended.

"Whose land is this?"

"Yours, sir."

"Whose niggers?"

"Yours, sir."

"Then why the goddamn hell aren't they in the fields?"

"Miss Fitzman . . . ."

"Damn Miss Fitzman! There's only one law here, my law. Only one word, my word. Only one say so, mine. Is that understood?"

167

"Yes, sir."

Ezra sighed, sat back in his chair, satisfied he'd put the fear into Butkis. "Very well, Mr. Butkis. It's a short while before noon. I want my darkies in the field within the next hour and I want them there and working until night-fall. Come morning I want to hear them back at it when I get up. And you tell those bumpkins that call themselves guards to lay the whip on. They had nearly two days of extra rest and I expect them niggers to work twice as hard for four, and they'll work Sunday to boot. You tell 'em that. And you tell 'em I'll personally be out and around. Every cotton plant, every corn plant I see chopped up, they'll pay for with sweat. You tell 'em that, too. Now get out of here. I'm tired."

Butkis started toward the door. He hesitated, turned back to Ezra. "Mistah Clayton?"

Ezra finished his whiskey, poured another. "Now what?"

"I hate to tell you now, but we got some trouble."

"What?"

"One of the field hands, a little girl, is missing. The niggers, they're kind of upset they can't find her."

"What happened?"

"Well, yestiday, things was kinda lazy like with the niggers not bein' in the fields . . . ." Ezra scowled, Butkis hurried on. "I was headin' over to the river to check on my men there and noticed Decater sneakin' off into the woods. Didn't give him too much thought, but did ask myself, why ain't that roister with the others? Well, sir, I didn't have no answer, but then it weren't much none of my business, him having the day off an' all. So I went on to the river. Now when I come back, I heard a bunch of noise. A girl callin' out. I follered the noise, keepin' outta sight an' come upon Decater with one of them little pick-aninnies from the field shanties. Lornie May's girl, I guess, the one they called Beulah. Couldn't be more'n twelve or thirteen.

"Anyway, ol' Decater was outta his drawers an' she was too. He's makin' her diddle him, but then he's want-in' more, wants to put it in. Well sir, she commences to squawk an' holler with him climbin' on her. She jus' weren't ripe for it. He jabs it in an' it hurt her so she screams an' carries on an' afore I know it, he grabbed her neck an' slammed her head down so fast I can't do nothin'. She was quiet then, an' he finished his job and rolled off'n her.

"All of a sudden-like it dawns on him she ain't makin' any sounds a'tall. Dead she was. He git all scared and covered her over with leaves an' the like, pulled on his drawers an' hurried off. Me, I'm thinkin' this sure is somethin' but I don't dare say nuthin', 'cause I figger them field niggers ever find out, Decater's life won't be worth swamp water. Anyway, the niggers are all fired up, an' I figgered you oughta know why."

Ezra drained his whiskey, turned to look out the window. Decater's life *wasn't* worth swamp water—or much of anything else—and for the first time that day something was going right. He smiled, the plan full-blown in his mind. Decater was going to play an important role in the continuing success of Ezra Clayton and Freedom Plantation.

"Very good, Mr. Butkis. A delightful recitation. Check outside the door, then come back and sit down." Butkis hurried to do as he was told, turned to see his employer set out a glass of whiskey for him. "Sit down, Mr. Butkis. We have some talking to do. . . ."

"Beaumarchant? Yo' mean yo' goana fight farmer Duggins' man?"

Rafe ignored Cat and concentrated on the red beans, rice and pork filling his wooden bowl. Grease seeped from the corners of his mouth, ran down his chin. He wiped it away with a hastily raised forearm and continued eating. Flies began to swarm and cluster on his arm. He ignored them as well.

"Dat scar-faced Cajun? Hell, he ain't eben human." Cat squatted in front of Rafe, knowing Dingo, Trinidad and several of the others were close enough to overhear. "Ah knows dat white man. Ugly as sin. Got a face dat would souah milk."

"I ain't fightin' the way he looks, boy. Looks don't count."

169

"If yo' was, an' if dey did, yo' be dead already. If'n looks was killin', dat man could nail yo' ass from a mile away."

Rafe scooped the last bit of rice from his bowl, gulped it quickly , then dipped the bowl into the tank and filled it to the brim with water. Sipping slowly, he savored the sweet cold water. His back felt stiff but did not pain him. Tomorrow he would clean off the poultice and get to work in earnest. The food had helped.

The sun was low in the west. Soon it would be dark. Rafe enjoyed evening. Another day closer to freedom. Cat continued to bait him, trying to worry him like a hound worried a bear. "Yassuh. Now dere one man I skeered of, an' dat de troof. Why, he so ugly Duggins gotta keep him away from de sugah cane, 'cause cane don't get sweet, it see him fuhst. Ooo-weee!"

"Cat, a fist don't never care whether a man's purty o' ugly. A fist jus' carin' about one thing. Bustin' flesh an' breakin' bones."

Cat cupped some of the water and splashed it on his face and neck. "Dat's anodder thing. Ah knows dis Beaumarchant. He ain't only ugly, he big. You knows Ah used to be Duggins' nigger afore he sold me ta Mistuh Clayton. I seen dat white man. Seed 'im poundin' iron. Seed 'im liftin' bales o' cotton lahk dey was no more'n a little baby. Seed 'im prowlin' de fields an' watchin' fo' some po' nigger who done fall asleep. He catch one ol'nigger one day when he feelin' ornery an' pop dat nigger's haid lahk it no more den a blue jay egg.

"Dat white man all mussed up in de haid an' he doan know right from wrong, jes' what Duggins tell him. Dat's one strong white man. Strong an' big. Stronger den yo' is, Rafe. An' bigger too."

"Yo' fo'gittin' dat pitchfo'k, nigger," Trinidad chimed in. "Boss ain't on'y strong, he move fas' when he gots to. Real fas'. He quick. Quick as yo' is, Cat." Trinidad nudged Dingo and the others joined in with their laughter.

"Yeah, Cat," Dingo added. "Why doan yo' go fin' dat pitchfo'k so's we can see how fas' Boss is again."

"Hesh up now, Dingo," Trinidad interjected. "Po' ol' Cat cain't fin' dat pitchfo'k 'cause it all busted up. All busted into pieces lahk dat Beaumarchant goana be when Rafe get finish wid 'im."

Cat scowled at his companions. He rose stiffly, his voice taking on a defensive tone. "All Ah sayin' is dat Ah done seen dat Beaumarchant. Dat's all. An' quick doan mean nuffin' when yo' dat big. Yo' hits dat white man all de live long day an' when it acomin' night time de moon a'laffin', 'cause dat man still be standin'. He all mussed up in de haid an' doan prob'ly know when to fall. Dat's all Ah'm sayin'.''

"Nigger, wha' fo' yo' chatterin' 'bout now?" Jomo asked as he approached the gathering of fighters around the spring.

"Nuffin'," Cat grumbled, brushing past him angrily on his way to the long house.

"When yo' goana up an' bus' dat boy's neck, N'gata?"

Rafe grinned as Jomo sat beside him. "When we in the pit, where it count for something. Cat got an itch in his craw, Jomo. Come the time, that itch is gonna do it for me. He gonna be so crazy mad to hurt me he won't think straight. When a man let temper guide him when he fightin', he ain't gonna be livin' long. Yessir, that boy Cat gonna be his own death."

The low weary sound of a spiritual carried through the wall of the compound. The field slaves were only now being herded in. "Dem po' niggers spent dem a long hard day fo' not startin' 'til pas' noon," muttered Jomo. "Look lahk Mistuh Clayton done decided ta make up fo' de day an' a half he done missed. Dem guards is layin' on de whip."

"Dey better not a had touched mah Bess. Dey bes' keep dat black snake off'n her back o' somebody git his belly cut open."

"Fool talk, Trinidad. Yo' talkin' fool talk. Dere's nuffin yo' can do but git a musket ball through dat head a' yores."

The spiritual broke up, drifted away into the dusky twilight. The field hands were at their shanties. Rafe rose and left, walking alone to his shack. The sudden crack of a whip and accompanying howl broke the silence. Rafe winced, reliving the cat, the night of the fight. What had

Crissa tried to prove by her intervention? A day and a half of merriment and rest. Did she think she could buy innocence so cheaply? Did she expect a day and half to erase uncounted years of drudgery? Life would be far harsher now Ezra was back. All she had done was give her field niggers a moment of hope, the more cruel because such hope was destined from the very first to be fruitless. Nothing had changed. They were still slaves. He drove the thought of her from his mind, replacing it with another more pressing.

He had let emotion rule, had rushed to Jomo's aid. To care about another human being, to call him friend, was a weakness he had not expected to find in himself. And in the pit, weakness meant death. In the pit only the strong survived. He glanced across the compound to Old Chulem's hut. The conjure man was in there staring at him. Rafe knew it. He could feel the old man's eyes through the board and animal-hide walls. Old eyes that had seen much. Too much, perhaps. Had they seen his weakness, read of his death? Had they seen what Ezra Clayton planned for him? The coming fight would be different, this he knew, for never before had he been told who he would fight before he stood at the bottom of the pit. Ezra Clayton must have something special in mind. Rafe shrugged the worry off and went into his shack to sleep. He was alive, his belly was full, and worry was for lesser men.

Ezra ate alone. The table was set for both Crissa and Micara but their places remained empty. The women had returned while Ezra was away with Butkis in the woods. He had expected them to show for the evening meal but Micara had sent word she was fatigued from her visit with Madame Bernard. Of Crissa he had heard nothing and was about to send Julie to inquire about her when she entered. She wore a gown of lavender silk that rustled deliciously as he seated her. "That is a gown I have not seen before."

"Madame Bernard gave it to me. It belonged to her daughter. She died only a year older than I."

"Yes. Too bad you missed the funeral. Marie Bernard

172

never could adapt to plantation life," Ezra said meaningfully, trying to bait her but getting no discernible reaction.

A young Negro man with a haughty, effeminate face entered. He was wearing butler's garb. "I'm afraid I dined without waiting for you," Ezra continued, taking a cup of tea from the servant.

"That's all right. I really wasn't hungry. Just some tea will do, please." The butler nodded and returned to the kitchen. Crissa had undertaken the trip to Bernard's for her mother's sake and was tired, but something within her demanded she face Ezra this evening. She knew the polite parrying would soon give way to cut and thrust, knew of his anger on learning the slaves had been given time off, and heard the field hands coming in late, singing their dark lament.

"It's good for Micara to get away," Ezra mused. "I have little time for the amenities of plantation life. Micara misses her amenities."

"Mother is a social creature, which is why she allowed you to stay when you stumbled out of the bayou five years ago." Ezra's face darkened, but before he could return the barb the Negro servant entered and placed cup, saucer and teapot in front of Crissa. "I'll let it steep a bit and pour it myself, thank you." The youth nodded, glanced at Ezra, and when there were no further orders, retreated once again to the kitchen. Crissa, her brows suddenly furrowed, watched him leave. Ezra noticed her puzzlement and smiled secretly. "Where is Tyree?" Crissa asked.

Ezra poured himself a glass of burgundy, holding it to the candlelight, studying the wine's rich color. "Who?"

"Tyree."

"The name escapes me." The wine cast a red glow on his face.

"Tyree was my father's valet. A trusted house servant for many years. I found him working in the fields like a common field hand. He is old and in ill health. I brought him back to the house and returned him to his former duties."

"Oh, yes. Now I remember. That cream-colored nigger I found in the hall this morning. I almost shot him."

173

Crissa paled. "You didn't. . . ."

Ezra finished his burgundy and refilled the glass. "No. I stripped him and sent him back to the fields."

"You what?"

"You heard me. If you'd wanted to contest the decision you should have been here instead of out and running around the countryside. A scrawny old nigger not worth the food he eats. I'll not have his kind in my house."

"He was a trusted servant."

"Not my servant."

Crissa could feel the anger rising in her like fearful, choking bile. Ezra remained placid, unconcernedly sipping his wine. He had recovered all emotional control since the morning's outburst. Now beyond her defenses, it was time for him to pursue the matter.

"It is my wish that . . . ." Crissa began.

"To the devil with your wishes," Ezra interrupted coldly. "Should I ever again return and find you have interfered with the running of this plantation I shall send you away with nothing more than the clothes on your back."

"What? You can't . . . ."

"I can and I will. I am master here. This is my land and I shall do as I please. Dammit, woman, do you still not understand?"

"I understand only one thing. You have defiled my father's name and that of this plantation. You are a cruel monster who delights in watching helpless creatures die."

"Helpless? That's good. I like that, Crissa. You're very perceptive." He rose from his chair, his voice like steel, hard and unrelenting. "You crawl down into my pit and face one of my pitbucks and see for yourself just how helpless they are."

"The practice is inhuman."

"What's this? Is your mother inhuman? Is Captain Bennett inhuman? Are all the townspeople, farmers, trappers and the like inhuman? They enjoy the gaming. Do I force the niggers into the pit? No. Do I force them to kill? No. They fight because they are savages. They would do so in the fields, in the shanties, in the forests. It

174

is for their betters, for cultured man, to appreciate the sport in their fighting, and it was for me to discover how to fight them successfully. Not just two ignorant cotton field niggers slashing at each other with knives for the pleasure of an uneducated few. No. I train my niggers. Train them to fight, train them to kill, train them to live, train them to win. Whether or not the idea pleases you, blood and gold have made Freedom the success you see. Blood and gold and my governing hand. I have told you I am a realist. Were I not, you would have returned from the east to find poverty and squalor, if anything. Your father," he spat, "bah! This plantation is mine, Crissa Elizabeth Fitzman, and don't you forget it. John Fitzman is dead. Everything here is mine!" He leaned on the table at her side, his gaze centered on her bosom, then rose to meet her eyes. "Everything," he said slowly, emphasizing each syllable. "Every thing."

Crissa caught his meaning only too well, shuddered inwardly as he finished his sentence. The revulsion of the suggestion drove her from the table in a panic. She fled up the stairs to her room, recoiling from the very walls as if they too bore the reddish-brown color staining the floor of the pit. And in a way, they did.

Ezra left the dining room feeling much better. There would be more to say later but he could wait. She had tested him and learned how he would react and respond —with brutal strength. Women were really too, too easy. She would walk a little more carefully in the future.

The lamp was already lit in the library. Tonight was the meeting with Patrick. His men were already moving, but there were still many details needing his attention. . . .

Decater ran his hands lightly over the white coat, the likes of which he'd never worn. He had always dreamed of owning fine things yet took little pleasure in the richly tailored broadcloth. The night was too hot, for one thing. Hot in more ways than one. The whole business stank. Damn that Beulah. Carryin' on an' caterwaulin' when ever'body knew nigger gash readied young. He had to kill her, even if he wasn't tryin' to. She'd left him no choice.

Little bitch screamin' loud enough to wake the dead. She hadn't no right. And Butkis, the bastard, followin' him an' watchin', stickin' his nose in other people's business, then holdin' back what he knew until this afternoon when Mistah Clayton called him to the house.

Sittin' across the desk from Ezra Clayton and listenin' to what he said scared the goose piss out of him. "No, sir," Decater said nervously. "No, sir. Anything but that. Ah cain't kill no white man. That's a hangin' crime."

Clayton led him to the window. Butkis was below with a buckboard drawn up close to the side of the house. Climbing in back, the overseer lifted a canvas tarpaulin and Beulah was lyin' there, starin' at him, her wide, dead eyes boring straight into him. If the field hands ever found out who, if word ever spread, he could never turn his back in the fields, never know when an accidental shovel or hoe or machete would slip from someone's grip. He wouldn't be able to stay with Clayton and he wouldn't be able to leave, for word would follow him wherever he went where there were niggers. He was trapped, hard-caught and no way out. There was nothing to do but what he was told.

He brushed the grit from his sleeve—from Clayton's sleeve—and stepped out from the clustered pecan trees. The Indian mound loomed ahead, a sleeping giant dimly lit by a quarter moon. The man would be there—somewhere.

Patrick could have had help. Long offered, right enough, but was told he should stay clear lest word of his presence get around. Folks knew about Long's filibustering and the military had been ordered to stop him. Anyway, Patrick Fitzman had his own plans. Lying silently in a slight depression atop the mound, he had an unobstructed view and a clear field of fire. Three hours he'd been there and not heard a sound, not seen a living thing other than birds and squirrels. He'd see if Ezra had not come alone.

Getting the money was no problem. Keeping it was another matter. If Ezra tried anything it would be after he'd passed the gold. Probably a waylaying, then the claim of robbery should anyone discover the deed. But Patrick had no intention of taking any road where he could be way-laid, neither to Natchitoches nor elsewhere. Nor did he plan on splitting the money. To hell with Long's filibuster into Mexico. Patrick had learned a lot in the past few years, knew his way around well enough to make his way north, melt into the swamps and disappear across the Sabine into Mexico. It would take time, but time he had. More than anyone would think, for he had prepared well-hidden caches along the way in little known places. A week here, two weeks there. They would abandon the chase after a month or two and forget him. He'd make his way through open country, then to the land he'd picked. There he'd settle like a king. Three thousand in gold would go far.

An owl flitted by overhead, soaring on silent wings, hunting for a kill. The bird glided down toward a cluster of trees, suddenly shifted direction and disappeared. Patrick tensed. Something was there to disturb the owl, for the bird had meant to land.

A figure in a white frock coat started out of the grove and toward the mound. No one else was that short, that stumpy. It had to be Ezra, carrying the gold in two sacks. Patrick listened intently. Had there been a sound behind him? There couldn't be anyone there. Only the line of sentinel trees. No. Ezra wouldn't take the chance. He wouldn't want shots fired so near the house. Micara and Crissa would waken and hear, demand explanations.

Men hunting possums or coons. . . . Suddenly Patrick didn't feel so safe. In his wide-eyed greed for gold he'd left too much to chance. He should have accepted Long's men. Better half than nothing. And now here he was lying hidden on top of an Indian mound and in the open. He forced himself to remember his plan. Get the gold and get into the swamp. Still, he felt fear, though without concrete cause or reason. He shivered in the sultry summer air.

Decater stopped as the form rose from the mound. The guard choked back a scream, telling himself this was only a man. He hadn't expected him to be waiting on top of the mound, though. Worse, he hadn't seen him lying

177

there, dressed as he was and not moving. He held the sacks out separately. They were heavy and he was tired of carrying them. His arms sagged. He would be glad to hand them over. The next task worried him. The man would have a pistol—maybe two—and be prepared to use them. Decater had to keep them from firing. If Ezra's plan didn't work, Decater would be a dead man.

He stopped and placed one of the bags at his feet. His head low and the wide brim of his white felt hat hiding his face, he held the sack out as if to pour a few coins in the man's hand. Patrick recognized the gesture, cocked the pistol in his right hand and held his left out. "No tricks, Ezra," he whispered softly. "Let's see the color of your gold. A few coins and then it's *adieu*."

Decater turned the sack over, sending his hand to the left, emptying sand, not gold, onto Patrick's pistol. Patrick squeezed the trigger but too late, for the flint struck the choking sand and nothing happened. He tugged at his second pistol as Decater leaped. Both men stumbled to the earth. The pistol caught on Patrick's shirt, and cursing, he freed it. Decater clawed for the weapon even as Patrick managed to cock it, shove it into Decater's stomach and pull the trigger. Decater rammed his hand across the frizzen. The hammer struck against his knuckles and the flint gouged into his flesh. He yelped with pain and tore free, ripping the gun from Patrick's grasp.

Suddenly figures were moving around them. Patrick staggered to his feet, tripped over Decater and tumbled down the slope of the Indian mound. The figures were closing in. He dizzily regained his footing and leaped for the shelter of the trees, slamming face first into the trunk of a pecan. Momentarily blinded, he staggered back. Someone gripped his shoulder and a flashing sliver of metal gleamed in the moonlight.

They formed a silent circle around their hapless victim. Decater groaned every now and then, rubbing the back of his hand. Patrick lay on his side, his hands clutching, fingers futilely attempting to plug his throat, ripped from ear to ear. Eventually he died. "Got 'im with mah razor," Milo proudly muttered. "It was worth the wait." They carried him into the brush and began digging.

Unseen by all of them, Old Ephraim crept back to his shack. There he sat out the rest of the night, rocking and weeping, rocking and weeping.

11

Crissa stood on the upper south gallery, her fingers clutching the railing. She could do nothing. She was powerless, totally incapable of influencing what would soon begin.

Little had changed in the five weeks she had spent at Freedom and she had nothing to show for her efforts. She had left two letters with Joe Terson to be forwarded to friends in Natchitoches and New Orleans, but had received answers from neither. Later, under the guise of visiting Steve, she travelled to Fort Jessup where she spent a clandestine hour in conversation with Major Reynolds. Sympathetic but of no help to her, he promised to forward a third letter to New Orleans. She pointedly avoided Captain Bennett.

With nothing left but to wait, she watched her twenty-first birthday come and go, a symbol of failure. She felt her chances of regaining her heritage slipping away irrevocably. Worse, all hope for assistance from Micara dimmed as her mother buried herself deeper and deeper in an alcoholic haze, driven there by constant pressure from Ezra. Crissa was positive Ezra was trying to drive her in the same direction, felt herself becoming weaker and weaker, more and more unstable as the taunts and insolent, obscene innuendoes eroded her self-esteem.

And the slaves. . . . Whatever Crissa had done to alleviate their hardships had been undone rapidly and with a vengeance. Despite her good intentions, her efforts had made life harder for the unfortunate blacks, for they worked longer hours and under a harsher regime than before the brief holiday she had given them. Only once, weeks earlier, had Ezra yielded to her demands. A little girl had been found dead in the woods and Crissa insisted she be buried and the slaves given time to mourn. Ezra strangely acquiesced and a weekday passed without the drifting chant of weary work songs. Instead, the wailing of a mother and the deep-throated spirituals hung heavily in the air.

The child's death, attributed to the vicious mayhem of a passing trapper, or perhaps an Indian, wrought a marked effect on the disposition of the field hands, and the next two weeks were marked by two attempted escapes. One black died in the swamp, preferring the deadly bite of a cottonmouth to recapture and retribution. The second, and Crissa felt once more her heart's pain and sorrow, was Tyree, John Fitzman's trusted manservant. His spirit broken, shattered by Ezra's cruel treatment, he fled, pursued down the long rows of cotton. But he was an old man, too old for such exertions, and his heart failed him in the end. The guards came upon his body on the fringe of the woods and left him to rot as an example to the others.

Ezra received no small measure of enjoyment at Crissa's expense, recounting to her Tyree's saddening demise over the dinner table. Crissa was beyond any outright display of grief. She denied Ezra that particular satisfaction. But late at night she wept in the privacy of her room. The next day, her birthday, she brooded on Tyree's death and wrapped herself in grim resolve. Ezra would one day be held accountable.

Pa-Paw Ephraim's absence was another disquieting factor. Several times over the past few weeks Crissa visited the pecan grove. Each time the old man was nowhere to be found, though a full pot of steaming tea was on the stove in his shack and she called his name until hoarse. Was he hiding from her? Why?

Rafe she had not seen since the night of the whipping, yet the raw, powerful nakedness, the searing savagery on his face as he turned to look at her, had indelibly marked her and left a permanent impression. As a young girl she wished he would speak to her more, but now as a woman some deeper and more mysterious emotion had been provoked. She found him impossible to forget, impossible to dismiss.

If she'd only been able to stop the fight! Ruefully she realized how truly powerful Ezra was. He would have his way. Soon it would begin and there was nothing she could do but mutter a silent prayer of appeal to a power higher than Ezra Clayton.

Had he known, Ezra would have cared less. He glanced about, studying each of the faces that ringed the pit. Bernard was there. And eleven others. Men of power —wealthy, arrogant, the proud aristocracy of a society already corrupt and increasingly degenerate. The true characters of these men were hidden under the veneer of elaborate trappings born of haughty self-esteem. All were masters of plantations far larger than Freedom, but none had the pit. Ezra's fighters had gained fame which accrued to their master, and the presence of the eleven gave proof of his reputation.

Bernard flushed jealously. Not a one of the owners would have made the three- and four-day journey to visit him. He took slight comfort from the fact they had not travelled so far merely to exchange niceties or do business with Ezra, but had come solely for the fight—to see the supposedly invincible nigger Rafe receive a much deserved comeuppance at the hands of the giant ex-soldier and white man.

Ezra, for the first time before a fight, felt uneasy despite the presence of his lofty guests. If Duggins won this night there would be only one recourse. To that end he had sent a detachment of armed guards along the Burr Ferry Road with instructions to make sure Duggins died and his corpse disappeared. With Duggins out of the way, Ezra would be able to claim the transfer of property had

183

never taken place, that Duggins had accepted cash value in lieu of the land, and that he, Ezra, could not be held accountable if the man had been waylaid. There would be talk among the small farmers and possibly an investigation by the army, but little concrete would happen. Of course, word would inevitably spread and Ezra's reputation would be tarnished. A cheap enough price. Time would heal such wounds, and though Freedom might languish for a year or two, the curious, the bloodthirsty, and the gamblers would soon be coming back.

He looked about him one last time. Everything was ready. The servants moved silently through the elite crowd. Ice, vastly more expensive than the liquor, tinkled in the glasses. Hushed conversations floated on the quiet air, conversations concerning thousands of acres and more thousands of bales of cotton. Somewhere back in the shadows Duggins waited with Beaumarchant. Butkis had yet to arrive with Rafe. Win or lose, one good thing out of all this would be to watch the impudent nigger learn what real fear was.

Rafe was thinking of fear. He had seen it in Jomo's face earlier. And now he stood alone, waiting. The rest of the pitbucks had avoided him like an evil charm. Looking relieved and glad they were staying behind, they watched silently from in front of the longhouse. And Old Chulem? Had he already seen the outcome, or was he huddled over a fire working his magic? Did he, too, watch?

Rafe was at the peak of condition. His body was lean and hard, over two hundred and twenty pounds of muscle, bone and sinew. Only a day ago he had bested five pitbucks, wrestling with them all at once. This Beaumarchant, this white man who practiced his strength breaking the backs and crushing the skulls of helpless field slaves. . . . Rafe felt a mounting rage swell in him. He was no field nigger.

Rafe stood naked, as he would fight. No weapons. Bare hands and feet only. He waited patiently for the guards, his body gleaming dully in the orange light of the single torch thrust in the ground near the gate. His shadow stretched across the compound to disappear in the secret darkness in the eyes of the watchers. No one moved.

A bolt rattled, shattering the heavy silence and thrusting it back on Rafe as the gate squealed open. Butkis strode in, stood with hands on hips in front of the only man who had taken his sword and lived to tell about it. His eyes searched Rafe's face, focused behind him to the silent shadows. "No need in waitin' tonight. This nigger's gonna die. He won't be back." The shadows shifted, held. "Yer a dead man, nigger," he said quietly. "I seen this Beaumarchant. No way you ken beat him. I don't know where I'm gonna hang yore black carcass. Maybe over the gate. Wherever, I'm gonna enjoy it. Now move."

He turned and strode out the gate. Rafe followed, ignoring the guards who fell in behind him. The path led him. The same path, with its ruts of fear. Rafe walked to one side, sniffed the wind, savored the cool air on his body.

The peaches reached out to him and suddenly Rafe left the path. "Hey!" Milo said.

Butkis turned, pulled his pistol. "What the hell? You stop there, nigger, or I'll put a ball through yore black hide."

Rafe ignored the overseer's threats. He walked to the nearest peach tree and plucked two of the largest fruits he could find. Butkis was bellowing at him as Milo and the others came on the run. When Rafe turned he was staring into the maws of six muskets. He walked back toward them. Butkis was fuming. "Have a peach, Mistuh Butkis," Rafe said laconically, tossing one of the fruits in the overseer's direction.

Butkis furiously batted it aside. "You son-of-a-bitch, I got a good mind to blow yer goddamn head off. Put that goddamn chunk o' fruit down."

Rafe, biting off large chunks of the peach, grinned as the sweet juice ran down his chin. "You ain't gonna shoot me, Butkis. A lotta folks got money an' come a long way to see me kill that white man. You ain't gonna disappoint 'em. An' neither am I." He spit the large, coarse seed out, wiped his hands on his naked belly and left the bewildered guards behind.

The last hundred feet. He entered the torchlit area. The men ringing the pit studied him in silence. His gaze ranged idly over them and came to rest on Ezra. The two stared at each other, Ezra searching for any sign of fear, finding only silent, mocking contemptuousness.

Duggins and two of his friends stepped to the edge of the far side of the pit. The farmer was grinning at the black man. "I have someone over here wants to meet you, nigger. You gotta god in that heathen place you darkies come from, you better say your prayers to him now." A figure loomed in the darkness, a figure of breath-taking proportions who stepped into the circle of light. And Duggins said quietly, "This is Beaumarchant."

There was a hushed murmur among the eleven planta-tion lords. Bets were revised, replaced. Three-to-one the nigger wouldn't last five minutes. Even odds on the nig-ger. Five-to-three the white would win but wouldn't walk away. Ten-to-one the nigger wouldn't fight at all and be killed by the guards as he tried to break and run.

Beaumarchant was huge. If Rafe was a giant, the Cajun was a behemoth; a misshapen grotesquerie tower-ing half a foot above Rafe, a herculean physique with shoulders and arms corded into knots of muscle, thighs as big around as most men's waists. His face was a ruina-tion, the whole left side from his eye down to his neck a single shining white and red sheet of scar tissue where the flesh had been seared. The left ear was a twisted mass of cartilage and part of his upper lip was gone, burned away to reveal the teeth and lending a skull-like appearance to the whole apparition. His head had been shaved, like Rafe's. Scars stood out, streaking Beaumarchant's chest and arms.

Is this how they felt, those who have faced me, a giant carved of black? Did they feel as I feel now, Rafe wondered. He remembered his father's words. "The lion is bigger and stronger than men, yet men kill lions. Re-member that, my son." The hulk across the pit was surely a lion of a man.

The elite were watching him, waiting for a reaction. Rafe suddenly imagined how Jomo would look beside this gargantuan. The little warrior would seem a small, furious doll. The notion amused him and he laughed aloud.

"Your nigger's crazed, Mistah Clayton. He's laughin'," Duggins called angrily.

Ezra ignored Duggins, inwardly fumed at the laughter. The nigger wouldn't be laughing long. "When Mr. Butkis fires, you jump into the pit," he ordered calmly. "Mr. Butkis, at your discretion."

The overseer nodded importantly and raised his pistol. The whispers died and the watchers edged forward. The torchlight sent a dozen flickering shadows dancing in the pit where clay walls glowed and pulsed with a life of their own. In his mind Rafe saw Old Chulem shaking his head and mouthing the ancient rites of a lost people. Chulem had seen his death, he knew. Rafe forced the thought away. Duggins touched his hulking friend on the shoulder, reached up and whispered something to him. Beaumarchant nodded and grinned his death's-head grin, the slash of revealed teeth and jawbone gleaming in the eerie light. Only the right half of his face moved. The brute silently pointed a finger at Rafe, singling him out. They stood their ground across the cavity in the earth, the black warrior and the monstrous Beaumarchant. Butkis' pistol spouted fire and a resounding clap of thunder.

Rafe, already tense, leaped high, landed on his feet, rolled and came up running, hurtling to meet Beaumarchant as the Cajun dropped sluggishly into the pit. Partially losing his balance and falling forward to the ground, he steadied himself with both hands, unable to avoid Rafe's attack. The black stopped, pivoted and drove his right leg in a powerful, thrusting kick which connected with Beaumarchant's disfigured face and lifted him to his feet. There was a sound like a club slapped against a log and the Cajun's head snapped back and he slammed into the wall. Rafe, his fists welded together in a powerful two-handed grip, followed his initial attack with a viscera-rushing blow to the Cajun's exposed belly. It would have killed a lesser man.

Beaumarchant doubled over, staggering forward into the clay arena. Rafe let him pass, then followed him, raining blow after head-clubbing, double-fisted blow onto the man. The Cajun stumbled, fell to his knees. Rafe drew back, breathing hard. His hands hurt. It was like punching stone, but the brute was down and wouldn't last long.

Rafe aimed his next kick for the kidneys and confidently closed in. Beaumarchant pitched sideways. As he fell, a rock-hard fist swung blindly into the pitbuck's legs, knocking him off his feet. Beaumarchant rolled again, this time onto Rafe, momentarily burying him. His hands grabbed Rafe's struggling wrists, pinned them to the earth. The drooling death's-head grin hung only inches away above Rafe's face, the gaping, torn scar tissue dripping saliva and blood into the pitbuck's eyes.

Rafe squirmed his legs free, locked them around the brute's waist and squeezed, the long-corded muscles of his thighs exerting tremendous pressure. Beaumarchant's eyes grew wide. He freed Rafe's hands and tried to roll away. The black stayed with him as the Cajun struggled to his knees, hammering at the legs that ground at his kidneys. Nearly bescrk with pain, Beaumarchant locked his fists together and began smashing Rafe's face, chest and abdomen. The black protected himself with his forearms, and only his own superb physique and the Cajun's growing weakness kept him from being killed. Even so, his torso was a mass of bruises and each slamming blow hurt worse than the one before. He exerted more pressure despite the terrible punishment until he could withstand the Cajun's jarring fists no longer.

Suddenly Beaumarchant was free. Rafe rolled away, jumped to his feet and attacked before his opponent could stand. A fist flattened the Cajun's nose, crushing the cartilage. A new fount of blood poured down Beaumarchant's face into the lipless mouth. Rafe swung again with his right fist. Beaumarchant ducked into it, catching the blow directly on his temple.

Pain shot the length of Rafe's arm and he howled in hurt suprise. Beaumarchant shook his head like a bull, and still on his knees, threw a diving, overhanded punch to Rafe's genitals, knocking the pitbuck off his feet. Rafe, doubled up and gasping for air, pulled himself across the clay floor.

Beaumarchant struggled slowly to his feet and stared dully at the black. The bruise on his temple was beginning to swell and his kidneys hurt from the punishing scissor-grip. The nigger had hurt him and now he was going to pay.

Rafe slowly dragged himself erect. His father had said . . . He couldn't remember, could only hear Cat. "Stronger den yo' is, Rafe . . . Stronger den yo' is, Rafe . . ." Over and over . . .

The fist, an obscenely huge bony crag of flesh, came out of nowhere and spun him back against the wall. Another grazed the side of his head and slammed into the hard clay as he slumped to one side. Rafe tried to move, couldn't, and watched as the swollen hands closed around his throat and began to squeeze.

There were no screams, no catcalls from above. Only empty time and the hoarse, rattling breath of Beaumarchant. Rafe's arms were lead, dangling to either side as Beaumarchant lifted him into the air and slid him up the wall. Rafe felt the pressure, tensed his neck. The Cajun's fingers dug deep but the neck did not crush beneath his grip. The brute's eyes widened in surprise. Used to the slaughter of old men, of helpless, weary field slaves, here was a nigger almost equal to himself. He scowled and squeezed harder.

Rafe gripped the Cajun's arms. He tucked his legs up and in a fluid motion planted his feet against Beaumarchant's chest, violently straightening them and flinging the brute away. Beaumarchant tripped and fell over on his back, the air whooshing out of his lungs.

For a moment both titans were down. Slowly they struggled to their feet and stood glaring at each other across the narrow space separating them. The pitbuck gingerly rubbed his throat, his flesh lacerated by Beaumarchant's powerful hands as they were torn from his neck.

Rafe began to warily circle his powerful foe, slowly regaining the use of his legs. His right hand hurt, his head throbbed, and pain shot through his groin, but he forced himself to disregard it. Like a hunting cat he circled the Cajun who waited, his pale flesh a garish orange in the

189

firelight. Minutes passed . . . a circle . . . another . . . interminable to those watching from above. Minutes to regain strength, to make the body work again. . . .

Rafe warily searched for an opening but Beaumarchant surprised him by attacking first. He lunged at the black who stepped aside and clubbed the back of the Cajun's neck as he rushed past. Beaumarchant slammed into the wall, rebounded and backhanded Rafe. The pitbuck, expecting the Cajun to be knocked half-senseless, caught the blow on the chin and fell reeling away. Beaumarchant pressed the attack, and even as Rafe spun from him, grappled two pale, brawny arms around the pitbuck's waist, encircling him from the rear in a crushing bearhug, hoisting him off his feet and squeezing the very breath from him.

Rafe's arms were pinned uselessly to his side, and struggle though he did, the irresistible pressure continued. Rafe's vision narrowed and bright ringlets of fire danced before his eyes, already bulging from their sockets. He smashed his head back into Beaumarchant's face, but the Cajun turned his face to one side and Rafe's head flopped uselessly to the white man's shoulder. The strength draining from him, he tried to raise his head but couldn't.

Above him the circle of white faces stared down. Was Crissa among them? Did she watch, too? He arched his body, kicked up and back, slamming a heel into Beaumarchant's groin. The Cajun grunted and tightened his viselike grip. Rafe repeated the kick. Once. Twice. Three times. The bear hug loosened. A fourth time. The pressure eased. A fifth time. And Beaumarchant thrust him from his arms. Rafe landed like a cat, rolled to his feet and promptly fell over on his buttocks, sitting against the wall of the pit, legs splayed out before him. Thirty feet away, Beaumarchant leaned against the opposite wall for support, his hands clutching his genitals, blood trickling through his fingers and down his inner thigh.

Now was the moment to press the attack. Rafe sat where he was, unmoving, pain lacing his left side in searing spasms. Beaumarchant was crippled, at least for the moment. *Now!* a voice screamed within him. But he could not.

And suddenly Rafe realized he was to die. Chulem had been right. He sat there, too tired to care. Beaumarchant shoved away from the wall and began to lurch toward him, step by staggering step, like some inexorable, invincible monster driven by malevolence and hatred—hatred, cruelty and grim satisfaction—for through his pain-dulled brain, Beaumarchant realized Rafe was beaten.

The pitbuck drew his legs up and attempted to stand, but Beaumarchant fell to his knees in front of him and slammed him back down against the wall with his forearm and held him there. Rafe's right arm ineffectually pummelled the Cajun's back. Beaumarchant grinned. His right hand grasped Rafe's left wrist in an unbreakable grip. He blocked the pitbuck's attempt to kick him in the groin and gradually drew Rafe's left hand toward him. Beaumarchant had remembered what his friend had said. "You can kill him as slow as you like."

Rafe tried to wrench his hand free but Beaumarchant was too strong. Too strong. "You be free," Jomo said. Beaumarchant would kill him, would win. Struggle only prolonged death, so he quit struggling and watched with curious aloofness as Beaumarchant's jaw closed around the base of his little finger.

And then pain. More pain than he could ever remember. Those grinding, tearing, grotesque jaws. Blood seeped from between the Cajun's clenched teeth. Rafe's blood.

And then the hand dropped free, spouting crimson gore where the little finger had been. Beaumarchant rocked back and pushed to his feet, his grisly prize jutting from his lips. Rafe lay back against the smooth, cool clay and felt the tears roll down his face while his lifeblood ran before his tear-dimmed vision and blotted in the somber clay.

Beaumarchant plodded to the center of the pit. He took the prize from his mouth and held Rafe's severed finger aloft. Some of the faces nodded up and down. Most smiled. Others laughed. A voice shouted, "That a boy, Beau! Kill that field nigger piece by piece. Bite off his pecker next."

And Beaumarchant's body shook, his travesty of a

mouth widening in silent, obscene laughter. Holding the bleeding length of human flesh and bone so all could see, turning in a circle, staring and grinning at the faces, his back contemptuously turned to the doomed black man. Three of the faces scowled and disappeared. They had lost their money and knew it. The others nodded and laughed. They'd won and now were anxious for the kill. With their money safe, they could enjoy the final moments.

They laughed. Duggins laughed. Beaumarchant laughed. Rafe stared at the faces, stared at the severed finger held high and outlined against the torches' glare. He stared at the silently chittering monster who held it; stared at his mutilated hand; the blood that was his; the walls of the pit stretching upward forever; back to the faces and the laughing, hulking white man who liked to kill field niggers.

And then rage. The fury grew in his belly and swelled to fill his whole being. He was not a field nigger! He would not die. Not alone. And Rafe, borne on a wave of rage, a terrible force filling his being, charged, blood spattering a trail in his wake. A scream tore his throat as he leaped high, springing onto Beaumarchant's back even as the Cajun started to turn toward the noise.

Rafe's legs wrapped around the giant's waist, wrapped and locked. His black arms enveloped the shaven white skull and began to twist. Beaumarchant staggered to his knees, rose despite Rafe's weight, despite the pain as his head was wrenched left. Rafe twisted, his hands like talons digging into Beaumarchant's sweat-slick skull. Beaumarchant locked his hands on Rafe's wrists. He pulled, his biceps swelling to phenomenal proportions. Rafe did not let go.

Beaumarchant hurled himself forward, bending to slam Rafe with bone jarring force into the wall. Rafe did not let go.

Beaumarchant fell forward and rolled on his back, then with herculean effort regained his footing, stood with back to wall and bashed Rafe against the wall again and again.

Rafe . . . did . . . not . . . let . . . go.

Beaumarchant clawed at the arms, clawed at the mutilated hand, clawed at the air and the lifeless, uncaring clay wall. Darkness was sweeping in on Rafe yet he held his body taut, ever fiber of his being, every vestige of his strength channelled into this last supreme effort.

And then a loud, wrenching crack like a limb torn from a living tree.

There was no more resistance. Beaumarchant's head was twisted almost completely around. Shards of bone jutted from his neck. A gobbet of flesh hung from his mouth where he had bitten through his own tongue. The massive white arms fluttered and the brutish body, dead already, took two steps and buckled.

Rafe fell with it, rolling off the corpse and into oblivion.

12

Images of fire. A house burning. Fiery animal tongues of flame and brimstone lap at the sky and turn it orange. Sound. The horrid crackling consumption of wood. The scream of a child, abruptly ended in a rising swirl of sparks. A face . . . Lord Lucas Clayton. Black arms drag him to safety, into the welcome coolness of night air where water waits. But his children, his wife . . . all are trapped inside. He breaks free from wiser, restraining arms and rushes into the blazing death trap as timbers sag and crumble, followed by a horrendous groaning crash drowning out the final, agonized scream of pain . . . of loss . . . of despair.

Visions of pale, cooling white. Rain sounds . . . raining on him . . . droplets cooling his flesh even as they turn to steam, condense and fall again. Seeping down into the grave, are they? Weary . . . why do the dead think? Closed eyes already closed, sleep while sleeping and dream of dreams.

Deprivation. Following Lord Lucas' brother. But why? Why follow the man who has no name? Forsaking the high roads and easy paths, keeping to the swamps, the waterways. Mud. Mosquitoes. Hunger. Following . . . his name is Ezra Clayton . . . to Freedom.

Kitchen smells! Awkward perusal of a girl. Pert,

friendly despite the color of his flesh. Danger! She is white. Black on white, white on black. Contrast. Don't touch. Don't think of touching. Don't think. Slaves don't think. The girl smiles, looks concerned. He is ashamed. Has she noticed how he cannot keep his eyes from her? She is a woman now, continues to stare. Is she concerned? She looks so. "Doan worry 'bout yo' nigger, Miss Crissa."

Wake to pain. Flames again. His hand is on fire, spouting crimson flames of gore. Throw sand on it! Someone dip it in the mud! Put out the fire! Quench the flames! Whose scream rends the night air? Whose scream dwindles rapidly into the depths of quiet tears and welcome unconsciousness? Who sleeps now, burned by fever, chilled by heat? Who tosses on the cloud of white? Black on white, white on black. Contrast. Cool white towels turned hot by black heat.

Another face leers like a contemptuous death spectre. Slowly drawing near, lurching across miles of open space. Unstoppable. The earth shakes, the staring faces shimmer with laughter. A towering hulk of sinew and bone, a swaggering monstrosity born of fire. Darkies in a row, kneeling, heads bowed. Down the line, the monster comes closer, popping heads with no more effort than eggs are cracked. Pop. Pop. Pop. Hands are tied. Must free them. Got to get hands free before the monster reaches him. Laughter and jiggling smiles from nodding, disconnected faces. Ezra Clayton has bound his darkie's hands, he's smiling into his darkie's face. Two brutish paws close around his skull. Pressure.

Lightning-blue flame. A thunderous collision among the clouds. The bed shook and Rafe woke but did not move. His shack? No. A real bed. And sheets. Sheets? Difficult to remember the feel of sheets, the soft surface of linen beneath his flesh. Rain pounded against a window, spattered, caused faint, besmirched shadows to coil and writhe on the opposite wall. He recognized the thick smell of soap. His body was clean and not perspiring in the rain-cooled room. A familiar room. . . .

His eyes searched the darkness, picking out and identifying shadows and silhouettes. His room. He was in Ezra

196

Clayton's house. This had been his room for a time five years ago, before the pit, before the one with the red beard, when he had been a house servant to Miss Micara, Mistuh Ezra and Miss Crissa. He used to see her every day, but then Crissa left and things changed. The red-bearded one died. The pit was dug. The pit . . . ? Beaumarchant.

Rafe pressed his left hand against his leg. Part of the hand was wrapped and bandaged. There was no pain, only a dull throb. I'm alive, he thought. Still he did not move, for some instinct cautioned him. Someone was near, in the room and moving in the dark. A rustle of silk like wind through the reeds. A clink of glass. The pressure of hands against him. The sheet covering him drawn away. Through slitted eyes he discerned a shape above him, heard the intake of breath as his awesome proportions were displayed in their naked entirety.

Woman-soft fingers played along the muscular ridges of his chest, then up to trace the hard line of his jaw, back down to his neck and shoulder, traversing his arm, stroking his belly and then lower, to cup, fondle and arouse. The soft fingers lifted him, cradled him, gently squeezed him, tugged and petted until, his fierce heart pounding in his breast, his blood coursing through limbs suddenly alive, Rafe felt himself grow taut and rise high and higher, harder and harder beneath the sensual strokes. His flesh radiated a fierce animal heat to her touch and he heard her whisper with a trace of choked fear in her voice, "At last, my black stallion. At last, at last."

He caught a glimpse of long, unbound hair and a pale shoulder. A cautioning finger touched his lips and the bed shook for a moment under her added weight. Then a flash of pale thigh across his loins and a leg swung over to straddle him. A hand pressed into his shoulder, another grasped his swollen manhood, guided it to touch and slowly enter the descending sheath of moistness and heat. The figure above him moaned softly. "Oh, my stallion . . . my stallion. . . ."

He could not contain himself. Rafe arched his back and violently thrust himself into her. The woman threw back her head and screamed inaudibly beneath a wall-

197

rattling thunderclap sounding in simultaneous fury. She arched back to touch his knees, pulled his hands to her heavy breasts and held them there as Rafe rammed himself deep inside her with increasing brutality. Her thighs gripped tightly to his hips and she matched his violent lovemaking with furious undulations of her own.

And suddenly she was convulsing uncontrollably even as he peaked and his fierce seed erupted into her eager cavity. The vehement words she spewed were not of love, but of hate. "Damn him damn him damn him . . ." until she fell forward, sobbing, burying her face in the hollow of his throat. Her body persisted in its contractions as his seed continued to flow languidly. He felt a tired, weary satisfaction. I am alive, he thought, alive. . . .

Her weight slid off him. A rustle of a silk gown and she bent over, kissed him on the lips and left silently. The taste of her lips provoked his memory as he drifted off to sleep again. He was a youth. Night had come and he was secretively pilfering Lord Clayton's personal spirits cabinet. Rafe's favorite was sherry. . . .

Morning. He could feel daybreak in his bones. He opened his eyes slowly to the hint of light from the single curtained window. He could see the room more clearly now, in greater detail. He had not been mistaken. Five years and he still remembered the room under the main house, the ground level where food and tools were stored. His old room. Suddenly the previous night flashed through his mind. He attempted to sit up but fell weakly back. Crissa? No, not her. He would have known and recognized her. A dream then? No. His lips still tasted faintly of sherry. And then he knew, for word of the mistress's one true affection, sherry, had been bandied about in the pitbuck compound. He lay quietly and wondered why, thought out the reasons until the answer came, and with it a new sense of despondency. Was he to be a weapon even as he lay in bed? To be involved in such a contest was more dangerous than his fight with Beaumarchant.

The door to his room opened and Crissa entered, only to gasp and turn away from his nakedness. Rafe pulled at the sheets, covered himself. When the rustling ended Crissa furtively looked back, then approached. "Oh, Rafe. You're awake. Good."

She remembered his name. The thought alone nearly shocked him speechless.

"Can you sit up?"

He nodded, staring suspiciously at her. She leaned over to adjust a pillow and her dressing gown parted to reveal a generous display of rounded, full breasts. Realizing what was happening, she backed away quickly, blushing and clutching her bodice, retying the ribbons. "I . . . I brought you a bowl of broth. I didn't know if you would be able to eat or not. You've been delirious at times and conscious at others. I've been able to get solid food in you only occasionally. Otherwise you might have wasted away entirely. Your eyes look clear now, though."

Rafe fumbled with the bowl, almost dropped it and didn't complain when she took it from him. Crissa pulled a chair close to the bed, sat and began to spoon the liquid into his mouth. His brain reeled with a myriad of thoughts. He could remember nothing except the fight and then last night. The broth was hot and tasted good. "How long have I been here?" he asked, measuring and pausing after each word. He was determined not to lapse into the compound dialect.

"Three weeks. Going on the fourth." His eyes widened. So much time asleep was impossible, yet there was no reason for her to lie. And the bearded stubble on his chin was further proof. "You were a terrible sight. All cut and bruised. And your poor hand. . . ." He eyes grew moist and a tear spilled down one cheek. She brushed it away quickly, smiled. "I'm sorry. Please forgive me. I don't know why I should cry. You're the one who was hurt. But Ezra is a horrible man. What he had you do was a terrible thing. I hate him and his cursed pit. How a man can delight in so much misery and suffering . . . there. That's the last of the broth." She brushed a cloth napkin across his mouth, found herself unable to meet his stare.

How could she tell him, make him understand what she believed and how she felt? Everything had gone wrong. The letter from New Orleans, telling her she had no recourse under the law to claim what was once her inheritance. She hid the news from Ezra, hoping to subdue his growing confidence and the liberties he took with her. She might have left had it not been for her mother and the plight of the slaves. And the night when Rafe was brought to the house like so much butchered meat. She remembered how Ezra had delighted in applying the white hot poker to the pitbuck's ravaged hand. Crissa promised herself Rafe would survive. Whatever else might happen, whatever other battles she may have lost or would lose in the future, this sensitive, oddly cultured black man who had been forced to become a killer would live. A killer. . . . She looked at his powerful torso, his silent brooding eyes. She felt very much alone in the room.

He lifted his bandaged hand. "You?" he asked.

She nodded. "It was bleeding terribly. Ezra cauterized it with a poker. I . . . I told him I'd take care of you. I was afraid of blood poisoning, of gangrene. At first he wasn't going to let me, but finally he relented and told me to do whatever was necessary. I remembered how the sla . . . field hands used to talk of the medicine man Chulem and his potions so I had him brought here to put something on your wounds. You caught a chill for awhile as well and lay there shivering for three days in spite of the summer heat. Other times you'd be up to eating, but I could tell you didn't know who you were or where you were."

He stared at her, and now his eyes were clear she was still unable to read his thoughts. Did he hate her? Did he consider her like all the rest? Why she should care what he thought bothered her more than anything else. What were her motives? Had she cared for him, bathed his feverish flesh with cooling wet cloths and fed him like a mother does a child only to spite Ezra? Or did she, God forbid, care about . . . .

Suddenly she wanted to be away. Crissa took the bowl and saucer and slid her chair back to the window. Why did he stare at her so, his eyes dark and brooding? Incriminating? She turned to go, stopped and whirled about. Had he started to speak? No. He was only staring. She left, closing the door quietly behind her. Odd, she could feel his eyes on her through the wood, watching her, following her. What was his silence trying to say?

Rafe would not have been able to tell her. She had tended him, true enough. No one except Old Chulem had ever tended him before, and Chulem didn't count. He was confused. He settled back against the pillow, listening to the morning stillness of the house and wishing Crissa hadn't left. But he was a fool. His weakness led to foolish thoughts. Why shouldn't she tend him? He was valuable property, worth more than a horse, or two mules. Dead, he was just another nigger, a hunk of meat to be buried and forgotten. Alive he was gold. Wagered gold. But if she hated Ezra as much as she pretended. . . . Damn! He had thought too much, and the broth made him drowsy again.

Micara's room didn't get the morning sun, but when she woke up she could see it brushing the very tops of the giant loblolly pines on the hill behind the house. She lay quietly, assimilating the sight. Morning sun! How utterly beautiful—bright gold on new green. How long had it been? She couldn't remember.

Her whole being was infused with languid bliss. Her body felt warm and cool at the same time. She looked down at herself, halfway on her side, one knee slightly bent, the other straight. Her right hand, palm up, lay gently relaxed on the sheet. She flexed the fingers, felt them move. The fingers she had . . . they curled of their own volition to memory's shape and her eyes closed to recapture and mirror the secret ecstasy of the night before.

Suddenly she rose from the bed and went to her dressing table, peered inquisitively at herself in the glass. Who was the woman she saw? Where had she come from? Where had she been? She couldn't remember. The horror which bound her to a slow, inexorable decline had snapped in the night and left her divorced from her past, left her giddy with a new sense of self.

She had dared, after all. The pride of accomplishment overwhelmed her and she sat back weakly, letting the realization creep into her slowly. She had dared! She would dare more. She rose quickly and wrapped a dressing gown about her sleeping attire before she stepped into the hall in time to see the door to Ezra's room open and Julie quietly back out. The girl wore a simple garment of cotton barely long enough to conceal her hips. Once in the hall she stooped to put on slippers. The smock lifted to reveal her buttocks, crisscrossed with bruises and welts. Micara audibly cleared her throat. Julie spun about, obviously startled. Seeing who it was, the mulatto girl recoiled against the wall, expecting the slap that was sure to follow.

Micara smiled at her. "Dear Julie," she said softly. "Come here."

The girl blinked in disbelief. "Ma'am?"

"Come here. I shan't hurt you." Julie walked slowly toward her. "You're such an attentive slut. And really quite lovely. Why, almost white. Almost."

"Yes'm."

Micara continued in sweet tones, as if truly affectionate toward Ezra's chosen bed partner. "The other day I noticed you coming out of the room downstairs. The room we've set aside for Ezra's pitbuck nigger. Several times, in fact."

"Yes'm. Ah went in ta see if'n he be aw'right."

"Your duty lies upstairs. I suspect there's more to your visit than concern for his health. We did not purchase you to service our studs. If service is what you wish, however, perhaps we could manage to turn loose some of the field hands with you for a few hours."

Julie held her own. "Mistuh Clayton, he doan 'low me to go near no field han's."

"I'm sure they'd love to have a chance to express their feelings for the nice little house nigger who pleasures the master they all love so dearly. Wouldn't they be fun? I can imagine how gently they would treat you."

For the first time in a long while Julie was suddenly afraid of her master's wife. Micara seemed very changed. Very capable. The girl had noticed a gradual change over the past week, but this was the first time it had been so visibly demonstrated. She nodded, her hands clenching the fabric of her shift. "Ma'am, Ah. . . ."

202

"Keep away from that room," Micara ordered harshly, the words hissing through her teeth. "I'm certain Ezra pumps away at you enough to keep you from scheming for even more seed, doesn't he? I imagine my dear husband would be more than a little displeased should he discover you in . . . that room."

Julie cringed at the very suggestion. "Miz Clayton, dat nigger was sleepin' ever' time Ah went in dere. Ah promise. Nuffin' happen. Ah'm a good girl an' do jes' lahk Mistuh Clayton tell me."

"Yes. You are a good girl. For as long as you do as you're told. Is that understood?"

"Yes'm," she answered meekly, anxious to be away.

"Very well. Run to your room and put some clothes on. I find it most unseemly to have a naked little pickaninny traipsing up and down my halls."

"Yes'm." The girl hurried to her room, a closed-off alcove at the far end of the house.

Micara watched her go, a grim smile of satisfaction on her face, then went to listen at her daughter's bedroom door. Not hearing anything she decided Crissa still slept. Better and better. She would be the first downstairs, the first to. . . . She heard footsteps, and suddenly apprehensive, hurried back to her room, leaving the door open a crack to see Crissa as she went into her bedroom. The door opened and shut. She frowned slightly at her temerity. Silly goose! To be frightened in her own house. What would John Fitzman say about that?

Very well. She had faltered, but not fallen. A moment of weakness, to be sure, but nothing irretrievable, and no one would know. She returned to her dressing table, let the dressing gown slip from her shoulders, then stepped out of her sleeping gown as well. She ran her hands over her stomach and up to cup her breasts. Forty-one years old. Her waist had thickened with age but not unpleasantly so. She could still give—and take—pleasure. The sound of a door closing across the hall alerted her to faint footsteps as Ezra passed by and descended the stairs. Micara rushed to her wardrobe and selected a dress suitable for the early hour. She was going to join Ezra at breakfast, for the first time in over two years.

His manservant bowed, placed a platter of ham in front of him. Ezra shoved his cup over. The young man bowed again and took the cup into the kitchen, returning immediately with a new cup, full and steaming hot. Ezra ate hungrily, listening with pleasure to the sound of the slaves heading for the fields. Satisfaction famished him. And he was satisfied. He had met all challenges and met them well. Patrick's threat had been removed. Duggins had been sent packing along with that foolish Statton fellow. And Rafe had won, beaten Beaumarchant, but not without a sufficiently demoralizing mauling by the Cajun. He'd never be the same, Ezra was certain. He would have to watch his bets from now on, of course. Win with his other pitbucks and begin wagering smaller amounts on Rafe. Perhaps even bet against him once in awhile and make sure the word got back to the compound, got back to Rafe and the other pitbucks.

Three weeks he'd kept that nigger under his roof. No telling how much longer he'd need before mending enough to fight again. But no matter. The process had begun and Ezra was not one to begrudge a dying man a little time to think over his coming death. He'd see Rafe was in the pit again before he was really ready. His spirits would erode even as his strength returned. And Ezra had the rest of the summer and fall to fight the giant black, to wear him down until he grovelled before his final foe, knowing he would never live long enough to taste his freedom.

Ezra anticipated watching him break, watching the hatred Rafe had flung in his master's face turn to supplication, to pleas for a mercy the lord of Freedom could never know and certainly never grant.

Suddenly his reverie was shattered and he paused with a cup of coffee halfway to his mouth, paused and slowly replaced the cup in its saucer. Micara seated herself across the table from him, relishing every moment of her husband's obvious surprise and discomfort. "Good morning, Ezra."

"Micara. . . ."

"Surprised? I'll have some ham and tea with cream,

204

thank you. There . . . there. . . . What a lovely morning! Did you see how beautiful the sky is?"

Ezra peered at her suspiciously, uneasy at what he saw and heard. Micara was different. Too different. He experienced a vague, unsettling pang of fear but quickly suppressed it. So she had risen early, applied some rouge to her cheeks. Nothing to get overly excited about.

"Did you pass a pleasant evening, Ezra?"

"I slept well. Always do," he responded gruffly, anxious to be away from the table.

"The rain cools the evenings so. And the breeze! Last night was almost pleasant, don't you think? Odd. Last July was such a stifling time."

He nodded, trying to figure her out. What did she think she was doing? He liked this less and less.

"Are you sure you slept well?" Micara asked, her voice taking on a tone of anxious concern.

"Yes, damn it."

"I only ask because your eyes look a bit puffy. Perhaps you forgot to open your window and your room was too stuffy."

"It was a night like any other," he answered roughly. A new tactic was needed. Shock. "Perhaps a little better. Julie invented a few new tricks. Nothing like a high yellow nigger wench for new tricks. They were delightful." He watched her face. That should have devastated her. She only smiled—an infernal idiot's grin, he called it—and poured her tea. Perhaps her senses had finally and totally left her, drowned in a vast sea of sherry and laudanum. Only there was a secretive confidence beneath this new placidity. His breakfast but partially completed, he slid his chair back and stood.

"You'll forgive me, Micara, but there are many things to which I must attend today. I shall be fighting Dingo in Natchitoches Saturday night and arrangements must be made in time to leave Thursday morning. The little nigger is proving to be a popular fighter."

"Why of course. I'll stay here with Crissa. We'll have a lovely time. And don't worry about Freedom. I'm sure I'll be able to look after things while you're away."

Ezra halted in the doorway, spun about as if to speak,

then faltered, at a loss for words. Micara was already intently involved with her breakfast. He watched her a moment more, brooding and puzzled over her behavior, then silently left.

Only when he was gone did Micara dare smile. She had won her first victory in over three years. She was determined there would be more. Many more.

13

Jagged shards of lightning tore the storm-darkened afternoon sky and though the rain ceased during the night, rolling tides of thunder threatened ominously until near first light. The previous day had been one of seemingly endless periods of sleep drifting one into the other. Crissa had not returned to see him and Rafe felt strangely disappointed and relieved at the same time. His solitary day had been broken only twice by the entrance of a manservant bringing him platters of food. He ate heartily each time, only dimly aware of what he was eating and how badly his body needed sustenance, how diminished was his strength.

Thursday morning brought a change. Sun streamed through the curtains over the window and brightened the small room. Rafe awoke fully aware of who and where he was, feeling rested and eager to be off his back. Then he thought of the pit and looked at his bandaged hand. Old Chulem had been wrong. They'd need more than a Beaumarchant if they wanted to kill him. He swung his legs over the edge of the bed and stood slowly, swayed for a second and fell back panting for breath, pain stitching his side. When the ceiling stopped whirling, he cursed softly and tried again. This time he made it with the help of the night table and the steadying influence of the wall. Taking one small cautious step after the other he traversed the small room and stood in front of the window. With his right hand he pushed the pane of glass. It stuck for a moment then slid upward with a loud, protesting squeak. A slight breeze ruffled the curtains, causing a delicate, whispering feminine sound he'd not heard for many years. The sound might have been insignificant to most, but not to a man who had spent four years waking to the hoarse cries of the guards, the stifling, harsh interior of the compound with its brutal inmates and equally vicious keepers.

He leaned against the wall, sniffed at the clean, summer morning smells and almost slept again, half dreaming of home. A home. The concept was murky, barely discernible. Only a dim idea of what the word meant. Curtains ruffling in the wind, strong honest labor, the sound of a man-child's laughter and a woman, one woman, the same woman at the end of every day.

Suddenly he began to tear at his bandaged left hand. This room, the smells, the bed, the dream, all lulled him from reality. The only reality. Why fool himself? The pit was home, was labor, love, hate, laughter, tears and even mother and wife. There was no other home. The cloth came away easily, sticking only in spots where blood or medication had seeped through and dried. He stopped at the inner bandage, then peeled it away as well, holding up his hand to the uncompromising sunlight. Softened, the skin was tender and shrivelled from being bandaged for so long. A gnarled, lumpish knob of tender flesh covered the nub of the severed joint. For a moment he wondered where his little finger was, if one of the guards had stolen it from the floor of the pit for a keepsake. Maybe Ezra Clayton himself kept it as a macabre memento.

The memory of pain swept over him and he relived the horrible mockery of the blurred faces above him and the agony of grinding teeth and the lipless smile, the burning, laughing eyes and finally his own blood welling from Beaumarchant's mouth as his mangled hand fell to his side. The shame of hot tears upon his cheek. His tears. . . .

He pulled himself erect with a shudder. "The past is to be seen through cold eyes," his father had told him. "Do not exult, do not weep. Learn." The remaining fingers and thumb felt stiff and painful when he flexed them, but flex them he did. Pain the teacher. He had learned more of pain than he ever thought he'd know, and from the pain, unsurpassed hate exploding into rage. Rafe had experienced a bloodlust that lay unsuspected in his character. His other battles had been won with cool, efficient action, not maddened, indiscriminate fury. The thought made him shudder. If Jomo or any of the others had been down there with him he would surely have killed them as well, even had they been fighting with him. Worse, had he been conscious, he would have clawed his way up the walls of the pit to wreak havoc on those above until he was shot down like a dog.

Rafe always pictured himself superior to the other pitbucks. He spoke better and had learned to read. But the blood-fury that came over him was not of a superior man, but rather of a rabid beast ready to kill the deserving and undeserving alike. Beaumarchant deserved death, he knew. Cat's tale of how the field slaves lived in mortal fear of the Cajun's indiscriminate killings was proof enough. But Beaumarchant's death was not the point. The point was how he had died—how Rafe had killed him—through unthinking, mindless rage. The thought was sobering, for how then could Rafe consider himself more a man than Beaumarchant or anyone else? Why should men not fear Rafe as a wild animal? How many black men had died at Beaumarchant's hands? Any more than at Rafe's?

"How many dark faces have I seen at the point of my machete?" Rafe asked himself quietly. "As many as I've seen watchin' me out of my dreams. I killed them so I could be free, just like they would a' killed me if they could a'."

But even as he spoke the words, he knew he was only hoping to exonerate himself from the guilt that had settled on him during the past weeks of feverish delirium and recovery. A man couldn't control his thoughts, laid up like he was. What thoughts? Could a man think while he slept? There had been too much time to dream, and the faces had come to him from the mist, each one accusing, each one a moldering symbol of his hunger to be free at any expense. He sought freedom, but would he ever be free from their faces? And the faces to come?

The door opened behind him and a manservant entered, a pair of coarse canvas trousers and a linen shirt over his arm. He raised his eyebrows at seeing Rafe out of bed, lay the clothes on the rumpled sheets and retreated hastily from the room. Rafe dressed, wishing he had mentioned the hungry ache in his stomach to the young Negro. As he was rubbing his flattened belly the door opened again and Crissa, as if on cue, entered with a platter of biscuits, bacon and honey.

"You're up. You have incredible powers of recovery. I should have thought you'd still be flat on your back. I'm still surprised you're even alive. Most men would have died."

"They would've," the black muttered, striding toward the food, then swaying dizzily, his knees weak and watery. He sat back on the bed, barely catching himself before falling.

"The clothes fit," Crissa went on as if nothing had happened. "They were the largest I could find in the storeroom." She put the platter by him on the bed, turned rapidly and stood behind the chair across the room. "There. I suspect you can well feed yourself."

Rafe was staring at Crissa, unable to tear his eyes from her in spite of years of training which had taught him no black man had the right to look so closely at a white woman. Her ripe figure more than attractively filled the summer dress and her hair fell about her face in a cascade of strawberry-gold ringlets. The faint trace of perfume tickled and provoked his senses and in a way angered him. Crissa was a symbol of everything he would forever be denied. "Why you carin' for me, Miss Crissa?" he suddenly blurted. "Did Mistah Ezra give you the orders an' you got to obey?"

Crissa sat down, unperturbed by the outburst. "Ezra Clayton did nothing of the sort. I was worried about you. There's no physician for miles about and I had no way of telling if you were going to live or die. I was determined to see you live."

"I'm livin', Miss Crissa. Don't you worry. There's more fightin' left in me. Yes, ma'am," he couldn't stop the sarcasm which dripped so bitterly from his voice, "I'll be butcherin' an' winnin' your stepdaddy his gold again before you know it, so don't worry."

"You don't have to be hateful. I was only trying to help," Crissa said angrily.

"What you tryin' to help for?" Rafe went on blindly, knowing he shouldn't be talking to the girl this way but unable to stop himself. "Help your nigger live to kill? Comin' in here in your finery, smellin' sweeter'n honey off a tree. That's all well an' good, but what am I goin' back to? Not the smell a' your sweet skin, but the smell a' ripped guts an' spilled blood. Not no gentle lady voice but the screamin' of dyin' men. Not the touch a' these here sheets and your coolin' hand on my face, but the feel of a hard wooden grip an' the weight an' balance a' my machete. I jus' a pit nigger, one a' your darkies an' you know it. Why you tryin' to make me feel like a real man?"

Her back straightened and a flush came to her cheeks. The words spilled out rapidly, an indication of her own pain, anger and frustration in the face of uncomfortable truth and unassailable logic. "Would you rather I'd let you die? What do you expect of me? Would you feel better if I treated you like an animal? And then what horrible things would you find to say to me? What else was I to do? What *can* I do?"

Rafe was silent under her outburst. He sat back against the pillows and shut his eyes, not wanting to see her face nor the hurt there. "When I was younger, five years younger, I used to watch you every chance I got. Steal a look at you doin' nothin' special, jus' bein', jus' . . . bein' you. The prettiest sight I ever seen, includin' all them fancy New Orleans women. You, jus' bein'.

"Then I figger if your mama ever found out, ever caught me gawkin' at you she'd fetch me up the side a' the head an' send me to the fields. No call for a nigger to be lookin' after a white woman, 'specially one jus' a girl. I didn't think you would a' minded, but everyone else sure would, an' raised a fuss. So I took to turnin' away every time you come around. Didn't matter. I found out I could shut my eyes an' still be seein' you."

"What are you saying?" Crissa asked tremulously.

"Nothin'. Jus' there's nothin' you can do, 'cept leave."

"I think I'd like to stay," she answered slowly, after a brief pause. "Finish your breakfast and I'll carry your plates back upstairs. It makes me feel useful." She paused again, a rueful smile on her face. "Carrying plates is about the only constructive function I can find for myself around here. Go on, eat."

Rafe forced any further reflection from his mind, concentrated on the taste of food and the pleasant nearness of Crissa Fitzman. She had changed, surely enough. The buds of youth had brought forth a woman. He finished the bacon and biscuits and slid the heavy coffee mug over, ladling several teaspoons of sugar and the entire contents of the small china pitcher of thick cream into the dark, aromatic brew. The result, sweet and heavy, was a luxury as well as a necessity if he wanted to rebuild his strength. He made the most of every drop.

Crissa sat and watched him. Perhaps Rafe had not changed all that much. Underneath the hardened veneer she was sure she detected a glimmer of the youth she had once barely known. She almost wished the five years had never been, wished they were back to the simple time she remembered so fondly.

"Why you grinnin' at me, Miss Crissa?"

"I was thinking about five years ago. You and Ezra had only just arrived. I was out playing on the gallery and saw you go into papa's library. No one, especially slaves, was allowed in that room. I hurried in to scold you but you looked so hurt when I started to speak I felt totally foolish and very much a little girl."

"You weren't seein' hurt. You were seein' scared. If'n your mama or stepdaddy found out, I knew I'd be in trouble. When it comes to trouble, ain't no one but the nigger gonna get his share an' then some."

"What really surprised me, though, was the fact you could read. For a moment I was angry because I didn't think slaves were supposed to be able to read. I'd never known one who could."

212

"I was the pride of Lucas Clayton's household," he responded, the bitterness seeping back into his voice. "His cultured, talkin', readin' nigger."

"It always comes back to that, doesn't it?"

"Why not? Sure, I used to sneak in your daddy's book-readin' room at night. Lord Lucas taught me to read an' gave me a hunger for words. So every night I fed myself on them books. Took to readin' whatever I could get my hands on the fastest. I'd sneak a book to my room an' read way into the night. One time Mistah Ezra almost caught me, but I stuck the book down the seat a' my britches an' then got it back when I had the chance. He never found out. If he had, it would've gone mighty hard for me. 'Course, after the compound was built, there wasn't any readin' to be done.

"Don't know how a man can get an' stay that mean an' keep from eatin' himself up with his own juices or cuttin' off his own limbs from spite. I guess 'cause he has his niggers to take it out on. That man doesn't have no heart. Maybe that's why he dug the pit, to match the hole he got on the inside where his feelin's ought to be. Can't understand why your mama tied her knot with him."

"Ezra was very dashing," Crissa explained. "And gallant. And knew the right things to say. Mama never was very strong. Independent minded, but not strong. She needed my father—or someone—around, couldn't handle things by herself. I was determined not to let myself get caught in a similar situation. When the opportunity came for me to go to school in Boston, I grabbed it. Now I wonder if I should have left at all, or come back. After four years I thought myself capable of meeting any situation. I should have known better. I'm not. In my own way I was taken in by Ezra too. He's too strong for any of us. I'm as much a slave as you. Of a different sort, but a slave all the same." She paused, sunk into herself. "When I was a child, slavery seemed very right. Father had slaves to work the fields. He never mistreated anyone and they seemed happy and at peace. It's strange. I learned in Boston how terrible slavery is. Now, seeing Freedom under Ezra Clayton and being under him myself, I've come to understand the difference between learning and

213

knowing. I wish I'd known earlier. Maybe I could have done something."

Rafe nodded. "My father once said, 'See the horns of the bush antelope, pointin' to where he has been. Like grief over wishin' you had done somethin' but didn't, or not done somethin' but did, it's better left behind you.' What's important is what you do, not what you wished you'd done."

"You said yourself there's nothing I can do," Crissa said angrily. She rose, agitated, and paced nervously back and forth like a caged animal. "Ezra will get his way in everything. Everything. He's made my mother an alcoholic and my father's land a symbol of corruption and greed. As for me, what he had planned . . . ." she paused, letting the words trail off. "And look at you. When I left you were a tall, shy, gawky young man. Now you're huge and frightening, the shy sensitivity replaced by an aura of menace and hatred toward all of us." Her face reddened as she realized what she'd said. "I'm sorry, Rafe. I didn't mean . . . ."

"No. What you sayin' is true. Mistah Ezra changed us all. I'm a fine one to be talkin' a' heart an' such. I got an emptiness where mine ought to be too. When all's said an' done, I don't care much who I point my knife at. Mistah Ezra made me a killer. Some needed killin', true enough, but others was jus' poor niggers more scared than me. But you're wrong about one thing, Crissa. I don't hate you. I never hated you. Ain't no way I could."

Her slim white hand reached out and touched the back of his mangled left hand, rested there despite the incongruous relief, the contrast of pale, lovely frailty to scarred and dark, fierce brutality. Suddenly she pulled back her hand as if burned, grabbed up the tray and left, leaving behind only a tantalizing hint of perfume.

Rafe spent the morning walking back and forth, flexing his hand. Around noon the manservant came with a tray piled high with food. Rafe ate every scrap, slept, and woke again to walk and flex, test and try his body, gaining strength with every step. The manservant came again shortly before sunset. This time he carried a lighted lantern and, on the tray next to a platter loaded with rice

214

and beans and a huge chunk of ham, a cloth-bound book. The manservant informed him in a nervous voice Crissa had sent the book as a gift. Eyes shifting from side to side, he obviously disapproved and Rafe could sense his fear of involvement. Rafe grumbled his thanks, told the boy not to worry. No one would betray him and he need not fear reprisal should Ezra return from Natchitoches and find the book in Rafe's possession. The slave deposited the tray and anxiously hurried from the room, glad to be away from the feared pitbuck.

The first book in over four years—since the compound had been built. Words. Would he remember how to read them? His mind whirling, he gingerly opened the book and stared with awe at the picture of a naked man on a beach. The man was kneeling, staff in hand, examining a footprint in the sand. Gold lettering glimmered on the frontispiece. *Robinson Crusoe* by Daniel Defoe. He turned up the flame on the lamp near the bed and, as he ate, began his struggle with the first page. . . .

The coal oil lamp had used much of its fuel and a dim shaft of moonlight struggled to be seen beyond the yellowish glow. The upstairs had been quiet for some time. He had reveled as the words, awkward and obscure at first, came easier and easier with each succeeding page. Some he remembered well, others he had to pronounce syllable by syllable. These words he sometimes stared at with awe, other times rushed past in eagerness to learn what lay beyond.

Suddenly his attention was interrupted by a wooden click as the latch on his door was released. Quickly he turned the lantern down and shoved the book under his bed. He knew the hour was late, had heard no warning sounds. Ezra wasn't due until Sunday, three days away. Nevertheless, suspicious of the presence behind the door, he dared take no chances. The door opened a crack and stopped. Whoever was there had paused, unable to decide whether or not to enter. Rafe felt his spine prickle with fear, for he was woefully weak and unable to defend himself. And if Ezra Clayton's wife came again . . . the game she played was not of his choosing.

The door opened all the way and Micara entered. Micara Clayton. The mistress of the house. Crissa's mother. The other night he had guessed it was she, and now he knew. Her hair was combed to fall in thick brown and silver curls, covering the swell of her bosom. Her figure was wrapped in a dark robe designed to hide her movements in the night and she held a single candle, only recently extinguished. A wisp of smoke rose from the red tip of the wick and trailed out into the hall until she closed the door. Her eyes glanced furtively to the shirt and breeches folded across the chair, then back to Rafe's dark form, sitting up, the sheet covering him from the waist down.

The dark robe fell behind as she walked toward him to reveal a white nightgown fit for a wedding bed. The gown diminished the slight thickness of her waist and hips and the fabric clung to her breasts to accentuate the erect nipples, already straining forward, swollen with anticipation and desire.

She drew closer, a beautiful woman nearing her decline and grabbing for whatever bit of sensation she could find in life, regardless of its clandestine, forbidden nature, aware only that from the first moment she had seen Rafe in the pit and then later, lying naked and unconscious in bed, there had been awakened in her a fierce sensuality appeased only by the driving rhythm and raging climax of two nights earlier. She sat on the edge of the bed, leaned over to press her face against his chest.

Rafe was a slave. Ezra Clayton's prize pit nigger. No matter Micara had come to him, the crime would be his should she throw her rutting ways in her husband's face. "What you doin' here?" he asked angrily. "You gonna get me killed. Worse than killed, probably. Go on back to Ezra's bed and wait for him. I don't need the grief you bring." The words were hard and biting, belying the urge he resisted to stroke her hair. There was something pitiable about her. She seemed a lost child.

"Are you afraid of Ezra? He's gone for the rest of the week." He tried to ignore the warm pressure of her breasts pressed against his stomach. Micara deftly undid the ribbons binding her nightgown. She shrugged and the slick fabric slid from her shoulders, gathered at her waist.

Her heavy breasts fell free, nipples taut, protruding hungrily from dark brown aureoles. She forced her breasts against his chest, drew them back and forth over his muscular, scar-covered physique, teased his neck and shoulders with kisses and teasing bites. "Are you afraid, Rafe?" she whispered huskily.

Her head sank to his belly and continued the arousing foreplay. Rafe's awesome member rose despite his attempts to disassociate himself from her caresses. He leaned over to push her away but she quickly stood and caught his hands, pulled them to her hips and slid the gown to the floor. Deftly she guided one hand to the dark triangle between her legs, and with her other hand swept the sheet to the floor and grasped him lightly, bringing him to a quick, limb-wrenching rigidity. His body shuddered ecstatically, her coos of encouragement and muted endearments, her playful fingers and tongue carrying him headlong to madness. As she leaned over onto him, his hand swept up her back, closed on her hair. He dragged her to him, rolled her over onto her back and covered her with his own demanding form, penetrating her roughly, ravenously. Micara wrapped her legs about him, forcing him deep into her, impaling herself on him, matching the animal rhythm of their mutual desire. Rafe's tongue probed and prodded her eager breasts, driving her further into an orgiastic frenzy. Her hands raked his back as she exploded into the uncontrollable, sobbing heights of sexuality. Her breath came in heaving, broken gasps until it seemed she ceased to expel any air at all, and still he thrust himself into her, faster and faster, harder and harder. Finally, no longer able to cry for him to stop, her eyes grew wide, then rolled up into her head. Her arms and legs dropped limply away from him. She was unconscious.

Rafe stopped, looked down at the now drawn white face, tried to feel hate and couldn't. This woman . . . beneath him, yet so far above him . . . deserved . . . what? He didn't know. He rose on his arms to look at her, down her body to where he disappeared inside her. Slowly, watching and feeling every inch of him move, he unsheathed himself and in so doing brought on his own orgasm. He watched his belly moving in and out with each driving breath, and below, his seed spilling on Micara's abdomen. He watched that as well.

Micara was breathing more easily now and her eyelids began to flutter. He wanted to believe he had succumbed to her out of spite for Eza, but felt only shame for his own weakness. Micara's hand stirred, sought his organ, pressed it to her. "You're my nigger, Rafe," she murmured sleepily. "You'll have a good life. I'll see you stay here. You won't ever have to go back to the pit. I want it to be like this. It can be good for a long, long time." She looked down at his manhood, glistening in the aftermath of its eruption. "My stallion . . . my stallion. . . ."

Something fell above them, was knocked over on the front gallery. Before the clatter died away feet were pounding on the wooden planking and then down the steps. A guard from far off shouted, "Hey!"

Rafe jumped from atop the woman as if struck by lightning. Micara bolted from the bed, quickly wiped herself and donned her gown and robe even as Rafe, his stomach knotted with panic, blew out the lamp. Outside, a musket fired, rupturing the still evening. Micara feverishly tied the bows and hurried to the door. The house was awake and stirring. Slaves were hurrying about in their rooms, dressing, running toward the front of the house. Micara looked back at Rafe, smiled and hurried out onto the dirt under the front gallery and up the stairs. Rather than try for her room she stopped halfway to the top of the stairs and turned back toward the front yard. "What is it?" she called to the first figure to run by.

The guard doffed his cap. "Saw someone movin' on the gallery, ma'am. Whoever it was run off. We'll track 'im, I 'spect." He rammed a load down the musket and hurried off. Other guards were running up from the barracks.

Crissa appeared on the gallery and ran to join her mother. "What's happening?"

"Nothing, dear. A trifling disturbance. I'm certain Mr. Butkis and his men will take care of it." Crissa was staring at her. "What is it, dear?" Micara asked.

218

"I didn't hear you in the hall, yet you were here ahead of me."

"Of course," the older woman answered pleasantly. "That's why you didn't hear me." She patted Crissa on the cheek and stepped into the dark house, dismissing the house servants and sending them back to their beds before she ascended the steps to her room.

Crissa stared perplexedly after her, finally followed.

The old man watched Crissa from the safety of the grove, wanting to go to her yet knowing the opportunity was lost. The guards would be searching all around him after ensuring the safety of the immediate grounds. Only the moon dropping behind a cloud had saved his life, enabling him to cross to the safety of his beloved pecans without being seen and shot. But the darkness would not last long. Ephraim hobbled off into the depths of the grove, bowed by a burden more terrible than his age.

14

The shay clattered over the rise out of Claytonville,
Ezra Clayton anxiously standing in the seat to inspect the
fields. His fields. . . . A guard on the perimeter of the
cotton field near the road briefly turned his attention from
the toiling slaves to doff his cap in salute as the shay
whisked by in a cloud of dust. Ezra ignored him, breathed
a sigh of relief. All appeared to be well. Staying in Natchitoches an extra day had been a calculated risk based
on faith in Butkis's ability to control the plantation in his
absence. He'd left the overseer with definite instructions
to carry on as usual should he arrive late, to accept and
implement new orders from no one. His faith was well-
placed. Butkis was a good man and the slaves were in the
fields and working. Good.

Still, he had left with definite misgivings. Micara was up
to something. Her new attitude puzzled and worried him.
The episode at breakfast the day before he left unnerved
him. After two years of sherry and subjection she'd evidently roused and wakened, and whether or not she knew
it, her new awareness had stuck in the back of his mind all
the weekend, plaguing him unmercifully and wreaking
havoc with his concentration. Damn the woman! And her
daughter!

There it was. Her daughter. Been working on Micara ever since she'd arrived back from the north where she should have stayed, a pox upon her. She'd brought him nothing but grief, now compounded by this apparently accomplished rehabilitation of her mother. Only two months and she'd turned his life upside down and inside out and now Micara, in an abrupt and unsettling change, had joined her. But that didn't make sense. The change should have been more gradual. There must have been some other factor he hadn't considered, of which he wasn't aware. He put the question behind him. His fields lay green and waving in the slight breeze. Everything was as it should be for the moment and he would handle new problems as they arose. He was in no mood for self-torment after a tiring weekend and even more exhausting long ride.

The lord and master of Freedom turned in the swaying seat and glanced back at the wagon just to the rear of his own carriage. Four pitbucks had ridden to Natchitoches and but for the driver, Dingo rode alone on the return trip. Dingo hadn't let him down. Dingo was a fighter of the first class. He'd faced a local nigger charged with thievery and killed him with style and at some profit to Ezra. Another five fights and he'd be as good as any other in the compound, including Jomo and Cat and perhaps even Rafe.

As an added draw Ezra had brought three of his younger bucks, each with only a fight or two to his credit. People would always gather to watch three Clayton pitbucks go at each other. So he had anticipated, and neither he nor the crowd was disappointed. The fight was hard and fast and bitter, leaving the crowd screaming in a blood frenzy. The one who survived the melee would have been the cream of his new crop, but the winner received a mortal gash across his stomach at the last moment. His eyes glazed with pain, he took three steps from the chalk circle and crumpled over, his guts in his hands. Ezra lost not only a potentially excellent pitbuck but a good future draw as well, for the boy had a natural flair, and after winning against two would have been popular the next time he was brought to town. The slave owner tried to take comfort from the fact that those who had come to watch were many, each paying handsomely to be there and betting heavily as well. With judicious side wagers, Ezra had made a profit in spite of the loss of the three.

The shay swung up the drive in front of the house and pulled to a halt as the wagon and escort continued to the compound. Ezra waved the driver of his shay away and entered the house, hurriedly doffing his waistcoat in the relief of the dim hallway, cooler by far than the bright afternoon sun. His manservant came forward and bowed nervously. "Rum. And chip some ice in it. There is still ice?"

"No, suh. Ah'm sorry, suh."

"Damn. Well, there'll be another shipment before the week is out. Scuppernong then. I'll be in the library." The manservant's eyes grew wide with fright but he said nothing, only nodded and hurried off to do his master's bidding.

Ezra, accustomed to and expecting fear from his darkies, ignored the young Negro. He entered the library, crossed to the huge oak desk and collapsed gratefully into the luxuriously plush chair. The chair, almost a throne of black walnut and leather and made to his specifications in England cost him a pretty penny but Ezra felt he deserved it. He stripped off his shirt and unhooked the heavy belt from around his waist, dropped it with a thump on the desk. For a second he stretched, feeling light after wearing the cumbersome burden for so long. He undid the ties and dumped the contents of the belt on the desk, sat and stared hungrily. A pile of coins like so many glittering, greedy eyes reflected the sun streaming in the window behind him and lent a malevolent, jaundiced gold cast to Ezra's face.

He allowed himself a moment of imagination. All the gold was won gold, all profit. The moment passed quickly, for in truth, he had brought half the coins with him. He sighed, took out the amount originally in the belt and placed it to one side. Subtracting his expenses, he added them to the new pile. After a moment of hesitation he gave in, took out the cost of the three slaves he'd lost, damn them all, and shoved more gold to the other side of the desk. Eight double-gold eagles left by the empty belt. Eight and no more. Still . . . eight was more profit than anyone else had seen. Not many men in western Louisiana could make a hundred and sixty dollars in gold on a week-end. A profit was a profit. He leaned back in the chair and let the tension drain from him, almost dozing until the boy returned with a decanter and glass on a tray.

"What the hell took you so long?"

"Scuppernong on the lower level, suh, where it stay cool." He poured some in the glass, his hand shaking so badly he spilled drops on the tray.

Ezra glared at him, a new tenseness, undefinable, creeping into him. "What's the matter with you, boy?"

The young slave jerked upright, almost spilling more wine. His eyes widened and he took an unconscious step backward. "Nuffin', suh. Ain't nuffin' wrong wid me. Ah's jes' fine, suh, Ah . . . ."

"Why are you shaking then? Come on, what have you done?"

"I ain't done nuffin', suh. Ah swears by de lawd Ah ain't done nuffin'," he gabbled, beads of sweat popping out on his forehead.

Ezra stared at him intently. The slave was frightened—so frightened he was lying, and a Clayton slave had to be damned scared to lie to his master. Perhaps Micara or her bitch daughter had been up to some new tricks after all. The slave shuffled back a few steps, kept turning his head left toward the books on the wall. Ezra followed his furtive, wide-eyed glances, saw nothing amiss.

"Kin Ah go now, suh?" he asked, staring assiduously at the floor. "Ah's got wo'k in de kitchen, an'. . . ."

Ezra saw it then, to his left and high above the fireplace. John Fitzman's portrait! The portrait he had removed so long ago! For a moment the shock left him senseless, his mind reeling in a nightmare. He couldn't be looking at it, couldn't believe what he saw. John Fitzman come back. . . .

He bolted upright, the chair slamming into the wall behind him and the terrified slave freezing in fear across the desk from him. Ezra's fingers turned bloodless from pressure as his knuckles dug into the desk top and a violent, animalistic howl of rage erupted from him, crescendoing painfully to a throat-tearing peak. He staggered from behind the desk and advanced on the painting, hands clenched into fists as if to strike that which was hopelessly out of reach.

He stood quaking before the stone mantel, beneath John Fitzman's benevolent gaze. Still staring, he groped about on the hearth until he found the iron poker. He reached up and swung the length of blackened metal but his brief height only allowed him to strike the deep and massive gilt frame bordering the hated portrait. Cursing, he struck over and over again, knocking away chips of wood which flew in all directions each time the poker made contact. Finally he succeeded in causing a great crack in the wood, but the painting itself remained unharmed.

Ezra paused, panting harshly, oaths of hate and frustration bubbling from his lips. He turned on the servant still cowering by the desk and started for him. The young Negro backed away, arms and hands vainly outstretched to protect his head and face from the raised poker his master bore, until he tripped on a chair and fell heavily against the wall of books. Ezra pounced, brought the iron poker down in a wicked slash across the slave's leg. The terrified Negro screamed once and fell the rest of the way to the floor, lay there writhing in agony and grabbing at his leg. "Oh, please, suh, please no moah. Ah din't do nuffin'. Ah din't do nuffin'," he broke off with a moan.

Ezra stood, face flushed, over the prostrate form. His breath rasping, he barely managed to speak. "Micara. Did . . . my wife. . . ."

"Yassuh. Oh, mah laig, oh, Lawd. Yassuh, Miz Clayton say fetch dat from de bottom level an' put it up in heah. She brung in two a' de downstair niggers to he'p her. Only not me, Mastah Clayton, 'cause Ah knowed . . . . Oh, it broke, it broke!"

"Shut up your damned whining mouth. Where is Mrs. Clayton?"

"She ain't heah, suh. Miz Clayton an' Missy Crissa goan to de town to hab tea wid Miz Leahy. Dey wid de Preachah's woman."

"Get out of here. I want that down and burned before . . . no. Wait. Not yet. Get out."

The manservant hobbled to his feet and stumbled painfully from the library, wincing every time he put his weight on his right leg though relieved the bone wasn't broken after all. Ezra took up the decanter and crystal wine glass. He stood in the center of the room, shirt off, sweat dripping from him as he stared up at the portrait. "I should have burned it when I first took the damned thing down," he muttered aloud.

John Fitzman only smiled in answer. That cursed, superior smile! "You're dead, God damn your soul to hell, dead!" he screamed. And still no answer, still only the mocking smile. Ezra flung the decanter. The glass exploded on the stone behind the portrait and sent shards and slivers slicing through the canvas, wine spilling across and down the delicate tints and hues, staining them bloody red. A gaping jagged hole rent John Fitzman's handsome features, leaving only one eye to stare enigmatically into space. Ezra gulped the contents of his wine glass and sent it after the decanter. The crystal struck the top of the frame and bounced harmlessly off, shattering on the wood floor.

Micara. The bitch! But how ever could he have expected this from her? There was only one solution. He would be rid of her—her and her daughter—and no questions asked. The advantages of keeping her around and in sight were now outweighed by those of having her as far away as possible. Damn the slut! He prided himself in the absolute control and sure-handed manipulation of those he allowed in his house; yet somehow Micara had recovered the spirit and confidence he had so laboriously eroded. She had changed under his very nose, and he couldn't understand how or why, could no longer predict her actions or reactions. She'd been a willful woman when he first met her. Lonely and inept at running a plantation, but headstrong and spirited in many other ways. What had caused her rejuvenation of spirit? What prompted such an insulting challenge to his command? Capricious defiance? He thought not. Something more. An unknown factor. Something new, deliberate on her part, unnoticed or unheeded on his. Nothing he could think of might have provoked this unwarranted attack on his authority. . . .

Rafe! Rafe! The thought struck him like a whip, sent him reeling back to lean on his desk, breathless at the very idea. He'd seen her watching the giant pitbuck as he fought, seen her breath quicken with excitement. And he'd heard her door close . . . when? Late the night before she'd come down to breakfast. But she wouldn't dare . . . wouldn't. . . .

The hallway inside the ground level where Rafe was kept was dim and needed sweeping. He'd call attention to the filth later. He stopped outside the door to Rafe's room, quietly checked the load and cocked the .69 caliber Army pistol. .69 caliber. Such a weapon was large enough even for Rafe, especially at such a short distance. Unbolting the door, he pressed his hand against the rough wood and pushed.

Rafe was awake, dressed and sitting upright in bed. The book he had placed beneath the pillow at his back the moment the bolt slid back. Ezra stepped into the room and Rafe made himself smile. For the first time in four years the two stood face to face with no one between them. The black man kept his eyes from the pistol, stared at the white flesh, flabby and sagging, then dropped his eyes quickly and respectfully lest insult be implied. The appearance of his owner, half-dressed and armed, surprised and alarmed him more than he cared to admit. Such a visit could only bode ill. "Welcome, Mistah Ezra," he said, his voice deep and melodious, reverberating in the small room.

Ezra glanced from right to left, found nothing to threaten him. He stood but six feet from Rafe, the Army pistol huge in his small hand. Rafe was not fooled into thinking his size or speed made any difference. Ezra would use the weapon if he had to and a lead ball that huge would rip through his belly and splatter his backbone over the entire wall. Gutshot, he would die ignobly, painfully.

"You scared, nigger?"

Rafe stared at the maw of the pistol. "I don't want to die. But I ain't feared of it, neither."

"I'm gonna see you gelded, boy. Have your balls and pecker in a jar of wood alcohol and put it on the mantelpiece. How do you like that idea? Pretty good?"

Rafe did not show the tight, gut-feeling of fear washing over him. Had Ezra discovered . . . ? And yet, how could he? He'd been in Natchitoches, arrived home only minutes ago, for Rafe had seen him through the window when the shay drove up. Surely he hadn't stopped in Claytonville on the way, for how would he know Micara was there? Still, Micara might have found some way to flaunt her indiscretion to her husband and so sealed Rafe's fate. Or someone, some quiet watcher, might have seen her in the night and, to curry favor, told the master of his wife's infidelity. Ezra seemed uncertain and Rafe took the chance and assumed he didn't really know. "I fought for you, Mistah Clayton. Even hatin' your guts the whole while, I fought for you. An' won. I figured you'd be grateful for the gold I won you."

Ezra's face paled. "Don't try to fool me, nigger. You played stud to my wife. You rammed that black pecker of yours up into my wife and shot your damn stinking black seed into her belly. No nigger's going to get away with that. Not you, not anyone."

Images of Julie flashed into Rafe's mind. Ezra could read the lie in a man's eyes so he had to say the truth. He drew himself up to his full height. "I haven't been with or done anything with your woman, Mistah Ezra." And Micara's not your woman, Ezra Clayton, if everything Micara told me is true, Rafe added silently.

"You're a high and mighty nigger. Always have been. Just because my brother gave you a bit of education you think you're white."

"I ain't never figgered I'm white," Rafe answered contemptuously.

"How many times did she sneak down here? Once? Twice? Every night I was gone? I'll bet she couldn't get enough. Bet you liked sticking it in a white woman, didn't you?"

"I ain't ever touched your woman, Mistah Clayton. You can believe me or not, but I know I'm talkin' true. Rafe don't lie, an' you not believin' what I say don't make me a liar."

Ezra realized he had lost his temper, let Rafe have the edge and possibly made a fool of himself. He watched the pitbuck closely, looking for signs of laughter. None. The nigger had sense and did seem to be telling the truth. He stared long and hard into the black, unwavering eyes in front of him. They stared back innocently, boldly and calmly, without fear. He was determined the nigger would not beat him, determined he wouldn't get away without learning fear. Forcing himself to remain calm, he pulled the chair to the door and sat down, being sure to keep the pistol pointed at the black man. "You've won a great deal of money for me, Rafe. And you shall win more. Perhaps I can find another Beaumarchant. Would you like that?"

When Rafe said nothing, Ezra continued. "Beaumarchant hurt you, didn't he? Hurt you bad. You wept like a little pickaninny."

"I didn't cry because he hurt me."

"You cried. Like a pickaninny. I saw you."

"But don't know why. Beaumarchant is dead," Rafe added.

"There'll be others."

The thought exploded full-blown in Rafe's mind, the sudden clarity of his decision surprising him. Rafe knew what he must do, knew where the three weeks of dreaming and sleep thinking had brought him. He knew, and a weight fell from him. Now there would be no more uncertainty, no more questions. He stood straight, facing the man with the gun. The white man. They stared at each other across the silent gulf, made vast by the pigments of their flesh. "I doubt it," he said calmly.

"I doubt it," Ezra sneered mockingly. "I doubt it. An educated nigger, too good for. . . ."

"Lord Lucas was a good man. He deserved respect."

Ezra bristled at the implied comparison. "Lucas was a fool," he countered harshly. "Giving an education to a

229

pickaninny was a waste of time and money. Well, I've given you the only kind of education a nigger can use. I made you worth something."

"Lord Lucas taught me readin' an' how to write. You taught me killin'. I killed for freedom, my freedom, and along the way I won gold for you. No Mistah Ezra, I made *you* worth somethin'. Me an' the rest of the pitbucks desperate enough to butcher an' die for a chance at a wagon, a woman, an' a place across the river. Only I'm thinkin' now that crossin' the river ain't worth it. Not when what's over there is bought with blood. I ain't no animal. I ain't no fightin' dog. I'm a man."

"You're a nigger. My nigger. That's all you're ever going to be! A nigger with six fights left in him and each one rougher than the one before. You and Jomo for instance. You two bucks are close, but not so close as one won't kill the other. You'll be at each other's throats like animals. Folks will pay a pretty sum to see Clayton's two best pitbuck niggers hack each other to pieces."

"They won't see nothin', Mistah Ezra. I decided, lyin' here all stove up. Ain't gonna be no more fights for Rafe."

Ezra stood, his legs apart, a diminutive figure of terrible authority. "You'll do as I tell you."

"Not if it's fightin' in your pit." Ezra, his face white and drawn with anger, raised the pistol deliberately, his finger tightening on the trigger. Rafe watched impassively. "An' pointin' that pistol won't work," he continued. "You shoot me an' none a' them'll ever fight again. What's the point of winnin' fifty fights if Mistah Ezra ain't gonna keep his promise? If the only freedom they gonna get is a bullet through the head there won't be one of them walkin' that path to fight for you ever again. They might as well take their chances on runnin' for the river, if they be gettin' shot anyway. Then where you be, Mistah Ezra? Where you be without your pitbucks? Where you gonna get the blood an' guts you like to watch?"

The gun lowered slowly. Rafe was right, Ezra had to admit. The nigger would have to be punished in the pit. Otherwise he'd be risking insurrection. Not that twenty or so darkies could do much against Butkis and his men, but a revolt would be expensive and hurt his reputation. Throw them in the pit and they'd fight, all right. More. They'd kill themselves off one by one and Rafe would be one of the first to go. In his mind's eye he could see the pitbuck dying slowly, painfully. A tight smile froze on his face. "It hurts me to think a nigger's right, Rafe, but for once I'm glad you are because I almost lost my temper and shot you. I am grateful, even. You stopped me from giving you a fast death. Now you may look forward to dying slowly. In the pit. You will fight again."

"No."

"I'll not send you to the fields, if that's what you're thinking. And you've lost your last chance to die fast. You'll go back to the compound to stay with the other bucks. I'll have you out of this house today. I know a dozen ways to make a nigger fighting mad and I expect Mr. Butkis can find a few of his own. By the time I'm done with you you'll beg for the chance to get down in my pit again. Only then it will be too late. You'll fight, but with fear in your throat slowing you down, helping you make mistakes. Little mistakes, big mistakes. You'll make them and I'll be watching from the rim of the pit, watching and waiting for you to cry again as you see death stalk, find and lay his hands on you. You'll cringe and cower like a dog and beg like the animal you are, and only then will I let you die."

"I saw you ragged, Mistah Ezra. I saw you cold an' hunted. I saw you hungry an' wet an' beaten an' I know you for what you are. You can't ever forget that, Mistah Ezra. You don't know it an' ain't nobody but me gonna tell you, but you're a froth-mouthed dog, even in your fine shirts an' cultured ways. You dug the pit out there on that hill, but what you don't know is you dug another an' bigger pit. A pit you fell in, don't know you're in an' don't know how to get out a'. I ain't killin' for you ever again."

"We'll see," Ezra leered. And then he was gone, the door bolted behind him.

Ezra hesitated on the other side, realizing he had not settled the question of Micara. No matter. He'd save her rutting for later, save her infidelity for his confrontation

231

with her. Whether or not she had actually lain with Rafe was of no import. He would accuse her and thus have excuse to be rid of her. Better yet, he'd never mention it to her; rather, send her to New Orleans and there spread the word of how she'd let a nigger have her. Later he would pretend to find out himself. By that time the nigger would be dead. He chuckled to himself. Both of them, by God, right where he wanted them. Micara's reputation would be compromised beyond all hope of repair and the nigger would die slowly and very, very painfully. He headed upstairs. Once inside he sent for Butkis.

Crissa and Micara arrived late, nearly at sunset, Crissa driving the team herself on her own insistence. She and her mother had passed a pleasant day with Rebecca Leahy, and for a few hours she had been able to forget her anxiety over Ezra's reaction to the restoration of her father's portrait. Now, the twin magnolias looming ahead, the hidden dread came into the open, strangely tempered by a sense of exhilaration. Did men, she wondered, feel that way when they went into battle? She stole a furtive glance at her mother. Rehanging the painting was Micara's idea, which surprised and delighted Crissa at the same time. Here was a mother she thought she'd lost, thought she'd never see again. The older woman's motives puzzled her but she feared to probe the newfound strength and confidence too deeply lest she accidentally discover something she didn't want to know, or worse, force Micara back into the fog of sherry and laudanum.

Butkis and two guards were escorting a heavily manacled Rafe away from the house as the carriage pulled up. Micara went pale at the sight, ordered Crissa to stop near the men. "Wait," she called to Butkis. "Where are you taking him?"

Butkis waved the men on and approached the carriage. "The nigger's bein' sent back to the stockade, Miz Clayton."

"But he isn't well yet," Crissa interjected.

"Well, now, Missy, he looks fine an' dandy to me. Fit as a fiddle."

"I order you to bring that man back immediately," Micara commanded.

Butkis grinned and spat into the dust. "Can't do so, Miz Clayton. Mistah Clayton's orders. Get the nigger ready to fight afore Sunday, is what he said." The overseer nodded curtly and walked away, paying them no more attention.

"He can't do this . . . he can't do this." Micara stumbled from the carriage and hurried into the house, half running, half falling up the stairs to the lower gallery. Crissa jumped from the carriage and handed the reins to one of the servants. By the time she entered the house Micara had already fled to her room. Ezra was in the library and Crissa went in to confront him. She stopped and stared at the ravaged painting of her father. "You . . . heathen," she swore. "You despicable, unconscionable swine."

Ezra unconcernedly sipped his brandy. "There is a boat out of Natchitoches for New Orleans. It leaves a week from tomorrow. You and your mother will go to see your good friend nigger Rafe fight Sunday, drive to Natchitoches Monday and be on the boat Tuesday."

Crissa stared uncomprehendingly at him. Ezra returned to his paperwork, dismissing her completely. He paid no attention when she left.

15

"Dat Beaumarchant put a yellah streak in him, dat's what Ah say."

"Shut up, Cat, a'fo' yo' mouf done talk itse'f into a fist."

"Yo' ain't got no call ta say dat ta me. Ain't got no call, Jomo. Ah ain't de one put all dis grief on us, dat got dem guards workin' us in de swamp an' runnin' de balls an' climbin' dat tall slick pole. Dat Rafe done it, him tellin' Butkis he ain't goana fight t'morrah. De whole week bin worse an' gettin' worser. Dem niggers in de field doan sweat hab as much as we done dis week. An' all account a' Rafe turnin' yellah."

Many of the other pitbucks nodded or muttered agreement. Jomo flared, defending Rafe. "Rafe got his reason. A man git dat hurt, he need time a'fo' tryin' ta git hurt agin. Dat's all."

"An' mean whiles we gots ta keep bustin' ouah asses."

"Tain't fair," agreed Dingo. "Cat's right, Jomo."

"He jump in an' fight dem wolves, standin' side by side wif me. If it weren't fo' him, Ah be in some dawg's gut by now. Rafe stood by me an' now Ah's goana stan' by him."

"Dat was near two month ago. Pas' is pas'. Yo' ain't

235

thinkin' right, Jomo," Cat retorted. "Ever'body else feel diff'rent."

"Yo' ain't speakin' fo' me," muttered Trinidad.

"Hell, Trinidad, you knows Ah'm speakin' de troof," Cat argued.

"Ah knows yo' speakin' an' nuffin' moah. Yo' always waggin' dat tongue moah den anybody else aroun' here. An' anybody who lissen to yo' got fools fo' ears."

Most of the gathering chuckled at Trinidad's remark, but Cat lunged at the pitbuck who had insulted him. Trinidad doubled his fists to meet the attack but Jomo quickly stepped between the two of them, violently shoving Cat away. "None a' dat. Mistuh Clayton gib y'all de fightin' yo' wants. No use goin' at it when it doan count fo' nuffin'."

Cat glared at both a moment more, then turned back to the younger pitbucks, to whom he was a leader of sorts. Jomo, Trinidad and Dingo walked together toward the shack that had once been Rafe's but was now assigned to Jomo.

"If he ain't skeered, den yo' tell me what got into him," Dingo demanded. All three made a point of not looking in Rafe's direction. The black giant was squatting in the shade of the cook shack. Near dusk, the sun had yet to dip below the horizon and heat waves still shimmered between them.

"Doan know," Jomo answered. "Touch a' fever still in his blood. Dat Beaumarchant could a' swatted him aside of de haid an' hurt him fo' sho'."

"May be, may not be. But dere jes' ain't no sense in gittin' Mistuh Butkis mad. All Rafe do is run an' exercise an' squat in de shade an' eat an' run some mo'. Doan speak to no one," Trinidad observed.

"Dat ain't all," Jomo added. "De way he jes' take what dey do to him. Took away his shack an' give it to me, dough I doan sleep in it none. An' dem guards trip 'im an' cuff 'im 'bout. He jes' get up an' keep on runnin', keep on workin'. Dey wake 'im up las' night an' make 'im run some mo' 'til he near drop. A man gotta be mussed up in de haid ta put up wid dat. An' he only gots ta fight six mo' time an' he be free. Cain't no one beat Rafe, 'cept maybe me. Him fightin' dis far an' jes' givin' up, Ah doan unnerstan'. Ah tells yo', dat Beaumarchant done hit him in de haid."

Rafe watched them from the shade of the cook shack wall. He knew what they were talking about. The subject, betrayed by too many sideways glances, was obvious. Only one person on their minds. Only one result of their thinking—Rafe was afraid, had turned yellow. He looked at the stub of his little finger. Perhaps he was yellow. But only a little. Fear wasn't the reason for the way he was acting and he knew it. Crissa . . . no. Not her, either. She was gentle, but did not understand. Perhaps he was wrong, though. Perhaps she did understand, if only a little. There was another, a deeper reason which he could not fully explain. He felt his father would have understood. He would have known and been able to tell him, put his feelings into words, make a story to fit the action. But his father was dead, killed by the same slavers who had captured him, torn him from his home, his land and family. Yes, his father would have understood.

The urge to run again tugged at him. Each circumvention of the compound was a different jungle trail in his mind's eye, one of a hundred remembered paths from a lost world he would never see again outside his dreams. He rose and set out to run the river path where he had killed his first antelope, a young and not too cautious buck. There the hollowed trunk of a fallen tree, home of the fierce bees whose gathered honey he had robbed more than once. Then into the trail in earnest, ducking underneath wide, sweeping fronds, bursting through a cluster of vines, his eyes searching the low-hanging branches for the friendly tree snake, searching the path for spoor, for traps, for the poisonous fangs of the quick death-dealing mamba, hidden in the bush. Monkeys chattered overhead. A bird of brilliant plumage swept low to scold. Down into the winding, tortuous river bed, dry but for a few stagnant pools and soon to burgeon with flood water come the rainy season. Up to cut across the tracks of a lion and her cubs, heading for the grassy plains. And so it went, oblivious to the following eyes of the pitbucks and the jeering shouts of the guard on the gate. Every step took him farther away beyond the cruel reach of his captors. For a moment he was home.

Micara fumbled with the decanter, her fingers clumsy and uncoordinated. The bottle tipped and the sherry spilled onto the coverlet, staining it violet. Cursing, she set the bottle upright, holding it with one hand while reaching blindly for the glass with the other. Her eyes blurred. When they cleared, the glass was filled and the decanter was back on the night stand. A careful inspection showed no more spilled. Hands trembling, she choked back a sob by swilling half the contents of the glass.

He was gone. Back to fight and die in the pit. Never again would she feel his raw strength inside her. "My stallion . . . my black stallion." Somehow the glass was empty again, drained. Numbed fingers let it slip away, drop and break on the floor. The slim green bottle was behind the pillow . . . behind the pillow. Laudanum would ease the choking pain, drown the agony in misty confusion. The bottle lifted, tipped of its own volition and the bitter almond-flavored fluid spilled down her chin and onto the lace-trimmed sleeping gown. She persisted, somehow managed to force down enough of the gagging liquid. Soon she would . . . .

Damn him damn him damn him. Ezra had taken everything. Her person, house, land and gold. Corrupting and abusing all he touched, now he would drive her out. Rafe . . . his massive form. Rafe had taken her, too. Driven himself into her, ravaged her, driven her to the heights of ecstasy. How jealous they would all be, how appalled. Micara Fitzman Clayton and her Nubian lover. Fitzman. Oh, John, you went and died. Fish have eaten out your pretty eyes, just like in the portrait. Nothing but a great hole. You had such handsome features. Such beautiful eyes. Went and died . . . my stallion . . . you were my beautiful stallion . . . black . . . .

The alcohol and opiate exploded in her system, ruptured veins, burst and seared burning images in her brain. Her eyes grew wide and a quiet smile, an ugly smile, a resigned, tortured, resolute smile grew on her face as she staggered to her feet, reached for the lamp and lurched across the room to the door, oblivious to the shards of glass which cut her feet.

Ezra was pleased with himself. Sending Micara and Crissa away was something he should have seen to a long time ago. It would cost him a pretty penny to put them up in a house and send them an allowance, but appearances had to be maintained. All in all their expenses would be money well-spent, as long as he didn't have to pay forever. New Orleans was a perfect place. He would spend to buy time until he could arrange for their permanent disgrace and removal.

Meanwhile, life went on and he was determined to pay as little mind to them as possible. Sunday would bring a festive event. Ambrose Pritchard, from the governor's office, was on a tour of western Louisiana and had stopped in Natchitoches to visit the thriving jumping-off point between the United States and Mexico before turning north to Shreveport. He was in Fort Jessup this evening and tomorrow would lunch at Freedom where he would be given a special entertainment such as only Ezra Clayton could conceive or execute. Three fights were slated, the third of which would feature Rafe against two young bucks to be brought in from Natchitoches. Butkis wasn't making much progress with Rafe at the moment, to be sure, but that worried him only a little. Butkis was positive Rafe would break and Butkis had never let him down. The big black would be in the pit and he would fight. He would win, too, of course, but in his weakened condition would be hurt again.

Pritchard's visit was important. As a representative of the governor he carried a great deal of influence. It wouldn't hurt to have a man of his stature carrying fond remembrances of Freedom back to the capitol. Of course, there was always the danger Ezra's less than illustrious past might be recalled, but the chance was small given the ferment of activity in New Orleans during the last few years and the shifting of most of the Army people involved. In any case, Pritchard travelled in better company than Patrick Fitzman had. Ezra hoped to be appointed to a governmental position in the west. Perhaps a judgeship. If a man became powerful enough, even petty rumors couldn't touch him. As a judge he would have ways of ensuring silence.

The lord of Freedom sat back in his chair, lifted a snifter of brandy in salute to the disfigured portrait of the man he had finally vanquished, sipped his drink with closed eyes and envisioned a manor in New Orleans, a host of fine carriages, servants and women to gratify his needs. And men for a new fighting pit designed to make him the talk of the coast. And power. Yes, power, for what ambitious dream does not include power?

He did not see Micara stumble past the door.

Crissa stared at the trunk in the center of the room. Almost everything she owned was carefully packed in the well-travelled wood and leather box. The rest of her belongings were crammed into travelling bags arranged near the door and waiting to be loaded on the wagon to follow them to Natchitoches. She had resigned herself to departure.

At first she couldn't believe Ezra would go to such lengths to be rid of them, nor that he could so easily turn them out from their own home. Only Freedom wasn't theirs, she forced herself to remember for the thousandth time. She thought of Pa-Paw Ephraim. Why had he hidden from her? What was to become of her old friend when there was no one left to protect him? The answer was painfully obvious—Butkis and the others would hunt him down and kill him. No. Send him to the fields again, free or no. Or worse, the pit for more of Ezra's sickly sport. She almost wept, picturing the old man cowering at the bottom of the grisly hole, waiting for whatever horrible death Ezra could devise. She forced the image from her mind and thought of trying the door to Micara's room once again. A useless venture. Micara wasn't seeing anyone and that was that.

How sad this room looked. Sad and empty, soon to be let to revellers, no doubt. How she had loved the four walls. How many hours had she spent looking out the window, watching the red sun rise blazing in the east? For how long would she remember before the memories blurred and faded?

The day after Ezra returned, sent Rafe back to the compound and issued his edict of expulsion, she had sneaked down and ventured timidly into that other tiny, empty and lifeless room on the lower level. There she had cared for him, bathed and fed him. She fought for his life and won. How small a victory his life seemed now, but a victory nevertheless. While straightening the bed and fluffing the pillow she found the book. *Robinson Crusoe*. She could tell he'd been reading, discovered the page where the dream had been interrupted. The very thought excited her. A slave reading. . . .

Slavery was wrong. She knew it in her heart and soul. The coffle of manacled humans in New Orleans; the old man in the hotel lobby; the field hands, their spirits broken, their lives shattered; the pitbucks, men turned into little more than ravaging beasts. Ironically, she had never totally understood how degrading bondage was until Ezra forced his will upon her. She had journeyed unescorted from the north, a nearly unthinkable adventure for a young woman her age. She had arrived so cocky and self-assured, and in the face of Ezra's treachery had still remained confident of her abilities to deal with the situation, restore her and her mother's inheritance, and expose Ezra for the evil man he was. Now she faced the bitter truth. Everyone knew exactly what Ezra was. They simply did not care. Either they were just as corrupt or looked away lest they become involved and find themselves called upon to take action. Perhaps a few cared but they were as powerless as she. The proof lay in the trunk and baggage which lay scattered on the floor around her.

The room darkened as evening folded around the house. Tomorrow morning she would go out and find Pa-Paw Ephraim if it took all day. Find and somehow convince him to accompany her to New Orleans. At least one part of the Freedom she had known and loved might be saved. An old man.

The sky burned crimson and gold, bidding colorful farewell to a sun passing beyond the lip of the world.

Rafe peered through the compound walls and watched the colors fade as evening overcame twilight and a chorus of cicadas in the trees signalled the end of another day. A torch flared, illuminating the front of the cook shack. A heavy-gutted Negro emerged from the wooden hut clanging an iron ladle against a strip of metal. Behind him a youngster struggled with a heavy iron pot of beans, rice and pot likker. Supper was late and the pitbucks, almost too tired to eat, shuffled wearily across the compound.

The guards had kept them cleaning swampland from can-see-to-can't and there was not a man among them who wasn't bone-tired. All had worked except Rafe who was forced to stay behind, ostensibly because he was still healing. The idea had been Butkis's, a plan to work up the other slaves' animosity toward the giant. Jomo, his plate already full, stepped forward and handed Rafe a plate and spoon. Most of the other pitbucks glared at the two from under brooding brows. Others looked away, either in disgust or fear, as Jomo left to squat down near the shack to eat and Rafe took a place near the end of the line. The men, resenting deeply the wrath he had brought down on their heads, ceased talking, shifted uncomfortably, none wanting to be near him. One pitbuck refused to stand behind him. "Ah a man," he grumbled. "Ah doan needs ta stan' behin' de lahks a' him."

Cat was at the head of the line. When he heard the angry answering buzz behind him he turned, saw what was happening and pulled his tin away from the cook's outstretched hand.

"What de hell?" the cook muttered. "Yo' wants food o' doan yo'?"

"Sheeit," Cat spat. "Dat mus' be food fo' de dawgs. Dey is a dawg in dis line awaitin' fo' his food. Ah doan eat de same vittles as no dawg." He stepped out of line, staring back at Rafe. The young pitbucks ahead of the towering black man looked at each other and at Cat, then followed their leader's example and walked away from the cook shack to cluster around Cat or stand out of the way.

Rafe feigned unconcern. The cook, his mouth open in

surprise, stood on the edge of the porch, the ladle in his hand full of the steaming gruel. All in all, fourteen pit-bucks had stepped aside. Rafe glanced at them, then slowly walked the distance to the cook and held up his plate. The cook stared at the empty plate as if he'd never seen one before, as if suddenly the harmless utensil bore a threat. Then the weight of the ladle bore his arm down and he dumped the food into Rafe's plate, filling it to the brim. Rafe glanced at Cat a moment, his eyes betraying his inner thoughts not a whit. Cat insolently held his ground. Everyone, the guard at the gate, the pitbucks, everyone knew Rafe was far below his normally fine-honed peak of condition. His weeks of confinement could only have served to rob him of much of his prowess, and his weakness was obvious in the way he had meekly submitted to a whole week of indignities from the guards and now this latest blatant insult from one of his own kind. Cat was confident and bold because he knew he could get away with more than usual. Yes, sir, he thought, Beaumarchant was the best thing to happen in a long while. The boss was just another nigger, and a gutless one at that. Rafe turned away and squatted in the shadow at the side of the shack, in the open space between it and the side of the long house.

"Now dat de dawg's been fed, Ah reckin' us mans kin eat," Cat laughed. The others joined him in line, their raucous jibes and laughter filling the night air.

Dingo and Trinidad, the two inseparable friends, squatted beside Jomo. "What Ah tell yo'?" Dingo asked in a low voice. "Yellah tru' an' tru'. Hell, if'n Cat done try dat wid any o' us, he fin' hisse'f countin' his teef as he pickin' 'em up off'n de groun'."

Trinidad shook his head from side to side. "Yo' wrong. Ah slip on ober ta see Ol' Chulem. He doan figger Rafe fo' bein' afeared. Sumpin' else wrong. He say he cain't tell fo' shore what, but it abuildin' an' acomin' ta a reckinin'. Rafe got a poison in him, jes' abuildin' up, an' when it bus' opin, yo' bettah watch where yo' be standin'."

Jomo said nothing as the two left to get in line. There was nothing to be said. Time now to wait. He had a gut feeling. Something, an instinct perhaps. Whatever, he was prepared. N'gata Rafe would have a friend when a friend was needed.

The gate to the compound swung open. Butkis, Milo and one of the duty guards entered. "Where is he?" Butkis growled.

"Over by the cook shack," the duty guard offered. "I been keepin' an eye on him, like you said, Mistah Butkis."

"That black son-of-a-bitch is gonna fight tomorrow or I'll know the reason why. He's about to break, startin' about two minutes from now."

"I'm keepin' my pistol handy," Milo said apprehensively.

"No need," Butkis sneered. "Put it in yore belt an' show him how much we ain't scared of him. That black buck got cut down to size. Bit down, I should say," he chuckled, pleased with his own joke. "He ain't half a' what he used to be. He'll be in the pit tomorrow, fightin' scared. By the time I'm finished there won't never be another nigger that won't fight when I tell him."

Rafe sensed their approach. The other pitbucks grew silent and shifted positions to better see what would happen. Rafe tensed for what was sure to come—more of the treatment he had put up with for the past week. He had endured in the hope they'd give up and send him to the fields. They hadn't and he was tired now, trapped and weary, harried and confused. They were pushing him into a corner, a corner with only two exits, one of which he would have to take, neither of which he liked, both of which he feared. Now it was only a question of time. How much longer before he'd break and go down in the pit again to fight for the man he hated? How much longer before he'd turn at bay, bring ruin on himself and those around him?

Butkis stood over him. The overseer sucked in his barrel-gut, flexed his broad muscular shoulders and planted his feet wide apart. He spoke gutturally, the words nasty and digging deep. "Nigger, how long you figger you gonna make these here other bucks do yore work for you?"

244

The pitbucks edged in closer, apprehensive and curious at the same time. Jomo stood in the shadows and moved silently to a position nearer Rafe, signalled for Trinidad and Dingo to follow him. Rafe spooned a mouthful of food from his still full plate, chewed slowly and swallowed.

"Nigger, I'm talkin' to you. We been lettin' you play the high an' mighty amongst these bucks long enough. Jus' cause you turned yella', jus' cause you ain't got the guts no more, don't matter. Mistah Clayton wants you to fight an' I told him you would. No big buck nigger is gonna make me out a liar. Tomorrow you are fightin', an' if I got to come here an' drag you so much the better."

Rafe spooned another mouthful of the greasy rice and said nothing. He heard the rasp of steel against leather, caught a gleam of the cutlass blade out of the corner of his eye. A second later the point pressed into his neck, the pressure slowly increasing until a trickle of blood began to well around the metal and trace a crooked line as it ran down his chest. Rafe held steady, refusing to move in the slightest rather than risk a real wound.

"Yore food looks a mite dry, nigger boy. Reckin' I oughta moisten it up for you." The overseer's thick, stubby fingers unbuttoned his fly and freed his manhood, guided a stream of foul-smelling urine into Rafe's tin plate. The urine spattered in the rice and beans, mingled with the grease. The sound was deafening in the silence of the compound. Rafe lowered his head to keep his face from being splattered. Butkis was laughing, a deep, rocking, malevolent laugh. Milo and the other guard, afraid not to join, were caught up in the overseer's mirth and guffawed loudly. Butkis sighed, chuckled in relief and shook off the last drops. "I want to see you clean that plate now, pickaninny."

"He ain't got no meat fo' his beans, Mistah Butkis," Milo exclaimed with mock sympathy.

"That's so, Milo. Stand up, nigger. You scared yella', let's see if you so scared you done give us a little meat ta fill out that gruel. If you have, we gonna put it in there an' then stand here 'til you eat everything in yore plate. Got to get yore strength back, so I want you to sop up every bit. Every drop, too." He broke into a fit of renewed laughter.

The point of the cutlass dropped away as Rafe stood, tin plate in hand, head bowed. Butkis slid the blade down along the inside of Rafe's muscular thigh, slicing the fabric of his breeches. Rafe's eyes were shut. He could hear the crackle of the flaming torch, the cicadas, the whispering wings of the hunting night owl, the subdued tones of frantic, scrambling prey, the laughter of the guards. Eyes shut, he could still see their faces. The scene shifted to Beaumarchant in the firelight. The wolves. The Indians and before them slaves from miles away, black and frightened and dying beneath his machete, over and over again. Still earlier, the red-bearded one, the first man to die by his hand. And then fire again, Lord Lucas Clayton's charred corpse, clutching twin-burned remnants of flesh and bone . . . still further the flesh-peeling chains . . . further still, squatting, lying in the hold of the ship, a boy torn from his homeland, fettered, beaten and afraid . . . the death of his father as he hurled himself between the muskets and his child, too frightened to run. Someone had laughed even then . . . my father . . . my father. . . .

The moan began deep within him. A moaning, keening wail of anguish that exploded in a blind and raging fury. His knotted left hand battered the cutlass away as his right hurled the plate full of beans and rice and urine in Butkis's face. The overseer, blinded and choking, flailed wildly with his hands. Rafe's fist slammed him back. Left fist and right, bone hard and awesome black, the swinging clubs crushed Butkis's chest, knocking him back against the wall of the longhouse, the wind smashed from his lungs, his mouth futilely gaping open for air. Rafe's fists splintered ribs, crumpled breast bone and drove hard white splinters through viscera. Blood bubbled from the overseer's nose, poured from his mouth. The powerful fists struck again and again, giving the lie to Rafe's supposed weakness and failing strength. Blows too numerous, falling too rapidly to count. And then he stopped. Butkis, his heart a burst ruin, bits of lung crushed against his spine and driven up into his throat, slowly slid down the

246

wall, his legs buckling grotesquely as he fell. It had all happened so quickly no one moved. Milo and the duty guard stared on, horror-stricken, unbelieving. Butkis was dead.

The pitbucks were stunned. Milo suddenly burst into action. He drew and cocked his pistol and raised his arm to aim at Rafe. A flash of unexpected steel whirred in the torchlight and the pistol fell uselessly to the earth, Milo's hand still clutching the grip. Milo stared in horrified fascination at the spouting crimson stump where hand and pistol should have been, unable to understand what had happened even as Jomo turned, swept the cutlass back and slashed him across the throat to stifle his scream. The other guard turned to run clear of the buildings and into the compound but Trinidad took three quick steps, tripped him and sent him slamming to the ground where Dingo grabbed his knife and sunk the blade in the writhing body, making sure to keep one hand over the youthful guard's mouth. The blade ripped into him five times before he died.

Milo continued to thrash a moment more. The pitbucks ignored him, except to dodge the blood spurting from his slashed throat. His vision dimming, Milo could barely discern the black faces surrounding him. And for just a moment, he thought he saw Patrick Fitzman sprawled on the earth beside him, frantically writhing, futilely clutching his torn throat, trying to tell him something. Milo listened, waited for the awesome truth. Too late. The last of his blood puddled on the hard clay and he died without having heard one word.

It was all over.

Jomo handed the cutlass to Rafe. The smaller man grinned. He, Trinidad and Dingo had acted in a matter of seconds. "What now, Boss?"

Rafe looked at the faces ringing him, the contempt of the last week replaced by total awe. They looked at him, each silently asking the question only Jomo had voiced. He gripped the cutlass for the second time, recalled the easy balance. Now it was his weapon. Light from the torch in front of the cook shack bounced from the bright steel and colored his scarred face with a grim red and yellow mask of diabolical intent, matched only by the hatred smouldering in the depths of his eyes.

When he spoke his voice was soft and clear, no longer trembling with rage but confident, menacing and fiercely determined. The time for fear and indecision was over. "We take our freedom," he said calmly.

16

Rafe studied each face. Eye-to-eye he considered the pitbucks separately, carefully, looking for signs of indecision or fear. When he came to Cat he lingered a moment longer until the thin, hot-blooded youth shrank back before the fierce stare. The killing of Butkis and the others left Cat totally unprepared. He had feared the overseer but feared the man who killed him even more. He had thought Rafe beaten, and called him a dog. Now the giant had risen and lesser men must tremble. "We're all together now. Say so if we ain't." Rafe spoke softly the words directed to all, but specifically to Cat.

Cat shook his head, "no," quickly changed it to "yes." "Ain't a nigger among us won't be held ta 'count fer killin' dese men. Ah din't ask fer no sech trouble," he muttered in a voice betraying his nervousness

"Ask or no, you got it, an' no choice offered," Rafe said matter-of-factly. "Tonight we takin' our freedom. Cat here's talkin' like a whupped dog, but I'm sayin' that come mornin' we'll be free."

"Or daid," Cat countered.

"You already dead," Rafe answered harshly. "We butcher each other so Ezra Clayton can win gold an' have his sport. But it's our flesh gets carved, our blood stains

249

the clay. Ain't no way to live. Hell, all a' us, we already dead, jus' walkin' around still. Ain't a man here who doin' any more. You all got only one choice. Walk out an' maybe live, or stay here an' for sure die." He paused meaningfully. "I'm walkin' out. I'm crossin' the Sabine. I'm gonna take what I can an' find me a new life."

"What we gotta do, Boss?"

"Take us wid yo'."

"Across de ribber? Yo' gonna lead us lahk Moses?"

"Dat guard above de gate got a scatter gun. How we gets pas' him an' out, we doan get blowed away?" The voices came in hurried whispers from the deep shadows.

A figure shuffled wearily through the gathered pitbucks who grew quiet with his passing. Rafe watched closely as the conjure man approached. Old Chulem looked from one corpse to the other, centering finally on Butkis. He stepped closer to the overseer's grisly hulk, leaned over and spat in the dead man's face, then turned back to Rafe, his eyes twinkling. He withdrew a hollow reed from the folded hides about his shoulders. In his hand he held a feathered dart for the blowing tube. A broad grin revealed his toothless gums. "Fo' dat guard above de gate."

Rafe returned the old man's grin. Quickly they stacked the three corpses together against the wall. Chulem, feeble and wizened, began a slow and apparently harmless crossing toward the gate. The guard would let him close and not feel threatened, even open the gate and let him out to go to the field hands' shanties if he wanted.

Rafe ripped the keys from around Butkis's waist. One was to the pitbucks' weapon bin just outside the gate. He did not know what the others opened but there would be time enough later to find out. Leaving the pitbucks to await his signal, he dulled the sheen on Butkis's blade with dirt, tucked a pistol into the waist of his pants and warily stalked off in the shadow of the walls, his speed and course designed to take him to the gate seconds before Old Chulem arrived. Butkis should have returned to the gate by this time and seen to the lighting of the torches, and since he hadn't, the guard on the platform would be getting suspicious. Rafe and Chulem would have to take him completely by surprise, kill him before he had a chance to ring the heavy brass warning bell above the gate and alert the whole plantation to trouble.

Jomo distributed the remaining weapons, keeping a pistol for himself. The wooden pistol grip felt uncomfortable in his hand and he longed for his axe. He peered around the corner of the cook shack. Chulem was nearly to the gate. Jomo searched the shadows beneath the wall and near the gate, thought he saw a flitting shape, a brief glimmer of steel.

"Dat nigger done goana get us all killed," Cat growled.

Jomo glanced over his shoulder, glared at the thin, restless pitbuck. "Cat, yo' jes' about said all yo' goana say, yo' heah me? Ah doan wan' no mo' shit from yo' mouf, yo' heah?" Cat saw the pistol aimed at his belly, read the intent in Jomo's eyes and shut up, withdrew even farther into the shadows.

Suddenly the bell was ringing. They all jumped, startled by the loud clangor of alarm. They'd been discovered! Jomo cursed aloud and peered around the wall. Chulem stood at the open gateway. What had gone wrong? Where was Rafe? When he heard the guard yell, "Fire! Fire at the house! Fire!" he relaxed. The guards were alerted, but not to the pitbucks nor the compound. A huge grin spread over his face. With the house on fire and the guards' attention diverted, they'd stand a good chance of getting across the Sabine for sure.

Rafe waved Chulem on and ran the remaining few feet to the gate. Chulem stepped through and raised the blowing tube. The guard looked down, saw the old man and still pulling the cord to the bell shouted down for him to get back inside. Rafe rounded the wall in time to see the guard clap his hands to his face, scream and pitch headfirst off the platform where he crumpled onto the tightly packed clay with a sickening crunch.

"Good thing he weren't much fu'ther up. Ah ain't gots much wind no mo'," Chulem cackled.

"You got enough, old man," Rafe replied. He fumbled with the padlock on the pitbucks' weapons bin while Chulem whistled for the other pitbucks and began to strip the guard of his weaponry. Two figures charged out of the dark. Rafe flung the lid open, spun aside as a musket ball splintered the wood where he'd been standing. A second later they were on him. Rafe parried a sword thrust with the cutlass and twisted to face his attackers as the guard with the empty rifle drew his own cutlass and fell to with his companion. Hard-pressed and with no room to maneuver, Rafe defended himself as best he could. A blade drew blood from his arm, another brushed his leg, nicking it. He dodged a third swipe at his head, ducked under and drove his cutlass up to the hilt in the guard's abdomen. He dragged the blade free, at the same time spinning the dying man into the path of his comrade's downward slash. The sword clove skull and brain and stuck. His hands sweating and his weapon caught in the bone, the second guard lost his grip and was left weaponless and at Rafe's mercy. The guard stared wide-eyed at the black man towering over him until he heard a slight puffing sound from behind him and felt a sting in the back of his neck. He reached vainly for the barb lodged there and tried desperately to pull it from him, then crumpled to his knees, not at all understanding how the rapid poison coursed through his system. His eyes glazed and he pitched forward, dead.

Jomo and the other pitbucks poured through the gate and into the weapons shed. They stripped the guards of weapons and emptied the bin of knives, machetes and axes, then milled about in confusion, none sure of what the next step should be. Rafe reloaded the fired weapon, sent Dingo up to the platform to retrieve the blunderbuss still leaning against the wall and made sure those with rifles and pistols knew how to use them. Jomo swung his axe in the night air, grinned at the comfortable heft, the sweet music of steel humming through open air.

Through the trees they could see the guards' barracks aglow with the glare of several lanterns. Beyond, on the crest of the hill, the plantation house stood, slender tendrils of flame beginning to lap from windows, climb to the roof and dance in the night sky. "Jomo," Rafe ordered, "take Trinidad and four more to free the field hands. Arm them with what you can find and bring them up to the house. There won't be many guards. The rest of you follow me to the barracks." The words barely out, he broke into a run up the path. Jomo rounded up four of the closest pitbucks and, already behind Trinidad who had sped on his way to find Bess, headed for the shanties.

Rafe bounded along the path, his huge strides pulling him ahead of the others. The guards had to be taken care of first, and quickly. Crissa and Micara were in the house, possibly trapped by the flames. Ezra, too, would be there. Tonight would be his night to die. But first the guards.

A figure loomed out of the darkness ahead of him. The man could only be a guard from the barracks but it was too dark for Rafe to recognize him or be recognized. The two figures approached each other on the run. Nearer . . . nearer . . . Rafe tugged at the pistol. The flint caught in the rope belting his waist. They were almost upon one another when Rafe recognized Boo, armed with a rifle.

Boo never expected to find a slave running up the path toward him and his momentary confusion saved Rafe's life. "Hey, who fired? Where's Butkis. . . . What?" He recognized the giant form, the dark skin visible now as he slowed and jerked his rifle up even as Rafe swung the cutlass with all his might, gripping the hilt with both hands. The blade was of the best steel, heavy and honed razor-sharp and Rafe fell to his knees from the momentum of the slash. Boo's head flew from his shoulders and bounced into the brush and weeds where it rolled upright, the mouth still open in an unvoiced wail of death. Empty eyes watched the body they'd just left as it continued running awkwardly into the bordering vines where it tripped, tumbled and thrashed grotesquely as the dying muscles continued trying to obey the last commands received. Dingo and the others appeared out of the darkness. Inured to death, they stripped the still twitching corpse of rifle, pistols and knife before following Rafe up a grassy knoll and into the clearing surrounding the barracks.

"Damn that Butkis anyway," muttered Decater.

"You sayin' somethin'?" one of the guards he was relieving asked.

"Naw, nuthin' any business a yores."

The guard to his left chuckled softly. Decater glanced sharply in his direction. He was a laugher, this new one, who never had anything to say. Decater didn't like him. Decater didn't like having to stand night guard duty alone at the field hands' shanties, either. He had seen Butkis coming from them earlier in the day. The overseer had grinned hugely at him, amused by some unspoken joke. Only one thing fit—the bastard overseer must have let slip a choice word or two hinting of the identity of Beulah's killer. Decater was nervous, all right, more so because he'd be alone until midnight. The double line of dark shacks, unpainted wood blending into shadows, spooked him. Even with Arvid and the laugher still around he didn't feel safe. The night was too quiet, too full of silent, threatening shadows.

And then the stillness broke. The pealing brass bell rang its monotonous clanging report into the night. Decater shot a startled glance toward the house and caught a glimpse of flames burgeoning from the plantation house. Fire! And a bad one, too, if he could see it clearly from the shanties. They'd need all the help they could get. Need it fast. "Fire! Fire at the big house!" he yelled at the top of his lungs to wake the blacks. "C'mon," he added roughly to Arvid and the laugher, shoving them toward the shacks. "Get yore asses on the move. Roust them niggers out! We gotta get 'em over to help with that fire. Move, damn it, move !"

Already the doors to the shanties were opening and field hands were pouring out into the barren yard. The three guards ran down between the line of shanties, pounding and slamming their musket stocks against walls and doors, raising a ruckus in an effort to hurry the slaves out. But there weren't enough. Where were they all? Decater lined up those in the yard, told them to wait and sent Arvid and the laugher to roust out the slaggards.

As the two disappeared into the night, Decater was left alone with the slaves in the yard. Were they staring at him funnylike? That som'bitch Butkis had told them for sure. The overseer and Clayton must have figured to get rid of him the easy way. Damn them to hell! The laugher appeared with a handful of youngsters and Decater relaxed, happy not to be alone. Arvid was still gone. What the hell was he doing, taking so long? They had a fire to fight, would be expected and missed. "Hurry up, Arvid!" Decater called. "Git yore ass on back. The hell with 'em. We ain't got time, got to git to the house an' help fight that fire."

The slaves were watching him. Only him. Clayton had sold him out, right enough, and all those black, staring, accusing eyes were proof enough. He cocked his musket, reassured by the feel of the weapon in his hands. Hell, he was all right. In spite of the fear, he grinned to prove there was nothing wrong. They'd need more than a few field niggers to handle him. Butkis and Clayton would find that out and the lesson would cost them a slave or two. And a guard who knew more than he was supposed to know, for he was determined to get out and away. The hell with them all. He patted the hefty wooden stock, nervously loosed his pistols. The slaves stirred restlessly, glancing to the house on the hill where they could hear the commotion of men rising to meet the emergency.

"Arvid . . . !" the laugher called. Decater listened intently. Too long. He'd been gone too long. When there was no answer he motioned the laugher to watch the niggers in the yard, then walked in the direction Arvid had taken. He rounded a corner and entered the deep shadows, moving more slowly during the brief moments his eyes would need to adjust to the darkness under the trees.

Silence. "Arvid?" he called softly. Nothing. He stepped forward and tripped on something not quite solid. His left hand shot out to steady himself and he reached down to feel a still warm corpse, the shirt sticky with blood. Decater jumped back from the dead man. "God damn!" he cursed, a horrid icy sensation freezing his blood. Suddenly the musket in his hands wasn't enough, not nearly enough. He turned and ran for the clearing, back into the moonlight, back toward the laugher and the waiting slaves.

The laugher watched Decater's panic-stricken flight out of the darkness, realized something had gone wrong and, suddenly frightened himself, stepped back from the slaves as a tongue of flame and the roar of a musket exploded from a darkened window. The laugher screamed and spun around, holding his arm. The slaves, as startled by the shot as the guards, broke and ran in all directions. A shadow near the corner of a building moved. Decater fired his musket and was rewarded with a yelp of pain. Tossing the musket aside he ran to the wounded guard and grabbed the musket he had dropped. More fire flashed from other doorways and a musket ball tore Decater's cheek. Another ripped the cap from his head as he dove behind the fallen laugher.

"Help me," the laugher moaned weakly, cradling his shattered arm. Decater roughly shoved him over, tore the brace of pistols from his belt and scurried for the safety of the wash shack, the only structure standing apart from the double line of shanties. A form leaped to bar his way. Decater fired the musket point blank and a slave was blown back into the darkness. Another figure, leveling a pistol, charged from the corner of the wash shack. Decater hurled the now useless musket into the startled assailant who stumbled back and fired directly into the sky. Decater shot him in the stomach, tossed the pistol aside and drew another. For a second all was quiet. Decater backed to the safety of the wall. The laugher screamed for him, screamed for him to come back.

Suddenly the screams ceased and a heavy, ominous silence broken only by distant shouts lay over the shanty town. Decater shuddered, cowered in the dark shadow of the overhung roof. What was going on? Who was shooting at him? Where did they get guns? He glanced around the corner. Flames were leaping high from the roof of the main house. No one would come to help him for they'd all be there, trying to put out the fire. He was on his own. A bunch of dumb niggers, that's all they were. He jerked his head at a new sound—gunfire, and from the barracks! Jesus God, that's how they got guns! The damned niggers . . . a revolt! He'd have to escape now for sure. The hell with the house. The hell with Clayton. Decater had himself to worry about. He'd have to escape. But where? The safety of the trees? But how safe were they?

Forms moved toward him out of the night. He shouted for them to stand back. Damn that Butkis, he thought. He told, he must have told. He fired at a shadow. Nothing. Another shadow moved, flung itself toward him. He fired again. Only two more shots left, unless he could reload before. . . . Something hard slammed against him from the side. He tugged one of the laugher's pistols from his belt but it was knocked away immediately. Frantic, he groped for his knife. Fists slammed into his mouth, sent him staggering back into the wall. He slashed with the knife and felt a hand on his wrist, the knife plucked easily from his grasp. They had him. They had him! He shrieked for mercy, to be let loose. "I didn't mean her no harm," he screamed. "I was nice to her, give her peppermint," he sobbed hysterically.

The hands quit hitting him, kept him pinned to the ground. "What yo' sayin', white man?"

"I didn't mean to kill her. I swear. She was a good girl. We was just funnin' until she went ta screamin' an' yellin'. I just tried to hush her up an' she hit her head. It was an accident, no matter what Butkis tole you. He was there. He seed it. He's guilty, too." And then he stopped, realizing what his fear and panic had caused him to blurt out.

A woman's voice, deep and resonant, came out of the darkness. "Mistuh Butkis tole us nuffin but dat mah Beulah be foun' daid. Now yo' tellin' us who done it. She was mah chile." There was silence for a moment until the voice went on, deep and wounded before the tears started. "A fool girl to go off wid de lahks a' yo', but mah little chile all de same. . . ."

"I seen Butkis," Decater started. "He come . . . ."

"Mistuh Butkis done come to check on us ever' day. Dis day was no diffrent from none oder."

"But he ain't never checkin' agin'." Decater shrank from the new voice. Jomo! Here? A torch flared. Decater tried to shield his eyes but couldn't move his arms. Jomo stood over him, his axe gleaming.

A fat, ungainly woman swam into focus. "Mah chile," the woman said, her voice husky but strong, overpowering Decater's cries for mercy. "He kill mah Beulah. Said it hisse'f. Oh, Lawd . . . an eye fo' a' eye, a life fo' a life. . . ."

Fingers, work-hard, calloused and blunt, tore at him. The other slave women joined in while the men held back and watched. Jomo tried to hurry them toward the main

257

house but the women were not to be denied. And worse for Decater, they were not to be rushed. Decater screamed until his voice was a hoarse, ragged shriek. Blood dripped from a torn ear. He felt his pants torn from him and an awesome pain rip through his groin. Something tore at his right eye. The women were making sure he died slowly. They had their ways. . . .

Ezra ran back in from the rear gallery. Flames were lapping at the walls on every side of the house. The lower storerooms had been set ablaze first, the kegs of coal oil spilled and fired. Only the heavy plank flooring was retarding the flames' eager progress, and that not for long and only inside the house. Where were the guards? Where was Butkis? What the hell was happening and why the shots?

Too late, damn it to hell. Too late even if they arrived on the moment, buckets in hand and full of water. How could a fire have started? Who? Julie and the other servants were beating at the flames with rugs, hoping to smother the spreading blaze. They did little more than delay the inevitable. Ezra rushed to the landing and hurried up the stairs to find Crissa in the hall, pounding on the door to her mother's bedroom.

Suddenly suspecting the worst, he shoved Crissa out of the way and drew his pistol to shoot the knob and lock away. The door slammed open and he leaped inside, Crissa right behind him. Micara stood poised by the window, coal oil lamp in hand. She smiled at both of them and, laughing maniacally, flung the lamp against the lace curtains. "You can have your house, Ezra," Micara laughed. "It's all yours now. All yours!"

Ezra screamed in rage and hurled himself upon her, knocking her down and pummelling her with the pistol butt. Crissa tore at him helplessly then lunged toward the bedroom fireplace. She grabbed the hearth shovel and slammed the flat side against Ezra's head, knocking him off her mother. He crawled away from Micara, staggered to his feet and, his head bloody, stumbled from the room, cursing them both. Crissa dragged her mother from the flame-swept curtains and sat her on the edge of the bed.

Micara's face was a mass of cruel welts and bruises. One hand fluttered weakly, gripped the coverlet beneath her. She stared confusedly at the bed while Crissa soaked a cloth in the water basin at the side of the bed and started to wrap her mother's face in order to take her through the fire. A figure loomed over her and she turned, hands lifted to protect herself. It was Ephraim. He was breathing hard, his eyes wide with fear.

"Oh, Pa-Paw. Help me. . . ." Crissa managed, choking back the tears.

"Miss Crissa, Ah tried ta come tell yo'. At fuhst Ah was afeared an' hid lessen yo' pry it from me an' wind up lahk po' Mistuh Patrick, but den Ah couldn't let it hide no longuh. Yo' had ta be to'd. Ah tried, but de guard almos' ketch me an' Ah had ta run fo' mah trees."

Crissa ignored him in her concern for her mother. "Pa-Paw, help me carry her out. We have to get her outside." The room was filling with smoke and Crissa tugged at Micara, trying to pull her from the bed.

Micara held on to the post with one hand, stared at the bedcover held in her other. When she spoke her voice was soft and distant, dreamlike, tender, and without rancor for the first time in years. "John bought this beautiful spread for me. Dear John. We spent our wedding night beneath these flowers."

"Mother, please. Not now, please. We have to hurry."

Micara pulled her hand away. Lost in memory, she smiled at Crissa. "Your father used to snore so. I tried everything I could think of to make him stop. And then he was gone. . . ." She faltered, near tears. "I would give anything to hear that man snore again . . . to feel him warm and sleepy at my side. . . ."

Crissa stood and pulled at her. Ephraim, coughing violently, stooped to help. Micara didn't want to come, held tight to the post. None of them heard Ezra reenter the room. He held a leather packet of papers and a second pistol. His eyes searched for Crissa through the smoke.

And found her. "You little bitch!" he yelled. Crissa whirled to face him. "You did this. It all began with you. I'll end it with you, too!" Crissa returned his stare, her face flushed from the heat but eyes defiant. As smoke from the curtains billowed between them, Ezra raised the pistol, fired and ran from the room. Crissa didn't realize Ephraim had stepped in the path of the ball until the impact flung him backward into the wall, his life's fluid leaving a trail on the floor.

Crissa let Micara go. Weeping openly she crawled to the old man's side and cradled his head in her arms. "Pa-Paw . . . Pa-Paw. . . ." Ephraim opened his eyes. Pink foam flecked his lips and Crissa wiped it away. "Pa-Paw. Please. . . . Oh, God . . . please . . . ."

"Miss Crissa, yo' de pretties' . . ." He coughed, tried to smile around the pain. "Jes' lahk dat ol' cottonmouf. Jes' lahk. . . ." He was dead.

The whole downstairs was a raging inferno, into which Ezra descended, fighting his way to the library. He kicked open the door to see flames greedily consuming the book-lined walls. The gold was in his desk. Ezra braved the choking smoke and searing heat, tore open the bottom drawer and withdrew two heavy sacks. He turned in time to see Martinson, his massive, obese torso stripped and bleeding from a dozen cuts and torn open blisters, stagger through the door.

"Mistah Clayton. I called but couldn't find you."

"Where the hell are Butkis and the others?" Ezra stormed, unable to hear the smattering of gunshots and musket fire being returned close at hand.

"They came at us, caught us by surprise. We had no warnin', headin' up to fight the fire."

"What the hell are you saying?"

"The pitbucks. They come at us out of the night. We turned guns on 'em but they were among us before we known it. An' Rafe was leadin' 'em."

"Rafe!"

"Yessir. I seen him myself. He's like a devil. I shot him. I think I hit him but he kept on comin'. They'll be here next. There's only five of us left."

Clayton considered briefly. Flight was the only reasonable course of action. He decided quickly. "Help me. We'll get out the front and cut our way to the stable."

Martinson nodded. Ezra slung the bags of gold, joined

as they were by a length of rope, over Martinson's flabby shoulders where they hung heavily, the rope biting deeply into the soft flesh. Like a dutiful beast of burden, Martinson followed Ezra out the front door.

Sporadic firing sounded at the rear of the manor but Ezra had guessed correctly and as the slaves attacked the back of the house, he and Martinson made their way unobserved around the south side to the carriage house and stable. Ezra held his rapier ready as they entered, ready for an attack from the inside.

The stable was quiet, the air cool after the inferno of the house. "Saddle the black gelding for me. I'll watch the door," Ezra commanded. Martinson handed him the pistol and got to work. By the time he finished he was sweating even more profusely and his breath came in ragged gasps. He turned to another stall to saddle a rangy bay. "That's good enough," Ezra said from behind him.

"But I got to saddle up the bay for me," Martinson protested. He turned back to the stall and never saw Ezra raise the pistol behind him and fire from only inches away. The blast slammed the guard's head forward and blew out his face, splattering the stall with bits of red and gray.

Ezra threw the gold over the gelding's back and swung into the saddle. Frightened as he was, it took little urging for the animal to break into a gallop as he cleared the open doorway. Dingo leaped from the shadows at the fleeing horse. His hands clutched at Ezra's clothing and the pitbuck half managed to clamber into the saddle before Ezra slammed the hilt of his rapier down on the pitbuck's skull. Dingo slid from the horse and his hands clutched around the first thing they found, the rope across the animal's back. Falling, he dragged the gold with him. Ezra hauled on the reins and started to dismount but a shot sounded nearby and figures rushed him out of the dark, almost hemming him in. He cursed aloud, dug his heels into the gelding and galloped past the hands reaching to tear him from the saddle. Seconds later he was free of the front lawn and had disappeared into the night.

The back door burst asunder as Rafe charged through.

He shouted Crissa's name, knowing full well his voice was a feeble whisper compared to the roar of the flames. A beam crashed in front of him as he neared the stairway. He leaped over it and ran up to the top floor, for he had caught a glimpse of a body lying near the top of the stairs. Crissa was draped on the steps where she had collapsed while attempting to drag Micara to safety. Micara's eyes were open wide and glazed by death.

Rafe lifted the girl from her mother's prostrate form, held her gently and began picking his way back down the stairs. A shower of sparks from a crashing segment of ceiling billowed around them but Rafe battered his way through, burning his arms and back, carrying Crissa in his arms to protect her from falling debris. Above him the rest of the ceiling was sagging, the beams clearly visible. A wall to his left collapsed. The front door was open wide and the wind from it stirred the corridor into a tunnel of flames lying between Rafe and safety. Without thinking he broke into a run, blindly trusting to luck the floor underneath them had not yet given way. Behind him the ceiling beams came down with an immense world-shattering groan. Rafe felt his pounding legs, sensed the fiery collapsing brimstone death around and above him.

And then a rush of cooling air and the steps down from the gallery to the ground. He was through. The beams exploded at his heels and burst into flaming shards as the house of Freedom collapsed on itself.

17

Like gaunt blackened bones the remnants of the house thrust bleakly into the pre-dawn darkness. Tenuous wisps of smoke swirled and drifted lazily, rose to join the mist seeping from the dense foliage. Birds neither chattered nor scolded among the nearby trees. No inquisitive animal came to poke or paw the ruins in search of food. Even the insects were strangely hushed. The world waited for the morning, waited and wondered what would happen next.

Crissa had dreamt of flames and dead wide eyes, of gaping wounds and billowing smoke. She watched her mother's face distort in maniacal laughter, saw her hurl the lantern over and over again. She had felt the flesh blister along her arms as she fought to drag the dying woman to safety, and though at the last she knew Micara was dead, kept struggling because she could think of nothing else to do, struggling down a miles-long corridor filled with choking smoke, her feet dragging, dragging ever so slowly. Pa-Paw kept jumping in front of her and getting shot again and again until his head was a bloody mutilated pulp. She bolted awake, calling for the old man who had saved her life and found instead Rafe's strong protective arm about her. Rafe, who had braved the flames and carried her to safety at last. She drifted back to sleep, deep and past dreaming.

She stirred. Night had passed and he still slept at her side, his arm pillowing her. He lay on the ground, a dark, magnificently muscled figure of dormant power and deep-set endurance. What had he said about watching her? *"Just being . . ."*? Crissa's fingers traced along the back of his hand, up the firm unyielding flesh of his forearm. The shirt had been burned from his back and he was clad only in torn breeches. And what of her? Her garment was in tatters, but at her side, neatly folded, lay breeches, soft moccasins and a linen shirt, all obviously meant for her.

She looked around anxiously. They were in the garden near what was left of the house. Through the hedge of rose bushes she imagined she could see other sleeping forms. They would waken soon, for already the eastern sky was taking on a barely discernible tinge of pewter and gold. Vaguely she remembered Rafe assuming command and directing a series of preparations, of posting men to guard and watch for activity on the road from Claytonville. Indefatigable, he alternately cajoled and bullied the mob into a semblance of order, refusing to let them celebrate their victory with dancing and partying. Instead, he insisted everyone rest in shifts in preparation for the long day to come, the day he would lead them to the river and across into Mexico.

She dimly recalled the sensation of being carried into the garden, of Rafe's strong arms setting her down, his hand stroking her face, soothing her. She clung to the hand and drifted off to sleep. Later she awoke when he lay down near her and hushed her when she started violently and almost screamed with the terror of a dream interrupted. And then she slept again, her back to him, cuddled in the warm cavity made by his body around her. She sighed, wishing for a return to that warmth, that safety. But their secluded garden spot would not be theirs for long. There would be prying eyes.

A section of charred wood crumpled over and fell into the pile of ashes, making no more noise than a sigh. Crissa thought of Micara, of Pa-Paw Ephraim, of the home her father had. . . . No. No. Better not to think at all

264

than continue on that course. Keeping an eye on the sleeping forms beyond the hedge, she slipped out of the tattered bodice, the ravaged fragments of her dress only barely concealing nature's gifts, the tone and firmness of hip, breast and thigh. The cool morning air tingled her naked flesh, refreshed and invigorated her, and in spite of the horrors of the night before she felt renewed and revitalized. Something evil, some horrid, necrotic malignancy had been expunged by the fire and she was surprised to find herself in an almost buoyant mood. The dewy grass beneath her buttocks was a cool invitation to sing for joy, to romp, frisk and play like some wild animal of the forest. She reached over and took the linen shirt, rising to her knees as she pulled it over her head.

Rafe watched her. Awake for several minutes, he lay quietly, scarcely daring to stir lest he disturb Crissa. He wanted to savor every moment of her body, warm and sleepy against his own. Suddenly she moved, got to her knees and stripped off the torn bodice, ripped the remnants of her skirt from around her waist. He had never seen her naked—never seen any white woman except for Micara naked—and his eyes narrowed with the illicit sight. He caught a glimpse of full breasts, each crowned by taut pink as she rose to pull on the shirt. Her thighs were pale and firm, buttocks rounded and whiter than white. A yellow petal fragment clung to one hip, pressed there by the pressure of her flesh and the moistness of the ground. The coarsely woven shirt reached to just below her waist. Still on her knees, Crissa leaned forward to fumble with the trousers, the shirt riding up her back. Rafe's hand, almost of its own volition, rose and fell lightly to the back of her knee.

Crissa stopped in midreach at the pressure of his hand. It was as if a cable had joined them, giving license to an interchanging flow of energy. The pressure of his hand made her tremble. Such a touch was forbidden, unspeakable, or so the social mores of her time instructed. But was this any more terrible than the slaughter of men for the amusement of their self-proclaimed betters? She doubted it. She had nursed Rafe back to health, bathed his fevered flesh, and he had risked life and limb to find and carry her to safety from the flaming wreckage of the house.

The sky was slowly brightening in the east. Towering cumulus clouds hung gray and motionless, frozen in the new light. The stillness. The waiting stillness. Thoughts raced through her mind. I should run, she told herself over and over again, flee the touch of his hand, the fingers travelling the length of inner thigh, up to stroke and caress her womanhood already betraying arousal, moist with its musky, sweet fluids. Then the rustle of cloth and two hands gripped her hips and pulled her onto her side, returning her to the heated cove of his body. She went willingly, shuddering at the touch of naked flesh. Two ebony hands reached in front of her, glided over her flat belly and the honey-colored triangle of hair, provoked and titillated the very bud of her desire. She felt Rafe's swollen manhood throb against the curve of her buttocks and opened her legs, arching her back to receive him. The quivering organ pressed against the half-open lips, parted them and entered. Crissa moaned and her fingers clawed the earth in front of her and the very cavity of her being gorged itself as Rafe slowly slid into her. There had been a dalliance in Boston, but nothing remotely like this. She caught his hands and pulled them up to cup her breasts, increasing her ecstasy, then pressed herself to him, pushing, pushing until his entire length was deep inside her. Crissa felt him move, slide out and back in once . . . twice. She tried to reciprocate, but found herself frozen as ecstatic spasms ripped through her. Three times, four. . . . Neither could prolong the moment. Rafe's lusty climax sent Crissa into a series of similar convulsions. When the grinding waves finally stopped, Rafe pulled her close to him and both dozed in languid bliss.

Rafe woke a half-hour later, rested and calm, ready to face the day ahead. They were still together and he didn't want to leave the warmth, the pleasant resting place. Slowly he eased himself back, eased himself out of her and heard her small sigh as, still asleep, her body missed that which it had so deliciously held. Rafe rolled back, pulled on his torn trousers and draped Crissa's torn skirt over her slumbering nakedness. He rose to his feet, made his way past the hedge and stepped quietly off toward the crowd on the front lawn. The sun was barely creeping over the horizon when Jomo hurried over to his giant friend. The smaller man grinned broadly. "Ah got men loadin' de wagons, N'gata. Mistuh Clayton set quite a store fo' de guards. We got enuff pistols an' muskets fo' mos' ever' man."

"Good. I'll roust out the others. We can't stay here any longer than we have to. Clayton got away an' maybe some others. They'll be sure ta bring help. I don't want ta fight any more than we have to. They," he indicated the field hands, "don't know enough about fightin'. They'll run the first time someone fires at 'em. We have ta get 'em out an' across the river. Fast."

Jomo nodded in agreement and ran off to oversee the gathering of provisions. Dingo and Trinidad were already instructing a gathering of field slaves in the use of musket and pistol. Painstakingly they explained each procedure of loading and firing, slowly went over the instructions again and again. Rafe aroused the sleepers in the garden. Julie was among them. She tried to catch his eye but he ignored her, crossing instead to the spot where he had slept with Crissa, only to discover she was gone.

Ezra's gold was still there. He slung the sacks over his shoulder and went back to the front lawn to find a milling, uncoordinated crowd of newly awakened slaves. Hastily he divided them, sending some to help Jomo and others to Dingo and Trinidad. That done he began to look anxiously for Crissa, finally spotting her standing under the half-burned magnolias in front of the ruins, dressed in the clothes he had left for her. He started toward her then hesitated. She was saying goodbye, putting the ghosts of the past behind her. This was a time for her to be alone.

Crissa stared at the empty, charred ruin of what had once been home, all brought to destruction because of one man and his greed. Ezra Clayton's ruthless ambition had exacted a terrible vengeance. Now all was ended. Or was it? Ezra escaped the wrath of his slaves, rode off into the night. To fight again? She couldn't imagine he wouldn't return. Not with the gold gone. There was something Rafe needed to know. Something she should tell him, but her mind was a welter of confused thoughts. The intimacy with Rafe, the loss of so much, Micara, Pa-Paw. . . .

Rafe studied her a moment longer then wandered away from the scene. Jomo and Trinidad had things under control and he took time for a brief moment alone for himself. He followed the path down behind the blackened ruins, past the barracks with its littered dead, past the compound ringed with cruel, iron-capped spires threatening the sky. The gate stood open and unguarded. He had never seen it so. Turning abruptly, he put his back to the compound and went on down the familiar dusty track of death to the pit. The peach grove was devoid of fruit, all of which had been gathered and either eaten or loaded for the coming journey. The grove was torn and shredded, limbs and branches ripped from the trees and littering the ground. The house burned, the guards dead and now the peach trees destroyed. Rafe could hardly blame anyone for the destruction, for when Ezra Clayton was in command all had reflected the master's power. He shook his head ruefully. How sad that a peach tree, its fruit forbidden to those who cared for it, should be a symbol of servitude.

He hesitated at the hard clay mound before him. It looked strange now, desolate, for no one ringed the pit and waited for him. Slowly he walked up the slight rise and to the edge of the hole in the ground. The hard clay felt cool under his feet, cool and silky smooth, as yet unwarmed by the sun. He stared down into the hole and faces, dim and shadowy, flitted across his consciousness. Would he never forget them? Carry them with him always? Yes. He thought of them often enough. With a sudden shock he realized he had known but few of their names. The red-bearded one. What was his name? The Indians must have been named by someone, must have been known by name to their companions. Beaumarchant, of course, had a name. He ran two-score faces past him, searching them for any sign of recognition. The five pitbucks he had fought were known to him by name.

And the others? Only one he could remember. A very short, wild, totally unpredictable man, his face scarred horribly with a thousand mysterious tiny nicks. Thor, they had called him, and rightly so, for he fought with a hammer, a wicked, fourteen-pound maul with a two-foot handle. Thor had died, too, name or no.

Dreams of torches, laughter, far white distant faces, blood, the whining rush of steel . . . . How odd, the pit wasn't very deep at all, yet from the floor, standing there with machete in hand and waiting to kill or be killed, how towering the walls had appeared. Too bad there wasn't time. He would have liked to fill in the hell-hole, to remove the gaping maw from the earth forever.

"Rafe!"

Dingo's voice broke the somber reverie, startled Rafe with its urgency. He turned to see the pitbuck running toward him, his face nervous and unsure. "Boss, dere's trouble up by de wagons. Dat Cat is causin' grief, an' he tried ta take Miz Crissa."

Rafe was moving before the sentence was out, hurtling back up the path. The mention of Crissa's name urged him to even greater speed. That damned Cat. If he so much as. . . .

He rounded the barracks and with a final burst of speed ascended the wooded slope, coming out behind a crowd of slaves, Cat at their head. An angry interchange was going on between Jomo and Cat. Rafe shoved his way through the field slaves who lost no time in making way for the wrathful figure. Most of the pitbucks were behind Jomo. Crissa stood alone, off to one side. She looked very tiny, very vulnerable, a single, frightened white in front of over a hundred angry, sullen black faces.

Cat ceased his shouting as Rafe drew near. Jomo wiped the sweat from his brow, leaving a glistening sheen of moisture on his forearm. "N'gata, dis nigger gonna ever be a thorn in mah side," he said angrily.

"Ah only sayin' what's right," Cat defended himself. "Dat woman got no business heah. She as bad as de res'. She white an' dey all de same. Ah'm sayin' we do to her lahk her Papa done to us."

269

Rafe glanced at Crissa's confused and frightened face then turned back to Cat. "You ain't touchin' no one, Cat. Crissa is goin' to Mexico with us."

The words fell like a bombshell and a sudden brittle hush fell over the crowd. Julie stepped forward and strode defiantly to Rafe. "She ain't got no right. She's one a' dem." Julie spat contemptuously. "Dat Miz Crissa jus' as bad as Mistuh Clayton, onlies' thing keepin' her purty white skin in one piece is dat Rafe cain't git enuff a' her bush. Black woman ain't good enuff fo' Boss. . . ."

Rafe slapped her across the mouth, knocking her down. "Ever'one here knows who shared Mistah Ezra's bed with him. Ever'one here knows who spread her legs for the white man she talkin' so bad about. Ever'body knows she done it glad. But," he paused meaningfully, "ain't no one sayin' Julie can't go with us. Crissa was Mistah Ezra's enemy jus' like us. She wasn't his girl an' ever'body know it. So you watch your mouth, little girl."

The crowd shifted silently. He turned back to Cat, took a menacing step toward him. "Now you, Cat, are tryin' me sorely. Best you get back to work an' keep your mouth shut. Crissa is goin' with us an' I ain't gonna talk any more on it." He stopped, letting the words sink in. The field hands watched silently, eyes neutral.

"Now, we gonna spend some of this mornin' bringin' as much food as we can from the fields. Split up an' go to the field you're used to workin'. Ain't none of us know how much food we gonna find in Mexico, ain't none of us know how long we gonna have to run afore they stop chasin' us. That food's our only chance."

"Hell, we ain't goin' to dem fields agin," one of the field slaves muttered.

"Yeah. Ah spent five yeah's workin' dat co'n an' Ah ain't 'bout to ben' mah back to it agin. Not while Ah is free," another agreed.

Other voices chimed in their accord. Rafe held up his hand to quiet them. "Listen to me," he shouted. "What you be gatherin' from the fields will be for *your* bellies. No one else's. No man is a slave when he workin' for himself. If you want to eat, you gonna have to pick crops."

"Dere is troof in dat," one of the blacks interjected. "Ah'll go. Ah done sweat ober dem crops. Ah got a right ta eat 'em."

Others nodded in agreement and started toward the fields. "Pick what we can take with us," Rafe called to them. "Corn. Beans. Don't take nothin' so ripe it'll rot before tomorrow. We gotta make each pound count. An' hurry back." For a moment the crowd milled around, then moved out, split into two groups, half behind a field slave named Eban, the other half following Cat.

Crissa hurried to Rafe's side. They stared into each other's eyes for a moment. "I just figured you'd be with me," Rafe said. "But you gotta choose for yourself. You can stay if you want."

Crissa looked puzzled, uncertain of herself, of what she wanted to, what she should do .She thought of earlier that morning, the two of them together, blushed and turned away. Rafe would have called to her, but instinct warned him against it. Her decision would have to be her own, freely made. . . .

"Damn!"

Rafe crawled out from under a light wagon on which he'd been working, one he wanted to take to Mexico with them. A half-hour had passed and the field hands would soon be back with their loads. Jomo stood atop one of the other wagons, staring in the direction of the fields. "What is it?" Rafe asked.

"Ha'f dem niggers never went to de fields. Dey follow-in' Cat down de road to town, an' damn near dere. Dat som'bitch done talked of burnin' de place, an' now it look lahk he goana try it. Ah neber figgered him fo' seein' it through. We best ride down an' get 'em back."

Rafe jumped to Jomo's side in time to see the tiny figures in the distance disappear over the hill into Clayton-ville. "Let him go," he sighed. "Only way to stop him is to kill him, an' I swore I'd not raise a hand against another black man again. There's an anger in those slaves. That town brought it on themselves."

"Ain't time fo' no such foolishness as dat," Old Chu-

271

lem scowled. "Dem sojers from de fo't goana be showin' dere colors an' we bes' be off afore dey come."

Rafe shook his head in disagreement. "Even if Mistah Ezra rode straight to the fort there ain't but twenty mounted horsemen there. Ever'body knows that. The rest is foot soldiers. They won't be bringin' jus' twenty men against us, an' it'll take a good while for them to round up enough horses for the others or to walk the distance. We got time."

"But you don't." It was Crissa, her face pale and drawn with worry. "I couldn't remember until just now. What Ezra said . . . . The fight today was to be in honor of a man named Pritchard from the governor's office in New Orleans. He was to spend last night at Fort Jessup. He was travelling with a heavily armed escort. They'll have horses enough, for they're all mounted."

Mounted! If that were the case then they could well arrive during the morning. At any time, realistically thinking. If Ezra rode through the night he would have arrived at the fort around one or two in the morning. If the soldiers left at three or four. . . . Damn! Rafe managed to suppress the panic welling inside him. They had to get away from the plantation, get across the river as fast as they could.

"Jomo. Take the wagon to the fields, load what there is and get everyone back here as fast as you can. Head them toward the river. Trinidad, Dingo. Take the pitbucks to the river. Take anyone else you can find with you. Take axes and rope an' set to tyin' together some rafts. We got no time to try to get to the landin' an' that little ferry boat I doubt will still be there. An' be ready to fight. When you see us comin', soldiers may be right on our tails."

Trinidad and Dingo left and started rounding up men and tools. Rafe swung into the saddle of a nearby gelding, one of the two mounts not hitched to a wagon. "Crissa," he called down, "take the mare an' ride to the river an' wait for me. Help if you can but stay out a' the way if you can't. Find a place where you'll be safe until I get back."

Crissa nodded and mounted the remaining grey. She noticed Bess watching her. The young black girl had not left Trinidad throughout the night and now she was alone, obviously lost without her man at her side. Crissa guided the horse close to her, held out her hand. Bess looked questioningly at Rafe, who nodded. The black girl smiled, took Crissa's hand and leaped up behind her. The two women galloped off, Trinidad, Dingo and the other pitbucks and the small crew they'd rounded up not far behind them.

Rafe watched them go, turned back to Jomo and nodded toward Claytonville. "If them soldiers catch Cat an' the fools with him in that town they'll be trapped with no way to run. I'm gonna get 'em out a' there if I have to gut me that damn nigger to do it."

Jomo grinned despite the urgency of the moment. "You done tol' me you swore. . . ."

"To hell with what I swore," Rafe said vehemently. "I can't let one fool drag the others down with him."

And then they heard the shots.

The citizens of Claytonville had watched in horror as the flames and gunshots wracked Freedom Plantation. Many had made their way to the top of the hill outside town, from which the fire was plainly visible. Some had ridden down the road to help but then rode back again, bearing frightening tales of carnage. In the end no one made an attempt to offer any assistance to the beleaguered plantation. Why should they? An insurrection was a dangerous thing. Someone could get hurt, killed even. Ezra Clayton could handle his own niggers. Few of the townspeople liked living under Clayton and none wanted to die for him. When they saw the owner pound through town they knew he was on the way to the fort. The army would arrive in the morning and take care of the slaves.

But night wore on and in the early pre-dawn hours their *laissez-faire* attitude gave way to one of concern. No soldiers had come. What if the trouble should spread? They were only three miles from the main house and it wouldn't take long for a bunch of aroused slaves to make the march and attack the town.

Men armed themselves and left their homes in the outlying district to help barricade the main street. Two wagonloads of women and children were sent east toward Jessup. Riders came and went, bringing news and bits of information, half-false, half-true. By daylight a ragged line of townsmen and a smattering of hunters and trappers eager for a fight lined the makeshift barricade across the street. They waited nervously, sleepless and tired, afraid for their women and children.

It was down this road the slaves marched. Nearly seventy-five men and women armed with guns, hoes, pitchforks and machetes. Cat had worked his followers up to fighting frenzy, calling to mind the cruelty and injustices perpetrated against them by their white masters. By the time they reached the hill above the town the burning hatred for their oppressors had been fanned into a white-hot flame. At the top of the hill they stopped to look down on the town, then started again, an inexorable black tide walking quietly, grimly, faces set in deadly purpose and following Cat into the very maws of rifles and muskets brought against them.

The quiet morning exploded in gunshot, flaming powder and smoking rifle barrels. Those of the blacks who had firearms returned the fire, though with no training the shooting did little more than lay a haze of black powder smoke in front of them, ruining the aim of those behind the barricade. When they swarmed over the wall of wagons and boards by sheer weight of numbers the trappers decided to abandon the fight and left as quickly as they had ridden to join. The townspeople ran to their stores and homes, hoping to protect what valuables they could.

Black Bedetta stood on the balcony of her brothel at the far edge of town. She watched and laughed, her corpulent frame quivering with each guffaw. Two of her girls —well-trained and with the scars to prove it—squatted to either side of her. Their hands toyed beneath the madam's dressing gown, titillating their mistress, bringing a shudder of ecstasy to accompany each echoing gunshot. Sweat beaded her brow and she laughed boisterously, then caught her breath and moaned. This was good. Her girls knew their job. Someone had fired a building. Another followed, going up in a billow of smoke. Shouts and frantic screams filled the air. A man, his head bloody, staggered past the brothel just beneath her. Reverend

Leahy. A pity he had never come to call. He would have. His kind always did. She peered away to the southeast. From her vantage point she could see, far away but coming at a steady trot, a detachment of men on horseback. Soldiers. How exciting. There would be a real fight, and after the fight, business enough to last her a week. She patted the girls. How lovely they were, how dexterous their fingers. Black Bedetta was having a good time.

Joe Terson's precious window was broken by Joe Terson himself when he went flying through it. A shard of the glass painstakingly protected all the way from New Orleans tore a bloody furrow across his chest as a burly field slave tossed him through the etched "T". When the slave turned the woman had disappeared, escaping through the back door and leaving the dry goods and foodstuffs to the rapacious attackers. She circled around to the street and desperately attempted to drag Joe from the board porch. His face was cut and blood was in his eyes. The gash on his chest was deep and needed attention. "I tried, Abby," he moaned. "That goddamn Elmer run off. But I tried."

"I know you did, husband," Abigail said, frantically trying to lift him to his feet. She wanted to remind him she had warned him about Ezra Clayton and the trouble he would bring, but the sight of the bloody, bowed man at her feet caused her to suppress the words, replace them, possibly for the first time in years, with protestations of endearment and encouragement. "Oh, Joe, please! You got to get up," she wept. "Joe? Please, Joe?" She tugged at his arm without effect. He was unconscious.

A rough hand pushed her aside. "Here's two more dat got dere debt ta pay." Cat faced them, a stiletto in each hand.

"Leave him alone," Abigail screamed, throwing herself at the lithe black man who threatened her and her husband. A knife point cut her deftly on the cheek and she screamed and fell back. Cat stared at her, his eyes crazed with bloodlust nurtured by years of hate. Joe Terson had laughed at him, even bet against him. "Goana gut dat ol' man an' leave him ta die, den cut yo' titties off, woman, less'n yo' runs real fas'. Yo' bettah run whiles yo' kin, o' stay an' watch. I'm goana stick 'im lahk a hog."

275

Abigail fell to her knees, tried to cover Joe's unconscious form.

"Leave them alone!"

Cat turned as Rafe leaped from his mount. "You blood-crazy as Mistah Ezra. Look what you doin'. More killin' an' bein' killed jus' like in the pit. No diff'rent from the white folks who watched. There ain't no call for this. You a fool, Cat. Long as you got that hate, you still ain't free."

Cat didn't say a word. He lunged at Abigail, his knives slicing down. Abigail screamed. Cat continued, his momentum carrying him as he fell dead by her side, his spine cracked open, the great nerves severed. Rafe had been quicker. Always had been. He sheathed the bloodied cutlass.

Abigail stared as if frozen to the spot. Desperately her mouth tried to move but no words came out. The black man lifted her husband's inert form as if it weighed no more than a doll and draped it over the horse he had been riding. "Take him away from here," he said to the trembling white woman, handing her the reins. "Get him away and patch him up."

Abigail nodded dumbly and lead the animal past Rafe, toward the forest bordering the town. She stopped momentarily to look back at the scarred giant who had saved their lives. He had killed one of his own kind to save her and her husband. Why? Why had he done it? The giant black was staring at the town and its pillagers, newly freed from bondage. How sad he looked, she thought. Which just proved there was no accounting for niggers. Abigail Terson frowned tightly and walked the horse to the safety of the trees.

18

Rafe realized the futility of any attempt to lead the rioting slaves from the town. The field slaves, after having endured Ezra Clayton's mistreatment for so many years, were in a frenzy of righteous destruction. The hour had come for them to demand retribution and exact payment and not one man, not even Rafe, had the power to stop them. Several buildings were aflame and the roadway was littered with piles of plunder. The slaves were milling in the street now, squabbling over the booty, arguing over which building to fire next. Rafe had to try. He jumped atop a wagon and called for them to listen, to follow him back up the road.

Bedetta had been the first to see the soldiers; Rafe was the second. The horsemen galloped into town, sabers drawn and gleaming in the sun. At the rear of the column, coatless and pistol in each hand, Ezra Clayton guided his mount recklessly, spurred on by demonic rage against the slaves who had revolted against him. Rafe leaped for cover behind the wagon, momentarily cursing his previous generosity in giving away the horse. No point in brooding. Escape was all.

The field slaves were caught in midroad and the soldiers rode them down. A few of the blacks had kept their firearms close at hand but of these only one or two had remembered to reload and their isolated shots offered no more than token resistance, ignored by the soldiers. Only the amount of goods littering the road served to retard the horses as they thundered toward the surprised blacks.

Captain Steven Bennett rode with grim resolve. For the white South the spectre of a slave uprising was too much to bear. Insurrection was totally insupportable and could never be allowed. Tried before and always ruthlessly put down, those involved in revolution were invariably slaughtered, for if one group was successful another would try: the very social fabric would be torn asunder, ripped to shreds.

If the niggers were real people it might be different. But they weren't. Childlike at best, they were without honor, lacked the ability to reason and couldn't be depended upon any farther than the nearest white man could watch. When it came right down to it they were animals, no more and no less. Domesticated they were useful, even desirable. Wild or unruly they must be eliminated before they infected the whole herd.

These had pillaged and burned, stolen and destroyed. Ezra Clayton's plantation was in ruins, the town on fire. They had very probably killed Crissa. Or worse! Unspeakable fantasies of rape and torture raged through Steve's head and the young captain put the spurs to his horse and charged them, a scream welling in his throat. He brought his saber down in a vicious arc powered by hatred, fear and horrifying images of Crissa's fate at the hands of the black devils. He stood in the stirrups and wheeled the great bay, slashed to either side, felt with grim satisfaction as the blade tore into black flesh, shattered black bone and spilled black blood. Angry enough for wholesale slaughter, he was a vindictive butcher, a wrathful white god ridding the world of vile black vermin.

Soldiers broke away from the center of the main street to ride down fleeing individuals. Ezra held back, glancing anxiously up the high road, cursing the delay in town. What had happened at Freedom since he'd ridden off in the night? Were his crops and stock left? Even now Rafe and the cursed pit niggers might be escaping. They'd head for Mexico, of course. The thought galled him, drove him to distraction. They musn't get away! They could not be allowed to succeed, had to be punished, had to pay with blood for the destruction of his house and land.

It was fortunate Pritchard brought such a large detachment of mounted soldiers to Fort Jessup. Fortunate indeed. The niggers didn't know what real trouble they were in. They'd had their party, burned their buildings and tasted a day of freedom, but Ezra Clayton would have the last laugh, a long, hard laugh over their broken and bloody corpses, over their bent and beaten backs. He'd work them like the beasts they were, work them until they fell and then leave them lie, each and every one of them food for the buzzards. As for the son-of-a-bitch Rafe, he hoped they took him alive. He'd see him nailed to a tree and then watch him rot. The very thought of revenge was sweet.

A breeze stirred the embers, fanned the flames of nearby buildings. Smoke billowed to enfold soldiers and rebellious slaves in shifting curtains of somber gray. Rafe judged the distance to the plantation house and knew his chances of getting back alive were nonexistent unless he had a horse. There were horses aplenty, the only problem being the armed soldiers riding them. He had no choice. Hefting his cutlass he raced around the back of Terson's store, dodged a gust of twinkling fiery embers and bolted across the alley between the burning shell of the barber and surgeon's shop and the battered but unfired tavern. A black woman ran screaming out of the smoke, chased by a young dragoon, saber raised for a killing swipe. He didn't see Rafe, only felt the cruel bite of steel as he charged his horse past a dark shadow coming from the side of the building. The violent tug across his middle almost knocked him from his seat. To regain his balance he reined up, pushing himself forward in the saddle. Had he hit a branch? a rope strung between the buildings? He looked down, his eyes widening with disbelief. Something pink and white was spilling from his belly, oozing down the saddle and hanging in great loops from the pommel. And then wetness and pain. Blood welled from the gaping line across his belly. His hands lost their grip on the saber as he sought to catch the slippery loops, sought to staunch the blood. Stunned, he turned to look back at what he had ridden into. The effort toppled him from the saddle and he screamed . . . once. The horse walked a few steps, nervous with the smell of blood and the weight of the trooper dragging on the stirrup. A huge black man caught the bridle, freed the booted foot and sliced the dripping viscera from the saddle while the youth stared at him, pain clouding his vision in his dying moments.

Rafe swung into the saddle, noticing with pleasure the two horse pistols to either side of the pommel. He looked about but the woman had disappeared among the trees. There was no time for her now. He had to get out without being seen, get back to warn the others, get them moving across the river where they could make a stand and an escape. He prodded the horse with his heels and the animal broke into an easy trot, then a canter. Behind him the youth no longer felt the heat from the nearby flames. On the contrary, his face felt oddly cool. Then he felt nothing at all.

Ezra rode through the town, impatient to be done with the work at hand and move on to the plantation. Behind him Captain Bennett inspected and reorganized the dragoons and found only one man for whom he couldn't account. The road was littered with the corpses of the slaves. Some had been lucky and gotten away but they would be rounded up easily later. Under the circumstances any further pursuit was fruitless. Time now to get to the plantation and finish off the rest of them. Ezra walked his horse down the street, scanning every body for signs of recognition. He halted at Cat's corpse. The back of the pitbuck's neck was sliced open and he lay face down, bony arms and legs splayed out in a grim paraphrase of life. He'd had great plans for Cat, damn it. Could have won a lot of gold on him. A horse bolted from the trees at the far edge of town and headed up the hill toward the plantation. Ezra glanced up and recognized the rider.

"Rafe!" he screamed, and fired his pistol.

Rafe instinctively ducked as he heard his name called and the shot fired. He turned and fired one of the horse pistols. Not waiting to see whether he hit anything he spurred the roan gelding up the hill. The animal was tired after the journey from Fort Jessup and Rafe wished he still had the fresher horse he'd ridden to town. As it was he had no advantage other than a slight head start and the fact the horses chasing him would be tired too. He'd have to manufacture an advantage. One man in the midst of many, if he acted unpredictably and with great daring, if he restricted their field of fire, just might outwit them all.

Ezra screamed in fury as he saw Rafe's pistol spout smoke and flame. The shot came nowhere near, but the very idea of a nigger shooting at him sent a wave of mad rage pouring through his system. He screamed Rafe's name again and spurred his horse into pursuit.

The response was instantaneous. Lead filled the air around Rafe as the soldiers sought to knock him from horseback. Steve recognized the giant black man and knew if any harm had come to Crissa, Rafe was most likely the perpetrator. Infuriated, he led the chase, his bicorn whipped from his head by the wind and his flaming red hair wildly dishevelled as he urged his horse up the hill.

Rafe disappeared over the crest, shifted his weight as the roan started down the long, sweeping hill to the flat stretch leading to the plantation. He risked a glance behind him and recognized Steve Bennett slowly closing the gap, the rest of the soldiers bunched up and not very far behind. The black man grinned and settled in for a fast ride, his back safe for the moment. They wouldn't be able to shoot at him without endangering their own captain.

The roan was a strong animal and bore his weight well, but twenty miles of hard riding, the fight in town and then the race up the hill and across the flats were taking their toll and the beast was rapidly weakening. The fields swept by him on both sides and he could see the magnolias and the front lawn. The wagons were gone. Rafe grunted to himself, pleased. Jomo and the others must have moved them out for the river. With luck they'd be there already, even starting to cross.

A lone, soot-blackened chimney pointed awkwardly to the left of the magnolias, concealing the charred shambles below. Time. He needed more time. If he took a straight route the soldiers would follow him directly down the river path to Clayton's landing. Rafe had no doubts about what would happen then. There had been no time for counting but it looked like at least forty or fifty soldiers, all heavily armed. Primed for battle by one bloodbath they would want more, would fight ferociously to put down the rebellion. The slaves could never sustain such an attack. Without a delay, without more time to get across the river, they would be massacred. He had but one chance, and a risky one at that. "Remember," his father had told him, "confusion is the most powerful weapon a single man has in the face of many."

He reined the roan off the road just before he reached the carriage lane to the burned house, jumped the ditch and guided the animal into the pecan grove. No more than twenty yards behind him, Steve chanced a shot which blew out a fist-sized chunk of bark from a tree as Rafe disappeared past the trunk. Steve jumped the ditch at a run and plunged into the grove at a gallop, Ezra and the dragoons following hard behind him into the dense stand of trees.

Inside the grove the quiet was shattered by the drum of hoofbeats and the shouts and curses of the soldiers. Rafe guided his horse between the trunks, back and forth, keeping to an irregular path and avoiding catastrophe by a hair's breadth. Many of the soldiers were not so lucky, and bunched as they were, found themselves slamming into each other and the trees themselves. Two or three were swept out of their saddles by low-hanging branches until Steve managed to spread them out, shouting at them to sweep the grove behind him and avoid firing lest they unwittingly shoot one another.

The grove darkened the farther in they ventured. Steve, still ahead of the others, managed to keep pace for he knew the grove well. The two men dodged one another among the pecans like children, but playing a deadlier game than tag. Suddenly Rafe swerved to the right and vanished into the dappled shadows. Steve followed, then abruptly reined in. His steed reared back and whinnied, protesting the halt. Rafe was nowhere to be seen.

Captain Steven Bennett sat and waited, listening for Rafe to make a sound and give himself away. Sweat poured down his face and into his eyes. Cursing the weight of his cloth coatee required by regulations, he tugged at the brass buttons and opened the garment to get some fresh air. Damn the regulations! A man couldn't fight bundled up so. He started to take off the coat. Quietly, careful not to make the slightest noise, he shrugged the shoulders down over his arms and at that moment Rafe broke from the brush to his right. Steve's face went taut as he struggled to free his hands and looked helplessly at his saddle pistols. Rafe brandished a pistol of his own. He charged his mount into the officer's, swinging the heavy-barrelled weapon to deliver a glancing blow to the captain's head as horse and man went down. Rafe's roan stumbled, recovered his stride and struck off toward the road and the plantation house.

Steve kicked himself clear of the thrashing mount, rolled over and got to his feet in time to see Rafe vanish once again among the trees. Cursing and yelling orders to his unseen command, he caught his horse's bridle and tugged the tired beast to its feet, tried to remount, losing precious moments when the horse shied from him. His face streaming blood and his senses rattled by the lump he'd received on the side of his head, he finally managed to regain his seat and head his horse after Rafe.

Rafe swerved the roan to miss a large hole, jumped a fallen log, and deftly guided the tired animal to the right and left, charging among the circling dragoons who had never expected a slave to display either horsemanship or bravery. A soldier swerved to avoid the massive black horseman and crashed into a tree. Rafe fired the second horse pistol. Surrounded as he was by enemies he could hardly miss and was rewarded with a howl of pain from a soldier behind him. He replaced the pistol in its saddle holster and grabbed the McKim's from his waist. One shot left. He bore down on two other dragoons who, confused and not wanting to fire into their comrades, turned and collided with a third as they attempted to cut him off. The roan galloped past the plunging, milling trio, heading for the road and running room.

A horse loomed in front of him. He loosed his final shot. The heavy caliber slug shattered the rider's knee and sent him skidding from his mount. The shot triggered a dozen more from the dragoons, still leaderless and flustered, angry at being played for such fools by one black man. Regardless of the proximity of their comrades they were not going to be fired at without firing back. Bullets tore the air, shredded leaves, ripped gaping chunks out of trees. Rafe dodged between the young soldiers who fired almost point-blank at the rushing figure, missed and shot into each other, one falling mortally wounded.

Rafe holstered his pistol and concentrated on keeping his horse swerving among the trees. Pandemonium reigned all around him as he ducked and bobbed under the branches. The sergeant had a clear shot at the ex-slave for a brief moment, but before he could fire a lead ball from a nervous private's pistol shattered his arm. The sergeant cursed mightily and the young soldier discreetly disappeared among the trees, hoping the wounded man hadn't seen who had fired the shot.

Steve rode through the grove, shouting for the men to assemble and cease fire. He was all too aware of Rafe's ruse now and knew they must regroup quickly and follow him before he could get to the other slaves. Other more seasoned men took up the call and soon the firing stopped. Steve slowed his horse to a canter. The men around him did likewise and massed together for orders. Finally, in some semblance of a formation, Steve led them back to the road.

The roan, lathered and heaving, barely made it across the ditch. Something sliced the flesh of Rafe's arm and thwacked into a tree. A pistol ball. . . . He turned and caught a glimpse of Ezra dashing back among the pecans. Old Ezra was too smart to follow the soldiers deep into the grove and had waited behind. "Here he is! Here he is!" he shouted frantically, summoning Steve and the troop.

Rafe felt the hatred well up in him but there wasn't a moment to spare for revenge, not even for Ezra. He urged the roan up the front lawn, around the ruins, past the barracks, the compound and the pit and down the river path. If only he had gained enough time. . . . If only the horse had enough left in him to make it. Rafe beat on the exhausted animal's flanks, beat him into a final, killing gallop. . . .

"What yo' want from us, white girl? Ain't yo' kine done enuff?" Julie demanded angrily. "What yo' doin', hangin' on where yo' ain't wanted?"

Crissa ignored her as she had ignored the suspicious stares of the others around her all the while she had helped load the raft each time it had landed on the east bank. She understood their resentment. What else could she expect of them? If only Julie would cease fanning their discontent and anger. . . . She lent a helping hand as another heavy sack of vegetables was handed onto the logs, slipping precariously in the mud when the weight shifted unexpectedly. The bag safely aboard and the raft shoved off, she staggered back up the slippery bank, suppressing a growing feeling of panic. There had been more gunfire coming from beyond the house. Rafe? Was he alive or dead? If dead, what would become of her? Unaccepted by one world and having forsaken the other for a black man and a slave, she would be an outcast, reviled by all. Rafe. . . . Yes, she loved him. She had fought the idea long enough, tried to convince herself the feelings were of pity. But now, especially since the morning, the fact was all too plain. She loved him. A fierce and gentle man, a man to stand by though the color of his skin made her a leper among her own kind. But then, what was her own kind? Surely not those leering patrons of Ezra's inhuman delights. No. Not them. She wandered off into the trees, away from the landing.

Unseen, Julie followed her, crept up behind her. The girl's fingers dug into Crissa's arm and spun her about. "Dat's right. Yo' jes' keep walkin'. Yo' gots no call ta stay," Julie said. The mulatto held a dagger before her, the blade pointed at Crissa's chest. What puzzled her was Crissa did not seem frightened. "Ah seen yo', turnin' yo' white ass to Rafe. Bringin' him ta dip in yo' bush. Yo' white girls gotta hab yo' black meat, doan yo'? Turn a po' nigger's haid wid yo' honey sweetness. Showin' yo' sof' purty white flesh dat ain't neber done no work. Rafe doan need yo', he need a black woman, he need his own kine."

Crissa stepped inside the blade and closed her hand firmly over Julie's fist "You must love him very much," she said softly.

The mulatto was taken totally off guard by Crissa's statement and seeming indifference to the length of steel at her chest. Her eyes began to grow moist, her lip trembled. The knife wavered and dropped to Crissa's feet and Julie wheeled around and ran back toward the river. Crissa would have followed but she heard Jomo shout, "Rafe! Rafe!" and saw the slaves' powerful leader rein in and jump from his lathered mount at the edge of the cypress lined shore.

19

"Yo' bleedin, N'gata."

Rafe glanced at the gash on his arm. "Ezra Clayton," he said shortly. Crissa gasped and brought a hand to her lips in a gesture of fear at the mention of her stepfather. "We knew he'd come, Crissa. Maybe it's better this way."

Rafe's voice was both warm and strong, giving her confidence. If anyone could get them safely across the Sabine, this man—her man—could. The pitbucks were gathering around them now and Crissa stepped through them, realizing there was nothing more to be said for the moment. Not until Ezra had been dealt with. If the lord of Freedom was there, he must have soldiers with him. Soldiers from Fort Jessup, which meant Steve would be riding with them. She shuddered at the lies Ezra must have told him. If she could get to him, talk to him—but what would she say? That the slaves were in the right? To Steve's way of thinking the slaves would have to be in the wrong. No explanation of hers could possibly reverse such a lifelong conviction. Would she tell him she loved Rafe? A slave and a killer? He'd never even admit he'd heard such blasphemy. Steve would never let her go. Crissa searched her mind for a way to stop the fight she knew must take place, fearing not only for the man she loved, but also for the man who was as a brother to her.

"How much more to get across?" Rafe asked.

Jomo gestured toward the river. "Another load. We split up de field hands. Only one mo' load to go an' dey all be ober. We hoped fo' de ferry, but dem guards Mistuh Ezra kep' here skedaddled wid it down de ribber an' we didn't hab no time ta build mo' den one raft. Soon as it take dem ober it come back fo' us."

"Ah swum dat ribber, Boss," Trinidad added. "Bess here foun' de pulleys an' rope in de stable an' Ah carried dem acrost ta de uder side ta hook 'em up an' pull de raf'. Sho' feel good ober dere. Feel free." His arm was around Bess. The diminutive black girl looked proudly at Trinidad.

Rafe studied the two briefly. That they idolized each other was evident. Whatever happened to him and the others he'd have to see they got across and away. He turned his attention to the river. The field hands grouped on the west side were hauling on the rope, pulling the final load of goods toward them. A smaller cluster left on the east shore watched Rafe, trusting him. The pitbucks were in a loose ring circling him. Rafe was one of their own, their leader. The soldiers would soon be coming down the river path and they waited for his directions.

Rafe surveyed his position. They needed more time. The field hands weren't fighters and once on the raft would be sitting ducks until in the trees on the other side of the water. Quickly he counted the pitbucks. They'd started out with twenty-two. Two, wounded in the fighting the night before, lay on pallets by the shore and would cross with the last of the field hands. Cat and one of the new ones were lost in town. That left eighteen, three of whom were new—Rafe didn't even know their names. Fifteen seasoned fighters, then. Fifteen who had survived at least a year as Ezra Clayton's fighting niggers. Fifteen against how many? Forty, perhaps, well-armed and mounted.

He grinned as the plan unfolded in his head. They could do it and still save Bess and Trinidad. He turned to the youth. "Trinidad, you take Bess and get on that raft with the others. They gonna need a leader an' you it."

"Boss, Ah. . . ."

"Ain't no time for arguin'. Do like I say." He turned to look up the river path. "We got to stop them soldiers. This path is too wide—eight or nine horses too wide. Drag them two empty wagons over across the road up there by that cottonwood an' tip 'em over. An' that fallen tree yonder. Bring it too." Jomo quickly jabbed his finger at eight of the men who broke for the wagons. Four more headed for the tree. "Get guns. All we have an' carry 'em to the wagons. We're gonna stop 'em right there. Dingo, soon's they get the wagon in place take them four men an' sneak out into the trees to the left. Jomo, you do the same to the right. Don't let no one see you. The rest of us will meet 'em head on. We'll empty our muskets an' pistols an' then rush into 'em. Jomo, you an' Dingo hold your fire. Soon as you see us jump the wagons, open up on 'em from the sides, then rush 'em with whatever you fight with. Tell your men if they ain't never fought a man on horseback before, watch out for over their heads."

Jomo grinned and raised his axe. "It goana be jes' lahk in de pit. One las' time. On'y Ezra Clayton be dere wid us." He chuckled evilly. "We see how he lahk it."

Dingo cocked the hammer on his blunderbuss. "Ah bet he doan lahk it a'tall," he muttered grimly. "Not one little bit a'tall."

There was time for no more talk. Already they could hear the thunder of hooves and see the first riders coming in the distance. Dingo and Jomo ran off to help finish with the wagons, then took their men and weapons and scurried into the heavy brush by the side of the road just in time to escape being seen by the mounted troop as it came in sight again and stopped at the last curve before the river path led straight to the water's edge. Rafe deployed the pitbucks left to him behind the wagons, reloaded and checked his horse pistols and the McKim. "Wait until I fire," he said calmly, "then blast away at them. Shoot fast an' thick, then follow me an' hit 'em as hard as you can."

The silence of waiting for violence hung heavily over them. Suddenly Trinidad was at his side, handed him a musket. "Ain't crossin' no ribber," he said. "Not unless we all do. Ah'm a pitbuck too. Ah gots as much right ta dis fight as any man. Ah fought more'n two yeahs fo' Mistuh Ezra an' Ah ain't goana miss dis las' fight now dat Ah'm fightin' fo' me."

Rafe watched the young pitbuck walk back to his position. Such was his right and Rafe could not change his decision, but Bess was armed too and stood beside her mate, her girlish face as determined as Trinidad's. Rafe started toward her to send her to the river. Aware of his intent the girl looked at him defiantly and edged closer to her man. Rafe grinned and remembered the last time another woman had tried to take Trinidad away from her. She had guts enough for any man. She smiled back, stepped to the barricade.

What were the soldiers doing? The path before them blocked, their edge was lost. Rafe scanned the shoreline where the field hands were pulling the empty raft back across the river. Only five minutes more and they and the wounded pitbucks would be aboard and safely on their way. He looked for Crissa. Certainly she wasn't on the Mexican side. He felt a growing uneasiness as he frantically searched the Louisiana shore for some sign of her. Where was she?

A drumming cannonade of hooves called back his attention to the river path. Captain Bennett and his soldiers were advancing. They halted some hundred yards up the path. There was no time to look for Crissa now. Only time to be ready. "Make sure your guns are primed and cocked," he told the pitbucks on either side of him.

Steve Bennett ordered his men to a halt, cautiously rode a few yards ahead of his command to study the barricaded path. Heavy, choking underbrush to either side prevented men on horseback from going around the tipped-over wagons. The only sure course was to charge, ride through them and come back with sword to cut down the survivors. "Rafe . . . !" he shouted. "You're outnumbered and your back is to the river. There is no escape. You will be punished for this insurrection that has taken the lives of so many innocent citizens. And I hold you personally responsible for the deaths of Micara and Crissa Fitzman. However, should you surrender I will guarantee lenient treatment for those with you."

Rafe leaped onto the wagon side, the added height making him look every bit some terrible ebony giant. When he spoke his voice was deep and resonant, carried through the humid air. "Crissa is alive and with us. Her mother died in the flames but we had nothing to do with the burning."

Crissa alive? Steve looked back sharply at Ezra, who only shrugged. The plantation lord had little liking for this jabbering. He had hoped the dragoons would sweep down onto the slaves and crush them in one fell blow. Talk made him apprehensive, all the more so if Crissa was still alive.

"Show her to us," Steve shouted back. "Send her out here. Release her and we can talk."

"She is here of her own choosing," came the reply.

Steve flushed in anger. "You're lying, nigger. Now . . . ."

Crissa burst from the foliage near the path and started running up the road toward Steve. She had made her decision, the only one she could make. No matter what the odds, she had to try to explain, somehow force Steve to listen to her while she told him what had really happened. With luck he'd listen to her before Ezra, and in any case her action would buy Rafe and the others time, time to escape the guns massed against them, time for a chance. "Steve! Steve!" she screamed.

Rafe started in surprise. What was she doing? Steve spurred his mount toward her but Ezra, recognizing the threat, kicked his horse past the line of dragoons and cut in front of Steve. His expression was one of a concerned father. "Wait here! As soon as I get her into the brush and out of the way, charge the black bastards." Without waiting for a reply he whipped his horse and sprang away down the road, leaving the startled captain behind.

Steve called for him to come back. Crissa stopped, shocked at the sight of Ezra riding down on her. He'd outfoxed her and even at a distance she could read all too well the malicious intent on his face. She turned and backed toward the dense foliage to her right.

"Don't shoot until I tell you!" Rafe shouted to his men. "Wait until they charge." He lay his musket across the side of the wagon, sighting along the barrel, leading Ezra as the plantation owner charged toward Crissa. Rafe fired. The unrifled musket, an inaccurate weapon at such a distance, belched smoke and flame but the shot went wide.

From Steve's viewpoint, it appeared the slave was aiming at Crissa, who stumbled and disappeared in the foliage, possibly hit. Seconds later Ezra plunged into the mass of wild berry vines and scrub cypress and Steve Bennett, eager to wipe out the last of the insurrection, angrily waved his command to the attack.

Rafe was torn between rushing after Crissa or staying with the barricade. The dragoons thundering down the road made his decision for him. Dropping behind the wagon, he rammed powder and ball down the barrel of the musket, poured a trace in the pan, brought the weapon to his shoulder and sighted along the barrel. "Get ready!" he shouted, and saw out of the corner of his eye the other pitbucks raise their weapons and wait for him to fire.

The dragoons quickly closed the distance between themselves and the barricade. Rafe was aiming dead center at Steve Bennett. A difficult shot, for there was little of the soldier exposed. He remembered Crissa telling him of the years she had spent with Steve and the childhood romance, ended on her part but never on his. Well, he thought, her friend would live, protected as he was by the horse. Rafe sucked in his breath, lowered the musket slightly and squeezed the trigger. The captain's mount buckled, head down and hind legs kicking high. Steve pushed himself free, rolling over in the mud, hands over his head to protect himself from the flashing hooves of the animals behind him. The dragoons swerved and leapt their mounts aside, trying to avoid trampling their captain.

The pitbucks held their fire a moment longer as if fascinated by the soldiers' attempts to ride free of the fallen man. Rafe dropped the musket and raised one of the horse pistols. "Shoot!" he yelled. "Shoot!"

The slaves at the barricade opened up and guns exploded to either side of him as Rafe fired, then rammed, primed and fired the horse pistol once again, fired his second horse pistol and then, McKim in one hand and cutlass in the other, leaped to the top of the wagon and charged.

The front line of horsemen slowed and the attack crumpled back as men pitched from horseback to lie wounded or dying in the mud. The milling horses and screaming men barred the line of attack for the soldiers coming from the rear, causing them to bunch dangerously in the center of the path. Sudden gunfire erupted from the trees to either side of them. The blunderbuss boomed, sending a load of shrapnel into the cluster of soldiers, blowing three of them from their saddles. The enfilade added further to the tumult and confusion.

Rafe, at the head of the charging pitbucks from the barricade, glared frantically through the thick haze of powder smoke toward the brush where Crissa had disappeared. Every passing moment brought her closer to death. Ezra might have caught her; she might have been hit by a stray musket ball. A dragoon on horseback suddenly loomed out of the smoke, his saber raised. Rafe grabbed at the horse's bridle, pulled the unsuspecting beast's head down and ducked under to come up on the other side, cutlass swinging. Steel bounced off steel and the cutlass sliced into the soldier's forearm, severing muscles and tendons, knocking him out of the battle.

Ahead of him, Rafe could see Steve on his feet and screaming for his men to dismount and fight afoot. Their horses made it impossible to maneuver in such a tight position. To his right he caught a glimpse of Jomo charging out of the swamp with his men, charging into the milling soldiers. Dingo would be doing likewise on his left.

The dragoons were not without training nor experience, but their great numbers worked against them as they had in the grove. Some of the more experienced formed into tight circles, sabers and pistols drawn and in hand, and as Rafe and the pitbucks charged into their midst the soldiers fired as one, for the most part shooting into a cloud of choking smoke, trusting pure firepower to wipe out most of their attackers. Two of the slaves staggered, wounded. Bess was slammed back into the mud. Trinidad leaped to her side, cradled her in his arms and, ignoring the gunfire around him, rocked her gently back and forth, crooning her name over and over again, holding her close so she couldn't see the great fount of blood spilling from the gaping hole in her chest. Bess stared at him, her eyes wide with pain and fear. She whispered his name once, shuddered and slumped to one side.

The dragoons attempted to reload but there was no time. The pitbucks were among them. Rafe parried a feeble saber thrust with the barrel of the McKim, slid it down the blade and fired point-blank over the hilt into the soldier's belly. The soldier spun from the impact of the lead ball that tore a fist-sized hole out his back. As he dropped, a companion leaped over him, cleaving the air with his saber. Rafe stepped aside and impaled him on the cutlass, flung the badly wounded man away and searched for another victim.

To his right Trinidad had gone berserk. Tears streaming down his face, screaming curses at the men in front of him, the youth brandished a pitchfork and charged half a dozen grouped soldiers. Crazy with anguish for his lost Bess, he used the wooden pole as a quarterstaff, ramming the butt into the gut of the first soldier then switching and slashing with the tines. The pitchfork whirled in his hands. He poked again with the pole, stabbed with the vicious prongs. Sabers opened a dozen wounds on him but the raging fury in his blood kept him upright and maiming and butchering all he could.

Minutes passed as seconds and the swirling, desperate carnage continued. Many of the soldiers were seasoned campaigners, determined fighters who had survived the recent war with England. Some were professionals who knew no other life but the charge, the clash of sabers, and fields of coiling powder smoke. In spite of Steve's warnings to the contrary, many made the assumption this battle would be no more difficult than the one they had just fought in town. The assumption was a fatal mistake and they underestimated their enemy and found themselves in battle with a veritable handful of demons. These were no ordinary field slaves, but black men trained and kept in the peak of condition to fight and kill. And there was one further and even more important difference. They were no longer fighting for Ezra Clayton. They were fighting for themselves, for their own freedom.

Rafe heard the roar of the blunderbuss brought into action once again. Soldiers loomed out of the smoke around him. He ducked past them, driving a rock hard fist to the groin of one, carving the leg of another. A blade struck sparks against his cutlass. He stepped inside the soldier's guard and rammed the cutlass through his side, kicked the wounded man away from him and into the pistol of a companion to his rear. The confused dragoon pulled the trigger and shot the wounded man in the back, killing him. A second later Rafe was flying through the air over the falling body. His cutlass clove at the uniformed shoulder and the dragoon dropped to his knees, groaning in agony as Rafe freed the blade. To his left he caught a glimpse of soldiers retreating. The attack was broken, the worst part over. He had to find Crissa.

An eddying breeze revealed a portion of the trail and Rafe leaped over bodies sprawled in death, the mark of Jomo's axe on three of them. Yelling for Jomo to take over and regroup behind the wagons, he ran to the relative safety of the trees. His eyes smarted from the stinging haze clouding the path, but as his vision cleared he made out more of the soldiers heading back up the trail.

Crissa. . . . Sudden panic overwhelmed him. He heard the whinny of a horse among the brush ahead and followed the sound to a small clearing. Ezra had picketed the animal, unable to ride among the overgrowth and soft mud. Crissa's flight and Ezra's pursuit were obvious. Rafe began to run, his long powerful legs carrying him swiftly into the swamp. The impulse was to tear through the underbrush and call for Crissa at the top of his lungs but he knew too well the man he stalked—a vicious, rabid animal whose appetite for cruelty recognized no bounds. A dangerous man who, if Rafe was not careful, could turn the tables yet. And Crissa was out there alone with him. How far? How long had he been in battle? His eyes ever watchful, he followed the footprints and broken branches his quarry had left in their wake. And then from the depths of the swamp, a pistol shot followed by a horrible scream . . . .

Crissa had read the murderous intent in Ezra's eyes as he galloped toward her and her only recourse had been the brush, for she had gone too far to get back to the barricade. When her stepfather continued his pursuit into the woods she had had no alternative but to press on. Suddenly the heavy foliage thinned and she found herself in the eerie twilight gloom of the great cypresses, brown stagnant water covered with green algae all around her. Always irrationally afraid of the swamps, she was now terrified. Vines grabbed at her, whipped her face, caught at her ankles and sent her stumbling into the evil-smelling muck. She crawled to solid ground and plunged again through the creepers, clawing her way through curtains of moss, fleeing from the violent sound of battle and the destruction awaiting her at the hands of Ezra Clayton.

She was lost, uncertain of the river's whereabouts. Ezra was screaming her name. He would be upon her soon. She continued her headlong plunge deeper and deeper into the swamp. Direction ceased to matter. Flight was all. She wallowed through a muddy course, sinking up to her knees. Her father's warnings of quicksand flashed to mind and a heart-thudding, icy fear gripped her as the ooze sucked at her legs. She managed to reach for and grab hold of a cypress root angling out of the muck and pulled free of the muddy trap, scrambling frantically under some concealing foliage. Ezra appeared, pistol in hand, stopped at the lip of the bog and peered intently around him. Crissa backed away as soundlessly as she could, rose and continuing to crouch low, retreated still deeper into the darkness, desperately keeping a large cypress between her and Ezra.

Suddenly the brush thickened again and she could go no farther. She was trapped on three sides by water. Behind her she could hear Ezra beating his way through the foliage. The stream in front of her meandered slowly, barely ten feet in width. It looked only a few feet deep at most but she couldn't really tell, so murky was the water. She could hear Ezra laugh and call to her. He was hard on her trail and she had little time left. A massive, ungainly bough hung across the stream. Reaching up she steadied herself on it and stepped into the stream. A shape glided toward her foot, a sinewy rope like shape followed by another and then a third. Water moccasins! The stream was alive with them. She jumped back with a squeal, glanced over her shoulder. Ezra was closing in fast. So little time. The bough. . . .

She swung up to the limb and, straddling it, edged her way to the opposite bank. If it failed to hold her weight . . . . All her life she had carried the memory of the striking reptile that had almost taken her life in the pecan grove and now she was dangling a few feet above a stream full of them. The bough shivered, the wood creaked and she wriggled the remaining yard and leaped to the bank, stood there exhausted, unable to run any farther. Ezra had destroyed everything: her home, her mother, her own dreams. His rapacious greed, his perverse and insatiable delight in blood and pain stunned her, left her filled with untempered disgust. She had tried to stand firm before him and failed. She had run from him and failed. Now she was through running and faced death. A whisper of sound behind her. She turned in time to see another snake slide into the water. I should have let them have me, she thought. Better them than. . . . Her breath caught at the boldness of the plan. Would he?

Ezra, his clothes torn and grimy, one boot missing, burst from the foliage across the creek and stopped at the water's edge. Crissa lay on the opposite shore, cringing against a huge old cypress knee. Not fifteen full feet away. He couldn't have asked for an easier shot. Ezra smiled, cocked the pistol. Crissa whirled at the sound, her eyes wide with fear. Her shirt was torn, the front ragged and open, her breasts nearly totally exposed, lovely despite the mud covering her. Ezra hesitated. Too bad, he thought. . . .

"Ezra. . . . Please, no!" Crissa pleaded, tears streaking her face. "Oh, please don't!"

Ezra laughed openly. He had waited two months to see her spirit broken, to hear her plaintive voice acknowledge his mastery. "You're going to die, Crissa Elizabeth. First you and then that nigger, if Steve and his soldiers don't beat me to him."

"Oh, God, Ezra. No. No, don't. . . ." He aimed the pistol. "I'll do anything, but please don't kill me, Ezra. Anything. You always wanted me," she rushed on, her voice filled with panic. "I'll be yours. It'll be good. You'll be the first, but I can make it good for you, I know I can. Please don't. Here . . . take me here. You'll see. The ground is soft, better than a bed."

A virgin. . . . Her breasts were beautiful. He had wanted her. And now she was broken. Frightened enough to do anything, to plead for him to put it in her just as he'd imagined. Why not take full satisfaction? Ream her and then put a bullet through her skull. Why not?

The pistol lowered. Ezra stared at the sensuous curves of her flesh, the trim, tight thighs beneath her ragged trousers. His smile changed to a leering grin and he stepped into the stream. Even as he took the first broad stride a change seemed to come over Crissa. A chilling look of triumph where seconds before there had been supplication and the promise of debasement. He took another step . . . .

"Crissa?"

She looked up. And saw Rafe. In the silence between them, Ezra's body was already turning black from the venom of a dozen strikes. The plantation lord had fallen with his head on the bank. His body extended into the water, feet waving gently in the sluggish current. He had fired into the water as the first set of fangs hit him, then thrashed and fought his way toward Crissa, cursing as the maddened reptiles struck over and over again at his limbs, torso and face. A water moccasin glided close, darted against Ezra's cheek, hung there a moment then slipped back into the water and disappeared beneath the surface. Crissa sighed low and long. It was finished.

"You ready, Captain?"

"No. Not yet, Sergeant."

"There can't be more'n a handful left behind that barricade."

"There weren't many more than that from the start. Count the darkies you see out there. Those behind the barricade are heavily armed. I can see that from here. No telling how many we'd lose before we took them. There's got to be another way."

Captain Steven Bennett stared at the battered remnants of his command. Over half his force dead or wounded. A straight-on charge would be near suicide and he had neither men nor time enough to infiltrate through the brush and take them from the sides. They'd be on the raft and across the river before his men could get close enough. There had to be another way. And what of Crissa? Hopefully Ezra had found her and the two were safely making their way back through the brush. He'd have to chance a wait.

Next to him the sergeant winced as he flexed his wounded arm and spat onto the moist earth. "I never seen the like of such niggers. Hell, I emptied four pistols into that darkie with the pitchfork afore he give up an' died. Lucky for us the British didn't fight like that when Andy Jackson generalled us at New Orleans. We'd still be runnin' instead of them."

"Captain," a youthful private called, handing him the glass. "Look there, comin' out of the trees."

Steve put the spyglass to his eye and studied the brush by the wagons. Crissa! And the niggers' huge, damnable leader, Rafe.

"Sheeit," the sergeant cursed. "Now we can't touch 'em. Not with a woman prisoner. Wonder what happened to Clayton?"

Steve watched as the two disappeared behind the barricade. She looked ragged but unharmed. Damn!

"What you figger we oughta do, Captain?"

"Wait, Sergeant. Just wait."

"Sir, supposin' they cross the river to Tejas an' take her with 'em? They'll be in Mexico where we can't foller."

Steve closed the spyglass, slamming it back into the

case. "Sergeant, if they take that girl with them we'll follow them straight to hell if need be."

Jomo watched and waited. He'd regrouped the remaining few behind the barricade and seen to the loading of the guns. Certain his friend would show up sooner or later, he was determined to wait however long it took. But the soldiers worried him. With only Dingo and two others beside himself he felt less than confident of their ability to survive another attack. Seeing Rafe come from the brush cheered him considerably. The white girl he wasn't sure about. White women were trouble. Still, they could trade her for their freedom. He shrugged his shoulders mentally, knowing there would be no trade. Rafe was Rafe. If he wanted the girl he'd have her, even if she did cause trouble, even if the rest of them had to fight because of her.

Rafe darted behind the wagons, squatted at Jomo's side. The giant grinned happily, swatted Jomo on the shoulder. "N'gata Jomo."

Jomo lifted the bloody axe. "A good fight, N'gata Rafe." He grinned back. Jomo would back his friend no matter what.

Rafe helped Crissa as she slumped down to rest, her back against the bed of the wagon. She closed her eyes. He thought of the corpses littering the path. Trinidad . . . Bess . . . so many more. "A hard fight, N'gata Jomo. So many dead. Trinidad and Bess?"

Jomo nodded his head in affirmation. "Dey choose to die. Dey choose. It make a difference, N'gata. Dey die free."

Rafe nodded. His friend was right. Dingo and the others were staring at him, waiting for instructions, looking apprehensively from him to the river and the field slaves gathered on the opposite shore. Rafe stood and stared down the path. The soldiers would not wait long. They'd have to come on foot if they didn't want to trample their wounded. Or through the brush. . . .

"Stay here," he told them, then turned and walked the twenty yards to the river's edge, took up the rope and began pulling the raft across to him, muscles bunching along his shoulders and back. Hand over hand he drew the raft closer and closer. On the other side Chulem instructed several of the men to handle the opposite line and help Rafe, then stand by to either cut the line or pull the raft back across.

"Rafe," Jomo called. "Dey must've see yo'. Dey comin' down de path. Dey holdin' a white flag."

Rafe left the line, let the raft drift in by itself as he hurried back to the wagons and climbed aboard one. "That's far enough!" His voice rang clearly, stopping the soldiers in their tracks. "What you want?"

"Talk," Steve called back. "We want to talk and we want the girl."

Rafe glanced down at Crissa, gestured for her to stay hidden. "What you gonna do if we give her to you?"

There was a pause. "Let you go."

Rafe laughed. "I tell you what, Mistah Captain. You pick up your wounded an' carry them back up the path to where you was campin'. Then we'll come out an' pick up our wounded, bringin' the girl with us in case you try anything. Then when we get back behind the wagons here, we'll let you know. But you gotta put down your guns an' walk slow."

There was silence from the soldiers. Steve recognized the bind he was in. There didn't seem to be much else to do except what Rafe had suggested. "We'll do it," he called.

"We know how many of you there are. We'll be watchin' an' countin' if you plannin' on leavin' a sleeper behind."

"I want the girl unharmed. We won't try anything." Steve laid down his musket and pistols, indicated the others should do likewise. When all the weapons were on the ground the men advanced slowly and picked up their wounded. Within moments they were back to their guns. They picked them up and headed back up the road.

Rafe laughed behind the barricade. "C'mon. Let's go. Crissa, you got to remember you a hostage now, an' act scared." The six came around the wagons and headed up the road, Crissa walking boldly in front, glancing back from time to time as if in fear for her life.

Only two were alive. A relative newcomer, a squat, burly man by the name of Jason had been knocked out by

301

a musket ball which had grazed his skull. They pulled him to his feet and headed him back for the wagons. Driver, a youth with some seven fights behind him had been cut cruelly on the arm and leg and had lost a lot of blood. They tied rags around his wounds and dragged him back with them. Silence hung over the path. They were back where they started ten minutes earlier.

"Mistah Captain?" Rafe shouted.

Steve took a few paces forward. "I hear you."

"We goin' cross the river. I ain't sayin' you gonna get her back an' I ain't sayin' you ain't, but we gonna take the girl with us. You want her hurt an' you shoot into us, you hear?"

"We won't shoot. But if you take her with you, I'll follow you until I see you dead."

"That be a long time, Mistah Captain," Rafe called, dropping down to the ground. "C'mon. . . ." He gestured with his hand and started for the river. Crissa dutifully stood and followed the others to the raft, waded through the shallows and clambered aboard. Dingo and Jomo grabbed the rope and started hauling, getting help from the slaves on the other side. The raft shot into the river. The soldiers were already on the move but Rafe could only hope they would hold their fire rather than endanger Crissa by shooting indiscriminately at the little party clustered so tightly together.

Steve and the soldiers rushed past the barricade and swarmed down to the beach. Two of the dragoons raised their pistols to fire but another soldier harshly ordered them to lower their guns. Rafe recognized Steve. He was glad he'd lowered his shot during the attack. Had the captain been killed the soldiers might have risked a volley and probably killed them all.

Steve watched helplessly as the raft was drawn up on the shore of Tejas. The freed slaves cheered wildly as the pitbucks disembarked and Rafe walked to the rope and cut it with his cutlass. The current slowly swung the raft downstream where it would soon be out of sight.

The raucous cheers stopped when someone pointed out Crissa. Rafe ordered the free men back into the trees, not wishing to waste another precious moment with their enemies just across the river. Soon the shoreline was nearly empty, only Jomo, Rafe and Crissa remaining, hidden from the prying eyes of the soldiers by a line of bushes. Crissa seemed reluctant to go. "We best join the others, Crissa."

Crissa looked instead at Jomo. "Jomo?" she asked. "May I talk to Rafe alone?"

Jomo shrugged. "I be waitin' in de trees," he said, drifting back from their hiding place at the water's edge.

Rafe knew what she was going to say before she said it. The knowledge didn't make the listening any easier.

"I'm not going, Rafe."

"You got to."

"You know what I have to do. And so do I."

"Stay with me. That's what you have to do."

"He'd follow. I know Steve. You heard him. As long as I'm with you he'll follow. The minute they think they can get away with it, they'll swim their horses across the river and be after us, treaty or no."

"We'll fight them," Rafe replied firmly.

"Yes. And more will be killed. Maybe Jomo. Maybe you. And how many others? Just so you could have your white woman."

"Don't say that."

"Rafe . . . . I love you, Rafe. I've been taught all my life how wrong it is and yet I love you. But we can't sacrifice everything else, all you've fought for, their freedom, so we can be together. It wouldn't be right. There's been enough death. Now is the time for life. If I stay behind Steve will turn back and let you go."

Rafe tried to interrupt but Crissa continued doggedly. "And what of the field slaves? Julie was only saying what they all feel. They'd never trust me. Their resentment would grow and grow until they'd no longer follow you, even if you are the only one who can lead them. They need you, Rafe."

Rafe stared at the sky. So now he would lose her. She was right, but for a few seconds he allowed himself the luxury of not believing her. His battle-scarred hands rose to cup her face as if seeking to remember the touch of her flesh. He brought his lips to her forehead. What had his father said? Nothing. There were no stories for the hurt that wrenched at his heart.

Suddenly he stood and faced the river. "White man! You come get your woman. A horse for you, a horse for her. No more."

He looked once into her eyes, then turned and walked up the hill to the bluff overlooking the river. Jomo was waiting for him. Rafe squatted among the brush and watched a lone rider with an extra mount swim his animals across the river toward the woman who waited alone on the shore.

The sun was settling into the western sky, bathing the scene in a reddish-gold light and adding a touch of crimson to the hair of the woman who waited. Rafe kept his vigil until the two were safely returned to the Louisiana shore. Then he turned away and without looking back, walked toward the western forest where there was freedom, real freedom to be fought for and won.

. . . and his people waited.

"A light read when you totally want to tune out the educational stuff. Two paws up."
—*Cleveland Plain Dealer*

"Loads of fun! Baxter's veterinary sleuth and her menagerie of animal companions are a great way to spend an afternoon. So pull up a chair and dive in."
—T. J. MacGregor, Edgar Award winner and author of *Category Five*

"*Dead Canaries Don't Sing* is top dog, the cat's pajamas, and the paws that refresh all rolled into one un-fur-gettable mystery entertainment."
—Sarah Graves, author of the *Home Repair Is Homicide* series

Also by Cynthia Baxter

DEAD CANARIES DON'T SING

PUTTING ON THE DOG

LEAD A HORSE TO MURDER

HARE TODAY, DEAD TOMORROW

RIGHT FROM THE GECKO

WHO'S KITTEN WHO?

And look for

MURDER PACKS A SUITCASE

The first in a new series!
On sale November 2008

Monkey See, Monkey Die

A *Reigning Cats & Dogs* Mystery

Cynthia Baxter

BANTAM BOOKS

MONKEY SEE, MONKEY DIE
A Bantam Book / August 2008

Published by Bantam Dell
A Division of Random House, Inc.
New York, New York

This is a work of fiction. Names, characters, places, and
incidents either are the product of the author's imagination
or are used fictitiously. Any resemblance to actual persons,
living or dead, events, or locales is entirely coincidental.

ISBN 978-0-553-59037-1

Printed in the United States of America
Published simultaneously in Canada

www.bantamdell.com

OPM   10 9 8 7 6 5 4 3 2 1